... ...er of an interior design ... ...me. She lives with her husband and two cats in Newport, Kentucky. This is her first novel.

'CeeCee Honeycutt is a sweet, perceptive girl with a troubled family, and this story of the summer that transforms her life is rich with hard truths and charm. This book unfolds like a lush Southern garden, blooming with vivid characters, beauty and surprises' Kim Edwards, author of *The Memory Keeper's Daughter*

'An absolutely delightful debut novel packed full of Southern charm, strong women, wacky humour and good old-fashioned heart. From the moment you first step into young CeeCee's unique world, you'll never want to leave' Kristin Hannah, bestselling author of *True Colors* and *Winter Garden*

'A confection so delightful readers will not be able to put it down. Beautifully written, brimming with decency and humour, and sparkling with a cast of women who are by turns wise, generous, and deliciously eccentric, this book is a joy to read. Beth Hoffman has written a debut novel to be savoured' Connie May Fowler, author of *How Clarissa Burden Learned to Fly* and *Before Women Had Wings*

'A refreshing dose of hope. There are gems of wisdom sprinkled throughout ... Saving CeeCee Honeycutt will chase your winter blahs' *Minneapolis Star Tribune*

'Anyone in need of a Southern-girl-power fix will find *Saving CeeCee Honeycutt* engaging. And it offers an invaluable reminder: even when things look bleak, a few good friends can turn your life around' *People*

Saving
CeeCee
Honeycutt

BETH HOFFMAN

ABACUS

First published in Great Britain as a paperback original in 2012 by Abacus

First published in the United States in 2010 by Viking Penguin

A CIP catalogue record for this book
is available from the British Library.

ISBN 978-0-349-00018-3

Typeset in Bembo by M Rules
Printed and bound in Great Britain by
Clays Ltd, St Ives plc

Papers used by Abacus are from well-managed forests
and other responsible sources.

MIX
Paper from
responsible sources
FSC® C104740

Abacus
An imprint of
Little, Brown Book Group
100 Victoria Embankment
London EC4Y 0DY

An Hachette UK Company
www.hachette.co.uk

www.littlebrown.co.uk

This book is dedicated to Marlane Vaicius,
the best friend a girl could ever hope to find. Marlane, you are my Dixie.
And:
In loving memory of my great-aunt, Mildred Williams Caldwell
of Danville, Kentucky, the remarkably generous and wise little woman
who ignited the flame that inspired this book.

Saving
CeeCee
Honeycutt

One

Momma left her red satin shoes in the middle of the road. That's what three eyewitnesses told the police. The first time I remember my mother wearing red shoes was on a snowy morning in December 1962, the year I was seven years old. I walked into the kitchen and found her sitting at the table. No lights were on, but in the thin haze of dawn that pushed through the frostbitten window, I could see red high-heeled shoes peeking out from beneath the hem of her robe. There was no breakfast waiting, and no freshly ironed school dress hanging on the basement doorknob. Momma just sat and stared out the window with empty eyes, her hands limp in her lap, her coffee cold and untouched.

I stood by her side and breathed in the sweet scent of lavender talcum powder that clung to the tufts of her robe.

'What's the matter, Momma?'

I waited and waited. Finally she turned from the window and looked at me. Her skin was as frail as tissue, and her voice wasn't much more than a whisper when she smoothed her hand over my cheek and said, 'Cecelia Rose, I'm taking you to Georgia. I want you to see what real living is like. All the women dress so nice. And the people are kind and friendly – it's so different from how things are here. As soon as I feel better, we'll plan a trip – just you and me.'

'But what about Dad, will he come too?'

She squeezed her eyes closed and didn't answer.

Momma stayed sad for the rest of the winter. Just when I thought she'd never smile again, spring came. When the lilacs bloomed in great, fluffy waves of violet, Momma went outside and cut bouquets for every room in the house. She painted her fingernails bright pink, fixed her hair, and slipped into a flowery-print dress. From room to room she dashed, pushing back curtains and throwing open the windows. She turned up the volume of the radio, took hold of my hands, and danced me through the house.

We whirled through the living room, into the dining room, and around the table. Right in the middle of a spin, Momma abruptly stopped. 'Oh, my gosh,' she said, taking in a big gulp of air and pointing to the mirror by the door, 'we look so much alike. When did that happen? When did you start to grow up?'

We stood side by side and gazed at our reflections. What I saw was two smiling people with the same heart-shaped face, blue eyes, and long brown hair – Momma's pulled away from her face in a headband and mine tied back in a ponytail.

'It's amazing,' my mother said, gathering her hair in her hand and holding it back in a ponytail like mine. 'Just look at us, CeeCee. I bet when you get older, people will think we're sisters. Won't that be fun?' She giggled, took hold of my hands, and spun me in circles till my feet lifted off the floor.

She was so happy that after we finished dancing, she took me into town and bought all sorts of new clothes and ribbons for my hair. Momma bought herself so many pairs of new shoes that the salesman laughed and said, 'Mrs. Honeycutt, I believe you have more shoes than the Bolshoi Ballet.' Neither Momma nor I knew what that meant, but the salesman sure thought he was clever. So we laughed along with him as he helped us carry our packages to the car.

After stuffing the trunk full with bags and boxes, we ran across the street to the five-and-dime, where we sat at the lunch counter and shared a cheeseburger, a bowl of French fries, and a chocolate milk shake.

That spring sure was something. I'd never seen Momma so happy. Every day was a big celebration. I'd come home from school and she'd be waiting, all dressed up with a big smile on her face. She'd grab her handbag, hurry me to her car, and off we'd go to do more shopping.

Then came the day when Dad arrived home from a three-week business trip. Momma and I were sitting at the kitchen table, she with a magazine and me with a coloring book and crayons. When my dad opened the closet door to hang up his jacket, he was all but knocked senseless when an avalanche of shoe boxes rained down on him.

'Good Christ!' he barked, turning to look at Momma. 'How much money have you been spending?'

When Momma didn't answer, I put down my crayon and smiled. 'Daddy, we've been shopping for weeks, but everything we got was for free.'

'Free? What are you talking about?'

I nodded wisely. 'Yep. All Momma had to do was show the salesman a square of plastic, and he let us have whatever we wanted.'

'What the hell?' Dad pounded across the kitchen floor, yanked Momma's handbag from the hook by the door, and pulled the square of plastic from her wallet. 'Damn it, Camille,' he said, cutting it up with a pair of scissors. 'How many times do I have to tell you? This has got to stop. No more credit cards.

You keep this up and you'll put us in the poor house. You hear me?'

Momma licked her finger and turned a page of the magazine.

He leaned down and looked at her. 'Have you been taking your pills?' She ignored him and turned another page. 'Camille, I'm talking to you.'

The sharpness of his words wiped the shine right out of her eyes.

Dad shook his head and pulled a beer from the refrigerator. He huffed and puffed out of the kitchen, kicking shoes out of his way as he headed for the living room. I heard him dump his wide, beefy body into the recliner, muttering the way he always did whenever he was in a bad mood. Which, as far as I could tell, was pretty much always.

My father didn't smile or laugh very much, and he had a limitless gift for making me feel about as important as a lost penny on the sidewalk. Whenever I'd show him a drawing I'd made or try to tell him about something I'd learned in school, he'd get fidgety and say, 'I'm tired. We'll talk another time.'

But another time never came.

He was a machine-tool salesman and spent much of his time in places like Michigan and Indiana. Usually he'd stay away all week and would come home only on weekends. And most times those weekends were filled with an unbearable tension that sprung loose on Saturday night.

Momma would get all dolled up, walk into the living room, and beg him to take her out. 'C'mon Carl,' she'd say, tugging at his arm, 'let's go dancing like we used to. We never have fun anymore.'

His face would turn sour and he'd say, 'No, Camille. I'm not taking you anywhere until you straighten up. Now go take your pills.'

4

She'd cry and say she didn't need any pills, he'd get mad, turn up the volume of the TV, and drink one beer after another, and I'd run upstairs and hide in my bedroom. Whole months would go by and I'd only hear an occasional kind word pass between them. Even less frequently I'd see them touch. Before too long even those things faded away, and my father's presence in the house faded right along with them.

Momma seemed glad that Dad stayed away so much. One day I was sitting on the floor of her bedroom cutting out paper dolls while she sat at her vanity and put on makeup. 'Who needs him anyway?' she said, leaning close to the mirror as she smoothed on bright red lipstick. 'I'll tell you something, Cecelia Rose. Northerners are exactly like their weather – cold and *boring*. And I swear, none of them has one iota of etiquette or propriety. Do you know that not one single person in this god-forsaken town even knows I'm a pageant queen? They're all a bunch of sticks-in-the-mud, just like your father.'

'You don't like Daddy anymore?'

'No,' she said, turning to look at me. 'I don't.'

'He doesn't come home very much. Where is he, Momma?'

She blotted her lips with a tissue. 'That old fool? He's not here because he's down at the cemetery with one foot stuck in the grave. And that's another thing. Never marry an older man. I mean it, CeeCee. If an older man ever sweeps you off your feet, just get up and run away as fast as you can.'

I set down my scissors. 'How old is Daddy?'

'Fifty-seven,' she said, rubbing a smudge of rouge from her cheek. 'And look what he's done to me.' She scowled at her reflection in the mirror and shook her head. 'I'm only thirty-three and I already have lines on my face. Your father is nothing but a Yankee liar. I can't tell you how many promises he made just so I'd marry him and move up here to this god-awful excuse for a town. But all those promises amounted to nothing but a five-hundred-pound bag of dog breath.'

As I was about to ask her what that meant, a strange, icy expression moved across her face. She gazed down at her wedding picture and slowly lifted it from the vanity. With her tube of lipstick she drew a big red X over my dad's face, then shrieked with laughter, fluffed her hair, and walked out the door.

What caused it, I didn't know, but after that day Momma's moods began to spike and plummet like a yo-yo. One day she'd pitch a fit and break everything she could get her hands on, and the next day she'd be as calm as a glass of water. Then, out of nowhere, she'd up and vanish. I'd panic and run down the street, calling her name while my heart hammered against my ribs. Eventually I'd find her going from door to door in the neighborhood, asking for donations for some charity nobody ever heard of. A few people felt sorry for her and would drop a coin or two into the jar she held in her hands, but most people closed the door in her face.

She became so unpredictable that I never knew what would be waiting for me when I got home from school — a plate of gooey half-baked cookies or muffled sobs leaking from beneath her closed bedroom door. I didn't know what was wrong with her, but I did know that none of the other mothers in our town acted the way she did. They'd come into school carrying trays filled with freshly baked cupcakes, and I'd see them walking along the sidewalks with their children and sometimes a dog. The other mothers were happy and seemed like they were fun to spend time with, but Momma wasn't fun anymore, and there were times when she acted so strange that she scared me.

Each year I watched her grasp on reality loosen as she slipped further away, but the worst part of her descent began on a breezy spring afternoon when I was nine years old.

I was headed home from school, enjoying the way the wind tickled my face, when three boys ran by. One of them skidded to a stop and poked me in the shoulder. 'Hey, Honeycutt, it's not Christmas, so how come there's a big fruitcake in your front yard?'

He let out a cruel, sputtering laugh and disappeared around the corner. When I turned down my street and saw Momma, a rush of heat scalded my cheeks. My brunette mother had bleached her hair white and was standing in the front yard wearing a slam-on-the-brakes horror of a yellow prom dress. It was so tight the seams were puckered up in some places and split open in others, and beneath the full, gathered skirt were layers and layers of stiff white petticoats.

She didn't look a thing like a fruitcake – no, she did not. My mother looked like a big lemon meringue pie. And if that weren't bad enough, sparks of light burst into the air from the rhinestone tiara that sat cockeyed on her head as she blew kisses to everyone who drove by.

'I love you,' she called, waving to a carload of teenage boys in a convertible.

The driver screeched to a stop and backed up. His greasy, slicked-back hair shimmered in the sunlight. He took a drag from a stubby cigarette and flicked it into the street. 'Hey, baby,' he called to Momma. 'That's some outfit. What's going on?'

'Please vote for me,' she sang out across the lawn. 'I'll make y'all proud of this great state of Georgia.'

All of the boys laughed, and one of them said, 'Georgia? What's the matter – you lost or something? This is Willoughby, Ohio.'

Oblivious to the truth of his words, she blew him a kiss. 'Now, don't forget to vote for me.'

One of the boys in the backseat motioned to Momma. 'Sure, I'll vote for you, honey. C'mon over and sit on my lap.'

She giggled and set off toward the car. Just as she reached the sidewalk, the driver hit the gas and laid rubber on the road. Clouds of smoke rolled into the air, but Momma kept right on blowing kisses.

I was so embarrassed, I thought I'd implode right there on the sidewalk. Though I knew I should grab her arm and haul her back inside the house, my shame sent me running in the opposite direction. With my books hugged to my chest, I ran full throttle until I reached the public library. I pushed through the heavy wooden door of the ladies' restroom, hid in one of the stalls, and opened a book. I read as fast as I could, gobbling up pages until the wild thumping of my heart subsided, until the story on the pages became real and my life became nothing but a story – a story that simply wasn't true. Couldn't be true. I stayed in the restroom until the maintenance man came in to wash the floors and shooed me out.

Not long after that day, Momma began walking to the Goodwill store. She'd buy all sorts of old prom dresses and formal gowns, and if she happened to find any dyed-to-match shoes, well, she'd buy those too, even if they were three sizes too big.

One afternoon I was lying on my bed, reading *Stuart Little*, when I heard Momma's footsteps on the stairs accompanied by the rustle of paper bags – always a surefire announcement that she had struck gold during her Goodwill shopping spree. I heard her laugh, giddy with anticipation, as she tried on the newest addition to her wardrobe. Within a few minutes she called to me, 'Cecelia Rose, come in here, darlin', and see what I found.'

I pressed my nose farther into the book and pretended not to hear, but Momma called again, and when I didn't answer, I heard the sharp *clickety-click* of her high-heeled shoes coming down the hall. She threw open my bedroom door and exclaimed, 'Will you just look at your momma! Isn't she something?'

She stood in the doorway, eyes glazed wide from her Goodwill shopping hangover. Then she gathered up the skirt of a raggedy old prom dress she'd just bought for a dollar and twirled into my room like a colorful, out-of-control top.

'Oh, how I adore this shade of pink. It suits me,' she said, stopping to admire her reflection in the mirror on my closet door.

I don't know what Momma saw in that mirror that delighted her so much, but it sure wasn't what I saw.

She put her hands on her hips, looked over her shoulder, and waited for me to tell her how beautiful she looked. It was all I could do to reach deep inside myself and push out the words she so desperately wanted to hear. 'You look nice, Momma,' I mumbled, embarrassed enough for both of us, then I lowered my eyes and went back to reading my book.

'Don't be sad, CeeCee. One day you'll win a beauty pageant, and then you can wear all these beautiful gowns too. I'm saving them for you, darlin'. I promise I am.' She grinned and sashayed out of my room.

Grateful that she'd finally left, I scooted off the bed and closed the door behind her.

Momma started wearing those tattered old prom dresses several days a week. The more she wore them, the more of a spectacle she became in our town. Even the nicest of our neighbors couldn't stop themselves from standing in their front yards bug-eyed and slack-jawed whenever she'd parade down the sidewalk in a rustle of taffeta. And who could blame them? With a neighbor like Momma, who needed TV?

In school I was the skinny girl who had a crown-wearing, lipstick-smeared lunatic for a mother. Nobody talked to me unless they wanted an answer to a test question, and nobody sat with me at the lunch table – well, nobody except Oscar Wolper, who smelled like dirty socks and bore a shocking resemblance to Mr. Potato Head.

After a while I didn't pay much attention to my classmates. It didn't matter what they said about my mother or what kinds of faces they made. I'd just walk in, take my seat, and keep my eyes glued to the blackboard. Besides, I always knew a smile would be waiting for me every Sunday.

Two

For as far back as my memory would take me, I had spent Sunday mornings with our elderly neighbor Mrs. Gertrude Odell. At eight o'clock I'd go down to the kitchen and watch for her porch light to go on; it was our signal that she was ready for me. The minute I'd see that light, I'd run out the door, across the yard, and up the back steps of her little brick house. Always she'd greet me with a smile, still with her thin white hair wound in itty-bitty pin curls, still wearing her nightgown and flowery snap-front robe that was frayed at the cuffs.

'Good morning, honey,' she'd say as I stepped into her kitchen. 'It's a beautiful day that just got more beautiful.'

Whether it was sunny, rainy, or even if a foot of snow had fallen overnight, to Mrs. Odell, every day was a beauty. I think she was just happy to have woken up on the top side of the earth.

Mrs. Odell lived alone. She'd had a husband once, but he died a long time ago. We helped each other a lot: she made my school lunch each morning, and I pulled weeds in her garden and helped her lift things that were heavy.

Our Sunday breakfasts were my favorite thing in the whole world. While I gathered silverware and set our places at the white enamel-top table that sat by the kitchen window, she'd shuffle across the green linoleum floor in a pair of broken-down, grandma-style shoes with mismatched laces and grill up a stack of pancakes. We'd sit down and have ourselves a feast while we listened to a church station on the radio. Mrs. Odell loved choir singing, and she'd tune in early so we wouldn't miss it. Most times we'd catch the tail end of the day's sermon, loudly delivered by an angry-sounding preacher. Every week it was like he was giving his listeners a big, finger-pointing reprimand.

One Sunday while licking maple syrup off my fingers, I looked at Mrs. Odell. 'Why is that preacher so upset? He always sounds real mad.'

She took a sip of tea and thought for a moment. 'Well, now that you mention it, he does sound a little crabby. Maybe he's tired of reminding people to be kind to each other.'

'Are all preachers crabby?' I said, taking a bite of my pancakes.

Mrs. Odell chuckled. 'I don't know if I'd say they're *all* crabby, but I think some do have a tendency to speak a little too force-ful at times.'

'Well, what I don't understand is why people get all dressed up and drive to church so they can sit there and get scolded. Seems to me it'd be a whole lot easier for them to just stay home in their pj's, eat pancakes, and get yelled at over the radio.'

Mrs. Odell laughed so hard she cried. But I was serious.

On my way home from school the following Friday, I heard the echo of a sharp *whack-whack-whack* rise above the trees. Up ahead, a man was hammering a sign into the ground in front of a local church. The sign was advertising a weekend fund-raising festival, and printed in bright red letters at the bottom were the words COME JOIN THE FUN – EVERYONE WELCOME. When I arrived home, I made up my mind that I'd go down there on Saturday morning and see for myself what all this church stuff was about.

Before leaving the house the next morning, I put on a pair of old sunglasses and tied a scarf around my head. Thanks to Momma's antics, even the adults in our town looked at me with something that was a cross between disgust and pity, so I tried to disguise myself whenever I ventured into town.

The festival was a swarm of activity, and I sunk into the shadows of the trees to watch. My first impression was that pies seemed to help people be kind to one another a whole lot better than any mean-talking preacher. In fact, there were more smiles around the bake-sale tables than I had ever seen in one place. Even the most ornery, stern-faced men in our town turned all happy and grinned like fools as they looked over the long tables lined with homemade cookies, pies, and strudels. Even Mr. Krick, the owner of the local hardware store, who was just about as grumpy as a person could be, picked up a pie. Under the watchful eye of a little gray-haired woman who stood behind the table, he held it beneath his nose and breathed in the aroma.

'Ida Mae,' he said with a goofy grin, 'you've created a masterpiece. This elderberry pie has been blessed by the Good Lord himself. I'll take it.'

Ida Mae blushed and packed the pie inside a box.

'Now, don't you worry about that broken latch on your screen door,' Mr. Krick said, suddenly jolly. 'I'll stop by tomorrow morning and get it all fixed up.' He handed Ida Mae a five-dollar bill, told her to keep the change, and disappeared into the crowd.

I made a mental note that if I ever needed help from a man I would make him a pie. I wondered if that's why my dad didn't come home much anymore. As far as I knew, Momma never once had baked him a pie.

Beyond the bake-sale tables stood a line of game booths, but

I steered clear of those when I saw a group of kids from my school. I watched from a safe distance as they threw balls, knocked over bowling pins, and won all sorts of prizes.

Once I'd seen enough of the festival, I took a shortcut through the grass and walked by the church. The door was wide open, so I climbed the steps and peeked inside.

It was almost dark. The only light there was came from a vibrantly colored stained glass window on the farthest wall. Beyond the rows of polished wood pews sat an altar draped in a cloth of deep red, its surface filled with dozens of burning candles that glowed from inside tiny glass cups.

Careful not to make a sound, I moved down the aisle. Three women were kneeling in the front pew, each one of them wearing a lacy square of fabric on top of her head. The women rubbed long beaded necklaces through their fingers, and one of them rocked back and forth to the rhythm of something I couldn't hear. I didn't know what beaded necklaces had to do with praying, but I guessed it was probably some secret code reserved exclusively for women.

For several minutes I watched the scene before me, wondering if a beaded necklace had the power to help my mother. I wondered about it the whole way home.

While walking around the side of the house, I saw Dad's car parked in the driveway. Just as I opened the back door, I heard Momma's voice burst through the air. 'No. Get out!'

'Damn it, Camille, calm down. We need to talk.'

There was a furious jumble of words, ending with the sound of breaking glass. I ran across the kitchen and hid inside the broom closet. Above me I could hear the shuffling of feet, and then Dad's words boomed through the house. 'Camille, you've got to stop this. Now, sit down and—'

Momma screamed, 'Don't come near me. I hate you!'

The slamming of her bedroom door shook the house, and a moment later Dad pounded down the stairs. I stood stock-still in the darkness of the closet, and when he came into the kitchen, I held my breath. When the screen door slapped shut, I pushed open the closet door and peered out the window. As I watched my father get into his car and roar away, I decided to give the praying business a try.

Later that night, while Momma was asleep on the sofa, I searched through a chest of drawers in her bedroom until I found the strand of pearls she kept tucked inside a pink satin pouch. After pulling an old doily from beneath a lamp and grabbing a Christmas candle from a box in the closet, I went into my bedroom and closed the door. I bobby-pinned the doily to my head, lit the candle, and got down on my knees by the window. Though I wasn't sure exactly what to do, I gazed into the sky and rubbed the pearls between my fingers until they grew nice and warm.

'Hello. My name is Cecelia Rose Honeycutt, and I live at 831 Tulipwood Avenue. The preacher on the radio said if we opened our hearts and asked, we'd be saved. He said it was that simple. So I'm asking, will you please save Momma? Something's wrong with her mind and it's getting worse every day. And while you're at it, will you save me too? There's nothing wrong with *my* mind, but I sure could use some help down here. I'll do anything you say. Thank you. Amen.'

I prayed for several weeks, counting off one pearl for each prayer. Every day I watched for signs of improvement, but Momma never got any better. There were sixty-one pearls on my mother's necklace, and if something didn't happen soon, I'd run out of prayers. One day it occurred to me that it was time to go directly to God. But I was a little worried about that idea.

Is God like the principal at our school who stays in his office and talks only with the teachers? Will God think I'm too bold if I call on him directly?

Though I was nervous about it, I decided I had nothing to lose, so I went ahead and prayed until I came to the last pearl on the necklace. But summer faded into autumn, and nothing in my life changed but the color of the leaves on the trees. Either God never heard me or had a whole lot more important things to worry about.

On a warm October night I sat outside and rested against a maple tree. I gazed at the branches above me, and while watching the moonlight ride the copper leaves as they let go and swirled to the ground, I wondered about all the prayers I'd said.

Where have they gone? Are they piled up in the corner of God's doorway the way the leaves mound beneath the trees? Will God one day open the door and be knocked backward when all my prayers tumble in?

When I went inside the house, I figured I'd said enough prayers to last a lifetime, so I tossed the doily and the candle in the trash, put Momma's pearls back inside the satin pouch, and went upstairs to read a book.

Books became my life, or maybe I should say books became the way I escaped from my life. Every day I studied my homework lessons until I knew them inside and out. And, in a strange, upside-down way, Momma's craziness helped me learn more and rise to the top of my class. For every dish, saucer, or glass she threw against the wall, I'd add a book to my reading list. And every time she cried, I'd read an entire column of words in the dictionary. By the time I was eleven years old I'd read a whole lot of books and knew a ton of words.

When the girls in my class raced home after school to play board games or make themselves up with their mothers' cosmetics, I turned and walked in the opposite direction. Down shade-dappled sidewalks I'd go until I reached the Willoughby

Public Library. I was happy sitting alone on the cool floor between the tall wooden shelves, but I'd be a liar if I said I didn't long for a living, breathing girlfriend to talk with. Laugh with. Just *be* with. Every day I ached to hear my footsteps walk in rhythm with those of another girl. When that ache got to be too much, I tried to pretend I didn't need anybody – including a mother.

But my pretending ended on a windy spring day when I was twelve years old.

When I came home from school and opened the front door, a cloud of gray smoke swirled into my face. I dropped my books and ran into the kitchen to find a saucepan burning on the stove. Coughing till I thought I'd choke, I grabbed a pot holder, put the scorched pan into the sink, and turned off the burner. After opening the windows and doors and fanning the smoke till the air cleared, I looked around to see how much damage had been done. Gooey cheese and burned macaroni were stuck to the stovetop and splattered on the cupboard doors, and the smoke had left a gray film on the ceiling. While I stared at the mess and wondered how I'd ever clean it up, I heard Momma wail like her hair was on fire.

I bolted up the stairs and found her sitting in the middle of her bed, wearing a red lace bra, a petticoat, and her tiara. She was crying so hard I could barely find her face behind all that blotched puffiness. Momma smelled real strange – like hair spray and Shalimar perfume mixed with urine.

As I moved across her room, my heart went wild, like a bird beating its wings against a closed window. I wrapped my hands around the bedpost to steady myself. 'What's the matter, Momma?'

Her face turned tragic. 'Look at this,' she said, lifting her scrapbook.

The picture she wanted me to see was a photograph of her smiling like a goddess in her white pageant dress. A green silk sash was draped from one of her shoulders to the opposite hip, and the words 1951 VIDALIA ONION QUEEN were written across it in glittery script. She was standing on a skirted platform framed by two wooden barrels overflowing with onions.

'My life is here; this is my *real* life,' she whimpered, poking the picture with a stiff finger. She wiped her eyes, smearing mascara across her cheeks. 'I was so beautiful and young.'

Knowing that compliments always made her happy, I took in a breath and said, 'You're still beautiful, Momma.'

Her chapped lips quivered. 'You think so?'

I nodded and tried to think of something to say that would bring her back to reality. 'But Momma, winning that pageant wasn't your life – it was only a *day* in your life – that's all. Mrs. Odell says life is what we make it. Maybe you'd be happier if you adjusted your thinking a bit.'

She looked at me with dilated eyes. 'Who's Mrs. Odell?'

My stomach started to churn, sending a wash of bile into my throat. I leaned my forehead against the bedpost and took in a slow breath of air. 'She's our neighbor, Momma. She lives next door. Remember?'

'Our neighbor is Colonel Braxton Griffin. He's a direct descendant of General Robert E. Lee and a fine Southern gentleman.'

'No, Momma, please listen to me. There is no Colonel Griffin. Mrs. Odell has *always* been our neighbor.'

She screwed up her face and looked at me like *I* was the one who was nuts. I had the horrible feeling that she had, once and for all, slipped over the edge. She began rocking from side to side, tears spilling down her cheeks.

Breathe, CeeCee. Breathe. Please, somebody help me. Please, God.

I walked to the side of the bed, sat down, and took hold of

her hand. I could hardly hear my own voice when I said, 'Momma. What's my name?'

She stopped rocking and stared at me for the longest time. The room grew quiet. The clock on her night chest ticked on and on. I swallowed hard. 'Who am I, Momma?'

The blank look on her face terrified me. As I was about to run next door and get Mrs. Odell, a small flicker of reality sparked in her eyes.

'Momma, what's my name?'

'Cecelia Rose,' she blurted. Then she crushed the scrapbook against her chest, flopped forward, and buried her face into the bedspread.

'You stay here. Everything will be okay. I'll be right back.' I rose from the bed, walked down the hall on shaking legs, and drew a hot bath. While the tub was filling, I returned to her bedroom. One by one I pried her fingers from the scrapbook, helped her out of bed, and led her into the bathroom. Why, I don't know, but Momma refused to take off her bra and slip. I didn't have the energy to argue, so after I gathered a wad of tissue and wiped bubbles of snot from her nose, I let her sink into the tub while I sat on the toilet lid and began reading aloud from one of my Nancy Drew books.

When Momma's tears finally subsided, she looked at me with swollen, red-rimmed eyes. 'Is Nancy Drew a friend of yours? I don't recall.'

My mouth dropped open in disbelief. I was so worn out by her illness that I wanted to scream. I stared at her, shaking my head. 'I don't have any friends.'

'You have lots of friends,' she said, scooping up a drift of soap bubbles and blowing them from the palm of her hand. 'They come in and out of the house all the time.'

A sudden, seething anger flared inside me. It was so powerful that my hands started to shake. I grabbed a hand mirror from the side of the sink and held it close to her face. 'How could I have friends? Just look at what you do to yourself.'

Her lips parted when she saw her reflection, and a slow, unspeakable sadness fell across her face. She turned away and gazed at the flowery wallpaper, as if the secret to her damaged life was hidden behind a faded petal or leaf.

I put down the mirror, ashamed by what I'd just done. 'I'm sorry, Momma. I didn't mean it.'

Without looking at me, she whispered, 'Nancy Drew is jealous because I'm a pageant queen and she's not.'

I lowered my eyes and went back to reading my book.

When the bathwater grew cold, I helped Momma out of the tub, peeled off her slip and bra, and dried her off. After getting her into a nightgown, she climbed into bed and fell asleep before I finished untangling the tiara from her hair. When I finally pulled it free, I set it on the night chest and went downstairs to the kitchen.

After filling a bucket with hot soapy water, I scrubbed the macaroni and cheese off the stovetop, then I stood on a chair and wiped down the cupboard doors. There was nothing to be done with the scorched pan, so I tossed it in the garbage. Once I'd cleaned everything up, I got down on my knees, reached behind the stove, and pulled the plug from the outlet. From now on Momma could eat cold sandwiches unless I was home to keep an eye on things.

Though I always tried to hide the worst of my mother's illness from everyone, that night I couldn't stop myself from running next door to Mrs. Odell's. I was too embarrassed to tell her the really bad parts of what had happened, but I managed to give her an idea of what had gone on.

She wrapped me in her arms. 'Oh, honey, your mother is a tortured soul. Shall I go over and see if I can help her?'

'She's sleeping,' I said, fighting back tears.

'Good. Then, you'll stay and have supper with me.'

Hungry for anything that even remotely resembled normal, I followed Mrs. Odell around her little kitchen, but she didn't seem to mind. We talked about what I was learning in school as she prepared our meal, and then she served it up on chipped porcelain plates while I set up TV trays in her living room. Pretty soon I all but forgot about Momma as we ate our supper and laughed at a rerun of *I Love Lucy*.

After we did the dishes, Mrs. Odell and I played Chinese checkers until it grew dark, and then she walked me home. She went upstairs to check on Momma, and returned a few minutes later with a sad look on her face. 'She's in a deep sleep, honey. Maybe tomorrow will be a better day.'

Mrs. Odell gave me a squeeze and left, her white hair glowing like a fuzzy moon in the darkness. As I stood at the window and watched her disappear, the truth blazed in my mind. There would never be a better day, because no matter what day it was, my mother, Camille Sugarbaker Honeycutt, the 1951 Vidalia Onion Queen, was crazy.

I blew a foggy circle on the windowpane and pressed my palm against it. The coolness of the glass was strangely comforting. While watching the mist evaporate around my fingers, I thought about Gloria.

Gloria used to live across the street. She and Momma were friends and had spent a lot of time together when I was real little. They would do each other's hair like the pictures they'd seen in magazines, and sometimes they'd dance around the living room while watching *American Bandstand* on TV.

When Momma started having her spells, it was Gloria who tried to talk to my father.

I remembered the day I was sitting in the grass by the side of

21

the house, playing with a toy bear. I looked across the street and saw Gloria unloading bags of groceries from her car. As I was about to call her name and wave, my father pulled into our driveway. When Gloria saw him, she trotted across the street, her short black hair shining in the sun.

'Carl, I need to talk to you. It's important. Something's wrong with Camille,' she said, folding her arms across her chest. 'I'm worried about her, and I'm scared for Cecelia. Please come over to my house so we can talk in private. I'd like to—'

'Gloria, I'll handle my own family,' Dad said, holding up his hand.

'I just think—'

But Dad turned and left her standing in the driveway.

Gloria was never the same after that day. She came over less and less, and then she stopped altogether. She'd always smile and wave hello whenever she saw me, but she didn't come across the street and talk to me like she used to. Then one day a big green moving van pulled up and parked in her driveway. Later that afternoon, Gloria and her husband locked their front door and moved away. She didn't even say good-bye.

And now here I was all these years later, staring into the starless sky, thinking about how much easier everything would be if my mother was locked up in a sanatorium. I sometimes even wished she were dead. It was terrible to think such a thing, but I just couldn't help it. I'm not saying I wanted to skip through life in a rosy blur from one Disney experience to the next – all I longed for was to know one whole happy day.

The following Saturday morning the phone rang, and when I answered, a woman's voice said, 'Oh, uh, hello. I'd like to speak to Carl.'

I recognized her voice. She had called several times in the past. 'He's not home. Who's calling?'

There was a long pause, and then she said, 'It's not important, I'll call back another time.' And she quickly hung up.

Late that afternoon she called again, and still she refused to leave a message.

Not ten minutes later I heard my dad's car roll into the driveway. I ran out the back door and watched him pull a six-pack of beer and a small suitcase from the trunk. Before he reached the top step of the porch, I blurted, 'You have to do something. Momma needs help. And I—'

'C'mon, CeeCee, move over,' he grumbled, pushing past me.

His face was as tight as a clenched fist, and he reeked of liquor, underarm sweat, and a three-day-old foul mood. I knew that smell was a big red flag warning me to stay clear, but I followed him into the kitchen anyway.

'Momma needs to be in a hospital, and she—'

'For God's sake. Can't I even walk in the door without getting hounded?' He grabbed a beer, shoved the rest of the six-pack into the refrigerator, and pushed the door closed with his foot. 'I took your mother to a big-deal doctor in Cleveland. He put her on so many pills the bathroom looked like a damn pharmacy. You know darn well she won't take them, and even when she does, none of them do much good.'

'There's a special hospital in Eastlake for mentally sick people. I looked it up in the phone book.'

He opened his beer and dropped the bottle opener into the drawer with a loud *clang*. 'Do you have any idea what that would cost? I'm not made of money.'

'But you're not here to see all the things she does.' I marched across the kitchen and yanked open a cupboard door. 'These are the only dishes we have left, and do you know why? Because when she gets mad, she throws them against the wall. Last week she threw the toaster down the basement steps, and then she—'

He grabbed hold of the back of a chair and squeezed until his knuckles turned white. 'My life isn't a walk in the park, either. I just lost a big sale yesterday. As it is we'll have to tighten out belts. I can't afford to send your mother to a hospital.'

'I can't take it anymore. If you won't send Momma to a hospital, then send *me* away.'

He leaned toward me, his breath foul-smelling and hot. 'Has your mother ever hurt you? Has she ever slapped you or paddled your behind?'

'No, but she—'

'Then just keep her inside the house when she isn't herself.' He looked away and rifled through a stack of mail.

'If you don't do something about Momma, then I will. I'll tell the nurse at school about it, or I'll ... I'll ... go the police, and ... ' My chin quivered so much I couldn't finish the sentence.

'And what do you think the police will do – arrest your mother for throwing a toaster down the stairs?'

I was so mad I started to shake. 'No. They'll make *you* do something about Momma.'

Dad's lips thinned. 'Who do you think you're talking to?'

'I'm trying to talk to you, but you won't listen! Where are you all the time? Why do you go to Detroit so much?'

'I travel for my job, you know that,' he said, ripping open an envelope. But it was the way he averted his eyes that stirred a suspicion deep in my gut.

I took a breath for courage and stepped forward. 'Some lady called here for you, twice, but she wouldn't give me her name. And today isn't the first time she's called, either. So is that why you're never home?'

Splotches of red bloomed on his neck and he glared at me. 'What kind of question is that?'

I held his gaze, matching his fury with my own. 'Do you have a girlfriend?'

'You know what? I don't know why I bother to come home anymore.' He pulled out his wallet, dropped some money on the kitchen table, and walked out the door.

And, like always, he was gone.

Late the following afternoon, I found my mother sitting on the back steps. She was still in her nightgown, and her hair was a snarled mess of bobby pins and rollers from the night before. With her knees hugged tightly to her chest, she sat quietly and gazed into a sky that was as brittle as charred tinfoil.

I went outside and lowered myself next to her. We didn't say anything. We just sat and watched the wind whip up angry gray clouds. The strange, electric smell of a storm filled the air, and when a roll of thunder sounded off in the distance, I reached out and touched her hand. 'You'd better come inside, Momma. It's going to rain.'

Her lips barely moved when she said, 'I'm watching that bird. Way up high in the tree.'

I couldn't see it, and I wondered if her imagination was playing tricks again. But a moment later three chirps sounded and a red-winged blackbird lifted out of the tree. Momma and I watched until the flash of his scarlet epaulets disappeared.

'I wish I could be a bird.'

'Why? What good would that do?'

She turned and looked at me with exhausted blue eyes. 'Then I could fly to Georgia and get my life back.'

I could tell she was about to cry, so I took hold of her hand and urged her to her feet. As we walked into the kitchen, Momma looked pale and seemed wobbly. 'Why don't you rest for a while?' I said, leading her up the stairs and into her bedroom. 'I'll make us some supper a little later.'

She sat on the edge of the bed, as limp as a worn-out rag doll. I pulled her slippers from her feet and placed them beneath her night chest, but when I reached out to remove the curlers from her hair, her hands flew over her head and she began swatting the air like she was being attacked by a swarm of mosquitoes.

'What is it, Momma? What's wrong?'

She jumped up and shrieked, 'I've wasted the best years of my life. Damn him. Damn him to hell. I wish he'd drop dead!'

Momma grabbed a container of scented talcum from her vanity and hurled it at the closet door. It exploded on impact and sent so much white powder into the air, I felt like I was standing inside a giant snow globe.

Three

There were three eyewitnesses, and each of them said the same thing: the Happy Cow Ice Cream truck came over a crest in the road and hit Momma so hard she was knocked clean out of her geranium-red satin shoes. A big-bellied policeman stood in our driveway and told my dad that Momma had died instantly.

'I'm sorry to be delivering this terrible news. Real sorry. It happened so fast she didn't feel a thing, Mr. Honeycutt – I can promise you that.'

My legs turned liquid, and I grabbed hold of my bedroom window frame to steady myself. *Red shoes? Yes, she was wearing her favorite red shoes.*

Ashen-faced, Dad glanced toward the house. For a brief, searing moment, his eyes locked with mine. A thousand unsaid words hung in the air between us. His voice broke apart when he turned to the officer and said, 'Where . . . where did you say this happened?'

'On Euclid Avenue, about fifty yards west of the Goodwill store. The driver of the truck said she ran right in front of him. He didn't even have time to swerve—'

Dad held up his hand, palm thrust forward and fingers spread

27

wide, as if trying to block any more words the policeman might say. 'Good God,' he said, slouching on the porch steps with a heavy moan. 'Good God Almighty.'

The policeman pulled a toothpick from behind his ear and slid it into the corner of his mouth. 'This is an awful shock, but I've got to ask you a few questions. Your wife was walking on the road wearing a fancy party dress, and she had a crown on her head. Now, I know she had a tendency to be a little ... well, a little colorful at times. And I'm wondering, was she on any sort of medication?'

Dad let out a low groan and shook his head.

'Mr. Honeycutt, do you know where she was going all gussied up like that in the middle of the afternoon?'

Dad hung his head and said no. But that was a big fat lie. He knew darn well Momma walked to the Goodwill store at least once a week, but I figured he was too embarrassed to tell the policeman why.

This was the first day in almost three weeks that Dad had been home, and he hadn't been in the house more than twenty minutes before the policeman knocked on the door. Though I teetered on the edge between feeling no emotion for my father and downright hating him, I was drop-to-my-knees grateful it was him talking with the policeman and not me.

I moved away from the window, collapsed on my bed, and took several slow, deep breaths. A rush of blood thundered in my ears and a strange heat snaked through my veins until I got so hot and sweaty I thought I'd throw up. Just when I was about to run to the bathroom, I cooled down so fast I shuddered. Whoever it was that said life can change in the blink of an eye sure wasn't lying. Less than two hours ago I had walked out of school with my year-end report card in my hand, feeling glad for the beginning of summer vacation. Now a policeman claimed my mother was dead, and I didn't know what to believe or think, much less feel.

The skin on my forehead tightened and my hands went numb, but not one tear leaked from my eyes. All I could do was stare off into space and imagine Momma flying through the air as the chiffon skirt of her beauty pageant dress billowed in the wind like a white gossamer parachute. I imagined her landing lightly on the side of the road, her dress splayed out prettily around her, and I could see her crinoline slip, full and stiff, standing up against the breeze – its lacy hem fluttering when motorists passed by.

I could picture all that so easily, but I couldn't picture Momma actually dead. Momma had always been the great pretender, and I half-expected her to twirl into my bedroom, giggle, and then flop on the bed and tell me that she wasn't even hurt – that it was only something she'd done just for fun. I could almost hear her say, 'I only did it to liven things up in this boring old town.'

I sat up and looked out the window. It struck me as odd how my dad and the policeman were talking as if they were friends. I wondered if maybe death does that – turns strangers into friends for a few minutes, or an hour, or maybe even a whole day. I was also struck by how the birds kept chirping, how the traffic kept moving past our house, and how the man across the street kept right on trimming his hedge. Even the neighbor ladies kept on walking by, pulling their wire carts filled with groceries.

Momma was dead, yet the day marched on as usual.

The remainder of that Friday is forever lost to me. The Saturday and Sunday following Momma's death are much the same – nothing but blurry bits and pieces that never quite fit together. I remember Mrs. Odell rubbing my back, and I remember waking up in the bathtub, hearing the phone ring and ring in the kitchen below. I have a vague memory of wiping vomit from the rim of the toilet, yet I don't recall throwing up. Mostly I stayed in bed, hiding behind the black screen of my closed eyelids, listening to the tree limbs scrape a sad melody across the roof. I have no memory of eating, but one night I woke to find a bowl of cereal tipped over in my bed, the milk soaked into the sheets, and a banana squashed beneath my arm.

But no matter how I've tried, those few things are all I can summon from the storehouse of my memory.

Momma was laid to rest on a bright blue Monday morning. Other than Dad and me, the gathering around her plain wooden casket consisted of a preacher whom I'd never seen before, Mrs. Odell, and Dottie McGee, the woman who ran the Goodwill store.

Mrs. Odell reached over and took hold of my hand when the preacher said a prayer and asked God to take Momma to heaven. Dad stood off to the side with his hands shoved deep inside his pockets, looking pale and waxy.

When the preacher finished speaking and closed his Bible with a soft but definitive *thump*, Mrs. McGee sniffled into a tissue. 'Camille was the best customer I ever had,' she said, dabbing her eyes. 'She was so funny and full of stories. I'll never look at a prom dress again without thinking of her.'

Whether that proclamation angered or humiliated Dad I couldn't say, but his lips thinned and he turned away.

Mrs. Odell had made up a bouquet of white irises and pink peonies from her garden and tied it with a white satin ribbon. She handed it to me, leaned down, and whispered, 'Here, honey, take these flowers and put them on your mother's casket. It's time to say good-bye.'

As I stepped forward, a high-pitched ringing began in my ears. And though I was swollen with a sorrow I'd never known, I stared at my mother's casket, dry-eyed and numb. My chest hurt and I could hardly breathe. I felt I might smother beneath a blanket of guilt.

Is this my fault? Were my prayers misunderstood? Did God intervene and decide this was the only thing He could do?

Mrs. McGee waddled away from the grave, blotting her eyes and shaking her head. I watched her get into an old green Volkswagen that sputtered as she pulled out of the parking lot. While Dad stared across the rows of chiseled gray headstones with glassy, lifeless eyes, Mrs. Odell touched Momma's casket and whispered, 'Rest well, Camille. Rest well.'

As we headed for the car, a red-winged blackbird let out a series of chirps as he flew low over the cemetery. I watched him swoop up and vanish over the top of an evergreen tree, and I thought about what Momma had said, how she wished she could turn into a bird and fly home to Georgia. I pointed to where the bird had disappeared and asked Mrs. Odell what direction it was.

'South,' she said.

I looked into the sky and smiled.

When we arrived home, Dad and I walked into the kitchen like total strangers who were none too happy about sharing the same space. Though it was only 10:45 in the morning, he pulled a glass and a bottle of liquor from the cupboard and sat down at the table. 'Cecelia, I want to talk with you, and I . . .'

I turned away and went upstairs to my bedroom.

After opening the window as wide as it could go, I flopped on the bed. A warm breeze washed over me, and with it came thoughts of Momma. I wondered what that brief interval between life and death was like. Did her life flash before her eyes? Did she see the face of Jesus? Was she in heaven like the preacher had said, or was Momma's place in the afterworld a giant-size Goodwill store packed with pageant dresses, prom gowns, and thousands of dyed-to-match shoes – all of them in her size?

Did heaven have a special place reserved for people who were mentally ill, or, if you were mentally ill and died, did you automatically get well? With my hands clutched beneath my chin, I said a prayer. 'Dear God, I'm so sorry my mother died. I hope it's not my fault. I was mad at her for a long time, and when I wished she was dead awhile ago, I didn't mean it. I swear I didn't. She wasn't very happy, and I think maybe she's better off with you. If she's not already there, will you help her find her way to heaven? She's not very good at directions.'

I also prayed heaven didn't have any beauty pageants.

I woke with a start, feeling sweaty and disoriented. When I rolled over and got a glimpse of the clock on my nightstand, it was 12:55 in the afternoon. I rubbed sleep from my eyes and scooted to the edge of the bed.

While I was buckling my shoes I heard the crunch of gravel. From my bedroom window I watched the most beautiful car I'd ever seen roll to a stop. It was a shiny plum red with a white convertible top and a big, gleaming chrome grill. The afternoon sun sent fireworks of light sparking off the hood ornament – a miniature silver angel with open wings and her arms stretched out in front of her, palms forward, as if she were ready to push aside anything that dared get in her way. The driver's side door opened and a round little woman slid from the seat. She was impeccably dressed in a dark blue suit, and on her head was a matching hat with a long, brown-speckled feather sprouting from its side.

The squeak of the screen door sounded as my dad stepped onto the porch. 'Tallulah? I can't believe it. You drove all the way up from Georgia?'

She came across the lawn at a brisk clip. 'Yes, I surely did. And this has been an ill-fated trip from the get-go. Traffic was just awful. I spent the night in Columbus and planned on being here early this morning, but I ended up out in the country. Someplace called Orwell. But anyway, here I am. I'm sorry I missed the funeral, Carl. Was there a big turnout?'

Dad didn't answer that question.

Moments later I heard her soft murmuring from the living room. Dad spoke in clipped consonants and hard-edged vowels that bumped into walls and faded before I could make out exactly what he'd said. I knew they were talking about Momma, but the last few days had worn me out and I didn't want to think about her anymore. I closed the door, lay on my bed, and read *Treasure Island*.

After reading several chapters, I looked at the clock. More than an hour had passed and they were still talking. I slid off the bed and soundlessly opened the door.

'I wish I knew. Maybe she tripped,' Dad said with a groan. 'Or maybe she—'

'Carl, from what you're telling me, I think Camille suffered from psychosis.'

I retreated into my bedroom and pulled out my dictionary. My chest felt heavy when I read:

'**Psychosis:** noun; a severe mental disorder in which thought and emotions are so impaired that contact with reality is lost. Characterized by bizarre behavior, hallucinations, and disorganized thought. Genetic inheritance can play an important part in close biological relationships. This is true of both schizophrenia and manic-depressive illness . . . '

I stared at those words for a long time and whispered, 'Genetic inheritance.'

Dad and the woman began raising their voices. I closed the dictionary, tiptoed into the hallway, and knelt by the railing.

'This isn't my fault, Tallulah. And I—'

'Hush up before Cecelia hears you,' she scolded. 'This is a tragedy we might never come to understand. I knew something wasn't right years ago when Camille stopped answering my letters. She never even cashed the checks I sent for Cecelia's birthday. Then, when Taylor passed away, I was so grief-stricken that I just wasn't thinking straight. But what I don't understand is why you didn't call and tell me about all this.'

'What could you have done, Tallulah? Nothing.'

There was a long moment of silence, and the little woman's voice softened when she said, 'All right, let's put all that aside for now and get back to Cecelia. That poor child has had twelve years ripped out of her life. There's no telling what she's seen and endured. It breaks my heart just to think of it. So please, give my offer some serious thought, Carl. That's all I'm asking you to do.'

'Okay, I'll call you tonight. Where are you staying?'

'Portman Inn. I'll be expecting your call by eight o'clock. I mean it, Carl, what's done is done – we've both got to let it go or it'll eat us alive. All that matters now is that Cecelia is taken care of properly. This is your chance to do right by your daughter. Without love and guidance there's no telling what will become of her. I certainly hope you're wise enough to understand *exactly* what I'm saying.'

They stepped out to the front porch, and a moment later I heard the roar of the car's engine. I raced down the steps and arrived at the front window just in time to see her vanish around the corner.

Dad walked inside the house, his face as red as a beet. Beneath his arms circles of sweat stained his shirt. When he saw me standing by the window, he pointed toward a chair. 'Cecelia, sit down. We need to talk.'

I sat and clamped my hands between my knees as he walked across the room and stood by the fireplace. 'Your great-aunt Tallulah was just here. She's your grandmother's sister, on your mother's side.'

'Tallulah? I've never even heard of her.'

'She and her sister, Lucille, came up here once when you were a baby, but you were too young to remember. Your grandmother had a falling out with both of her sisters. She stopped talking to them before I met your mother.'

'Why?'

'All I know is that your great-grandfather owned a jewelry store. When he passed away, Tallulah and Lucille wanted to keep it in the family, but your grandmother, Bernice, wanted to sell it. Things went downhill after that.'

Why haven't I heard of these people? Why had Momma kept them a secret?

'Cecelia, I want you to listen to me.' Dad looked out the window and took a long, slow breath. 'With your mother dying and me traveling for my job, things have got to change. All your grandparents are gone, and other than my cousin Judd, the only relatives left are Tallulah and Lucille.'

Every nerve in my body snapped to attention. 'So what does this have to do with me?'

He never even looked at me when he said. 'Tallulah asked if you'd like to go down to Savannah, Georgia.'

'For how long? You mean for summer vacation?'

Dad rubbed the back of his neck and began to pace. 'No, I mean . . . I mean to live with her. Permanently.'

My stomach dropped. Time stalled. A rush of blood thundered

in my ears. *He's sending me away? Momma's gone and now he wants me gone too?*

I looked up at him. 'Live with her?'

'Tallulah's a fine woman. I think it'll do you good to get out of this town and have a fresh start. This is the best solution for everybody. And—'

I shook my head. 'No. I'll go live with Mrs. Odell.'

Dad pushed his hands into his pockets. 'I know she's important to you, but think how hard it would be on her if you moved into her house. Mrs. Odell is over eighty years old. Besides, in Savannah, you'd have a new school and new friends.'

What an idiot. How can I have new friends when I don't have any old ones? I glared at him, wishing he'd vaporize into a puff of smoke.

The muscles in his jaw tightened. 'C'mon, CeeCee, don't look at me like that. I'm trying to do the right thing here. And I—'

I rose from the chair and walked to the front window, my ankles weak and my throat so full with hurt that I couldn't swallow.

Across the street two girls from my class at school were walking down the sidewalk. They stopped and looked at our house, and I could tell by the way they leaned their heads together and talked that they'd heard about Momma's death – red shoes, tiara, Happy Cow Ice Cream truck, and all. Most likely the whole town was talking about it. Eventually stories of my mother's final day would be distorted by the countless mouths that repeated them, of that I was certain.

I leaned my forehead against the windowpane and closed my eyes.

Dad's voice sounded like it was a million miles away when he said, 'One day you'll thank me for this. Believe me, you will.'

He reached out and touched my shoulder, but I shrugged him away.

The heaviness of his footsteps shook the floorboards as he walked away. I heard him grab a beer from the refrigerator, and a moment later, the screen door slapped closed behind him.

I stood at the window in a foggy stupor of confusion and disbelief. I'd never even spent the night away from home before, and now here I was, about to move far away and live with someone I didn't even know. And I had not one word of say-so in the matter. Momma had been gone for only three days, and already I was facing the single biggest lesson of my life: death changes everything.

Later that afternoon, Dad came banging up the stairs with an old brown suitcase. 'It's all set,' he said, walking into my bedroom and avoiding my eyes. 'Tallulah will come get you tomorrow morning,' he muttered, hoisting the suitcase onto the bed.

'But what about my books?' I said, pointing to the stacks of books lined up on the floor across from my bed. It had been a while since I counted them, but there had to be at least two hundred.

Dad hadn't set foot inside my room for years, and he stared at the books with a blank expression on his face. 'Where'd you get all those books?'

'Every year the library has a sale. Ten books for a dollar. Mrs. Odell buys me books too.'

'You've read those books?'

'Yes. I've read some of them two or three times.'

'Now, wait a minute,' he said, rubbing the crease in his forehead. 'You're telling me you've read *all* those damn books?'

I nodded but didn't speak, couldn't speak. *How dare he call them 'damn books'?* A raw hurt burned in my belly, and I wanted to tell him that he obviously didn't know a *damn* thing about me.

The corners of his mouth tightened. 'Well, we can't ask Tallulah to haul all those books to Savannah. So pick out a few of your favorites. The rest I'll have to give away.'

'No. You can't do that.' I pulled my report card from the drawer in my nightstand and shoved it toward him. 'Those books helped me do *this*.'

He leaned against the doorjamb and scanned down the column of grades. 'You got As – in *everything*?'

I didn't know why he was so shocked. He'd never once bothered to look at any of my report cards, so what was he expecting?

'Well,' he said, placing my report card on the bed, 'you're a smart girl. You should be proud of yourself. I never got As. Anyway, I'll get a box from the basement and you can pack it up with a few of your favorite books, but only one box.'

One box, that's all? He's sending me away and won't even let me take my books?

My hands began to shake, and the words 'I hate you' tumbled out of my mouth.

We stood and looked at each other until the room grew so quiet I could hear the air move through the window screen.

Dad gave me a tired look and nodded. 'I don't blame you.' When he walked out the door, I heard him mutter, 'If I were you, I'd hate me too.'

The truth fell on me like a piano. Though I had no idea what lay ahead, there was one thing I knew for sure: wherever I was going, it had to be better than where I was.

I spent the rest of the afternoon sorting through all my books. Every time I set one aside in the pile to be left behind, I felt numb with anger. Finally I selected my favorites and packed them into the box: *The Chronicles of Narnia*, *Gulliver's Travels*, and every Nancy Drew book I had.

Later that night, Dad left the house, saying he'd be back in an hour or so. After he pulled out of the driveway, I walked down the hall and stood outside my mother's bedroom door. The house was so still and hushed, I could hear the ticking of the clock by her bed. Slowly I reached out, turned the doorknob, and pushed the door open. I stood for a moment and peered into the shadowy darkness, then I stepped inside and turned on a light.

Her bedroom was a perfume-scented battlefield. Above all else, it was a testimony to her illness. The mirror above the vanity table was cracked in half. Hair rollers and tubes of lipstick were scattered across the floor like spent bullet casings – all of them sad reminders of Momma's long-fought interior war. Deep within the grooves of the dull wood floor, I could still see remnants of the talcum powder she'd hurled across the room, and the vision of it exploding in the air made a lump rise in my throat.

From the cedar chest I removed her scrapbook and slowly leafed through the pages, touching my mother's most precious memories – memories that were smeared by fingerprints and dulled by the passage of time.

The bed was covered with mounds of her favorite dresses – a sorrowful pastel landscape of rumpled chiffon and taffeta. I gathered a handful of hangers, and one by one I hung each dress in the closet, smoothing out the wrinkles as best as I could. When I finished, I stepped back.

And there they were – Momma's frayed old pageant dresses and prom gowns, all lined up in a row, arranged by color like a worn-out tattered rainbow.

'Good-bye, Momma,' I whispered, taking her scrapbook and heading for the door.

I don't know if I actually heard it, or if it was just a memory that played vividly in my mind, but as plain as day my mother's voice floated through the air: 'One day you'll wear all these beautiful gowns too. I'm saving them for you, darlin'.'

I shook my head. 'No, I won't, Momma. Not ever.'

Silently I closed the door behind me.

Four

She was sitting on the weather-worn porch swing. The rusty chains creaked back and forth in a slow, easy rhythm that I knew by heart. Other than my parents, she was the only person I'd known all my life. I purely loved her.

I stood for a moment and watched her, and a sweep of panic stole my breath when I realized that I might never see her again. I jumped from the steps and ran across the lawn as fast as I could go. When Mrs. Odell saw me coming, she stood and opened her arms, and like a baby bird returning to its nest for the final time, I flew right into them.

Neither one of us said anything for a long time. We just stood and hugged each other. 'Oh, honey,' she said, easing herself down on the swing and patting the seat next to her, 'come sit with me.'

I buried my face against her shoulder, and, like always, she smelled of freshly ironed cotton. She kissed my temple and pulled me close. 'Your daddy came by a little bit ago. He told me you're moving to Savannah. I've never seen it, but I hear it's pretty down there.'

As she began to slowly swing, I nuzzled closer. 'Mrs. Odell, couldn't I live with you?'

'I wish you could,' she said, pressing her cheek to mine. 'But that's not the way it's written in your Life Book. This is the beginning of a big adventure, and you won't want to miss it. Your Life Book is about to reveal a brand new chapter, and so is mine.'

I sat up and searched her face. 'What do you mean?'

'The winter months are hard on me. A few weeks ago my cousin Adele called and asked me to move down to Florida, to live with her. I knew it would be a nice warm place to spend the rest of my days, but I just wasn't sure if that's where I belonged. So I thought about it awhile, and after your daddy told me that you're moving to Savannah, I decided I'd go ahead and accept Adele's offer. Life is full of change, honey. That's how we learn and grow. When we're born, the Good Lord gives each of us a Life Book. Chapter by chapter, we live and learn.'

'But, Mrs. Odell, I've never even heard of a Life Book.'

'It's not a book you can see or touch. It's a book that's held deep within your heart. It's guarded by your spirit.'

'My spirit?'

'Yes,' she said, smoothing a loose strand of hair from my face. 'When a chapter of your Life Book is complete, your spirit knows it's time to turn the page so a new chapter can begin. Even when you're scared or think you're not ready, your spirit knows you are.'

'Really?'

Mrs. Odell nodded and her voice cracked with emotion. 'You and I have shared a wonderful chapter, Cecelia. You'll never know how much joy you've brought into my life. I love you more than I can say. When my son James was killed in the war, and then Elmer passed away so unexpectedly, all of a sudden I was a widow with no family close by. There were times I was so sad and lonely I could hardly get out of bed. Those were dark days.

'Then, one summer morning, a page turned in *my* Life Book. I'll never forget it. I was sitting at the kitchen table, trying to glue the broken handle of a teacup. I was feeling sorry for myself. It seemed like my hopes and dreams got all chewed up like an old moth-eaten sweater. I was thinking life just wasn't worth living anymore. Right when I had that thought, somebody knocked at the back door. I looked up, and there was your mother holding you in her arms. You were so tiny, only a few months old. She asked if I'd watch you while she went to get her hair cut. Well, of course, I said yes. When I reached out and took hold of you, do you know what happened next?'

'What?'

'My sadness fell away. If you want to know the truth, I think I needed you that day a lot more than you needed me.' Mrs. Odell's eyes glistened when she said, 'Oh, CeeCee, what memories we've made, and there will be more to come. Florida isn't all that far from Savannah. I believe we'll see each other again. I really do.'

I took my finger and traced the blue ropes of veins in her hand.

My first clear memory of Mrs. Odell was on the afternoon of my fourth birthday. The snow had melted, and the sun was shining in a bright blue sky. Mrs. Odell knocked on our back door and asked Momma if she could have me for a while. Momma said yes, and Mrs. Odell took my hand and walked me toward her house. Bobbing from a long string tied to the rail of her porch was a bright red balloon, and when we climbed the steps, I saw two frosted cupcakes sitting on the potting bench by her back door. Stuck in a thick swirl of chocolate frosting on one of the cupcakes were four little candles. Mrs. Odell pulled a pack of matches from the pocket of her sweater, lit them, and grinned. 'Now make a wish, honey.'

My wish – which I loudly declared – was that she'd teach me to read storybooks.

'We'll start this afternoon,' she said with a wink.

After we ate our cupcakes and licked every last crumb from our fingers, Mrs. Odell untied the string of the balloon and offered it to me. 'This is filled with a special air called helium, so hold on tight,' she said, leading me to the middle of her back-yard. 'All right, now you get to make another wish. But this time it's a secret wish. Don't tell me what it is, just think about it real hard in your mind.'

A sudden gust of wind swirled around me and took hold of the balloon as if to say, 'Hurry, follow me for the ride of your life.' The balloon bobbed and tugged in an effort to escape, but I gripped the string tightly and made the secret wish that Mrs. Odell and I would always be together.

'When you're ready, let go so the balloon can carry your wish into the sky.'

'But where's it going?'

Mrs. Odell leaned down close and said, 'It's a mystery. We just have to believe.'

I let the string slip through my fingers. The balloon took flight, weaving back and forth as if uncertain where to go. A moment later the wind swept it high in the air, and Mrs. Odell and I stood side by side and watched it disappear.

And now here we were, saying good-bye.

How long we sat on her porch swing I couldn't say, but when Mrs. Odell pressed her cheek against mine and said, 'Write to me, honey, and I'll write to you too,' I was so sad I couldn't even speak.

I woke so early the following morning the birds were still asleep. As I pushed back the covers and sat up, I felt a twinge of sadness. This was the last morning I'd ever wake up in my bed-room. And even with the cracked ceiling and the dingy blue walls, I knew I'd miss it. My skin felt tight against my ribs as I slid out of bed and went downstairs. Dad was asleep on the sofa, still wearing the clothes he'd worn to the cemetery. An empty whiskey bottle and an overturned glass were lying on the floor by his side. I looked at him, feeling nothing but cold contempt, then I turned and crept into the kitchen. After pouring a glass of orange juice, I stepped out to the back porch.

While sitting on the steps in the sleepy half-light of dawn, I drank my juice and took mental snapshots of what stood before me. The picnic table, which long ago had surrendered to dry rot and years of neglect, lay in a dilapidated heap of moss-stained boards. From a distance it looked like the ribs of a dinosaur carcass protruding from the earth. And off to the side was the thin shadow of Momma's clothesline, hanging slack between two maple trees.

I turned and gazed at Mrs. Odell's house. I wanted to remember her garden, her old porch swing, and the morning-glory trellis that brought the hummingbirds to visit. My eyes followed the path I'd beaten through the grass from our back door to hers, a path that was now a narrow ribbon of smooth brown dirt. The pain of knowing I'd never travel along it again was so unbearable I had to look away.

A cool breeze ruffled the hem of my nightgown, the birds began to chirp and sing, and the first sparks of sunlight brought the dewdrops to life. I took one last look at all that surrounded me and slowly rose from the steps. When my fingers touched the knob of the back door, something inside me shifted – I could actually feel it. I knew Mrs. Odell was right. I felt the flutter of a page turn deep within me as a chapter in my Life Book came to a close.

Five

While I was standing in front of the bathroom mirror, braiding my ponytail and chewing the inside of my lip till I tasted blood, Dad called up the stairs, 'I put your suitcase and box of books by the front door. I'm going to the hardware store.'

'Who cares?' I mumbled under my breath.

'CeeCee, did you hear me?'

'Okay,' I called back. I spit a mouthful of blood into the sink and rinsed it down the drain. My stomach did a series of flips when I walked across the hall and into my bedroom. I was so nervous the skin at the back of my arms itched. From a stack of books I pulled out an old atlas, sat on the floor, and turned to the map of Georgia. While trying to figure out how many miles away Savannah was, I heard a *beep-beep* from the driveway. I scrambled to my feet and looked out the window as my great-aunt's car rolled to a stop.

The door opened and she slid from the seat. The skirt of her green-and-white polka-dotted dress moved softly in the breeze, and a small straw hat was perched on her head. After giving her white gloves a quick tug, she headed toward the house. My heart all but pounded clean through my chest when she knocked at the door.

What should I do? What will I say to her?

The knock on the door came again, followed by a cheery 'Woo-hoo – anybody home?'

I took a deep breath, pried my feet from the floor, and descended the stairs on rubbery legs. When I opened the door, her grin stretched from ear to ear. 'Cecelia Rose, just look at you. You're as precious as you can be.'

I moved aside. 'Please come in.'

She stepped inside and offered me her hand. 'I know you couldn't possibly remember me. We met when you were just a wee little thing. I'm your great-aunt Tallulah Caldwell, but everyone calls me Tootie, and I'd be pleased if you would too.'

I could barely hear my voice when I said, 'I'm glad to meet you, Great-aunt Tootie.'

She winked. 'That's quite a mouthful. Let's forget about the "Great" part, shall we? Why don't you just call me Aunt Tootie? Would that be all right?'

Feeling tongue-tied and inadequate in every way imaginable, I could do nothing but nod.

She gave me a gentle squeeze. 'I know you've been through quite an ordeal, and I can't begin to tell you how sorry I am. Your daddy and I have had several conversations, and he told me you'd like to come live with me.'

A soft fringe of silver-gray hair framed a gentle face that was lightly etched with fine lines. Her watery brown eyes grew large behind the lenses of her glasses. They were kind eyes.

'Your mind must be swimming right now, but I want you to know that I've got a big ole house with plenty of room, and I'd sure love to have you.'

Those six simple words echoed around me and filled the room with light: *I'd sure love to have you . . . I'd sure love to have you . . .*

My shoulders began to shake, and to my disbelief, hot tears

47

spilled from my eyes and ran down my cheeks. Aunt Tootie wrapped me in her arms and pulled me close. 'Oh, honey,' she said, stroking my hair, 'everything will be all right. If I'd known about all the problems your momma was having, I'd have come to get the both of you a long time ago.'

Right then and there I felt my life pass fully into her white-gloved hands.

It felt so good to be held that I cried until I got the hiccups. Aunt Tootie led me into the kitchen, sat me down at the table, and got me a glass of water. Through a blur of tears I watched her retrieve a handkerchief from her shiny black handbag. She sat down next to me and pressed it into my palm. 'Here, take this and dry your tears. The worst is behind you.'

Her handkerchief smelled as wonderful as she did. Edged in delicate lace with tiny violets embroidered along its edges, it was the most beautiful thing I'd ever seen. But after I'd wiped my eyes and blown my nose, it looked like a soggy bouquet lying limp in my hands.

'You go ahead and keep the hankie, honey. I have lots more in my handbag.' She leaned forward and looked into my eyes; her smile was so tender and generous I felt its warmth touch my cheeks. 'Cecelia Rose, why don't you show me your bedroom so we can pack up your things?'

My lips quivered. 'I already packed my clothes, and I have a box of books too.'

She stood and offered me her hand. 'Well, then, show me what all you're bringing.'

I led her into the living room, and when I pointed to the suitcase and box of books, she said, 'That's it? I have lots of room in my car, Cecelia. Is there anything else you'd like to bring?'

Though I wanted to ask if I could take all my old books, I shook my head. 'No, I don't need anything else.'

'All right, then, let's take these things out to the car, shall we?'

As I helped her lift my suitcase into the trunk, she said, 'Cecelia, do you have something to remember your momma by – pictures, jewelry?'

I thought of my mother's scrapbook and nodded. In an effort to move the conversation away from Momma, I said, 'This is the prettiest car I've ever seen. What kind is it?'

Her eyes shone with pride. 'This is a Packard Victoria. I've had this car since the day my late husband, Taylor, and I picked it out from the showroom.' She closed her eyes and thought for a moment. 'Let's see. That was the summer of 1948. Almost twenty years ago.'

'Does that mean it's an antique?'

She laughed. 'Well, I guess so. I suppose we're both antiques.'

'Where did you get her?' I asked, walking to the front of the car and running my fingers over the silver angel's wings. They were warm from the sun and as smooth as glass.

Aunt Tootie came and stood next to me. 'That's Delilah. Taylor had her made for me. He wanted me to have a guardian angel to take care of me on the highway. And so far she's done a fine job. Delilah will get us back to Savannah safe and sound.'

We stood, looking at each other, and everything went quiet. Time caved in around me. This was it. I was leaving Willoughby, Mrs. Odell, and my books.

Aunt Tootie reached out and touched my shoulder. 'Cecelia Rose, are you ready to go?'

'But what about Dad? Aren't we going to wait for him?'

The lines beneath her eyes deepened. 'Your father isn't coming to say good-bye. He thought it would be easier this way – less painful. I'm sorry.'

Not coming to say good-bye?

She opened her handbag, pulled out an envelope, and handed it to me. 'He wanted me to give this to you.'

I stared at the envelope in her outstretched hand, and something went flat inside me.

My aunt's words were so soft I barely heard them. 'Shall I save it for later?'

I shook my head, took the envelope, and pulled out a note.

Dear Cecelia,
  I'm sorry for everything that has happened.
  But I know you'll be happy in Savannah.

  Love,
  Dad

Nineteen words. I counted them. That's all he had to say to me. Nineteen meaningless little words.

And that's when my father died to me — right there in the driveway. I was, as of that very moment, an orphan. Both my parents were dead, and if I was to be honest with myself, they'd been dead for a long time. It just took me awhile to figure it out.

I shoved the note back into the envelope and stuffed it deep in my pocket. Though I could feel Aunt Tootie's eyes on me, I couldn't bring myself to look at her. I turned and took one last look at Mrs. Odell's little house, and my throat tightened when I saw her peek through the slats of the venetian blind in her front window. That did it. I took off running toward her house. She opened the door, stepped onto the porch, and threw her arms around me. Neither one of us said a word; we just clung to each other like it was the end of the world. And in many ways it was.

'Oh, Cecelia,' she whispered into my hair, 'this is so hard.'

I burrowed my face into her shoulder. 'I love you, Mrs. Odell.'

She leaned close to my ear. 'And I love you. Don't be scared, honey. Remember what I told you about your Life Book?'

I looked into her eyes. 'Yes.'

She kissed my forehead. 'This is a wonderful new chapter for you. Everything will be fine. I promise it will. You'll see.'

I took a deep breath and turned to see Aunt Tootie standing at the bottom of the steps.

'I'm ready,' I said, not believing it but saying it just the same.

Aunt Tootie winked at Mrs. Odell. 'I'll call you when we reach Savannah, Gertrude. I'll take good care of Cecelia. I promise.'

Mrs. Odell nodded, lowered her head, and walked inside her house. A part of me went right through the door with her.

Aunt Tootie took hold of my hand, and we walked toward the car. 'How do you know Mrs. Odell?' I asked.

'Your father told me how close the two of you are, so I stopped by to see her earlier this morning before I came to get you. She's a lovely lady, and she sure thinks the world of you.'

Aunt Tootie opened the driver's side door and looked at me. 'Cecelia, let's go home. Delilah will lead the way.'

I walked to the passenger side, took a deep breath, and climbed in. I'd never been in such a fancy car. It had tan leather seats as plush as sofas, and sprouting from the dashboard were all sorts of knobs and gizmos. In the backseat were three round floral boxes tied with silk ribbons.

'Those boxes are pretty,' I said, wiping a tear from my cheek. 'What's in them?'

'Hats,' she said, adjusting herself on the seat. 'I started collecting them when I was in my twenties and haven't stopped since. Would you like to wear one?'

'Okay.'

She reached over the seat and pulled one from its box. 'I think this one will suit you just fine,' she said, handing me a white straw hat with a red flower pinned to its wide yellow band.

I pulled it on and tucked in my bangs.

Aunt Tootie tilted her head and smiled. 'You know what, Cecelia? That hat looks better on you than it ever did on me. I think it's time it moved on. If you'd like to have it, I'd be pleased to give it to you.'

I learned over and looked at myself in the rearview mirror. 'Thank you.'

'You're welcome, sugar. All right,' she said, pushing her glasses onto the bridge of her nose, 'we're on our way.' She revved the engine and put the car in reverse, but the car lunged backward and knocked over a reflector at the end of the driveway.

'Don't worry,' she said with a laugh. 'I do a whole lot better when the road is in front of me.' She put the car in drive and roared down the street.

As we left the town of Willoughby behind, I turned and rested my chin on the back of the seat. From the rear window I watched the only town I'd ever known disappear behind us. I don't think I could have spoken if I'd tried, which turned out to be just fine. As she zoomed down the road, the sunlight dotting and splashing across the windshield, Aunt Tootie twittered on about everything from the herb garden she'd just planted to how much she loved old houses, antique clocks, and Boston cream pie. The farther we traveled, the more I calmed down, and after we had stopped for lunch, I found my voice and was able to share a little bit in the conversation. I told her how much I loved to read, and how I'd learned about flowers from Mrs. Odell.

'So you like working in the garden?'

'Yes. I even like to pull weeds.'

'Oh, that's wonderful. Maybe you'd like to help me with my gardens too. Now, let me tell you about the things I planted on the north side of the house . . . '

I'd never met anyone who could talk as much as Aunt Tootie. She kept right on talking until the sun disappeared beyond the horizon, pulling wispy violet-blue clouds behind it. It wasn't until the moon rolled over the tops of the trees that she wound down her storytelling and asked me to help her watch for a place to stay for the night.

'When Taylor and I traveled, it was my job to find a motel. As soon as it started to get dark, he'd say, "Tootie-girl, it's time for you to be the scout," and then I'd watch for a place to stay.'

'Where did the name Tootie come from?'

Her eyes lit up and she let out a little laugh. 'When I met Taylor I'd never driven a car. In fact, I'd always been scared to death at the thought of it. Taylor said it was imperative that I learn to drive; he said all women should savor their independence. So, despite my protests, which I can assure you were many, he taught me. But when I got behind the wheel, I was so nervous I could hardly think straight. Every time a car got close, I'd wave my arms and toot the horn like crazy to warn everyone to keep clear. Taylor laughed and laughed. He thought it was the funniest thing he'd ever seen. That's when he nicknamed me Tootie. All my friends picked up on it, and pretty soon nobody called me Tallulah anymore.'

As the wind whistled through the open windows and the scenery flew by in blurry smears of gray, I got a pretty good idea why Aunt Tootie's husband had a guardian angel made for the hood of her car. I looked at my aunt and said, 'Looks like you're not afraid to drive anymore.'

Oh, how she laughed.

I watched out the window and read every sign we passed. Finally I saw one that advertised a motel. 'Look,' I said, pointing to a dimly lit sign at the side of the road. 'Mountain View Travel Lodge – ten point five miles.'

'Good job, sugar. We'll be relaxing in bed in no time.'

The headlights carved a hole through the foggy darkness as she zoomed down the highway. I felt like she was driving me straight into a silver-edged dream. I had no idea where we were, and to be honest, I don't think Aunt Tootie did, either. All I knew was that I was flying through the night in a fancy car with a woman who showed up out of nowhere and offered to take me, messed-up life and all, to a place called Savannah.

It was nearly five o'clock the following evening when we approached a narrow, vine-covered bridge. Three words were written on a sign at the side of the road, and as we roared by, I whispered them to myself: 'Welcome to Savannah.'

The biggest trees I'd ever seen reached out to one another as if trying to hold hands over wide, brick-paved streets, and grand old houses stood tall and proud on smooth shade-dappled lawns. Like a curious spaniel, I leaned my head out the window and breathed in. The air was warm and sweet with the scent of freshly cut grass.

Aunt Tootie slowed and turned onto a shady street called West Gaston. 'Well, here we are,' she said, pulling to a stop at the curb. 'Welcome to your new home, sugar.' She gestured to a house surrounded by lush gardens and an iron fence that looked like countless yards of black lace. The house, which was made of stucco and painted the color of lemonade, was three stories tall and had lots of arched windows. Wide stone steps stretched high above the street and ended at double front doors.

'We'll leave the car here. After we unload the trunk, I'll pull it around back to the garage.' She grabbed her handbag and we climbed out of the car. While she headed up the steps, I lagged behind and craned my neck to see all that surrounded me. I had the sensation that an unseen hand had plunked me into a giant slingshot, pulled back, and let go. I was catapulting into a new world and nothing could have prepared me for it.

The front hall – which Aunt Tootie called the foy-yay – was, to my way of thinking, a room unto itself. An alabaster chandelier sent a wash of mellow light over walls the color of peach sherbet. The ceiling soared over my head and was framed by elaborately carved moldings, and to the left was a stairway that had a wide ribbon of flowery carpet running down its center.

My aunt chattered like a sparrow as she flitted from room to room. 'This is your home now, honey, and I want you to know where everything is so you feel comfortable. You have no idea how much I love this old house. It was built back in 1858. Thanks to General Sherman, Savannah was spared the ravages of the Civil War . . .'

I tried to listen to all she said, but her voice faded into the plump upholstery and richly patterned carpets. Each room was a vision of beauty, and each had vases overflowing with all sorts of fresh flowers.

'Oh, look what Oletta did,' Aunt Tootie said, stopping to smell a vase full of yellow roses. 'Aren't they pretty? She went out to the garden and cut all these flowers while I was gone. I love coming home to a house full of bouquets – it makes me feel happy.'

I studied the face of a tall grandfather clock and lightly touched its beveled-glass door. 'Who's Oletta?'

'She runs my house, and she's the finest cook I've ever known. Just wait, you'll think you went straight to heaven when you taste her chocolate cream pie.'

'But if you live alone, why do you need a cook?'

Aunt Tootie pulled off her gloves and dropped them on a

marble-topped chest. 'Oletta has been with me for years and years,' she said, removing her hat and scratching her scalp. 'Lord knows I tried, but I never was much of a cook. Taylor just loved good food – eating was one of the greatest joys in his life. We needed Oletta back then. When Taylor passed away, I kept her on. She's family to me. I honestly don't know what I'd do without her.'

When we climbed the steps to the second floor, I was weak-kneed from sensory overload. A pair of blue-and-white vases, as tall as I was and filled with flowers the size of basketballs, flanked the arched corridor at the top of the staircase. I all but got drunk on the perfumed air as we headed down the hall.

'There are four guest bedrooms up here. This one faces the front of the house,' she said, stepping into a room and turning on the overhead light. The bed had four carved posts and was so high off the floor there were little wooden steps to reach it. Long ivory-colored draperies were covered with acres of embroidery and tied back with huge green tassels. Between two windows sat a chest of drawers the size of a refrigerator.

'It's yours if you want it, Cecelia, but we'll take a look at all the others before you decide.'

The other bedrooms were much the same as the first – big and fancy – all with their own private bathrooms that had shiny white tubs supported by golden feet that looked like the claws of giant birds.

My aunt chattered away as she continued her tour. I followed, keeping my arms glued to my sides so I wouldn't bump into anything. As breathtaking as the house was, Aunt Tootie wasn't even the slightest bit show-offy. In fact, she seemed tethered to the earth and as homey as a comfortable chair.

At the far left side of the upstairs hallway was an alcove with an arched door. 'What's in there?' I asked.

'I'll show you.' She opened the door, flicked on a light, and led me up a narrow stairway. 'There are two bedrooms and a storage room at the end of the hall. And this,' she said, dramatically opening a door, 'is the sleeping porch. Isn't it the sweetest thing you've ever seen?'

She walked around the room and flung open tall moss-green shutters to reveal floor-to-ceiling screens. A light breeze rolled in and my aunt took a deep breath. 'It smells divine up here, doesn't it?'

The wooden floor was painted a soft robin's-egg blue, and the ceiling was pale yellow. An iron bed shaped like a sleigh was smothered with colorful pillows, and when I touched the white comforter, my fingers disappeared as if I'd plunged them into a mound of whipped cream. The room was like a happy tree house made just for girls.

I stepped across the floor and pressed my nose against the window screen. I was up so high I had a bird's-eye view of the entire garden. 'Wow. Is this your bedroom?'

'Oh, no, honey. My bedroom is at the end of the hall on the second floor. When we go back downstairs, I'll show you.'

A smile tugged at the corners of my mouth. 'Aunt Tootie,' I said, turning to face her, 'could *this* be my bedroom?'

She was quiet for a moment, and I wondered if I shouldn't have asked, like maybe this was a room reserved for special guests. But then she put her arm around my shoulders and nodded. 'If I were your age, I believe this is the room I'd pick too. Consider it yours, Cecelia Rose. In the winter months you'll have to use one of the other bedrooms – this room gets cold – but for now I think it'll be perfect.'

She gave my shoulders a squeeze. 'All right, let's get your suitcase out of the car and get you settled. Then we'll have a bite to eat and go to bed. I don't know about you, but I'm plum worn-out.'

Six

I woke to the sound of children's voices, as faint as the tinkling of wind chimes. The voices grew louder and erupted into gales of laughter. I listened until the laughter faded away.

The bedsheets were damp with humidity and sleep, and from the pillowcase I detected a familiar scent: it was just like the lavender sachets Mrs. Odell made every year as Christmas gifts. I rubbed my eyes and tried to sit up, but I was nestled deep in the feather bed, like a baby bird in a nest. Once I freed myself, I sat up and looked around the room. My dented brown suitcase looked out of place on the pretty floral rug, and my scuffed-up penny loafers looked just plain wrong sitting beneath the delicate antique chair with its crisp, eyelet-ruffled seat cushion.

Thoughts of Momma surfaced. It seemed like she died a long time ago, an event that was now fuzzy and out of focus, from the passage of years instead of days. A terrible ache spread across my chest when I thought of Mrs. Odell. I wondered if she was thinking about me too, and if her chest hurt like mine. My thoughts drifted to the adventure of traveling all those miles to get here, and how only a few hours ago that sign had appeared at the side of the road, spelling out the three words I knew would forever change my life: WELCOME TO SAVANNAH.

All those thoughts swirled in my mind like confetti in a windstorm. I actually felt dizzy, flopped back on the pillow, and closed my eyes. I must have dozed off, because I was startled when a voice boomed from above me.

'You're sleeping your life away up here. This ain't no hotel. Time to get up.'

I bolted upright and blinked. Standing at the end of the bed was a tall, thickly built woman with skin as smooth and brown as a chestnut. A bright yellow-and-blue-striped scarf was coiled around her head, and a white apron hung loosely over her shapeless graydress.

Her brown eyes narrowed. 'I ain't got time for no lazybones today. You need to get up and get yourself dressed.'

She propped her hands on her hips and waited for me to say something. But my tongue had turned thick, and all I could do was stare.

'You got five minutes to get downstairs – that's all. Understand?'

A strong breeze pushed through the windows and lifted the edge of her apron like a sail. She smoothed it down and headed toward the door. As she disappeared I heard her grumble, 'Lord, next time I climb this many steps it best be on the stairway to heaven. That's all I gotta say.'

I listened to the slow *thump, thump, thump* as she lumbered down the stairs. When the sound of her footsteps faded, I bolted out of bed, brushed my teeth, and got dressed.

When I descended the stairs and entered the room Aunt Tootie had called the foy-yay, an overwhelming longing to be back in Ohio washed over me. It was so powerful I had to stop for a minute and collect myself. I looked down at my rumpled clothes, and while trying to smooth out my T-shirt, I knew I didn't belong in this beautiful house.

Her voice thundered down the hall behind me. 'Hello! I'm speakin' to you.'

I snapped to attention and turned. Framed in an open doorway at the end of the hall, she stood on a pair of thick legs that sagged into boxy brown shoes. 'C'mon, breakfast is ready.'

My heart raced and my bare feet slapped against the shiny wood floor as I scurried down the hall. I followed her shadow through an arched doorway and into the kitchen.

'The table's in there,' she said, tilting her head toward a door. 'Miz Tootie went to the beauty parlor, and then she's goin' to a board meeting. She won't be home till after lunch.'

I nodded, gingerly pushed open the door, and stepped into a sun-splashed room that overlooked a garden. A round table draped in a pink-and-white plaid tablecloth sat in the center of the room. Fancy silverware engraved with swirling initials sat atop a linen napkin, and on the table were two white china plates. Carefully I picked one up and held it to the light. It was so delicate I could almost see right through it.

The door from the kitchen swung open, and I quickly returned the plate to the table. She walked in with a tray in her hands and set it on the table. Silence filled the room as we considered each other.

'Are you Oletta?'

'Umm-hmm.' From a gleaming crystal pitcher she poured orange juice into a glass and set it on the table with a loud *thunk*. 'This is a fine home,' she said, leveling her dark eyes on me. 'And fine homes have *rules*. And one of them rules is wearin' shoes to the table.'

I looked at my bare feet and felt my cheeks flame.

Her voice softened a bit when she said. 'Just remember for next time. Okay?'

I nodded.

'Now, sit yourself down so I can serve breakfast.'

Oletta placed a starched white doily on the plate in front of me while I pulled out a chair and sat down. On top of the doily she set a bowl covered by a dome-shaped silver lid. Next she set out two small glass bowls that looked like they were carved from ice; one was filled with raspberries and the other with brown sugar. With a pair of silver tongs she placed a frosted cinnamon roll on a small plate. Her eyes bore a hole right through me when she hooked her finger through the handle of the domed lid and lifted it to reveal a bowl of steaming hot oatmeal. She replaced the lid with a sharp-sounding *ting*, turned, and left the room.

Oatmeal.

I remembered a blustery cold morning back in 1963. I had walked into the kitchen to find Momma standing at the stove. Steam rose in the air, and beads of moisture dripped down the windowpane as she frantically stirred a pot. When she saw me in the doorway, she smiled and told me to sit at the table while she finished.

A few minutes later she ceremoniously placed a bowl of oatmeal in front of me, propped her hands on her hips, and smiled. 'I made a special surprise for my sweet little honey-bunny. Happy birthday.'

I peered into the bowl in disbelief. Sprinkled on top of the lumpy oatmeal were chunks of broken candy canes, and if that wasn't bad enough, Momma had topped it off with a sprinkle of paprika and three shriveled-up green olives. I stared into the bowl, stupefied.

But worst of all: it wasn't my birthday.

I pushed that memory aside and gazed out the window at Aunt Tootie's garden. Mounds of creamy-white flowers billowed over the edge of the brick patio like runaway soapsuds. I thought about Mrs. Odell – how much she loved flowers – and me. Next thing I knew tears flooded my eyes. I pressed my palms to my cheeks and tried to grab hold of myself, but I was powerless to stop the avalanche of emotions that crashed in on me.

Coming to Savannah was a colossal mistake. I didn't fit in and I knew I never would. I buried my face into my hands, let out a muffled sob, and wondered how much it would cost for a bus ticket back to Willoughby. I had fifteen dollars shoved inside my suitcase, and I'd use that to get as close to home as I could. I'd walk the rest of the way if I had to. I didn't know when I'd ever felt so low or cried so hard. Probably never.

I was startled when something pressed against the bare flesh of my arm. I looked up to see Oletta standing next to me with a scowl on her face as she tapped a box of tissues against my skin. I took one and blotted my eyes.

'What's the matter with you, child?'

I blew my nose. 'Everything's the matter with me.'

Her eyebrows lifted into high arches. 'Everything? Well, that's a *whoooole* lot.'

I don't know what happened, but my hands began to shake, and my scalp felt like it was on fire. Something deep within me let loose, and I broke wide open. Before I could stop myself, I told Oletta about Momma's Goodwill shopping sprees, her fits of rage, and how my dad had walked out on us. The more I told Oletta, the more I cried, pulling one tissue after another from the box she'd set on the table. I couldn't believe all the things I heard myself say.

What are you doing? Are you crazy? Stop it, CeeCee. Shut up. Shut up.

But my mouth had disengaged from my brain, and I jabbered on and on.

Oletta's eyes grew as round as silver dollars as she listened to my tear-soaked autobiography. She never said a word; she just pulled out the chair next to me and lowered herself down with a tired-sounding groan.

'Nobody liked me,' I mumbled into a wad of soggy tissue. 'The only friend I ever had was Mrs. Odell. And now I'll never see her again.'

When I finally grabbed hold of myself and realized I'd exposed the worst of my shame, I clamped my mouth shut and looked down at my hands. I wanted to crawl into a hole and die for all the things I'd just revealed.

'Sorry,' I whispered.

Oletta reached over and lifted the lid off the oatmeal. 'Eat your breakfast before it gets cold.'

My stomach was tied in knots, but I didn't want to insult her by not eating the breakfast she'd prepared. Halfheartedly I dipped my spoon into the oatmeal, but when it touched my tongue, my taste buds snapped awake.

Oletta reached out and spooned some brown sugar onto the oatmeal, followed by some plump berries. She never took her eyes off me as I emptied the entire bowl and gulped down a glass of orange juice. I had the sinking feeling Oletta had summed me up pretty fast, and I was sure the word *pathetic* was in her mind.

'Miz Tootie left in a hurry. I didn't catch what your name was.'

'My name is CeeCee. CeeCee Honeycutt,' I said, plucking the cinnamon roll from the plate. I took a bite and an involuntary moan of pleasure pushed past my lips. It was the most extraordinary thing I'd ever tasted. A rush of sugar exploded into my veins, and with my mouth full of that sugary, buttery sweetness, I let out a nervous laugh and started crying all over again. 'I'm the daughter of the 1951 Vidalia Onion Queen.'

Oletta slapped her hands on her thighs. 'Sweet baby Jesus. That's some kinda crazy life you was livin'. *Um-um-um*. No wonder you're cryin' and carryin' on.' She pressed her lips together and looked at me with such intensity, I got a sudden chill. I could see a storm of questions gathering in her eyes. 'How old are you, child?'

'Twelve.'

'Twelve? You sure is tiny for twelve. I thought you was about nine or ten. There ain't much to you but skin and bones.' She rested back in the chair and shook her head. 'So, your daddy didn't want to face all the problems your momma was having and he up and walked out, leaving you all alone without your momma's hand to guide you. That's a sad, sad story. C'mon over here, child,' she said, patting her lap. 'Let me give you some sugar.'

I had no idea what she meant, but at her urging I got up from the table. As she eased me onto her lap, I leaned against her shoulder and inhaled her scent. She smelled of warm cinnamon and kindness.

'Those are some mighty wild stories about your momma. Ain't nobody could make up something like that. When Miz Tootie said you was havin' a real hard time up north, she sure was tellin' the truth.'

Oletta patted my back with her wide, strong hand as if I were a baby and she wanted me to burp. 'I was crabby this morning and made you feel bad. I'm sorry. I was just in a bad mood from havin' to climb up all them stairs to wake you up. I worked in my vegetable patch yesterday and my legs ache something awful. It didn't have anything to do with you.'

'That's okay,' I said, wiping away a tear, only to feel another one form in the corner of my eye.

'Child, child,' she said with a heavy exhale. 'You've got a

whole lot of healin' to do. But the Good Lord sent you to the right place. Ain't nobody walkin' this green earth got a bigger heart than Miz Tootie. Once you settle in and let me get some meat on your bones, you'll feel a whole lot better.'

Oletta leaned back to look into my eyes, and there came a deafening crack, as if a bolt of lightning had exploded into the room. Next thing I knew we pitched backward and crashed to the floor. After I got over the shock of it, I crawled to my knees. But Oletta just lay there, motionless, splayed out across the floor.

'Oletta. Oh, no. Please wake up.' I patted her hand but she didn't move. I called her name again and squeezed her fingers, watching for her to breathe. 'Oletta ... Oletta?' Finally she blinked her eyes open and looked at me, dazed. I leaned close. 'Oh, my gosh. Are you all right?'

She lifted her hand and grimaced when she rubbed her forehead. 'What happened?'

'The chair broke.'

She was quiet for a moment and seemed disoriented as she slowly looked around the room.

'Are you okay?' I asked, touching her arm. 'Should I call an ambulance?'

Oletta let out a grunt as she struggled to sit up. She reached out, picked up a splintered piece of the destroyed chair, and examined it closely. 'I don't need no ambulance, but this chair sure does.'

I nodded. 'I think a coroner is more like it.'

Oletta gave me the strangest look, and then she launched into the finest laughter my ears had ever heard. It was a rich, gorgeous sound, as thick and smooth as pudding. I sat on the floor next to her, and pretty soon we were both laughing like fools.

I knew my wish had come true: I had a girlfriend in Savannah.

Seven

On my second full day in Savannah, Aunt Tootie and I had breakfast together. When she finished her coffee, she stood and dropped her napkin on the table. 'I've got a meeting with the trustees of the Historic Savannah Foundation a little later, but would you like to go for a walk through Forsyth Park before I get ready?'

'Sure.'

Before leaving the house, Aunt Tootie put on a sun-bleached straw hat and grabbed a bag of sunflower seeds from the pantry. While we strolled around the park, we talked and tossed the seeds to the birds and squirrels.

'Aunt Tootie, do you have children?'

'Taylor and I were never blessed with children, but I do have a lovely young girl in my life.'

'What's her name?' I asked, feeling an odd twinge of jealousy.

My aunt put her arm around my shoulders and gave me a squeeze. 'Her name is Cecelia Rose Honeycutt.'

I smiled up at her.

'Savannah is so pretty. I love the trees,' I said, looking up into a maze of moss-draped branches. 'Have you always lived here?'

She eased herself down on a bench in the shade and I sat next to her.

'I was born in Brunswick, Georgia. My father had a small jewelry store and we lived in the apartment above. My sister, Lucille, still lives there – she took over the store when my father passed on. When I met Taylor, this is where he'd lived all his life. So after we married, I left Brunswick and moved into his house in Ardsley Park. It's just a few miles from here. I liked his house just fine, but it was downtown Savannah that I loved. The first time Taylor drove me down Gaston Street, it was just like coming home – as if that was where I'd always belonged. But so many folks had lost their money during the Depression, and a good number of the big old houses were in disrepair. It made me feel so sad to see such magnificent homes fall to ruin. I told Taylor it was a crime and he agreed, but he didn't say much more about it.

'Well, I couldn't get those wonderful homes out of my mind. One evening during dinner, I asked Taylor if he'd consider buying one as a rehabilitation project. He put down his fork and looked at me like I'd lost my mind, so I dropped the subject. But every time we'd go out for a drive, I'd ask him to go down Gaston Street, and he'd take me.

'There was this one old house that stole my heart. It had been boarded up so long that even the paint on the For Sale sign had begun to peel. Well, one Sunday afternoon, Taylor took me out for ice cream. We drove around for a while, talking and having ourselves a gay old time. He turned down Gaston and pulled up in front of that house I loved. He turned off the engine and said, "Look, Tootie, the FOR SALE sign is gone. Looks like somebody bought your house."

'I was crushed. Taylor got out of the car and climbed the front steps to the house. He rattled the door and then reached over and ripped a board from one of the windows. I jumped from the car and asked him what on earth he was doing. He pulled a key from his pocket, unlocked the door, and called out, "Well, c'mon, Tootie. Don't you want to take a look at your new house?"'

'He bought you the house? The one you live in now?'

She nodded, smiling at the memory.

'Wow. I bet you were surprised.'

'I certainly was. I flew up those steps and into his arms. My sweet husband bought me that old house even though he thought it was a huge mistake. It took a team of workmen almost two years to bring the house back to the pride it once had, and I'm sure it cost Taylor a small fortune, but never once did he complain. He said as long as I was happy, well, then he was happy too.'

She tossed a handful of sunflower seeds to a gathering of birds and let out a sigh of contentment. 'I planted all the gardens myself, and then one day I got an idea and founded the Ladies of Savannah Garden Club.'

'What's that?'

'Oh, it's more social than anything,' she said with a chuckle. 'I get together with seven of my dearest friends on the first Thursday of every month. We rotate so we all have the chance to play hostess once a year. We play cards, drink oodles of Long Island iced tea, and talk about gardening and gossip till dinnertime. It's so much fun, we always laugh ourselves sick.'

I turned and looked at the giant fountain, trying to imagine having seven girlfriends to laugh with. 'But if you have so much fun, then why don't you get together more than once a month?'

She looked at me like a wise old owl and winked. 'Do something too often and it stops being special.'

After we returned home, Aunt Tootie changed clothes and

left for her meeting while I browsed through the books in her library. Floor-to-ceiling bookshelves lined three of the four walls, and there was a tall wooden ladder that rolled back and forth on wheels that ran along a shiny brass track bolted to the ceiling. Most of the books were about world history and biographies of famous people – Abraham Lincoln, Winston Churchill, and the like. As far as I could tell none of the books was anything I wanted to read, so I climbed off the ladder and wandered into the kitchen.

Oletta was singing some song about Jesus and collard greens while she worked at a butcher-block table that sat in front of the window. Flour covered her hands like thin white gloves, and beads of sweat glistened on her forehead as she beat a mound of dough with a wooden mallet.

'Whatcha doing?' I asked.

'I've gotta whack this dough at least two hundred times,' she said, hitting it so hard that puffs of flour rose in the air and dusted her chin. 'The secret to my beaten biscuits bein' the best in Savannah is 'cause I whack the dough till it blisters up real good.'

I wrinkled my nose. 'Beaten biscuits? I've never had one.'

She stopped and raised her eyebrows. 'Never had a beaten biscuit? Well, then you ain't lived. There's nothing better than a beaten biscuit with butter and honey. Do me a favor, child. Fetch the roll of wax paper from the pantry. It's in the third drawer on the left.'

As I entered the pantry there was a knock at the back door, followed by a shrill 'Helloooooooo, anybody home?'

From where I stood I could see Oletta. She turned toward the door, rolled her eyes, and called out, 'Miz Tootie's gone for the day.'

The screen door creaked open, and a moment later a short,

big-busted woman stepped into the kitchen doorway. Her pudgy body was stuffed into a strawberry-pink dress that was so tight I could see the seams of her girdle. The neckline was cut so low, I was sure her breasts would explode into full view if she took a deep breath. She had the biggest mound of teased-up blonde hair I'd ever seen.

'Well, I was just over at Sissy-Lynn's havin' my weekly manicure,' she said in a high-pitched, singsong voice, 'and I heard there's a new resident of Savannah named Cecelia who just so happens to be living here with Tootie. I *had* to come over right away and see if it was true.'

Oletta kept right on beating the dough. She never even looked up when she said, 'Afta-noon, Miz Hobbs. Like I said, Miz Tootie's out for the day, but I'll tell her you stopped by.'

It was obvious Oletta didn't like this woman, so I shrunk back into the pantry, but my head banged into the teacup holder and set the cups rattling.

'There she is!' the woman bleated, shimmying across the kitchen in a pair of pink high heels. She looked me over with the bulgy eyes of a Chihuahua. 'You must be Cecelia. I'm Violene Hobbs, and I wanted to be among the first to welcome you to Savannah.'

'Thank you.'

'You poor thing,' she said, cocking her head in that irritating, sympathetic way that grown-ups do when they think you're pitiful. 'I heard your momma passed away. Such a tragedy. Once you get settled, you'll have to come over and tell me *all* about it. But I just can't stop myself from askin' – how in the world did she get hit by a truck?'

I was stunned speechless. *Who does she think she is? What kind of person would ask a question like that?*

'I've learned the more we talk about things the better we feel.

70

I talk about everything, and I know that's one of the reasons why I never so much as catch a cold.' She pinched my cheek and grinned. 'But now that you've been rescued by Tootie, I'm sure everything will work out just fine.'

The more she talked, the louder Oletta whacked the dough. Each time she brought down the mallet, I thought the table might break.

Miz Hobbs just babbled away, paying no mind to the death-blows Oletta was inflicting on the dough. She didn't even flinch when Oletta brought down the mallet so hard it made the window rattle.

'You'll like Savannah, it's the gem of the South,' Miz Hobbs gushed. 'I live two doors away – the house with the swimming pool. Did you know I'm one of the *only* people in Savannah who has one?'

'No, ma'am.' I said, trying to edge my way closer to Oletta.

Miz Hobbs followed me across the kitchen like a bloodhound on a fresh scent. 'Like I said, you'll have to come over sometime soon so we can talk about how you lost your poor momma. I just can't imagine how devastated you must be, bless your little heart. You must be beside yourself.'

'I'm fine,' I mumbled.

Her lips formed a pitying grin, and the thin veneer of her phony graciousness fell away when she said, 'I heard you were a Northerner. You have a sweet face, but it's hard to see it. Your bangs are too long – looks like you're hidin' behind a raggedy old curtain. When's the last time you had your hair cut? I see those hippies hitchhiking on the side of the road in their dirty torn clothes and sandals, and I just don't understand it. I can practically see the bugs crawlin' in their hair. That whole hippie thing started up north, didn't it? Or maybe it was California. I forget.'

71

Oletta looked over her shoulder and gave Miz Hobbs a nasty look.

With fingers as plump as Twinkies, Miz Hobbs reached out and touched my ponytail. 'If your hair gets much longer you'll be sittin' on it. I'm sure you don't want to look like one of those dreadful hippies. But don't worry – my beautician can fix you right up. You'd look nice in one of those short pixie haircuts. I think those are so cute. I'll be sure to mention it to Tootie.'

It was all I could do not to slap her hand away.

'Well, I'd love to stay and chat, but I'd better skedaddle on home. The day is runnin' away from me, and I've got *sooooooo* much to do. Buh-bye,' she chirped in a syrupy-sweet voice as she headed toward the door. But she stopped midstride and looked down her nose at Oletta. Her voice was filled with a superior bite when she said, 'Later this afternoon I'll be expecting you to drop off some of those *wonderful* beaten biscuits. Last time I mentioned it you never did bring them by. But I'm sure you just forgot, isn't that right?'

Oletta didn't answer. She just kept right on whacking the dough.

Miz Hobbs waved her hand in the air. 'I'll be waitin' for your visit, Cecelia.'

She made a ridiculously grand, sweeping exit as if she were auditioning for a remake of *Gone With the Wind*.

When the slap of the screen door sounded, Oletta stopped bludgeoning the dough and let out a snort. Her eyes narrowed as she leaned forward and looked out the window. 'The devil will invite Jesus to Sunday supper before I'll give that woman a crumb of my cookin'.'

I walked across the kitchen and stood next to Oletta. We watched Miz Hobbs wiggle across the patio until her wide, strawberry-pink rump vanished around the side of the house.

'She's always pokin' around in everyone's business, thinks she's gonna die if she ain't in the center of everything going on in this town.' Oletta looked at me thoughtfully. 'You be careful of her. Mind every word you say. Don't tell her about your momma, 'cause if you do, it'll be all over town in less than five minutes. Miz Hobbs ain't nothin' but an ole flap-jawed busybody.'

'Is she a friend of Aunt Tootie's?'

Oletta wiped her hands on her apron and frowned. 'Lord, no. She nice to her because that's how Miz Tootie is, but far as I can tell ain't nobody friends with Miz Hobbs. People just put up with her, that's all. I guess they feel sorry for her.'

'Why?' I asked, brushing a drift of flour from the edge of the table.

'She lives all alone in that big house, and nobody stops in for a visit. She has two grown daughters, but I ain't seen either one of 'em in years. Far as I know they never come back, not even at Christmastime.'

'Miz Hobbs doesn't have a husband?'

Oletta shook her head and began rolling out the dough. 'Not anymore she don't. Her husband owned a bank right here in town. He was a nice man. Real quiet and gentlemanly, always had something nice to say to everybody. Story goes that one Saturday mornin' he was sitting in the kitchen reading the paper when Miz Hobbs walked in flappin' her jaws about somethin'. Nobody knows what all she said, but I guess he couldn't take her big mouth no more. He didn't have the nerve to kill her, so he up and shot himself instead.'

At first I thought it was a joke, some story Oletta had made up to make me laugh. But when I saw the look in her eyes, I knew the story was true.

While Oletta's biscuits were in the oven, we took a plate of egg salad sandwiches out to the porch and had lunch. It felt so good – just Oletta and me sitting in the big white rockers, sharing some quiet time. I watched her from the corner of my eye: how she chewed her sandwich real slow, and how, after she swallowed, she'd rest her head against the back of the chair, seeming pleased with the taste that lingered on her tongue.

She wore no jewelry except for a narrow silver ring. Though I didn't want to seem nosy, I thought it was probably okay to ask her about it. 'Are you married, Oletta?'

She glanced at her hand. 'No. This here ring was my momma's. I put it on the day she passed away and haven't taken it off since. Makes me feel close to her. I was married once, but that was a long time ago. His name was Henry. We was only married six years – then the mule-kick did him in.'

I'd never heard of anyone dying from the blow of a mule's hooves. I imagined an ornery mule letting out a deafening bray and hauling off and kicking the life out of her husband. The thought of it made me shudder.

'That's awful, Oletta. Did the mule kill him on purpose, or was it an accident?'

She looked at me with the oddest expression and laughed. 'Oh, child, mule-kick is liquor – you know, *booze*. Henry ain't dead, least not far as I know. He was just lazy and drank too much. Couldn't hold a job more than a few months at a time, so I had to throw him out of the house. That's when I came to work for Miz Tootie. Been here twenty-nine years. Lord, time goes so fast.'

Oletta stretched her legs and sighed when she looked at her thick, broken-down ankles. 'My legs keep telling me to retire, but I don't see no sense in sittin' around waitin' for my final day. Besides, I like to cook, and Miz Tootie's always been real good to me.' She took a sip of sweet tea and said, 'Yes, she sure has treated me fine. Mr. Taylor did too, bless his sweet soul. I

74

couldn't have asked to work for finer folks, that's for sure. I turned fifty-five last May, and Miz Tootie gave me the whole week off with full pay. She said a double-nickel birthday was something to be celebrated by relaxing. So that's just what I did. I was at home sitting on the porch when a truck pulled up. A man got out and said he was there to deliver a new color TV and a leather recliner chair. I told him he had the wrong address, but he said they was gifts from Miz Tootie.' Oletta leaned back and closed her eyes. 'Best chair I ever did sit in. Every day I go home, sit myself down in that chair, and take a nice long nap.'

Just then I heard a rusty squeak. Through the row of open windows on the back wall of the garage, I saw a glint of light spark from Delilah's wings as Aunt Tootie pulled the car in and parked. A moment later she came walking toward us at a brisk clip.

'Oh, we had such a productive meeting this morning,' she said, climbing the steps of the porch. 'We've been trying to save the Pemberton place from that nasty wreckin' ball for months, and we finally did.' She sat in a chair next to Oletta with a satisfied smile on her face.

'You mean that old house over by Lafayette Square?' Oletta said, furrowing her brow. 'Lord, ain't much left to save, is there?'

Aunt Tootie gazed across the garden. 'It's in critical condition, there's no doubt about it, but that house is a wonderful example of Italianate architecture. Oh, you should see the moldings and balustrades. And the fireplaces are gorgeous beyond words. Today we got another sizable donation, and finally we've raised enough money to buy that wonderful old home.'

'What will you do with it, Aunt Tootie?'

'I hope we'll find someone to buy it and have it rehabilitated.'

'Can I see it sometime?'

'Oh, I'd love to show it to you, sugar. As soon as we take

possession and get the keys, I'll take you over. And guess what else I did today? I went shopping for *you*. It was so much fun. Wait till you see what all I got. Will you help me with the bags?'

Together we hauled more than a dozen bags from the trunk of her car, lugged them upstairs to my room, and piled them on the bed. Aunt Tootie sat in the chair by the desk. 'Open them up, honey. Let's see how everything fits.'

Inside the first bag was a shoe box. I lifted the lid and peered down at a pair of dark blue sneakers with white laces.

'Red Ball Jets.' I was so excited I kicked off my scuffed-up loafers, sat on the floor, and put them on. All my life I'd dreamed of having a pair.

'Do they fit all right?'

I rose to my feet and walked around the room. 'They're perfect.'

I tore through the remaining bags and pulled out enough summer dresses to clothe all the debutantes in Georgia. And there were shorts, blue jeans, sweaters, T-shirts, underpants with flowers on the waistbands, and then there were jumpers, pajamas, and a pair of shiny black patent-leather party shoes. Inside the last bag was a large pale blue box.

Aunt Tootie clasped her hands beneath her chin, looking so excited that I couldn't imagine what was inside. I removed the lid, unfolded the crisp tissue, and lifted out a fancy white party dress. When I got a good look at it, my throat tightened.

Oh, no. Oh, God, please, no.

The dress in my hands was nearly identical to Momma's pageant dress, just a miniature version.

'Isn't it beautiful?' my aunt gushed, her eyes gleaming. 'The moment I saw it in the window of Betsy's Belles I had a fit over it. I just *had* to get it for you.'

A long-forgotten memory flashed through my mind.

It was a breezy spring day, the kind of day where the air is so fresh and clean it makes your nose tingle. Mrs. Odell and I had spent the entire morning turning the soil in her garden in preparation for planting. As we returned the tools to her shed, she invited me inside for a lunch of grilled cheese sandwiches and tomato soup. But my socks were wet, my shoes were caked with mud, and my feet were cold. So I told her I'd run home, change my shoes and socks, and be back in a few minutes. As I approached the house, I heard the radio blaring from an open window. I left my shoes on the back steps and walked into the kitchen. Momma's white pageant dress was draped over the ironing board. Whenever I saw that dress a siren went off in my head – Momma was in trouble.

I turned off the radio and glanced into the living room. Momma was standing on a hassock in front of the living room window, her face slathered with cold cream. She was talking into a wooden spoon as if it were a microphone.

Other than the fuzzy yellow slippers on her feet, she was totally naked. This was a stunt I hadn't seen before, and desperation clawed its way up my spine. I bolted to the front widow and pulled the curtains closed. 'Momma! Get down from there,' I said, grabbing her hand and all but yanking her off the hassock. 'For Pete's sake, put some clothes on!'

Her eyes blazed with outrage. She threw the spoon on the floor and screeched, 'You just *ruined it*!'

'Ruined what?'

She pushed past me, ran up the stairs, and slammed her bedroom door.

When she was like this, there was nothing I could do. I was about to head back to Mrs. Odell's when I thought, *Oh no. What if Momma stands in front of her bedroom window and somebody sees her!*

I dashed up the stairs.

As I knocked on her door, begging her to let me in, I realized I had just taken my father's place: there I was, standing outside her locked bedroom door, frustrated and helpless and just plain tired. Tired of it all.

Aunt Tootie's voice startled me. 'Sugar, is something wrong?'

'No,' I said, plastering a smile on my face. 'Everything's fine. I'm just so . . . so happy. Thank you for all these pretty clothes and shoes.' I averted my eyes and picked up a shoe box.

'You're welcome. I had so much fun picking everything out. I know I should have taken you with me, but I wanted it to be a surprise.'

While we hung my new dresses in the closet, my aunt said, 'Would you like to go out for dinner and a movie tonight?'

'Yes, ma'am.'

'I just love a good movie,' she said, smoothing the skirt of a pale yellow sundress before hanging it in the closet. 'Did your mother take you to movies?'

'No. But Mrs. Odell did a few times.'

'What kinds of fun things did you and your mother do together?'

I just stood there, staring blankly at my aunt. What was I to say – that living with Momma was about as much fun as living with a hurricane stuffed in the closet?

Aunt Tootie grew quiet and studied me. 'Honey,' she said, cupping her hand beneath my chin, 'I don't want to pry, but I think we need to talk about your mother.'

I looked away. 'Not now, please?'

She hesitated, then rested her hand on my shoulder. 'All right. But soon.'

After gathering the empty bags, she stepped toward the door. 'I'll go look at the newspaper and see what movies are playing.'

After she left the room, I got down on my knees and pulled Momma's scrapbook from its hiding place beneath the mattress. I flipped to the page that held the glossy eight-by-ten color picture that was taken when she was crowned Vidalia Onion Queen. I was right. The party dress Aunt Tootie had bought me was eerily similar to Momma's pageant dress: crisp white with a full gathered skirt, sleeveless, scoop neck, and a zipper up the back. It even had layers of crinoline petticoats. The only real difference I could see was that Momma's dress didn't have a sash at the waist and mine did.

Momma had been wearing that dress on the day she died, and though her casket had been closed, I imagined she was still wearing it, along with her red shoes, when she was lowered into the ground. It wasn't a vision I could wipe easily from my mind.

I closed the scrapbook and shoved it back under the mattress.

As I smoothed the comforter into place, terrifying thoughts bumped around in my head. *What if the dress Aunt Tootie bought me is an omen of the worst possible kind? Has Momma's illness been passed down to me? Am I genetically doomed? Will it only be a matter of time before my mind corrodes like hers did?*

Wanting the dress as far from sight as possible, I walked to the closet and pushed it all the way to the end of the pole, then I rearranged and fluffed up my other dresses so it all but vanished behind cotton prints, checks, and stripes. With any luck, maybe Aunt Tootie would forget all about it.

Eight

Friday was a busy day in Aunt Tootie's house. She was out the door before eight o'clock in the morning to attend a special meeting of the Historic Savannah Foundation. Around nine-thirty, a light blue van rumbled its way down the alley behind the house and parked next to the garage. Two men came through the garden gate, one carrying hedge clippers and a tote bag filled with gardening tools, the other pushing a lawnmower. Within minutes I heard the *snip, snip* of the clippers, and soon the roar of the lawnmower rolled in through the open windows, growing loud, then soft, then loud again as it was pushed up and down the yard.

Oletta was busy too. With the fan humming at the kitchen ceiling, she was baking bread and cinnamon rolls for Aunt Tootie and me to eat over the weekend. Though I'd lived in this big old house for only a few days, already Oletta and I had established a morning routine. As sweet, yeasty aromas filled the air, I'd sit on a stool by the chopping block and read aloud to Oletta from one of my Nancy Drew books.

'That Nancy Drew sure is smart,' Oletta said, shaping bread dough into a pan. 'You read real good too – got yourself a nice voice.'

Her words made me blush. 'I've read this book so many times I know it by heart. I looked at the books in Aunt Tootie's library, but they all seem kinda boring.'

She slid a bread pan into the oven. 'Most all them books was Mr. Taylor's, rest his sweet soul. Too bad you never got the chance to meet him – finest man I ever did know. A real gentleman.' She shook her head. 'They don't make 'em like him no more.'

'What did he die from?'

'Heart attack,' she said, leaning over the stove to set the timer. 'He passed away sittin' in his favorite chair in the library. Oh, how that man loved to read. Every night after supper he'd sit himself down and read till bedtime.'

Oletta headed for the pantry, and I slid off the stool and followed. 'How did he get so rich?'

'Mr. Taylor bought a lot of land in Florida way, way back,' she said, lifting a sack of flour from the shelf. 'When he sold it, he made himself bushels of money. He had something to do with mining too, not coal, but them big stone quarries. He was a powerful man and a kind, kind soul. Usually them two things don't go together.'

We returned to the kitchen and I held the canister steady so Oletta could pour in the flour. 'Most of the books in the library are history books. He must have liked history a lot.'

Oletta nodded. 'He sure did. But I don't think none of them books would be anything you'd like. Later this afternoon I'll walk you down to the public library. I'm sure they got lots of books for children.' She looked at me and winked. 'Even real smart ones like you.'

From behind me a woman spoke – had it been a color, her voice would have been a velvety shade of purple. 'No need to go to the library.'

I looked over my shoulder and sucked in my breath. It was like the universe had cracked wide open. Poised in the doorway, one perfectly manicured hand on her hip and the other resting on the doorjamb, was the reigning empress of some strange, exotic land. Though she'd long since passed the zenith of youth, unmistakable remnants of a mysterious beauty oozed from the pores of her porcelain-white skin. Swirling around her ankles, as light as smoke and the color of midnight, was a silk caftan splashed with bits of silver glitter. Her wavy red hair was pinned high on top of her head like the plumage of an alien bird.

'I have a library in my house that doesn't get a lick of attention except for an occasional dusting,' she said from the reddest lips I'd ever seen. 'You're welcome to come have a look and borrow anything you'd like.' She smiled a slow, catlike smile. 'I take it you must be Cecelia.'

Oletta grinned. 'How you doin', Miz Goodpepper? This here child is Cecelia Rose Honeycutt, Miz Tootie's grandniece. And Cecelia, this is Miz Thelma Rae Goodpepper, she lives next door.'

'It's a pleasure to meet you, Cecelia,' she said, floating toward me in a pair of silver lamé slippers. She extended her hand, and perched on her right pointer finger was a deep green ring the size of a walnut.

I didn't know if I should kiss her ring or curtsy. Finally I took hold of her outstretched hand and managed to push out the words 'Thank you.'

Her blue eyes twinkled. 'And like I said, please come over and go through my library. I have thousands of books, and I'm sure you'd find several to your liking.'

She flashed a sideways glance at Oletta. 'I was sitting in my garden, having a cup of coffee, when the most heavenly ambrosia floated through the air. And I said to myself, "Thelma Rae, Oletta's making her fabulous cinnamon rolls."'

Oletta pointed to the rolls with pride. 'Your nose was right. I got a dozen of 'em right there on the rack. When they cool, I'll ice 'em up real nice.'

Miz Goodpepper closed her eyes, pressed a hand to her breast, and inhaled deeply. 'Oletta, you are the culinary goddess of Savannah. I know it's shameful how I come over here sniffing the air like a dog, begging for your baked goods. But I'd love to have one or two if you've got them to spare.'

Oletta beamed like neon. 'You know I always make extra for you. I'll send Cecelia over with 'em after I make the icing.'

'You're such a treasure,' she said with a breathy exhale. 'You know, I kick myself every day – I should have snapped you away from Tootie years ago.' She lifted her slender fingers to her lips and blew Oletta a big, lip-smacking kiss, turned, and disappeared, leaving a swirl of spicy perfume in her wake.

It was at that very moment when I first felt the powerful undertow of beauty.

Later in the day, Oletta placed three thickly iced cinnamon rolls on a paper plate. 'These should make Miz Goodpepper happy. I gave her the biggest ones.'

'She looks like . . . well, like she's from a foreign country or something,' I said, dipping my finger into the icing bowl.

'Miz Goodpepper's lived in Savannah all her life, but she does dress a little strange at times, I'll grant you that,' she said, smoothing tinfoil over the top of the plate and pinching down the edges. 'Take these over to her, will you? There's a path at the side of the garden that leads into her backyard.'

My heart made a flip-flop. What it was I couldn't have said, but something about Miz Goodpepper scared me. I took a step back and chewed my lip.

Oletta furrowed her brow. 'What's the matter, child?'

'M-m-maybe-e-e you could go with me?' I sputtered.

She studied me through squinted eyes. 'Is you afraid of Miz Goodpepper?'

'I . . . well, maybe a little.'

'Oh, Cecelia,' she said with a laugh. 'Ain't no reason to be. Miz Goodpepper's just as nice as she can be. So don't you worry.' Oletta handed me the foil-covered plate and nodded toward the back door. 'Now, go on, I've got to keep an eye on the oven.'

Knowing there was no way to wiggle my way out of it, I took the plate and headed out the door. Already I felt tongue-tied just from the thought of being alone with Miz Goodpepper.

I walked beneath a giant live oak, and found a small opening in the hedge shrouded by a ferocious twist of moss-covered branches. I took a deep breath and stepped into Miz Goodpepper's yard. Grateful that she was nowhere in sight, I moved along a path that led to the back porch of her house, hoping I could leave the plate by the door and skedaddle back home.

The yard was a sea of living color. Never had I seen so many flowers in one place. Classical music sailed across the extravagant garden. Where it came from I didn't know, but it was like an orchestra was hidden in the lush foliage. I walked beneath a vine-smothered trellis, and Miz Goodpepper's house came into full view. It was a colossal monstrosity of gray stone that looked more like a mausoleum than a place where someone actually lived.

I was startled by a screech and turned to see a peacock standing in a sunny spot on the lawn. He was so beautiful I caught my breath. I stood still as he took a few tentative steps toward me, and then he stopped, tilted his head, and scanned me from head to toe. I figured he was disappointed in what he saw because he flattened his topknot and strutted away.

I heard a splash followed by a gurgle, and turned to see Miz

Goodpepper's head appear above a thick hedge. Her hair was dripping wet.

'Well, what a nice surprise,' she said, wrapping her head in a towel. 'Let me get something on. I'll be out in a second.'

A moment later she appeared, wearing a pale, silvery-blue satin robe and a pair of iridescent pink flip-flops. When she saw the look on my face, her lips curled ever so slightly. 'I take it you've never seen an outdoor bath before,' she mused, tightening the belt of her robe. She gestured toward a perfectly clipped opening in the foliage. 'Come have a look.'

I took a few steps forward and peered in. On a slab of thick gray marble sat a moss-stained, claw-footed bathtub. Frothy soapsuds spun down the drain, gurgling as they went. Next to the tub stood a life-size marble statue of a naked woman with her arms outstretched. Draped over one of her hands was a damp towel.

Miz Goodpepper gazed at her tub fondly. 'It's charming, don't you think? I call it my secret garden spa. You'll have to come over and try it sometime. I especially like to use it late at night. There's nothing more relaxing than to lean back and watch the stars.' She nodded toward the peacock. 'I see you've met Louie. He's such a handsome boy, though he isn't very social. He belongs to a neighbor, but wanders over here quite often.' She flashed the bird an intimate look. 'Louie's a bit of a voyeur – he likes to peek through the bushes and watch me bathe.'

I didn't know what to say about her secret garden spa or the peacock being a voyeur, so I offered her the foil-covered plate. 'These are from Oletta.'

'Thank you, darling,' she said, making an elegant gesture toward her house. 'Welcome to my home, Cecelia. Please come inside.'

A warm breeze sent her robe fluttering around her ankles,

and the faint scent of bubble bath wafted through the air as I followed her. Louie let out a deafening squawk and headed in the opposite direction.

When we entered Miz Goodpepper's kitchen, I glanced down at my wrinkled shorts and dusty Red Ball Jets, feeling frumpy – like Daffy Duck standing in the presence of a great blue heron. The next thing I knew, Miz Goodpepper grabbed hold of my hand and whisked me down a long cool hallway.

'This is the library,' she said, stepping into a room that smelled of old leather and books. Above a massive fireplace hung a faded photograph of a military officer, staring out through the dusty glass, looking glum. There were no drapes on the windows. Instead, hanging from various lengths of string nailed to the top of the moldings were crystal prisms, hundreds of them, all sizes and shapes. They caught the afternoon light and sent miniature rainbows shimmering across the walls and ceiling. From a hook by one of the windows hung a gold birdcage with its door propped open.

'Do you have a pet bird?' I asked, looking around the room.

'Oh, heavens, no. I'd never cage a bird. I can't imagine a worse fate, can you? I bought this cage at a market in Peru several years ago. I hung it here and wired the door open to remind myself how delicious freedom is – financial and otherwise.'

Her lips formed an odd smile, and she turned and gazed out the window. The trancelike look on her face made me uncomfortable, so I picked up a copy of *Vogue* from a chairside table and said, 'I like to look at magazines. The librarian back in Willoughby used to give me old copies.'

Miz Goodpepper blinked. 'I'm sorry, what did you say?'

'I was saying that I like to look at magazines, especially the pictures.'

She reached out, slid the magazine from my fingers, and

studied the woman on the cover. 'I used to look *just* like that. But after I turned forty it was a daily struggle to keep myself up. I turned forty-five this past February, and let me tell you, every day is nothing but an insult.' She tossed the magazine on the table with disgust. 'Aging is a terrible slap in the face. My body betrays me every chance it gets.'

She lifted her chin and tightened the towel on her head. 'Oh, well, I'd much rather die with one of Oletta's cinnamon rolls in my mouth than a lousy stalk of celery. Anyway, as you can see, I have tons of books. Pick anything you'd like. If you need me, I'll be in the kitchen.'

When she turned and left the room, the hem of her robe opened to a full sweep, sending dust motes spinning across the floor. As the rhythmic *slap-slap-slap* of her flip-flops faded down the hall, I began scanning the sagging shelves.

There were books on everything from the healing powers of crystals to studies on the Mayan ruins to a book titled *Exploring the Sacred Fires – A Beginner's Guide to the Kama Sutra*. I'd never heard of a place called the Kama Sutra and figured it was probably some boring old volcano, so I returned the book to the shelf.

Before too long I had found at least twenty books I wanted to read. Not wanting to appear greedy, I narrowed my choices to seven and found my way back to the kitchen. Miz Goodpepper was standing at the counter, folding clothes and pushing them into paper grocery bags. Hooked over a knob of a china cupboard was a red taffeta party dress with rhinestone spaghetti straps. The dress was really, *really* fancy, and really, *really* red. Bright, screaming Crayola red.

She looked up and smiled. 'I'm glad you found some books that interest you. Would you like a glass of lemonade?'

Though I was hoping to thank her for the books and be on

my way, I didn't want to seem rude. I nodded and set the stack of books on the counter. While Miz Goodpepper pulled a pitcher from the refrigerator, I asked, 'Is the Kama Sutra a volcano?'

She gasped and splashed lemonade across the kitchen counter. The strangest look streaked across her face as she sopped up the mess with a wad of paper towels. 'Well, I suppose some might think it's a volcano of sorts, but I can say with absolute assurance you wouldn't enjoy that book.'

'That's what I thought,' I said, feeling pleased with myself, 'so I put it back on the shelf.'

She let out a barely audible sigh. 'Good.'

'That's pretty,' I said, pointing to the red dress. 'Are you going to a party?'

She handed me the lemonade and turned her gaze toward the dress. 'It is pretty, isn't it? But no, I won't be wearing that dress again. I'm donating it to the local animal shelter for their annual rummage sale.

'That dress cost a king's ransom. It's a shame I only wore it twice,' Miz Goodpepper said with a wistful smile. 'I bought it to wear to a charity ball back in 1959. I felt wonderful in that dress. It suited my personality. But when my husband and I got in the car to come home that night, he said I'd embarrassed him. He actually had the gall to say I looked like a prostitute. He told me *never* to wear that dress again.'

She leaned her hip against the counter and folded her arms across her chest. 'So I tucked it away at the back of my closet and all but forgot about it. But, wouldn't you know, three years later I had the opportunity to wear that beautiful dress one last time.' Her lips formed a twisted half smile and her eyes gleamed. 'I wore it to court on the day I divorced my husband.'

I didn't know what to say. *Was it a joke, or was she serious?*

She let out a brief, wicked laugh, grabbed a bottle of wine from the counter, and pulled a razor-thin goblet from the cupboard. 'Come sit with me for a while.'

I took my glass of lemonade and followed. As we stepped off the porch, violin music poured from an open window. It swelled across the garden and ended in a vibrant crescendo. Miz Goodpepper rested back against a cushioned chaise lounge that sat beneath a canopy of gnarled vines. I sat in a rocking chair at her side.

'What is this?' I asked, running my fingers over a smooth twist of bark.

'Wisteria,' she said, pulling the towel off her head and fluffing her damp hair. 'In the spring it blooms with the most beautiful purple flowers you can imagine. Wisteria is my favorite flowering vine. Do you know why?'

I shook my head. 'No, ma'am.'

'Because it's strong — just like me. But if you don't take care of it, wisteria will grow wild. It can heave a porch right off its foundation. I remember once . . . '

She talked about plants and the wonders of nature with a passion that lit up her eyes, the whole time drinking wine like it was water. Every time she moved, her silky robe slid off to the side and revealed her long, slender legs.

'My love of nature is one of the reasons why I play music in the garden. See that camellia bush?' she said, pointing toward the far edge of the property. 'It's particularly fond of Mozart's Symphony Number 12 in G Major. And my roses adore anything by Chopin. And once, when my oldest sago palm looked sickly, I played a Puccini opera as loud as my hi-fi would go, and do you know that old palm perked right up.'

I'd never heard that plants liked music, but I didn't want to seem stupid by asking about it, so I grinned as if I understood.

'This garden is my greatest joy. It soothes my spirit and elevates my awareness to great heights. Every day I commune with nature. I owe my serenity and love of all living things to His Holiness, the Dalai Lama.'

'Who's that?'

'He's the supreme head of Tibetan Buddhism and a master of spiritual teachings. One of the most important things he teaches is that we're never to cause harm to any living thing. Not ever. It makes for terrible karma.'

I took a sip of lemonade. 'Karma? What's that?'

She rested her head against the cushion and thought for a moment. 'Karma stems from mental, physical, and verbal action. It's the sum of all we've said, done, and thought, be it good *or* bad.'

I sat quietly and listened to all she said, but the karma business was way over my head. And when she started talking about how we reincarnate to clean up our karma so we can eventually reach someplace called nirvana, I figured it was time for me to go home. But as I was about to stand up and excuse myself, Miz Goodpepper began spouting off about the countless wrongs people do to the earth and the animal kingdom.

'Right there is a prime example of *terrible* karma,' she said bitterly, pointing to a tree stump by the hedge that separated her yard from Miz Hobbs's swimming pool. 'That poor withering stump is all that's left of a beautiful magnolia. It was the most glorious thing you could possibly imagine. Every spring it was smothered with thousands of blooms that smelled so wonderful it'd make your heart ache. I loved that tree. Every morning I'd sit beneath its cool shade and meditate. That magnolia had such a wonderful energy force, I could feel it pulse through my body whenever I leaned against its trunk.' She took a big gulp of wine and her face turned hard. 'But that beautiful, defenseless tree was *murdered*!'

I jolted, splashing lemonade on my shorts. 'Murdered?'

Her voice had a venomous sting when she replied, 'Yes. Murdered in cold blood. While I was out of town in April, my neighbor, the great gaping vagina otherwise known as Violene Hobbs, murdered it.'

I didn't know what to think, much less say. A heavy silence fell across the garden as we stared at the patch of vivid blue sky the magnolia had once occupied.

Miz Goodpepper smoothed a stray lock of hair off her forehead. 'Murdering anything is just plain criminal, but a Southerner murdering a magnolia? Well, that's an unforgivable sacrilege against nature *and* the South. Violene Hobbs is the black widow of Savannah. Stay clear of her, Cecelia. Behind that drippy-sweet voice lies nothing but pure evil.' Miz Goodpepper let out a bitter, humorless laugh. 'There aren't enough years left in my life to cauterize the wounds that wretched woman has inflicted upon me.'

Without a doubt this was the most fascinating conversation I'd ever taken part in. I shifted in my chair to get more comfortable. 'Why did she murder the tree?'

Miz Goodpepper poured herself more wine, swirled it around in the glass, then drank it down in one long, slow gulp. Her eyes narrowed to slits of blue as she tightened the belt of her robe with an angry tug. 'She murdered that beautiful tree because she was worried a strong wind might come and blow it into her swimming pool. Now, isn't that the most ludicrous thing you've ever heard?'

I had to agree.

'From the first day I met her, I knew Violene was a pea-minded idiot. I've known ferns with higher IQs than hers. But I still can't believe she murdered that magnolia. I can hardly bear to think about it. That beautiful tree was a home to countless birds and squirrels. Oh, I wish you could have seen it. It was like breathing in a bit of heaven.'

She paused to finish off the bottle of wine and added, 'But now after it rains, all I can smell is death. Have you ever smelled a dying tree after it rains?'

'No, ma'am. I don't think I have.'

'Well, I hope you never do,' she said, spinning the mysterious green ring on her finger. 'I can assure you it's a smell you'll never forget. Mark my words, one day all the wicked deeds Violene Hobbs has done will gather together and form a big black boomerang of karma that will spin through the sky and strike her down.' Miz Goodpepper closed her eyes and sighed. 'I only hope I'm around to see it.'

I stared at my hands, not knowing how to respond. I'd never heard of a holy man named after a llama, I'd never heard of a great gaping vagina, and I didn't know a thing about the black boomerang of karma. All I knew for sure was this: I had been plunked into a strange, perfumed world that, as far as I could tell, seemed to be run entirely by women.

Nine

I woke the following Monday morning to realize I'd overslept. Oletta served breakfast promptly at eight-thirty, and it was almost nine o'clock. After dressing quickly, I scrambled downstairs. As I trotted down the hallway toward the kitchen, I heard Aunt Tootie talking to Oletta. 'Cecelia won't discuss her mother, and it worries me. I've tried several times to get her to open up, but she won't. And she doesn't show any signs of grieving. What should I do?'

I crept into the den, and hid behind the door. There was the sound of a cup meeting a saucer, and then Oletta said, 'Miz Tootie, I've told you everything Cecelia's told me about her momma. I have the feelin' she's not grieving 'cause she ain't sorted things out yet. That child's been through a whole lot, and the dust ain't even settled. She'll grieve when she's good'n ready. And when she does, then I believe she'll open up. We was young when my pappy died. My sister, Geneva, wanted to talk about him all the time; it was her way to make sense of things – her way to heal. But me, I was a lot like Cecelia. It took me a long time before I could bring myself to talk about him. It ain't my place to tell you what to do, but since you asked, I think it's best you give Cecelia more time to adjust. Let the child feel happy and safe, then you can . . .'

I closed my eyes and leaned against the wall. *Why can't Aunt Tootie just leave things alone?*

The slap of the screen door sounded, and, thinking Aunt Tootie had left, I waited a minute and then walked down the hall. I entered the kitchen to find Aunt Tootie sitting at the table with the newspaper and a cup of coffee.

'Good morning, sugar.'

'Hi, where's Oletta?'

'She just left for a dental appointment. I thought I'd take you out to breakfast. There's a little diner I'm fond of. It's a hole-in-the-wall place, but they make wonderful omelets and all sorts of pancakes.'

'Do I need to change clothes?' I asked, looking down at my shorts and blouse.

'You look just fine,' she said, folding the paper. 'I'm starved, so let's go.'

When we arrived at the diner it was crowded, mostly with businessmen in suits and construction workers wearing heavy boots. The smell of strong coffee and the sound of clanging silverware filled the air as we wound our way toward an empty table all the way at the back. A ballet of nimble-footed waitresses moved among the tables, taking orders and sliding them beneath the clips on a silver carousel above the cook's window. Both Aunt Tootie and I ordered blueberry pancakes. But as good as they were, I have to say they didn't come close to Oletta's.

'When we leave here, remind me to stop at the post office,' Aunt Tootie said, dabbing her mouth with her napkin. 'I'm running out of stamps.'

'Okay.'

Just as I swallowed the last of my orange juice, two men at the table next to ours began talking.

'A demolition company brought in a crane early this morning. The old Pemberton house sure was something back in the day.'

The other man took a gulp of his coffee and nodded. 'I've never been inside, but my mother used to play with the Pemberton kids when she was a girl. She said the moldings were spectacular. Did a salvage company come in and take them?'

Aunt Tootie stiffened.

'I don't know,' the other man said. 'And if they didn't, it's too late now. By nightfall that house'll be gone.'

'Excuse me, gentlemen,' my aunt said, turning in her chair. 'I couldn't help but overhear your conversation. Did you say there's a wreckin' ball at the Pemberton place?'

'Yes, ma'am,' one of the men said.

Aunt Tootie nodded her thanks and fumbled with her wallet, quickly tucking money beneath her coffee cup. 'C'mon, Cecelia Rose,' she said, rising from her chair. I followed her as she rushed down a narrow hall toward a pay phone, but it was being used. She turned and was out the front door so fast I had to run to catch up with her.

When we reached the street, she said, 'Hurry, get in the car.'

'What's wrong?'

She fired up the engine and barreled down the street, passing cars and honking the horn. 'That's the house we saved from the wreckin' ball. There must be some mistake. As of yesterday, we own that house. Sara Jane picked up the key last night!' she said, turning a corner so fast I slid across the seat.

I grabbed hold of the armrest and looked at her. 'What are you going to do?'

'First thing I've got to do is make a phone call.' She pulled into a gas station and screeched to a stop. 'Wait here,' she said, jumping from the car.

95

I watched her race inside the gas station and shove coins into the pay phone by the front window. She hadn't talked for more than thirty seconds when she hung up and made another call. A moment later she pushed through the door and ran toward the car.

'All right, let's go.' She tromped on the gas and zoomed away, the sun glinting across the windshield in blinding bursts of light.

'Cecelia Rose, we have become a throwaway society. Instead of honoring and preserving our past, we tear it down, shove it aside, and just go on our merry way. Well, I won't have it. We have to stand firm for what we believe in. Only in the most dire circumstances should a structure of historical significance be demolished.'

She came to a jolting stop in front of a three-story brick house that sagged in on itself like a ruined soufflé. A statue of an angel stood off to the side of the front garden. Her nose was broken and her moss-stained eyes gazed toward a big yellow crane that had a steel ball dangling from its long arm.

'Oh, my word!' Aunt Tootie gasped, cutting the engine.

Parked in front of us was a black pickup truck. Two men were sitting on the tailgate, eating doughnuts and drinking coffee from paper cups. Aunt Tootie climbed out of the car. 'Good morning, gentlemen. Who's in charge here?'

One of the men, a big burly-looking guy, put down his coffee and slid off the tailgate. He had a dusting of powdered sugar on his chin. 'I am,' he said, tipping his hardhat. 'Grady Tucker.'

'Mr. Tucker, my name is Tallulah Caldwell, and I'm a board member of the Historic Savannah Foundation. We just purchased this house and—'

There came a deafening roar as the crane operator started the engine. The earth shook beneath my feet as the crane moved its wide steel treads toward the house.

Aunt Tootie raised her voice above the loud rumble. 'You've got to stop. There's been a mistake.'

'Ma'am. This house has been scheduled for demolition for a long time. I have all the paperwork in the truck. I'll show you—'

'Mr. Tucker, you are not listening to me. We *own* this house. It is impossible to overstate the importance of this.' Aunt Tootie turned and looked at the crane – it was moving into position, the heavy black ball swaying. 'Cecelia, you stay right here.'

To my astonishment, she turned and began marching across the yard, her chin held high, her handbag slapping against her hip. 'Please, turn that thing off!' she called to the operator.

The foreman's voice boomed. 'Now, hold on! You can't go up there. It's dangerous.'

Aunt Tootie ignored him and kept on marching. He spit out a cuss word, lifted his fingers to his lips, and let out a sharp whistle. 'Pete, stop the crane. Jesus Christ, *stop!*'

The crane slowed to a stop but the engine remained idling as the operator stood to see what was going on.

'Ma'am, now I mean it, come back here,' the foreman said, walking toward her and shaking his head.

Just as she turned to face him, a screech of tires sounded. Car after car pulled to the curb, doors flew open, and women of all shapes and sizes poured out. They came rushing across the lawn like a stampede of buffalo in flowery dresses.

'The demolition permit was revoked!' a woman wearing a pink dress called out, waving her arms in the air.

'That's right,' said a woman with rosy cheeks and curly gray hair.

The foreman held up his hands like a traffic cop. 'Whoa. Now, y'all hold on.' But the women had him surrounded and began talking all at once, pointing their fingers at the crane.

'You're not to touch a single brick of this house,' a woman with tight silver curls scolded, her jowls shaking with fury. 'Now, tell your man to turn that thing off!'

He looked over at the crane, made a motion with his hand, and yelled. 'Shut her down, Pete!' The rumble of the crane's engine wound down, then it stopped with a belch of blue smoke. The crane operator lit a cigarette, leaned back on the seat, and put his feet up. He looked like he was enjoying the show.

A police car pulled up and an officer strutted toward the house. 'What's goin' on here?'

'I have a permit to tear down this house, but these women are—'

'No you don't. I have the key to this house right here!' the woman in the pink dress said with anger in her eyes.

'Now, Mrs. Wells,' the policeman soothed, 'calm down a minute. We'll get this straightened out.' He turned and looked at the foreman. 'Let's see that permit.'

'I don't care *what* permit he has,' my aunt said evenly. 'We own this house and it's not to be touched.'

When the policeman saw Aunt Tootie, he tipped his hat and said, 'Well, good mornin', Miz Caldwell.'

'Good morning, Doug,' she said pleasantly. 'How's your mother feeling? I know she had her gallbladder removed. I sent her flowers.'

'Yes, ma'am, and she sure appreciated 'em.'

Just then a tall man in a dark blue suit walked briskly across the lawn, a black briefcase swinging at his side. 'My name is T. Johnson Fuller. I'm an attorney representing the Foundation. And you are?' he asked the foreman, who still had powdered sugar on his chin.

'Grady Tucker of Wilder Demolition Company,' he said,

shaking the attorney's outstretched hand. 'This house is scheduled to be demolished today. I got all the permits in my truck,
and—'

'Well, Mr. Tucker, I'm afraid there's been a gross error. The city
building department committed an oversight,' Mr. Fuller said,
pulling papers from his briefcase. 'An injunction to stop the
demolition was filed, and Judge Goodwin ruled in favor of the
injunction. Yesterday this house was sold to the Historic Savannah
Foundation, and . . . '

I clutched Aunt Tootie's hand, marveling at all the hullabaloo
going on just for a saggy old house. She stood, all prim and
proper in her blue chambray dress and little straw hat, smiling as
if this were a church social.

I don't know, maybe I got all caught up in the excitement and
it was just my imagination. But as strange as it sounds, when it
became obvious there would be no demolishing, I thought I
heard that old house let out a creaky groan, as if it were grateful to be saved from the grips of death.

Mr. Fuller set down his briefcase and pulled a card from the
breast pocket of his jacket. 'Why don't you come over to my
office so we can sort this out? I'm just a block from the courthouse.'

The foreman took the card and looked it over. 'What time do
you want me to stop by?'

'I'm heading back to the office now, and I'll be there for the
rest of the morning.'

'All right,' the foreman grumbled. 'I'll wrap things up here
and be over within a half hour or so.'

All the women sighed with relief. Aunt Tootie grinned, put
her arm around my shoulders, and gave me a squeeze.

The policeman tipped his hat to Aunt Tootie and her friends.
'Glad this all worked out. Now, you ladies have a nice day.'

'Thanks so much,' the woman in the pink dress said.

Aunt Tootie patted his arm. 'You be sure to give your mother my best.'

'I'll do that, Miz Caldwell.'

We all watched as the lawyer and the policemen walked to the street, climbed into their cars, and drove away.

Aunt Tootie looked at the foreman and smiled. 'Mr. Tucker?'

'Yes, ma'am?'

'Powdered sugar,' she said, dusting her hand over her chin.

He looked a bit embarrassed as he wiped it away, then he turned and instructed Pete to start up the crane and move it off the property. All the women smiled triumphantly as they watched it rumble across the lawn, leaving gouged-up pieces of earth in its wake.

Aunt Tootie introduced me to her friends, making a fuss and telling them how lucky she was to have me. 'I can't tell y'all what a joy it is to have Cecelia Rose living with me. She's just a delight and such a big help in the garden. She even loves to pull weeds.'

The woman with the rosy cheeks laughed and looked at me. 'Honey, you can come pull weeds in my garden anytime.'

We all talked for a few minutes, and then the women began to leave.

'Sara Jane,' my aunt said, 'could I have the key to the house? I'd like to show Cecelia the inside.'

'Of course. You can give it back to me at Friday's meeting,' she said, retrieving the key from her handbag. 'You know, Tootie, this was sheer providence. Thank heavens you overheard those men talking about this at breakfast. Can you imagine? We would have had a title to nothing but a pile of bricks.'

Aunt Tootie nodded. 'Well, as the saying goes – the Lord works in mysterious ways.'

'That He does,' Sara Jane said as she turned and headed toward her car. 'That He surely does.'

After we waved good-bye, Aunt Tootie and I walked toward the house. 'Now, be careful when we go inside,' she said, unlocking the front door. 'There are shards of glass everywhere, and some of the floorboards are broken. I don't want you falling through to the cellar.'

'You've been inside before?'

'Oh, yes. The members of the Foundation came here several months ago; that's when we knew we had to save it.'

She pushed the door open and we stepped into an entrance hall. The sunlight could barely push through the grimy windowpanes, and scattered across the dusty hardwood floors was a carpet of dead wasps and flies. Dingy floral wallpaper had loosened from the walls in stiff, cracked sheets, and the ceilings were covered with scales of peeling paint. To me the house was a disaster, but from the look on Aunt Tootie's face, you'd have thought we'd entered Buckingham Palace.

'Look at this gorgeous staircase. Even under all that awful paint, I can see that the balusters are magnificent.'

I smiled up at her, but I didn't see what was so special about them. It looked like a bunch of chubby spindles all slopped up with paint.

'Come look at this,' she said, leading me into a room and pointing out a crystal chandelier swathed in dirty cobwebs. 'I can't wait to see it restored. Oh, Cecelia, can you imagine how many lively dinner parties took place under the glow of this chandelier? You know what surprises me most?'

'What?' I said, stepping over a rolled-up rug.

'That so many of this home's original details survived all those years of abuse and neglect.'

She walked to the far wall, where a pair of tall windows

flanked an enormous fireplace. 'This fireplace was crafted from two solid pieces of marble – one piece for the mantel and the other for the entire front. And these,' she said, gesturing to delicate flowers cascading down each side of the fireplace, 'were all hand-carved by a fine Italian craftsman. His name was Alphonse Brunalli, and he was well respected for his artistry. Such talent to carve these flowers, can you even imagine?'

I smoothed my fingers over a dusty petal. 'It's beautiful, Aunt Tootie. This fireplace looks like it belongs in a museum.'

'You're touching an important piece of history, that's for sure.'

She showed me the rest of the house, words I'd never heard falling easily from her lips – *parquetry, guilloche, corbel* – and then, like the curator in a museum, she'd tell me what they meant. I followed her from room to room, amazed. Not so much by the house, but by her knowledge and enthusiasm. But by the time we reached the third floor, I had to admit that I felt a small stirring of hope for the old house.

When we descended the back stairway, dried bug carcasses crunched beneath our feet. 'It sounds like we're walking on Rice Krispies,' I said. And my aunt laughed.

Just as I thought we were going to leave, Aunt Tootie stopped in the hallway and closed her eyes. 'Oh, Cecelia, isn't it a wonder?' she said with a look of ecstasy on her face. 'This house is alive with history. I can feel it humming through the soles of my shoes.'

I looked down at the floor and waited. But I didn't feel anything.

'All right,' she said, guiding me out the door, 'let's go home.'

As we headed to the car, I looked up at her. 'You sure do love saving old houses.'

'Oh, yes, I do. It's my fire.'

'Your fire?'

She glanced over her shoulder at the house, which was now bathed in a warm tint of yellow from the sun. 'Yes. Everyone needs to find the one thing that brings out her passion. It's what we do and share with the world that matters. I believe it's important that we leave our communities in better shape than we found them.

'Cecelia Rose,' she said, reaching for my hand, 'far too many people die with a heart that's gone flat with indifference, and it surely must be a terrible way to go. Life will offer us amazing opportunities, but we've got to be wide-awake to recognize them.'

She rested her hands on my shoulders and looked into my eyes. 'If there's one thing I'd like most for you, it's that you'll find your calling in life. That's where *true* happiness and purpose lies. Whether it's taking care of abandoned animals, saving old houses from the wreckin' ball, or reading to the blind, you've got to find your fire, sugar. You'll never be fulfilled if you don't.'

I thought about what she said, and as we climbed into the car I looked at her thoughtfully. 'But how will I know what my fire is?'

She pulled the keys from her handbag and started the engine. 'Oh, you'll know. One day you'll do something, see something, or get an idea that seems to pop up from nowhere. And you'll feel a kind of stirring – like a warm flicker inside your chest. When that happens, whatever you do, don't ignore it. Open your mind and explore the idea. Fan your flame. And when you do, you'll have found it.'

As she stepped on the gas and pulled away from the curb, my aunt's words settled deep within me. What my fire was, I didn't know. But I promised myself that I'd find out.

On the drive home, I thought about Momma and all those lost years of her life. *If she had found her fire would she still be alive? And if, sometime in her life she did find it, what had put it out?*

Ten

I was changing the sheets on my bed when Aunt Tootie called from the bottom of the stairs, 'Cecelia Rose?'

'Yes, ma'am.'

'I've got a surprise. I'll be right up.' I listened to the creaking of the stairs, and a moment later she appeared in the doorway with a package and an envelope in her hands. She smiled, and offered me the envelope first.

'It's from Mrs. Odell!' I squealed, ripping open the envelope. I opened the ivory note card and read:

My dear Cecelia,

I think of you every day. Remember the zinnias you planted in my border garden? They're already blooming. They're the prettiest zinnias I've ever had. I think you have a special touch. When you can, please write and tell me how you are. I miss our Sunday morning breakfasts so much.

All my love,
Mrs. O

As I set the note on my desk, Aunt Tootie handed me the package. 'This is just a little something I thought you might enjoy.'

I opened the bag and pulled out a square box. 'A camera! I've never had one.'

'It's a Polaroid. You know, the kind that takes those instant pictures. I don't know exactly how it works. When it comes to things mechanical, I'm dumber than a jaybird, but there's a booklet inside that explains everything.'

I opened the box and pulled out the camera and the instruction manual. 'Wow. This is great. I've seen ads for these on TV. Thank you.'

She patted my shoulder and smiled. 'I hope you'll have fun with it.'

'Oh, I know I will.' I stood on my tiptoes and kissed her cheek.

Later that evening, Aunt Tootie and I went for a leisurely walk. I took my new camera and snapped pictures along the way. Each time I pressed the button, the camera made a whirring sound and spit out the picture, and we'd both laugh; it was like making a miracle happen.

'Oh, look,' Aunt Tootie said, stopping by an iron fence. She pointed out a white water lily floating in a pond. 'It looks like a cup and saucer, don't you think?'

I nodded, leaned over the fence, and took three pictures: one for Aunt Tootie, one for Oletta, and the third I'd send to Mrs. Odell.

'You're good at picture taking,' my aunt said as we turned down Bull Street. 'I'm going to frame this and put it on my desk.'

'You think it's that good?'

'Yes, Cecelia Rose. I do. I think you are a *very* smart and talented young lady.'

Her words made me smile.

While heading home, Aunt Tootie said, 'I'm having lunch

with my sister, Lucille, and her best friend tomorrow. They live down in Brunswick. It isn't all that far away, and it's a nice drive. Would you like to go with me?'

'Yes, ma'am. I love riding in the car with you.'

'Wonderful. I can't wait to tell Lucille – she'll be tickled you're coming along. We'll leave around ten o'clock in the morning.'

During our drive to Brunswick, Aunt Tootie told me about her sister. Lucille was once married to an Irishman called Dutch. She had been young and happy and pretty, and Dutch was older and handsome – a big jokester kind of a guy who loved to bet on the horses.

Dutch laughed and sang his way into Aunt Lu's heart and married her less than three months after they met. Two years later, while she was minding the store on a rainy Tuesday afternoon, Dutch emptied her savings account, stole her mother's antique diamond watch, and laughed his way out of town, driving Aunt Lu's brand-new Chevrolet coupe. All this happened so fast that poor Aunt Lu never knew what hit her.

That experience did something to Aunt Lu – something real bad. From that day forward she wanted nothing more to do with men, and she never did get another car. She spent her days tending the jewelry store, and her nights locked away in the apartment above it, with her Perry Como record collection, her knitting, and her one-eared cat, Napoleon.

Aunt Tootie sighed and glanced over at me. 'But as hard as that awful ordeal was on Lucille, she's made her peace with it.'

When we arrived in Brunswick, Aunt Tootie pulled down a wide street lined with all sorts of shops. She parked the car and pointed out a narrow brick building that was three stories tall. Peeling gold letters spanned the small front window and spelled out the name: BRUNSWICK FINE JEWELERS.

'My father opened this store way back in 1887. It's been in the family ever since.'

Aunt Tootie opened the door of the jewelry shop and a small bell tinkled overhead. Lining the walls were long glass cases, each of them brightly lit and filled with jewelry displayed on puffy black velvet pillows.

A door swung open at the back of the store and a prim little woman appeared. 'Tallulah!' she said, fumbling to remove a pair of magnifying glasses that were strapped over her head. She set them on a jewelry case and rushed forward to give me a hug. She smelled like lily of the valley cologne. 'Welcome, Cecelia. I remember holding you when you were just a baby.'

'Really?'

Her watery blue eyes twinkled when she nodded. 'I rode all the way up to Ohio with Tallulah not long after you were born. I'm so glad to see you again.'

From somewhere outside a clock sounded twelve loud *bongs*.

'Lunchtime,' Aunt Lu said, pulling a small key from her pocket. She opened the cash register, slid two nickels from the change tray, and scurried out the door. From the window we watched her pick an empty parking spot. She leaned forward and listened to the whir of the coin counter as she pushed the nickels into the parking meter. A moment later she came inside and said, 'Will you give me a hand?'

While she and Aunt Tootie hauled an old vinyl-topped card table out to the parking space, I followed, lugging three folding chairs.

'Where's the fourth chair?' Aunt Tootie asked.

'It broke so I tossed it out. Rosa is bringing her chair. I'll be right back.'

After she disappeared inside her shop, I looked at the old card table. 'We're having lunch out here?'

Aunt Tootie smiled. 'If you ask Rosa and Lu about it, they'll tell you the story of how it came to be.'

Aunt Lu returned with a basket filled with sandwiches, cookies, and drinks. After smoothing a crisp linen tablecloth over the table, we settled into our chairs. A minute later a loud, metallic clacking noise filled the air as Rosa Cicero, Aunt Lu's best friend, came down the sidewalk, rolling her desk chair in front of her. Her stiletto-heeled shoes made a sharp *clickety-click* on the pavement and an unlit cigarette was stuck between her red lips. Unlit, Aunt Lu said, because Rosa had quit smoking years ago but could never entirely give up the idea of cigarettes.

Rosa was a remarkable-looking woman. Remarkable in that she wasn't what most people would call beautiful, but she oozed a raw femaleness that I was certain made most women uncomfortable and sent men walking into walls. And when she smiled, well, that was magic.

Rosa earned her living as a bookkeeper for Wilma Jo's Beauty World, which stood just a half block from Aunt Lu's jewelry store. Aunt Tootie said Wilma Jo's was touted as *the* place to go for bouffant hairdos and dye jobs. Aunt Lu claimed it provided the best entertainment in town.

'See what I mean,' Aunt Lu said as two women appeared from beneath the sun-bleached, pink-and-white-striped awning. One had a blonde beehive teased up as high and frothy as carnival cotton candy, and the other walked out with her auburn hair done up in a perfectly round bubble. It was lacquered so heavily that not a single hair moved when a gust of wind blew. As I watched the women come and go, there was no doubt in my mind that Wilma Jo's produced the greatest cavalcade of big hair this side of Savannah.

'So, how did this street picnic begin?' I asked, taking a bite of my sandwich.

Rosa laughed. 'Well, years ago I was married to a man named Frank. He bounced from one job to another, usually with months of unemployment in between that were spent on the golf course. After nineteen years of supporting him and my son, I woke up one Friday morning, sat up in bed, and screamed, "Enough!" And I kept screaming as I went on a rampage through the house, throwing my son's dirty clothes in the trash and emptying the refrigerator of my husband's beer bottles.'

Rosa leaned back and laughed. 'My son ran out the door to join the army. Frank ran out with his golf clubs in tow, and I ran out behind them and rented a one-bedroom apartment that had a pink-tiled bathroom and shag carpeting. That same day I bought myself a purple velvet sofa.'

Aunt Lu chuckled and said, 'The purchase of the sofa was how the Friday street picnics began. Rosa wanted to celebrate every paycheck she had all to herself.'

Rosa nodded. 'Friday is a purple-velvet-sofa day for some poor woman who's finally reclaimed her life. A purple velvet sofa is a gal's symbol of freedom.'

'Lu, it was your idea to set up a lunch table outside the store, wasn't it?' Aunt Tootie asked.

Aunt Lu took a swig of her Vernor's ginger ale and nodded. 'That way I could enjoy our celebration of financial independence, but not miss a sale if someone wandered into the store.'

'How long have you been friends?' I asked.

'Since we were nine,' Rosa said, popping a potato chip into her mouth and crunching loudly. 'See that?' She pointed to the small window of Aunt Lu's store. 'To the rest of the world it's just another jewelry store, but to me that's where I can always find my best girlfriend. When we were kids, I'd knock on that window every morning, and Lucille would grab her books off the jewelry case and come out the door so we could walk to school together.'

109

Aunt Lu swallowed a bite of her sandwich and said, 'I bet you'll make lots of friends in Savannah. There's nothing better than having a good girlfriend.'

'So, CeeCee,' Rosa said, 'what do you think you want to do with yourself when you grow up?'

'I'm not sure. Maybe I'll be a librarian or a writer.'

'Well, if you end up writing, make sure you write about me and Lucille. We're interesting as hell, aren't we, Lu?' she said, knocking her elbow into my aunt's arm.

I flushed with delight at being in the company of a woman who used cuss words so freely.

Aunt Lu gave Rosa a wry smile. 'You're the one who's interesting. I just hang around for the laughs and the stories.'

'What stories?' I asked. 'I love to hear stories.'

'These two have more crazy stories between them than the *National Enquirer*,' Aunt Tootie said. 'Rosa, tell CeeCee about the day you fried your hair.'

Rosa took a cigarette, and held it, unlit, like a movie star. 'Well, I'd been divorced for a little over a year when a salesman dropped by the shop to show Wilma Jo a new line of depilatories.' She looked at me and wrinkled her nose. 'It's gooey stuff that rips hair off your upper lip. If anyone *ever* tries to use it on you, run like hell.

'Anyway, that man had the most beautiful blue eyes I'd ever seen. His name was Stan Cole. About ten minutes after he'd packed up his bag and left, the phone rang. When I answered, a man's voice said, "I'm calling to speak to the raven-haired beauty at the front desk." I all but melted. It was Stan. He asked to take me to dinner the following evening. Well, of course I said yes. I was so excited. I felt like a teenager again.'

Aunt Lu shook her head. 'You acted like one too.'

'I did, didn't I?' Rosa chuckled. 'Well, I got this nutty idea

110

that I wanted to perm my hair before I went out on my date, but it was prom weekend and all the beauticians at Wilma's were booked. That night I stopped at the drugstore and bought a home permanent. On Saturday morning I wrapped my hair on the perm rods and drizzled on the solution. While my hair was cooking, I decided to have an apple. When I took a bite, the crown on my front tooth came off. My dentist's office was closed, so I called Lucille in a panic. A few minutes later she showed up at my apartment with a tube of jeweler's glue.'

Aunt Lu swallowed a bite of her sandwich and said, 'Once I got the glue inside the crown, I pressed it into place and held it there for a few minutes. But some of the glue had seeped out from under the crown, and when I tried to let go, my finger was cemented to Rosa's tooth. I tried to slice the glue away with a paring knife and ended up cutting my finger. That's when Rosa remembered her perm and started screaming.'

'I dragged Lucille to the kitchen sink so we could rinse off the perm solution, and when we removed the rods, half my hair came out right along with them.'

'When Rosa saw her hair in the sink, she threw a fit. And my finger was still stuck to her tooth! I couldn't stop the bleeding. So I suggested we hurry down the street to Floyd Webber's, but Rosa refused.'

Rosa laughed so hard she snorted. 'Of course I refused, Lu. Floyd's a butcher.'

'He trimmed meat better than anyone I'd ever seen, so I thought he'd do a fine job of trimming my finger from your tooth,' Aunt Lu said with a defensive sniff. 'Anyway, once Rosa calmed down, we knew we'd better get to the hospital. So we climbed into Rosa's car. What a sight we were – I was practically sitting on her lap with my finger stuck in her mouth. I couldn't stop laughing, and Rosa was in tears. When we got to the hospital, a doctor sliced my finger free from her tooth and wrapped it in a bandage.'

Rosa shook her head. 'I've never been more mortified in my life.'

Aunt Lu laughed. 'Oh, sure you have, Rosa, lots of times.'

I gulped down a bite of my sandwich and asked, 'What did you do about your hair? Did you get it fixed up for your date?'

'No. My hair looked like I'd doused it in gasoline and lit a match. There was no way I could go out with Stan, but I didn't know how to reach him to cancel our date. And I sure didn't want to sit in the dark all night with the lights turned off pretending I wasn't home.'

'So Rosa wrote him a note that said she'd had an emergency and taped it to her door. Then she packed an overnight bag and came home with me,' Aunt Lu said.

Rosa sighed. 'And that was the end of Stan. I was so upset that when I went back home on Sunday, I spent the entire day in bed. I was a sniveling basket case of wrecked humanity. That night, Lu came over with a pizza, and we sat on my sofa and talked. I was feeling sorry for myself, fussing about my ruined hair and missing my date with Stan. Well, Lucille looked me right in the eyes and said, "What's wrong with you, Rosa? Did you forget why you bought this sofa? Are you that anxious to go out and find your next *ex*-husband?"'

Rosa, Aunt Tootie, and Aunt Lu burst into laughter. It took me a moment to get the joke; then I laughed too.

'And she was right,' Rosa said, leaning back and taking another pretend drag from her cigarette. 'I realized I was happy with the way things were, so why mess it up by bringing a man into my life? I've got my job, my apartment, my purple velvet sofa, and the best friend in the world,' she said, grinning at Aunt Lu.

Just then a sharp *ding* sounded, and a little red flag popped up inside the window of the parking meter.

'Time's up. Back to work,' Rosa said, folding her napkin.

'Wait. Don't go anywhere.' I ran to the car and grabbed my new camera. 'I want a picture of you two.'

Rosa pressed her cheek against the side of Aunt Lu's face, and I took their picture. As I watched it develop, I wondered if I'd ever be so lucky to have a girlfriend I'd grow old with, a girl-friend who knew my secrets, my fears, my hopes – and loved me anyway. A purple-velvet-sofa kind of girlfriend.

Two weeks later I was passing through the kitchen when the phone rang. Aunt Tootie was out in the garden, so I answered. I heard nothing but sobs echoing over the phone line. Finally I realized who it was.

'She's gone,' Rosa cried. 'My best girlfriend is gone!' With gulps and tears punctuating her words, she told me that Aunt Lu had died only a couple of hours ago.

I was so shocked, I slid down the wall and landed on the floor.

As Aunt Lu would have wanted, Rosa was with her when she left this earth. And as only God himself could have ordained, Aunt Lu died while sitting at that old card table as she and Rosa enjoyed what was to be the last of their Friday street picnics.

Rosa blew her nose and said, 'I can't believe it. Just a few hours ago we were having lunch, and I nearly fainted when Lucille told me she'd paid her dues in life and had finally earned her freedom. She told me she'd decided to retire and was clos-ing the store at the end of the summer.' Rosa whimpered and blew her nose again. 'Lucille laughed and asked if I'd help her find a purple velvet sofa to celebrate her retirement. So we made plans to go shopping on Saturday.'

By this time I was crying myself. I climbed up from the floor and wiped my eyes on a paper towel. But my tears flowed again when Rosa told me how Aunt Lu's eyes had twinkled when she'd laughed and said, 'Can you imagine it – *me* with a purple velvet sofa?'

According to Rosa, Aunt Lu was still laughing when she stiffened and pitched forward, dropping dead of a massive brain aneurism, right there at the card table. Rosa wept uncontrollably when she told me that the moment Aunt Lu died, the parking meter whirred and the little red time-expired flag popped up into the window and sounded its customary *ding*.

'I'll never get over it,' Rosa sobbed. 'Never.'

Before going to bed that night, I pulled the photograph I'd taken of Aunt Lu and Rosa from my bureau drawer. I sat on the edge of the bed and studied their faces, how the sparkle of their friendship lit up their eyes. Anyone who saw the picture would never doubt they had loved each other.

The next afternoon, Aunt Tootie and I packed our suitcases and headed to Brunswick to make funeral arrangements. We drove in silence for a long time, and then I looked at her and said, 'It doesn't seem real. We just saw her.'

'That's the way it is sometimes when people leave us – one minute they're here and the next minute they're gone.'

I nodded and stared at the hem of my dress, thinking about Momma and wishing I hadn't brought up the subject.

Picking out a casket was a somber experience that left me thinking cremation was a good idea. As Aunt Tootie spoke with the funeral director, I stared at the room full of caskets on display – their lids gaping open like hungry mouths, waiting to swallow up the newly departed. I decided I'd much rather exit this world in a crackle of flames and a swirl of smoke through my ribs than be cooped up for all eternity in a dark box surrounded by puffy white satin.

After we left the funeral home, Aunt Tootie drove to a cement-block building that sat on the edge of town. The sign above the door read: JOE BODACCI AND SON CONSTRUCTION – NO JOB TOO BIG OR TOO SMALL. Her eyes swam in a pool of tears when she parked the car. 'Wait here for me, honey,' she said, pulling a handkerchief from her handbag and blowing her nose. 'I won't be long.'

Though I wondered why she'd driven to a construction company after picking out a casket, I thought it was best not to ask about it.

The day after Aunt Lu was laid to rest, Aunt Tootie and I went to Rosa's apartment for lunch before we headed home to Savannah. Rosa had adopted Aunt Lu's old cat, Napoleon, and when she greeted us at the door he was curled up in her arms. 'Look at him. He's in mourning, just like I am.'

The three of us sat at a pink Formica table by the kitchen window and had lunch, the whole time Rosa crying and laughing while she told stories about Aunt Lu. Aunt Tootie and I laughed and cried right along with her while Napoleon sat on the windowsill and gazed out through the screen with sad green eyes.

While Rosa was telling us another story, there came a knock on the door. 'Who could that be?' she said, lifting her napkin from her lap and blotting her eyes. She got up from the table and walked to the living room.

Aunt Tootie pressed her finger to her lips and said, '*Shhh*,' then stood and motioned for me to join her at the kitchen doorway. Rosa unlocked the dead bolt and was speechless when she opened the door. In walked Mr. Bodacci and his son, and in their hands they carried the front window from Aunt Lu's store, its peeling gold letters spelling out the name BRUNSWICK FINE JEWELERS. The window had been professionally framed and backed with a mirror, making the letters stand out as if they were floating on a sheet of ice.

The single largest tear I'd ever seen rolled down Rosa's cheek as she reached out and lightly ran her fingers over the frail gold letters. Aunt Tootie, Rosa, and I stood holding hands as we watched Mr. Bodacci and his son carefully hang the framed window on the wall – directly above Rosa's purple velvet sofa.

For several days following Aunt Lu's funeral, friends of Aunt Tootie's would stop by the house. I'd feel the atmosphere lift when they arrived, only to sense it fall when they left. At dusk, Aunt Tootie would go out to the garden and sit on the bench beneath the live oak – her shoulders hunched forward and her hands clasped at her knees. She wore her sadness on the outside, like a heavy winter coat. Though I knew I should go out there and be with her, I couldn't. Something inside me had slammed shut when Momma died, and whatever it was, I needed to keep it that way. I felt selfish and small as I watched my aunt from the kitchen window. She had given me so much, so freely, yet I was unable to do something as simple as sit at her side.

Then one morning, as I headed out the front door to take some pictures, I heard a *clackety-clack*. From around the side of the house came Aunt Tootie with her rusty gardening wagon in tow. A gust of wind snatched her straw hat from her head and sent it sailing. I put down my camera, raced down the front steps, and chased it to the far end of the lawn.

When I returned the hat to my aunt, we stood facing each other. Then she looked into the sky. 'Lucille always loved a strong breeze. She said it was nature's way of blowing away our sorrows.'

Just then another gust of wind whipped around us. Aunt Tootie smiled. I smiled too. 'Would you like some help today?' I asked.

'Oh, sugar, that would be lovely.'

I reached down, took hold of the wagon's handle, and together we headed for the garden.

Eleven

It was a warm Thursday evening. Aunt Tootie and I had just finished dinner, and she settled into a chair in the den to work on her cross-stitching and watch a rerun of *The George Burns and Gracie Allen Show*. I wasn't in the mood for TV, so I wandered to the back porch and began reading one of the books I'd borrowed from Miz Goodpepper.

I loved this time of night, how everything softened and lost the hard edges of day, and how, if the wind moved just right, the live oaks would murmur tender green words across the shadowy lawn. Sitting with a book in the warm circle of light from the table lamp had become my favorite way to end the day.

While reading *The Call of the Wild,* I came across something that looked like a piece of old money pressed between the pages. It was faded and dry and had a picture of a sailing ship etched in the center. Above the ship was the word *Confederate*. I walked into the house to show Aunt Tootie, but she was sound asleep in her chair. I turned off the TV and quietly went back to the porch.

The white blooms of Miz Goodpepper's rosebushes glowed in the moonlight like tiny lanterns. Just beyond the trellis I noticed something flutter. I stood on my tiptoes and saw Miz

Goodpepper move across her patio. Wanting to return the money I'd found, I hopped off the porch, cut through the opening in the hedge, and entered her backyard. I called her name softly as I approached.

She looked up with surprise. 'Cecelia?'

'Yes, ma'am. It's me. I was reading one of the books I borrowed from you, and I found this inside.' I offered her the money. 'There's a date on it – 1861. It's even older than the book.'

In her hands she held a rubber pancake flipper and a Mason jar. She set them on the ground and took the bill from my outstretched hand. 'This was my granddaddy's,' she said, smoothing the bill between her slender fingers. 'He was fond of old paper money – had the habit of using it as bookmarks. He's been gone for nearly thirty years, and I still find all sorts of bills tucked inside his books.'

She thanked me for returning the money and slid it into the pocket of her emerald green caftan. 'Oh, look – there's a big one,' she said, grabbing the pancake flipper and jar. She scurried to the brick walk, bent down, and scooped something up. 'This one will do *lots* of damage.' She tapped the pancake flipper on the edge of the jar and something the size of a sausage link fell to the bottom. 'This is an all-time record. I've collected at least a dozen of these fellows tonight.'

'What are they?' I asked.

She held the jar to the moonlight. 'Slugs. They're such bad, bad boys – the silent destroyers of my garden. Though I must admit they're rather pretty in a slimy, prehistoric way. After I water my gardens they come out in droves, but I've outsmarted them,' she said with a throaty laugh. 'I come out here and scoop them up; then they go for a nice little trip.'

I'd seen a slug or two in Mrs. Odell's tomato patch, but never

had I seen anything as big as the ones Miz Goodpepper had collected. 'What do you do with them?'

'Follow me,' she commanded, plunging into the shadows.

We walked to the edge of the property, to the exact place
where the murdered magnolia tree had once stood. Miz
Goodpepper gathered the length of her caftan and stepped on
the stump. Her lips formed a devilish smile when she shook one
of the slugs onto the end of the pancake flipper. She held out
the jar and said, 'Will you hold this for a minute?'

I wrinkled my nose but did as she asked.

With her right hand she held the handle and with her left she
pulled back the top like a slingshot and said, 'Enjoy the ride.' She
let go and the slug catapulted through the air and disappeared
into the darkness of Miz Hobbs's backyard.

Though I didn't much care for the creatures, I thought it was
cruel to hurl them through the air like that. Plus, it was the exact
opposite of all the things Miz Goodpepper had told me when
we first met, and I couldn't stop myself from saying so. 'Miz
Goodpepper, you said killing anything was wrong. You said it
would bring lots of bad karma. So why are you killing the slugs?'

She let out a low, haunting laugh. 'Oh, I'm not killing them.
I'm just sending them on a little ride. Slugs like to fly. They look
forward to this – it's their only sport.'

Their only sport?

I stood, stupefied, and watched her catapult the slugs, one by
one, over the hedge. When the jar was empty she stepped down
from the stump with a satisfied smile. 'Well, with any luck those
slugs will eat half of that evil witch's garden before morning.'

A squeak sounded and I turned to see Miz Hobbs push open
her screen door and step out onto the back porch. She struck a
match and lit a row of candles that were lined up on the railing.
Miz Goodpepper motioned for me to duck, and we crouched

down low and peered through an opening in the hedge. She poked my ribs with her elbow and whispered, 'Look at that outfit.'

Miz Hobbs was wearing a yellow see-through robe with its hem and sleeves trimmed in white feathers. Backlit by the glow of the candles, I could see she was naked underneath, and I mean *totally* naked.

Miz Goodpepper whispered, 'Isn't she ridiculous? She looks like the centerfold in a poultry catalog.'

Just then a man's voice boomed through the air, 'You're a wild one, Violene.'

Miz Hobbs turned around and giggled as a short, pudgy man stepped onto the porch. It wasn't the baggy white underpants that left me wide-eyed. It was the black, Zorro-like mask. Dangling from his fingers was a brassiere. I could hardly believe my eyes when he began twirling it over his head like a lasso.

'C'mon, Violene, shake it for Big Daddy,' he whooped, spinning the bra faster and faster. 'Do that little striptease again.'

'Stop that, Earl.' She giggled, reaching for the spinning brassiere, but he snatched it from her fingers and sent it hurling into the shrubs. Miz Hobbs let out a scream. 'Now, you go get that.'

'I'm gonna get *this* instead,' he said, grabbing her butt.

She slapped his hand and stepped away. That's when I noticed her feet. They were crammed into high-heeled shoes that had feathery pom-poms on the toes.

'C'mon, honey, do that striptease again.' Earl begged, reaching out and grabbing her breasts. Miz Hobbs squealed and her high-heeled shoes clacked across the wooden floorboards as she ran to the other side of the porch.

'You're a naughty boy, Earl,' she called from behind the porch swing. 'If you don't behave I might have to spank you.'

'Ohhhhhh, baby, you sure are frisky tonight.'

I thought Miz Goodpepper might choke when she elbowed my side and whispered, 'That masked man is Earl Jenkins. He's a policeman *and* he's married. Just look at him. I've always said he was only one step above a bait-shop dealer.'

I didn't know what that meant, but Miz Goodpepper thought it was so funny, she buried her face in her hands.

Earl began chasing Miz Hobbs around the porch. 'Now, you leave me alone,' she shrieked, running down the porch steps. But her feet flew straight out in front of her, and in a flash of feathers she was airborne. She landed at the bottom of the steps with a sickening *thump*.

The man's laughter died in the night air, and his belly jiggled like a bowl of Jell-O when he ran down the steps. 'Violene? Are you all right? Awwww, shit,' he said, pulling the mask from his face and kneeling by her side. 'C'mon, Violene, stop kidding around.'

Earl patted Miz Hobbs's cheeks and called her name, but no matter what he did, he couldn't wake her. He sputtered a few words I couldn't quite hear, then he ran up the steps and into the house, returning a few minutes later dressed in his police uniform.

Miz Goodpepper pushed aside a branch of the hedge so she could see more clearly. 'Earl's such an ignorant whore-hound,' she murmured. 'I wonder how he's going to get himself out of *this*.'

'Violene?' he said, leaning down beside her lifeless body, 'Aww, man, you're bleeding – you've gone and busted your head open. I called an ambulance, but dammit, don't you tell anybody we were together tonight. I'm gonna say I found you like this. Okay? Violene – can you hear me?'

A siren screamed in the distance. It grew louder and louder, and a minute later two policemen rushed into Miz Hobbs's backyard. 'What happened?' one of them asked.

Earl gave an innocent shrug of his shoulders. 'I don't have any idea. I was just doing my nightly rounds as usual, checking on the neighborhood. I was heading back to my car when I glanced over the hedge and saw her lying here. Looks like she might have tripped and taken a bad fall down those steps. I tried to wake her up, but she's out cold.'

Miz Goodpepper pulled a rosebud from the bush, held it to her nose, and smiled like Mona Lisa.

One of the policemen turned on his flashlight, bent down, and took a closer look at Miz Hobbs. 'Yeah, her head's cracked open, she's bleeding pretty good. But what the hell was going on here? She's almost naked. What was she doing out here wearing *that* getup? Will you look at all those feathers. She looks like a half-plucked chicken.' He moved the beam down to her feet and stopped. 'Well, Jesus jumpin' Christ. Look right there – *there's* your perpetrator. That's a smashed slug on the bottom of her shoe.'

Miz Goodpepper and I exchanged a wide-eyed sideways glance.

'A slug?' the other officer said. 'Are you sure?'

'Hell, yeah, I'm sure. Look for yourself.'

Earl piped in, 'Will ya look at the size of that thing. Slugs are slippery little shits. She must have stepped on it and had her feet go clean out from under her.'

All the policemen knelt to have a closer look at the squashed slug. 'Eww, that was a juicy one,' one of them said.

Earl wiped his hand across his face. 'Yeah, yeah, I bet that's exactly what happened.'

Miz Goodpepper's eyes gleamed triumphantly. Unable to contain her laughter, she let out a snort. Quickly she slapped her hand over her mouth.

One of the policemen stood up. 'Did you hear that?'

'What? I didn't hear anything,' Earl said.

The policeman began to scan the backyard with the beam of his flashlight. He moved slowly across the patio and around the swimming pool. Miz Goodpepper leaned back and held her breath. I did too. I was terrified when he moved closer and stopped. The beam from his flashlight skipped across the top of the hedge, stopping directly over my head.

'Good God,' the other policeman called out. 'There's a whole mess of slugs over here on the patio. Look at 'em all. There's no crime here – just a bunch of garden slugs.'

The flashlight's beam nearly blinded me when the policeman turned and headed back toward the house. Miz Goodpepper leaned forward and watched him move away, the whole time plucking petals from the rose in her hand and dropping them onto the ground. When the policeman reached the porch, I covered my face with my hands and breathed a sigh of relief into my sweaty palms.

A siren sounded, and a moment later whirling red lights ignited the leaves on the trees with an eerie, shimmering fire. Two men carrying a stretcher came around the side of the house. Within minutes Miz Hobbs had been lifted onto the stretcher, covered with a sheet, and loaded into the back of an ambulance. Miz Goodpepper and I didn't utter a word until all the policemen left and the night fell quiet.

I retrieved the pancake flipper from the grass, stood, and handed it to Miz Goodpepper. 'Is she dead?' I whispered.

She pushed herself up from the ground, dropped the pancake flipper inside the jar with a plunk, and looked into the sky. A strange blue tint of moonlight washed over her face, and she stood for a long moment, smiling at nothing. 'No. It would take a lot more than a slug to kill *that* woman.'

I glanced over my shoulder at the scene of the crime. 'When Miz Hobbs slipped on the slug and hit her head, was that kinda like the black boomerang of karma you talked about?'

Miz Goodpepper clutched the empty jar to her chest and slowly turned toward me. 'You are a very smart child.'

Twelve

It's true what they say about people being drawn back to the scene of a crime. I woke early the next morning with thoughts of Miz Hobbs bumping around in my head. I pushed back the covers, threw on some clothes, and crept down the stairs.

The house was sleeping and filled with the thin light of dawn. I moved past the living room and the fragrance from a vase of lilies hovered in the air. Quietly I padded down the hall and into the kitchen. Careful not to let the screen door slap closed behind me, I stepped onto the back porch and headed for the opening in the hedge. Across Miz Goodpepper's yard I ran, kicking up a cool mist of dew that dampened my legs. When I reached the spot where we'd been the night before, I had to remind myself to breathe, and when I did, the scent of secrets and bruised rose petals filled my nostrils.

I got down on my hands and knees and peeked through the hedge. On the fourth step of Miz Hobbs's porch was a reddish-brown bloodstain the size of a serving platter. I sat back on my haunches and gasped. I figured that much blood surely meant that Miz Hobbs was dead.

The sound of air brakes hissed through the morning air. I

jumped to my feet and peered over the top of the hedge just in time to see Oletta step off the bus.

Oh, no. What's she doing here so early?

Knowing I had to beat Oletta home, I ducked down low and hauled my butt across Miz Goodpepper's yard as fast as my legs could go. I didn't slow down until I reached my bedroom, feeling so hot and winded that my chest heaved.

I sat on the edge of the bed and tried to cool down, the whole time thinking about Miz Hobbs's death and the part I had played in it. Never had I been more scared. My stomach was bound in knots when I took a shower, and I couldn't stop my hands from shaking as I zipped up my shorts and tied the laces of my shoes. While making my way down the stairs, I heard the soft mutterings of Oletta and Aunt Tootie.

As I entered the kitchen, the phone rang and Aunt Tootie picked it up. Oletta was busy stirring something in a bowl and didn't notice when Aunt Tootie's face drained of color. But when Aunt Tootie clutched the collar of her robe and let out a gasp, Oletta stopped what she was doing and listened.

'Oh, no. This is just awful. When did this happen?' Aunt Tootie said, lowering herself into a chair. 'Last night? But she lives alone, who found her?'

This was it. I was in big trouble. Miz Hobbs was dead, and I was partly to blame. I imagined a swarm of police cars pulling up in front of the house. I'd be slapped in handcuffs and hauled away while Aunt Tootie and Oletta cried out their protests. After taking my photograph and fingerprints, the police would shove me into a dimly lit cell where Miz Goodpepper would already be waiting. I could picture her sitting on a narrow cot, her mysterious eyes void of all emotion.

I wandered down the hall, unlocked the front door, and went

outside. Feeling lower than low, I plunked down on the steps and hugged my knees.

Will there be a trial? Will I be sentenced to spend years behind bars? Will Aunt Tootie and Oletta come visit me? Or will they be so ashamed I'll never see or hear from them again? And what about Mrs. Odell? Will she stop writing to me?

While envisioning the soon-to-be-revealed miseries of my ill-fated life, I heard the door open. Oletta's shadow loomed over me. 'What are you doin' out here lookin' all hangdog?'

I glanced up at her. 'Waiting.'

She scowled. 'Waitin' for what?'

'When Aunt Tootie gets off the phone I'll tell you about it.'

'Well, she's off the phone now. So c'mon inside.'

I followed Oletta into the house, wondering how I'd tell her and Aunt Tootie what had happened last night.

Will they be mad at me even though I wasn't the one who had catapulted the slugs through the air? Do they know about the black boomerang of karma?

Just when we entered the kitchen, the phone rang again and Aunt Tootie picked it up. 'Hello. Oh, good morning, Thelma. Yes . . .'

I couldn't bear to see the look of shock that would soon overshadow my aunt's face, so I turned and walked into the breakfast room. How long I stared out the window, I don't know, but I was startled when Aunt Tootie spoke from the doorway.

'Cecelia Rose, something awful has happened.' She looked frail and tired as she moved across the room and eased herself down at the table. 'I'm so upset,' she said, dabbing her eyes with a handkerchief.

I pulled out the chair across from her and slowly sat down, waiting to hear the words that would forever ruin my life. I was so nervous I couldn't stop my right foot from tapping against the rung of the chair.

'I just hate leaving you, but I have to go away in a few days. I don't know for sure, but I suspect I'll be gone for the better part of a week. When you were outside, I asked Oletta if she'd stay here at the house with you, and bless her heart, she said she would.'

The door swung open, and Oletta walked in carrying a tray. She served us waffles and juice, and while she was pouring coffee into my aunt's cup, Aunt Tootie reached out and touched her arm. 'Oletta, this is a sad, sad day.'

Oletta nodded and patted my aunt's hand.

'Frankie Mae was the first friend I had in college. She was such a sweet-tempered girl, and oh, was she smart. I remember the time when we . . . '

Frankie Mae? Who is she talking about?

When Aunt Tootie finished telling her story, Oletta took the tray and left the room. I watched Aunt Tootie shake out her napkin, drape it across her lap, and pour syrup on her waffles.

'Aunt Tootie, I'm confused. Who called this morning?'

'The first call was from my friend Estelle Trent. She was letting me know that poor Frankie Mae suffered a stroke last evening. She's in the hospital up in Raleigh. Estelle and I are driving there to see her.'

'But . . . but then Miz Goodpepper called.'

'Oh, yes. Thelma called to ask where I'd bought the silver polish I'd been raving about.'

Deciding it was best to not to say another word, I began eating my waffles.

Oletta walked in with the morning newspaper and placed it on the table. As she turned to leave, Aunt Tootie opened the paper and gasped. 'Good heavens. Oletta, did you see the front page?'

'No, I didn't. What's it say?'

'Well, wait till you hear this.' Aunt Tootie angled the paper into the morning light and read, '"Local widow suffers severe head injury caused by garden slug . . ."'

I nearly choked on my waffle.

Aunt Tootie read the article aloud. Miz Hobbs was in the hospital with a concussion, and it sounded like she'd needed a ton of stitches in her head. She was reported to be in a serious but stable condition.

'Isn't that the strangest thing?' Aunt Tootie looked at Oletta over the top of her glasses and shook her head. 'In all my days I've never heard of anyone slipping on a slug. I wonder if they had to shave off Violene's hair to stitch up her head,' she said with a tiny smirk. 'She'd just hate that.'

Oletta showed no emotion except for the way the skin around her eyes crinkled into little pleats. I knew she was trying not to laugh.

Aunt Tootie put down the paper and took a sip of coffee. 'Well, Violene surely isn't one of my favorite people in this town, and Lord knows I don't have one thing pink to say about her. But, no matter what, she *is* a neighbor. I suppose I'd better call the florist and have some flowers sent over to the hospital. Sounds like she'll be there for a while.'

Oletta rolled her eyes. 'That'd be a waste of money if you ask me. But if you feel you've got to send her something – then send her a nice big bouquet of belladonna and sign my name to the card.'

Aunt Tootie chuckled and shooed Oletta away with a wave of her napkin. I heard Oletta laugh as the door swung closed behind her.

'What's belladonna?' I asked.

My aunt's lips edged toward a smile when she said, 'Poison.'

That afternoon Aunt Tootie, Oletta, and I climbed into the car and drove through the shady streets of Savannah. We wound our way along narrow streets lined with itty-bitty houses, and then Aunt Tootie pulled to a stop in front of a yellow house trimmed in violet. Clay pots filled with flowers lined the edge of the front steps, and on the porch sat a wooden rocking chair.

'Oletta, you go on in and take your time packing. I'm heading over to Mr. Hammond's vegetable stand to see what he has. I'll be back to get you in about a half hour or so.'

'Can I go with you, Oletta?' I asked.

She hoisted herself out of the car. 'If it's all right with Miz Tootie.'

My aunt nodded, and I scrambled from the backseat and waved good-bye as she pulled away.

Oletta opened a wooden gate and we walked to her front porch. While she hunted for keys in her handbag, I looked around. Dangling from a hook in the porch ceiling were wind chimes made of old silver spoons. I flicked my finger and sent them into a happy, out-of-tune melody. A narrow gravel driveway ran along the side of the house and led to a small garage.

'Do you have a car, Oletta?'

'Not anymore. Cars and I never got along too good. I like takin' the bus – it suits me just fine. If I can't get somewhere on the bus, then I figure I don't need to go. C'mon in,' she said, unlocking the front door.

I followed her into a living room that had a lime green area rug and a brightly patterned floral-print sofa. A brown leather recliner chair sat off to the side – its seat cushion bore the soft, round imprint of Oletta's behind. Directly across from the chair was a TV, and on the front windowsill was a statue of Jesus.

She led me past a tiny kitchen with a red linoleum floor that gleamed like a polished mirror. I followed Oletta down a narrow hallway, past a sewing room, and into a bedroom that was so clean it was like breathing in a basketful of fresh laundry. Above a chest of drawers there hung a photograph of a black man with dark, intense eyes. A thin silver chain was draped over one corner of the frame, and from a loop on its end dangled a wooden cross.

'Who's that?' I asked, stepping closer to the picture.

Oletta's eyebrows shot up. 'As smart as you are, you don't know who that is?'

I shook my head.

Her eyes warmed with reverence as she eased herself down on the bed and gazed at the picture. 'That's Martin Luther King. He's a great, great man. I got the chance to hear him speak when I was visiting my sister, Geneva, in Birmingham. It was something I'll never forget. The minute I heard him speak, I knew he was sent here by the Good Lord himself.'

I figured the man must be important to have a cross hanging over his picture. 'Is he something like a saint for colored people?'

She let out a little laugh. 'Child, I get a kick out of how your mind works. But in a way, you're right. Martin Luther King is a saint to me, and to lots of other folks too. Mark my words, that man is gonna change this world. Next time he's on the radio, I'll let you know so you can hear him speak.'

'Okay.'

On a table next to the bed was a photograph of a young girl with wide, inquisitive eyes and the whitest teeth I'd ever seen. 'She's really cute,' I said, picking up the picture. 'Who is she?'

'My sweet daughter, Jewel. She was about your age when that picture was taken. You remind me of Jewel in a lot of ways. She was real smart and curious about things, just like you. That child asked questions from morning till night.'

I smiled at Oletta. 'I didn't know you had a daughter. Will I get to meet her?'

She glanced down at her hands and shook her head. 'Jewel is with the Lord now. She passed away when she was only thirteen years old.'

I reached out and touched her shoulder. 'Oh, Oletta, that's so sad. What happened?'

'Jewel got spinal meningitis. The doctors tried everything, but they couldn't save her. I was right there with her when she closed her eyes and went home. She went real peaceful.'

Though I wondered what spinal meningitis was, I knew this wasn't the time to ask. Gently I replaced the picture on the table. 'I'm sorry, Oletta.'

She let out a barely audible moan. 'Me too.' And with those two simple words the depth of Oletta's grief revealed itself to me. As if to beat away the painful memory, she slapped her thighs and said, 'Anyway, we better hurry up. Miz Tootie'll be back soon. There's a suitcase under the bed. Pull it out for me, will you?'

When she'd finished packing, Oletta pulled something from the closet that looked like a metal broom handle with a beat-up silver platter attached to one end.

It looked so weird, I laughed out loud. 'What is that thing?'

'This here is my fortune finder,' she said with a chuckle. 'Works pretty good too. Last year I found some old Spanish coins and a solid gold watch. Made me some nice money off them things.'

I'd never heard of a fortune finder. 'How does it work?' I asked, smoothing my fingers along its handle.

'Well, I turn it on and then I walk real slow along the beach. If I hear a crackling noise, I know I'm real close to something that might be worth some money. Maybe while Miz Tootie's gone we'll go over to Tybee Island and do us some treasure huntin'.'

Just then a familiar *beep-beep* sounded.

'Miz Tootie's back,' she said, pulling the suitcase off the bed and heading for the door.

I followed, carrying her fortune finder.

When we arrived home, Miz Goodpepper was weaving her way through Aunt Tootie's garden. She was wearing an immaculate white suit and a wide-brimmed black hat that dipped low over her left eye.

'The mailman delivered this to me by mistake,' she said, waving an envelope in the air.

'Thank you, Thelma. You look lovely. Where are you off to all dressed up?'

'I'm driving up to Charleston to attend an art show, then I'll have dinner with some friends.'

Miz Goodpepper's gaze drifted toward me. Her ruby lips formed a strange, conspiratorial half smile, and her long silver earrings glittered like the tails of twin comets when she stepped forward and said, 'Cecelia is so sweet. Did she mention that she stopped over to see me last night?'

'She did?' Aunt Tootie said, turning to look at me.

'Yes. She brought me an old twenty-dollar bill she found in one of Granddaddy's books. We've become great friends, haven't we, darling?'

I nodded and looked down at my shoes. She was testing me. I was sure of it.

Aunt Tootie lifted her hand and shaded her eyes from the sun. 'Thelma, did you see the morning paper?'

'No. Was there something of interest?'

Aunt Tootie nodded and the corners of her lips quivered when she said, 'Violene is in the hospital. She slipped on a slug last night, right in her own backyard. From what I read it sounds like she cracked her head wide open. She's got a concussion too.'

Miz Goodpepper gave a slight shrug to her shoulders. 'I heard a siren, but I didn't pay much attention. A slug? Is that what you said?'

'Yes, a simple old garden slug.'

'Well,' Miz Goodpepper said with a wry smile, 'Violene's so thickheaded I'm sure she'll be just fine.'

Aunt Tootie and Oletta chuckled.

Though I'd never dare to utter a word about what had really happened, the threat of it being revealed stood between Miz Goodpepper and me, as big as a Ferris wheel. She seemed pleased with my unspoken vow of loyalty and touched my cheek. The current that passed through her fingertips brought the hair straight up off my neck.

Miz Goodpepper glanced at her watch. 'I'd better be going.' She turned and headed for home, her high-heeled shoes leaving a trail of tiny holes in the grass behind her.

'Thanks for bringing my mail,' Aunt Tootie called out.

'Anytime,' Miz Goodpepper said with a wave of her hand.

I pressed my fingers against the spot on my cheek Miz Goodpepper had touched, and as she dipped her hat beneath a tree limb and disappeared, I thought about the black boomerang of karma.

Thelma Rae Goodpepper was a mystery to me: wise and funny and kind, yet she also possessed a darkness that was as smooth as silk and as dangerous as a slim blade. Something formidable shimmered in her cool, blue eyes. I didn't know what to think of her. But I did know, with searing clarity, that I'd never want to fall out of her favor.

Thirteen

While Aunt Tootie packed a suitcase for her trip to Raleigh, I sat on a dainty upholstered chair by the side of her bed.

'Cecelia Rose, I just hate leaving you,' she said, folding a sweater. 'With all the work I'm doing on the Historic Foundation and now having to go to Raleigh, you must think I run in circles like a dog chasing his tail.'

I ran my finger along the silky cording of the chair. 'I understand. I've got plenty of books to keep me happy.'

Aunt Tootie slapped her forehead. 'How could I have forgotten,' she said, moving across the room. She flung open the door to her walk-in closet and disappeared, returning a moment later with a paper bag in her hand. 'I bought this for you the other day.'

I opened the bag and pulled out a new, leather-bound dictionary.

'I know you're always running downstairs to look up words in that big old dictionary in the library, so I thought it'd be nice if you had your own to keep in your bedroom,' she said with a wink.

'Thank you, Aunt Tootie.' I lifted the dictionary to my nose and breathed in the leathery smell.

'You're welcome,' she said, walking into her closet again. I heard the metallic clink of hangers and the soft rustle of dry-cleaning bags. 'I've got to find my favorite traveling dress. I know it came back from the cleaners.'

Oletta walked into the bedroom with a stack of towels in her arms and headed for Aunt Tootie's bathroom. I could hear her happily humming a song as she put them in the linen cabinet.

Just then the ring of the doorbell sounded.

I put down the dictionary and headed for the door. 'I'll get it.'

While I was bounding down the stairs, the doorbell rang again. I fumbled with the dead bolt and pulled open the door. I couldn't have been more stunned had someone pulled out a gun and shot me.

Standing on the steps was my father.

He offered me a thin smile. 'Hello, CeeCee. I'm on my way to Chattanooga. Thought I'd take a long detour and stop by.' He nervously shoved his hands into his pockets and glanced toward Forsyth Park. 'Savannah's a pretty place. That's some park over there.' He took a step backward and looked at the front of Aunt Tootie's house. 'So, how's it feel to be living in the lap of luxury? This house is something, isn't it?'

When I didn't answer, he started jangling loose change in his pocket. 'I've got something for you in the car,' he said, nodding toward the street.

From behind me, I felt hands on my shoulders, strong and warm. Oletta's voice boomed over my head, 'What can I do for you, sir?'

'Oh, uh, hello. I came by to drop some things off for Cecelia. I'm Carl Honeycutt, her father.'

'Is that so?' Oletta said, squeezing my shoulders. 'Well, you just wait a minute.' She never took her eyes off my dad as she nudged me from the doorway. To my astonishment she closed the door in his face and bolted the lock. 'Run upstairs, get Miz Tootie. Hurry up.'

Oletta stood by the door like a five-star general while I raced up the stairs, and when Aunt Tootie and I came down, she was still standing there with her arms crossed over her chest.

Aunt Tootie took a breath and opened the door. Dad was sitting on the steps. He quickly stood and brushed off the seat of his pants. 'Hello, Tallulah.'

Her voice sounded stiff and frosty. 'Why, Carl, this is quite a surprise.' She waited a moment before she said, 'Won't you come in?'

Dad sheepishly stepped inside while Oletta stared him down. 'I don't want to interrupt anything,' he said, nervously rubbing a finger over his right eyebrow. 'I was telling CeeCee that I was on my way to Tennessee and thought I'd swing by. I've got some things for her.'

'Oletta,' Aunt Tootie said, 'will you bring us some iced tea, please?'

Oletta shot my dad a sharp look, turned, and headed for the kitchen while Aunt Tootie led Dad and me into the formal living room. I huddled close to her on the sofa while Dad sat on the edge of a yellow velvet chair, looking pale and uncomfortable.

'Well, like I said, I can't stay and I don't want to interrupt your day. I was—'

'Savannah's quite a drive from Tennessee. What's on your mind, Carl?'

Stunned by the crisp bite in Aunt Tootie's voice, he held up his hands and said, 'I'm not here to cause any trouble. I just wanted to talk to CeeCee for a few minutes and give her some things. That's all.'

After Oletta brought the iced tea, Aunt Tootie stood and gave my arm a gentle pat. 'All right, I'll leave you two alone for a few minutes.' She took her glass of tea and headed out of the room, but then she stopped and turned to me. 'Cecelia Rose, I'll be in the library if you need me.'

Like two edgy cats, Dad and I stared at each other from opposite sides of the fireplace. He took a slow drink of iced tea and forced a smile. It was a broken, tired smile. 'So, how are you making out here?'

'Everything's fine,' I said flatly.

'Cecelia,' he said, leaning forward and clasping his hands between his knees, 'I know what you probably think of me, and whatever it is, you're right. I ran out on you and your mother when things got rough. There's no excuse for it—'

'Then, why did you?'

'When the psychiatrists couldn't help her, I got tired – just gave up. And when the traveling sales position came up, I grabbed it. I guess I thought it'd be easier that way.'

'Easier for you!'

Dad's face reddened. He stood and peered out the front window. For the longest time he didn't say anything. I watched him cave in on himself as each moment of silence ticked by.

'Sure is pretty down here. The trees are something else, aren't they? The South must agree with you, CeeCee,' he said, turning to face me. 'You look good, real good.' He jingled his pocket change again, waiting for me to respond. 'Anyway, I've got some things for you in the car.'

I stood and shook my head. 'I don't want anything.'

Dad walked into the front hall, opened the door, and nodded toward his car. 'The things I've got in the trunk are important to you.'

I glared at him with so much loathing that my ears heated up. 'How would *you* know what's important to me?'

138

He rubbed the back of his neck and said, 'Okay, I had that coming. But, please, at least come out and see what I've got. Fair enough?'

I rolled my eyes and reluctantly followed him out the door.

Dad fished the keys from his pocket and unlocked the trunk. I took a few steps forward and peered in. The trunk was jammed full with cardboard boxes. I pulled back a flap of the closest box and could hardly believe what was packed inside. My books. I reached in, grabbed a box, and lugged it to the sidewalk. Dad and I unloaded the trunk, never once speaking a single word.

When the trunk had been emptied, I looked him in the eyes and managed to say, 'Thanks.'

'Let me help you get them into the house. They're heavy.'

'No. I'll take care of them from here.'

He let out a sigh of defeat and slowly closed the trunk. 'Okay. Well, I don't suppose you'd like to take a walk over in the park, so we could talk?'

I shook my head and backed away.

'All right, maybe another time. I guess I'd better hit the road.' But instead of getting in the car, he stepped forward. 'CeeCee, will you listen to me for a minute?'

'What?' I said, crossing my arms over my chest.

'I'm sorry things happened the way they did. But you've got to understand that it's not all my fault. When I met your mother, I knew she was high-strung and emotional at times. But she was beautiful and fun. I thought her moods were just part of her young age. I didn't know that an incurable mental illness was starting to take hold of her. All I knew was that she made me laugh and I loved her. I did. She gave me a new lease on life – made me feel young again.'

Dad's shoulders sagged. 'Now, did I screw things up? Yeah, I did. I admit it. But I didn't know what to do. I couldn't divorce your mother and take you away from her. It would have killed her. Do you have any idea how much she adored you? I know you might not remember that, but she did. You were the only one who could reason with her. Hell, it got to the point where she didn't know me from Colonel Sanders. Half the time she didn't even know my name. But she always knew your name. Did you ever notice that? And she'd listen to you too. You always handled her a lot better than I ever did.'

Angry words burned my tongue, and I spat them out. 'And while I was *handling* her, my life got ruined.'

He looked down and tapped the curb with the toe of his shoe. 'I know that, and I came here to tell you I'm sorry. I was a lousy father, Cecelia.'

I chewed the inside of my cheek. Who did he think he was, showing up here and thinking he could erase all those years of hurt with a few words and that sad look on his face?

Mrs. Odell once told me that forgiveness had a whole lot more to do with the person doing the forgiving than it did with the person in need of forgiveness. She said holding on to hurt and anger made about as much sense as hitting your head with a hammer and expecting the other person to get a headache. But too many years of resentment were swollen inside me, and I had no forgiveness to offer my dad.

I stood tall and took a deep breath. 'I want the truth. You *owe* me the truth.'

'All right. What do you want to know?'

'Do you have a girlfriend?'

He squeezed his eyes shut and didn't answer.

'I know you do, and I'm not the *only* one who knows, either. But I want to hear you admit it.' That was a downright lie, but I didn't care. I wanted to see what he'd say.

Streaks of red spiked above his collar. I waited for his answer, but he just lowered his head and stared at the sidewalk. Car after car went by, whipping up hot dusty air. He never looked at me when he cleared his throat and said, 'It's not what you think. Believe me. But I was lonely and—'

'You were lonely!'

He took a tentative step forward. 'Now, hold on a minute, CeeCee. You're old enough to know there are two sides to a story. If you'll just calm down and let me explain—'

'No. I don't want to hear anything more you have to say.'

While a full minute of silence fell between us, I realized there simply was no better way to sum up his character than to say this: my father, Carl Dwayne Honeycutt, was a total jerk.

But I had to admit that bringing my books was the nicest thing he'd ever done for me. And jerk or not, I at least had to give him that.

'Well, I can see this was a bad idea. Anyway, here,' he said, dipping his fingers into his shirt pocket and pulling out a folded piece of paper. 'I moved to Detroit, and this is my new phone number – in case you ever want to talk.'

He reached out and offered me the paper, but I clasped my hands behind my back. 'I want you to be happy, CeeCee,' he said, placing the paper on top of a box. 'I know you don't believe me, but I do.'

He waited for me to say something, and when I didn't, he turned, climbed into the car, and started the engine. As he pulled away from the curb, a light breeze blew the paper from the box. It spun end over end and swirled into the street. I left it there and watched my dad's car disappear.

It was a familiar sight.

Fourteen

Early the next morning, Aunt Tootie carried her suitcase down the stairs while I followed behind with two hatboxes. She stopped in the foyer and turned to me. 'Here, honey, just leave everything by the front door. Estelle will park out front.'

'How come you're not driving to Raleigh?' I asked, setting the hatboxes on the rug.

'Estelle and I always take turns driving whenever we go out of town. This is her turn.' Aunt Tootie put her arm around my shoulders. 'Are you sure you're all right? This is such bad timing for me to leave, especially after what happened yesterday.'

'I'm fine.'

Though I never spoke of the things my dad and I had discussed, I figured Aunt Tootie had a pretty good idea that nothing good had come of it. I wasn't even upset anymore, at least not like I was yesterday. I made up my mind that my father was just a chapter in my Life Book that finally came to an end. I actually felt relieved to have it over with. Besides, I got my books.

'I'm sure going to miss you,' my aunt said. 'I'll call every day.'

Estelle Trent pulled up in front of the house and beeped the horn. She and Aunt Tootie loaded the trunk, looking like a pair of aging twins – each wearing a flowery-print dress and a little straw hat. Oletta and I stood on the front steps and waved good-bye. The minute they were out of sight, Oletta headed for the kitchen and dialed the telephone. She talked for several minutes, and when she hung up, she grinned.

'It's all set. Nadine and Chessie will pick us up tomorrow morning. We're goin' to Tybee Island to do us some fortune huntin' and have a picnic.'

'We are?'

'Um-hmm. I asked Miz Tootie if it was all right, and she said yes.'

I let out a squeal and danced around the kitchen. 'I'm so excited. I've never seen the ocean.'

'Well, then, you're in for a big surprise.'

The alarm clock blasted me awake at six-thirty in the morning. I dressed quickly, my eyes still blurry with sleep. After tying the laces of my sneakers and grabbing the hat Aunt Tootie had given me, I bounded down the stairs.

Oletta was standing at the kitchen counter, packing a cooler with food. Wound around her head was a pink-and-green-striped scarf, and she was wearing a sleeveless dress splashed with giant orange flowers. Propped up by the back door was her fortune finder.

She looked up and smiled. 'I made us a nice lunch. We got ham and cheese sandwiches, potato salad, lemonade, Coke, and raspberry cobbler. I even got a bag of them cheese puffs you like.'

I stood on my tiptoes and looked inside the cooler. 'Wow, Oletta, there's a lot of food in there.'

'The ocean will stir up your appetite something fierce – make you hungry as a bear.' As she closed the lid the phone rang. 'That must be Nadine. I bet she's runnin' late,' Oletta said, heading for the phone. She talked for only a few seconds, and when she hung up, her face fell. 'Nadine's car won't start,' she said, shuffling to the sink. 'Looks like we'll be staying home today.'

I was so disappointed I could hardly stand it. While Oletta washed out the coffeepot, I pulled a banana from the fruit bowl and plunked down at the kitchen table. I wanted to go to Tybee Island so badly I would have gnawed through a cement wall to get there. While looking out the window and halfheartedly eating my banana, I got an idea. 'I know how we can get to Tybee Island. Let's take Aunt Tootie's car.'

Oletta dried the coffeepot and shook her head. 'Child, I haven't drove a car in years.'

'But what about Nadine? She could drive it, couldn't she?'

'There's no way for Nadine and Chessie to get here. They don't live on the bus line. I know you're disappointed, I am too, but we'll go to Tybee another time. C'mon, help me unpack this food and put it in the refrigerator.'

'How far away do Nadine and Chessie live?' I asked, handing her a container of potato salad.

'I don't know mile-wise, but only about fifteen minutes or so.'

Just then the phone rang again. 'Oh, good,' Oletta said. 'Maybe Nadine got her car started. Grab that for me, will you?'

I ran to the wall phone and answered. It was Aunt Tootie calling from Raleigh. We talked for a few minutes and then she asked when we were leaving for Tybee Island. I told her about Nadine's car not starting, and though I was sure she'd most likely say no, I went ahead and asked if Oletta could drive her car. When Oletta heard me, she closed the refrigerator door with a sharp bang and shook her head.

Aunt Tootie was quiet for a moment, and then she said, 'Sugar, would you please put Oletta on the phone?'

I stretched the cord across the counter and handed Oletta the receiver. She didn't say much, just seemed to be listening. When Oletta said good-bye and hung up, she shot me warning look. 'Now listen to me, and listen real good. Don't ever speak for me again. Understand?'

'I'm sorry. Was Aunt Tootie mad?'

'No, she wasn't. She said I could drive her car over to Nadine's, but I ain't gonna do that.'

'But why? Couldn't we—'

'Hold your tongue and let me finish,' she said, wagging her finger. 'I already told you that I ain't drove a car in a long time. I wasn't good at it back then, and I sure as blazes won't be good at it now.'

'Okay,' I said sheepishly. 'I'm sorry, Oletta. I didn't know you were afraid to drive.'

The look on her face just about knocked me over. 'Who said I was *afraid*?' she sputtered.

Clearly I'd hit a nerve. I stared at her, not knowing what to say.

'Oletta Jones ain't *never* been afraid of anything or anyone,' she said, turning away with a scowl on her face. 'I said I wasn't *good* at drivin' a car – I never said I was afraid.'

As she washed off the countertops, I settled at the table and began working on a crossword puzzle. But I couldn't get Tybee Island off my mind. I leaned back in the chair and twirled my pencil from one finger to the next. 'Oletta, how much did you get for that gold watch you found?'

'A hundred dollars,' she said, rinsing the sponge in the sink. 'That was some lucky day.'

'Maybe, whenever we do end up going to Tybee Island, it'll be another lucky day too. Just think, there could be a diamond ring or another gold watch out there, or maybe even a ruby bracelet. I hope Nadine gets her car fixed so we can go some-time soon.'

She dried her hands and gazed out the window, lips pursed. There was no mistaking the hunger for adventure that glittered in her eyes.

'Well, Miz Tootie did say it was all right with her. Guess there'd be no harm. If we leave now, it's so early there won't be many cars on the road.'

I jumped from the chair and threw my arms around her. 'Oh, thank you, Oletta.'

'We better hurry up before I come to my senses.'

After she called Nadine, we quickly put the food back into the cooler, grabbed the fortune finder, and hauled them both out to the garage. 'Okay,' I said, closing the trunk, 'let's go have some fun.'

Oletta backed the car into the alley, her lower lip jutting out so far I could see the soft pink of her gums. When she nosed the car into the street, she leaned forward until her chin nearly touched the steering wheel. 'Lord,' she said, inching toward the intersection, 'if we get there in one piece, it'll be a miracle.'

I laughed. 'You mean if we get there before next week, it'll be a miracle.'

'Now, you hush up and let me drive.'

We hadn't gone three blocks when beads of sweat began trickling down Oletta's face. 'I should have my head examined,' she grumbled, nearly driving off the side of the road when a big truck passed us and tooted his horn. 'I don't know why I let you talk me into this. Trouble is just waitin' on us. I can feel it in my bones.'

I didn't talk Oletta into anything – she did all the convincing herself. But I just smiled and kept that thought to myself. By the time we left the city behind and were rolling along a country road, she relaxed a bit and even seemed to be enjoying the sun-dappled scenery.

We drove in silence for a few minutes, and then Oletta let out a sigh of relief. 'Thank you, sweet Jesus. We made it.'

Though there weren't any cars in sight, she flicked on the turn signal and rolled the car into a narrow dirt driveway. A small wooden sign was nailed to the post of a mailbox, and written across the top were the words Custom Jewelry by Nadine, and below that was Stone Readings by Chessie.

'Nadine makes jewelry?'

'Yes. She's real good at it too. Got herself a nice business. She works part-time as a nurse over at the hospital, but she makes fancy beaded jewelry on the side.'

'What does Stone Readings mean?'

Oletta headed up the long driveway at a snail's pace and said, 'Chessie's got a bag of old stones that have some kinda ancient designs on 'em. She claims they have the Power – whatever that means. People come to her when they're in trouble or upset, and Chessie pulls out her stones and reads what they have to say.' Oletta shook her head. 'She charges five whole dollars for one reading. That's a lot of money to stare at a bunch of stones, if you ask me. But I guess some folks is willin' to pay anything for hope.'

Ahead was a white clapboard house with grass-green shutters and a flamingo pink front door. As Oletta pulled up and parked the car, a short woman opened the front door and stepped outside. Her hair was gathered into a thick curly knot on top of her head, and she was wearing white pedal pushers and a stretchy orange tube top. She planted her hands on her hips, and in a voice of someone three times her size, she called out, 'Oletta Jones, when you told me you was driving here, I thought you was tellin' a tall tale.'

Oletta climbed out of the car, visibly relieved to have the driving over with. 'You know I don't lie, Nadine. But take a good look, 'cause after today, I ain't never drivin' again. So what's wrong with your car?'

'I don't know. The dealer just towed it away. Makes me so mad – I go and spend all that money on a brand-new Oldsmobile and what good is it?'

From around the side of the house there appeared a hefty, broad-shouldered man. His skin was as black as midnight and his hair was shorn close to his scalp. Baggy denim overalls hung shapeless over his faded plaid shirt. While ambling toward us, he waved and called out, 'Hey, Oletta. I can't hardly believe my eyes.'

It was then when I realized the person in the overalls was not a man but a woman. A tall, barrel-shaped woman. I mean tall like a giant. And her hands? Well, it's no exaggeration to say they were the size of rump roasts. Nobody would have guessed these two women were sisters. But they had generous, almost identical smiles, which they offered freely.

'We sure have heard a lot about you,' Nadine said.

Chessie looped her thumbs around the straps of her overalls and grinned down at me, as big and happy as you please.

'Well, let's get a move on,' Nadine said, gathering folding chairs from beneath a tree. I helped her carry them to the car while Chessie went inside the house and hauled out a blanket and a red beach umbrella. They tucked everything into the trunk and hustled back inside the house. Nadine returned wearing sunglasses and a fluorescent green baseball cap. Over her shoulder she carried a fortune finder similar to Oletta's. Chessie lumbered out of the house with an armload of magazines and a dark blue velvet bag cinched with a string.

'Sweet mother of all that's holy, this is one fine automobile,'

Nadine said, smoothing her hand over the hood of Aunt Tootie's car. 'Nobody makes cars like this anymore. Let's put the top down.'

'No. We can't do that,' Oletta said, shaking her head.

Nadine put her hands on her hips and tilted her head. 'And why not? Now, you tell me, what's the sense in drivin' a convertible if the top ain't down?'

'I mean it, Nadine. No. Miz Tootie ain't put it down in years. We can't just—'

'Oletta Jones, you need to lighten up,' Nadine said, dismissing Oletta's protests with a wave of her hand. She slid behind the wheel and searched the levers and buttons on the dashboard. 'I think I've got it,' she called out. 'Now, y'all stand back.'

She started the engine and a moment later there was a rusty squeak followed by a loud pop. The metal frame lifted high in the air, and slowly the canvas top folded into neat accordion pleats behind the backseat. Chessie was so excited she let out a whoop.

'C'mon, girls, hop in. Momma Nadine is gonna drive us to Tybee in style.'

Oletta gave Nadine a sharp look. 'All that road dust is gonna fly in and make a mess.'

'Don't worry,' Nadine said with a laugh. 'I'll drive real fast so it just blows away. Now, quit your frettin' and get in.'

I jumped into the backseat, raring to go. Oletta, looking annoyed, climbed in next to me while Chessie eased herself down in the front. Nadine sat straight and proud as she turned the car around, and then she hit the gas and blasted down the driveway.

'Watch where you're goin'!' Oletta yelped, slapping her hand against the back of Nadine's seat.

Nadine glanced in the rearview mirror and arched one

eyebrow. 'Oletta, why are you so wiz-pickled? I've been drivin' all my life, and I ain't never had an accident.'

'Oh, yes, you did. You hit your old boyfriend Clem Riley, knocked him clean into a ditch. That poor man still walks with a limp.'

Nadine laughed. 'I've got news, sistah, that wasn't no accident.' She turned on the radio and scrolled through the stations. When she found a song she liked, she cranked up the volume.

Oletta joyously called out, 'I love Martha and the Vandellas!' She began singing the words to 'Nowhere to Run,' holding her clenched fist close to her mouth like she was singing into a microphone. Nadine and Chessie sang in harmony, the whole time moving their shoulders in ways I'd never seen. Though I tried to imitate the way they bobbed their heads and rolled their shoulders, I felt stiff and ridiculous. I must have looked ridiculous too because Oletta burst out laughing.

From her handbag she removed two pairs of sunglasses. 'Here, I bought these for you,' she said, handing me a pair. They were bright red with lenses shaped like hearts.

'These are crazy,' I said with a giggle, leaning forward to look at my reflection in the rearview mirror.

Oletta slid on the other pair of sunglasses. They were shaped like cat's eyes and studded with yellow rhinestones. She looked at me and grinned.

They were so goofy I collapsed against the seat and howled. I got a glimpse of what Oletta must have been like as a young girl when she called into the wind, 'If you wanna be cool, then you gotta *look* cool. And Lord knows there ain't nobody cooler than Oletta Jones!'

Fifteen

Streaks of gold shimmered in the morning sky, and off in the distance a string of cream-puff clouds seemed to bump into the treetops. Nadine drove over a bridge that was surrounded by a swampy marsh. The thick scent of warm, muddy soil and stagnant water smelled both putrid and oddly sweet at the same time. There was something about its strange aroma that urged me to close my eyes and breathe it in.

Nadine turned down a road that had little cottages painted in all sorts of mismatched colors, parked the car beneath a pine tree, and cut the engine. 'Okay, girls, let's unload the car and get down to the beach.'

We pulled everything out, and after Nadine, Chessie, and Oletta tucked their handbags into the trunk, Nadine pushed it closed and shoved the keys deep into her pocket. With me holding one end of the cooler and Chessie the other, we followed Nadine and Oletta along a path that wound its way through a stand of trees, around a pair of dunes, and toward the sound of waves.

My first view of the ocean left me knee-deep in awe. Never had I witnessed anything that pulsed with such beauty and imminent danger at the same moment.

151

Oletta pushed the umbrella into the sand and asked, 'So, what do you think of the ocean, child?'

I watched the waves roll and crash as mounds of white foam raced onto the beach. 'It's the most beautiful and scary thing I've ever seen.'

Chessie unfolded a beach chair and looked at me. 'Everybody needs to respect the power of the ocean. Those waves can knock you clean off your feet and haul you under before you know it.'

'Don't worry. I won't go in the water,' I said, untying my sneakers and digging my toes into the sand. 'I don't know how to swim.'

Oletta's eyebrows shot up. 'Don't know how to swim?'

Nadine opened a bottle of Coke and took a sip. 'All young'uns should know how to swim.'

'I remember the day my pappy took me and my sister, Geneva, down to the watering hole behind our house,' Oletta said, fiddling with her fortune finder. 'We was just babies. He set us inside an old inner tube and waded us into the water. We kicked and splashed and had ourselves a gay ole time.' Oletta shook her head. 'Seems like that was a hundred years ago.'

'Could you teach me to swim today?' I asked.

Oletta shook her head. 'Not in the ocean. You gotta learn in a pool or a pond; someplace where the water's nice and calm.' She handed me a small garden spade. 'C'mon, let's go treasure huntin'. You get to be my digger.'

'Digger?'

'Um-hmm. If I find something, you can dig it up and save me from bending these old knees.'

I took the spade, and we set off along the beach. Nadine took her fortune finder and headed in the opposite direction, while Chessie plopped down in one of the chairs with a magazine.

Gulls flew low, skimming over the waves as they hunted for

152

breakfast. I was fascinated by how they'd take aim, dive, and pluck out an unsuspecting fish. The higher the sun lifted into the sky, the more people showed up at the beach. They slathered themselves with oil and flopped on their backs to broil in the sun like lizards.

Oletta gazed at the ocean and inhaled. 'It just don't get any better'n this.'

'I know this is the same sky that hangs over Ohio, but the sun seems bigger here. Everything seems bigger.'

She pursed her lips and thought about that for a moment. 'Maybe your eyes is just more open.'

There were times when Oletta would say something, and the sheer profoundness of it would stun me.

I smiled to myself as I bent down and picked up a seashell. 'Do you come here a lot?'

'I try to. Wasn't all that long ago that colored folks weren't allowed. Not just at the beach, but on the whole island – unless they worked here. Then one day a group of colored kids got together and came down here to swim. Lord, they was brave. They swam in the ocean and had a gay old time until the police came and hauled 'em off to jail. That started a whole bunch of protests. One thing led to another, and not too long after that, Tybee was desegregated. I been comin' here with Chessie and Nadine ever since.'

We turned and walked down the beach, Oletta moving her fortune finder from side to side. Sometimes it would send out a crackling noise, and she'd stop and watch with hopeful eyes as I dug through the sand, only to find a tangled piece of wire or a rusty bottle cap. I got a little bored with the whole fortune-finding business, but she was content to plod along, humming to herself.

Off in the distance a few couples were walking along the beach, holding hands and sometimes kissing.

'Oletta, do you have a boyfriend?'

She looked at me kinda funny and furrowed her brow. 'Lord, no. I lost interest in men a long time ago. The last man I went out with was real nice, but he talked too much. After a while it got on my nerves. Besides, his name was Scrub Hardy, and it was hard to take a man serious with a name that sounded like a cleanin' product.'

I eyed her suspiciously. 'Is that true, or just some story you made up?'

'It's true,' she said with a nod. But the twinkle in her eye told me otherwise, which made me laugh.

As I was about to ask if I could go stand closer to the waves, the fortune finder crackled up a storm.

Oletta's face brightened. 'Ooooo-wee, we got something. Dig right there,' she commanded, pointing to a spot in the sand.

I got on my knees and dug a hole, but there was nothing to be found.

'Keep diggin'. There's something there.'

I plunged the spade deeper, pulling the sand free with my cupped hands. 'Nope. False alarm,' I said, squinting up at Oletta.

'You sure?'

I pushed my hand deep into the hole. 'There's nothing here . . . oh, wait.' I flinched as something pricked my finger. I pulled it free from the sand and handed it to Oletta. Dirt and sand fell away as she rubbed it on her dress. It looked like a slim knitting needle topped with a red gemstone.

Oletta raised her eyebrows. 'Well, I'll be. It's an old hat pin.'

'Oh, my gosh. Oletta, do you think this is a ruby?' I said, touching the faceted stone.

She pursed her lips. 'Looks like cut glass to me. Take it over to the water and wash it off, will you? Just don't go in too far.'

I trotted to the water and gingerly waded in. The foamy surf lapped against my ankles and tickled my skin. After rinsing the hat pin as best as I could, I ran back and handed it to Oletta.

She examined it closely, turning it in her hand. 'Well, don't look like it's worth much, but it sure is pretty.' She reached up and stuck it through the back of her headscarf. 'How's it look?'

I laughed. 'You look like you've got an antenna sticking out of your head.'

Oletta reached up, ran her fingers over the hat pin, and smiled as if she liked that idea. 'Let's go have some lunch,' she said, resting her arm across my shoulders. 'I got to get off these legs for a while.'

When we arrived at our spot on the beach, Chessie was down by the water, dipping something into the waves. Beneath the shade of the umbrella, Nadine was sitting in a chair, sliding beads onto a thin silver wire. 'Find anything?' she asked.

'Just this,' Oletta said, easing herself down in a chair and leaning toward Nadine.

Nadine lowered her sunglasses to the end of her nose. 'What you got stickin' outa your head?'

'An old hat pin,' she said, stretching out her legs. 'Did you find anything?'

'No, I gave up about an hour ago,' Nadine said, working the ends of the wire with a small pair of pliers. 'I came back here and made this bracelet. Here, CeeCee, this is for you.'

'Really? You made that for me?'

'Sure did. Go ahead and try it on. Just slide the two ends of the wires apart.'

The bracelet was made of glass beads in all sorts of colors. It fit perfectly. 'Thank you, Nadine. I love it.'

'You're welcome.' She slid her box of beads and pliers into her beach bag. 'Next time I'll make—' Nadine gasped and sat

155

up straight in her chair. 'Oletta, you won't believe it till you see it. That's my old neighbor Royal Watson, and she's in a bikini.'

Oletta jerked up her head. 'A bikini?'

Walking through the sand by the edge of the water was a round, busty woman wearing a tiger-print bikini. 'Hey, Nadine,' she called, 'whatchu doin' at the beach on a Tuesday?'

Nadine's lips thinned when she called back, 'Even us workin' folks take a day off now and then.'

Oletta reached over and tapped Nadine's arm. 'Don't let her get under your skin. She ain't worth it.'

Nadine's eyes narrowed as she watched Royal saunter away. 'Ever since she married Joe Baker and moved into that new house, she acts like she's too good for the rest of us. That woman gets on my last nerve. See how she walks? Looks like she's squeezin' her life savings between her cheeks.'

Oletta leaned back in her chair and laughed.

Chessie walked across the sand toward us. The legs of her overalls were soaked to the knees, and in her hand she carried a sack that was dripping wet.

'Get your stones electrified, sistah?' Nadine asked.

Chessie eased herself onto the blanket and opened the soggy bag. 'Yep, soaked 'em real good,' she said, spreading the stones in front of her.

I leaned over to have a better look. There were seven in all – each was the size of a chubby silver dollar with a primitive-looking design carved on one side. 'Where did you get these, Chessie?'

She patted the blanket. 'Come closer and let me tell you about Omu.' Her voice grew low and serious, and the lines in her forehead deepened when she said, 'These stones is almost two hundred years old. They belonged to my great-great-great-grandmother Omu. She had healin' ways in her hands and carved the designs on each one of these stones. Omu was born in a village on the West African coastline. It ain't there no more, but way back then it was called Moboko . . . '

I listened, totally enthralled, as Chessie gazed out across the ocean and told me the story.

On a brilliant, clear-skied day, Omu was conducting a sacred dance in the crystal-blue waters of the Atlantic Ocean. It was a ritual she always did on the morning of the full moon. As the waves tumbled toward her, Omu dipped the stones into the water and quietly chanted a string of secret words. The stones were smooth and wet in her hands, electrified by the mysteries that pulsed in the crashing waves. As she neared the end of her ritual, Omu felt a vibration in the sand beneath her feet. She thought it was the ocean bringing her great power, but when she finished blessing the final stone, the vibration grew ominous.

Omu turned to see a band of men thundering toward her. Quickly she gathered the stones in the hem of her dress and took off running down the beach. But as young and fast as she was, the ghost-faced men soon had her surrounded. Their skin was the color of death, and as they moved closer she could smell their evil stench. As they bore down on her, Omu tossed her magic stones toward the ocean. They spun in the air, and in the brief moment before they fell into the waves, the stones exploded with light and transformed into seven tiny white birds. The birds fluttered their wings and soared high in the air, circling above Omu as she fought off the slave traders. Within minutes she was beaten into bloody submission. Days later she was chained in the bowels of a giant ship that set sail and took her away from her homeland. Week after week the ship grew more bloated with the moans of the dying and those who wished they would die. And when that ship arrived in America, Omu was sold to a plantation owner.

One blistering-hot night, Omu lay quietly crying on a

157

narrow bed in a slave shack when she noticed a shadowy flutter by the window. She sat up, wiped her eyes, and watched in stunned silence as, one by one, seven tiny white birds landed on the windowsill. Omu rose to her knees and lifted her hand toward the birds. The moment her fingers reached the window, the birds fluttered their feathers one last time and transformed themselves back into her seven magic stones.

Omu hid her stones beneath a loose floorboard by her bed. She believed if she could find a way to reach the ocean, she could soak her stones with enough magic to create bigger birds – birds so powerful they could carry her back to her homeland. But the years passed, and the only ocean Omu ever saw was the one that flooded her dreams.

When Chessie finished the story of Omu, she picked up one of the stones and turned it over in her hand. 'These stones been handed down from one generation to the next. When I was a child, my momma told me the story of the stones, and before she passed away she gave them to me.'

'What do the stones do?'

'They tell the truth of things,' she said, leaning so close I could see flecks of gold in her dark eyes. 'Let's see what the stones have to say to you.' She pushed them across the blanket toward me and turned them facedown. 'Now, close your eyes, and empty your mind. Feel the ocean waves move through you. Let your heart soar high into the wind till you feel free as a bird. Now, put out your hand and touch each stone. Wait till one feels just right, then go ahead and pick it up. But do it slow, take your time and let the stones speak to you.'

While I let my hand fall across the stones, feeling their smooth, damp coolness, Chessie began to hum. It was a soulful, haunting sound that rolled up from someplace deep inside of her.

I waited a moment and then picked one.

'All right,' Chessie said, 'now open your eyes.'

The design on the stone was a zigzagged line inside a triangle.

Chessie looked at the stone and nodded thoughtfully. 'That's Jakuni. It's a powerful stone. Even when there's trouble in your life, Jakuni says if you hold on tight and be patient, the sky will clear. Jakuni says you have protection all around you.'

'I do?'

Chessie nodded. 'Now, go ahead, pick up another stone and—'

'C'mon you two,' Oletta said. 'Enough storytelling. Lunch is ready.'

With our bellies stuffed with lunch and the rhythmic sound of the waves lulling us to sleep, we reclined beneath the shade of the umbrella to take a nap. I dozed for a while but the soft tug of the wind lured me toward the water. With my hat on my head and my new bracelet on my wrist, I headed across the sand.

I waded into the water and stood ankle-deep. The waves licked my skin as I gazed across the ocean and thought about Omu. *How old was she when was captured? Was she ever happy again? Was she a slave until she died?*

The heat of the sun prickled my cheeks, so I turned and walked along the edge of the ocean with the burning rays at my back. Every so often I'd stretch out my arm and admire my new bracelet, marveling at how the faceted beads took hold of the light and sent it spinning through the air with nothing more than the slightest turn of my wrist.

My imagination took flight, and I began dancing on the edge of the foamy white waves. I imagined Omu dancing next to me, splashing through the surf as droplets of water gathered on her skin, gleaming in the sun like liquid jewels.

'You havin' fun?'

Startled, I turned to see Nadine walking up behind me. 'Hi. I'm having a blast. Look how my new bracelet sparkles in the sun,' I said, turning my wrist in the light.

She smiled. 'All of us girls like sparkle. Last week I ordered some pretty glass beads that have specks of silver on the inside. When I get them, would you like me to make you a necklace?'

'Sure. I'd love a necklace,' I said, glancing at the golden chain around her neck. I pointed to the round pendant that held an icy-white stone. 'Your necklace is beautiful, Nadine. Is that a diamond?'

'Yes, it is,' she said with pride, lightly touching the stone. 'My husband gave it to me for my fiftieth birthday last year. I haven't taken it off since.'

She looked at my shoulders and raised her eyebrows. 'Oooo, you sure are pink. You got too much sun today. Good thing we're goin' home now. Chessie and Oletta already took the cooler and chairs up to the car,' she said, nodding toward our spot on the beach.

Side by side we wandered through the sand, talking and examining seashells along the way.

'We're just about ready,' Oletta said, brushing sand off her fortune finder while Chessie closed the umbrella. Nadine handed me the blanket, swung her beach bag over her shoulder, and we headed for the car. Oletta and Chessie lagged behind, laughing and kidding each other like schoolgirls.

I followed Nadine across the beach, around a windswept dune, and down a narrow path. Just as we passed beneath a shady stand of trees, a man wearing a cowboy hat stepped from the shadows. He raised his hand and a *click* sounded. A silver blade flashed in the sunlight.

Nadine gasped. I froze.

He moved toward Nadine, his eyes ferocious with something I'd never seen before. 'One word, one move, and I'll cut your throat.' He reached out, took hold of her necklace, and ripped it from her neck with so much force that she lost her balance and fell in the sand.

His eyes fixed on me, round and wild. A nameless horror clawed at my throat. I was so terrified I nearly shook clean out of my skin. The blanket slid from my hands. Then his eyes darted back to Nadine.

'Gimme the watch,' he said, pointing the knife at her nose with one hand while he shoved her necklace into the pocket of his jeans with the other.

Nadine fumbled, her hands trembling as she tried to loosen the clasp.

'Hurry up, you stupid nigger,' he growled, shaking the knife in her face.

Nadine freed her watch from her wrist, and he reached out and yanked it from her fingers.

'One sound and you're dead,' he said, glaring at us with so much hate that my arms went weak in their sockets. He took a few steps backward and looked over his shoulder. From the corner of my eye I saw Chessie moving through the sand like a barge, spinning her bag of stones at her side. She stepped from the shadows and stopped, the whites of her eyes bright.

A glint of sunlight sparked off the knife's blade. He smirked, moving toward Chessie, step by slow step, like a lion eyeing his prey. But Chessie just stood there as solid as a mountain, staring down at him as she spun her bag of stones. Oletta appeared behind Chessie, her eyes wide and her fortune finder poised over her head like a weapon.

There came the sound of a *whoosh, whoosh, whoosh* as Chessie spun the bag faster and faster. His eyes flashed from left to right, and just as I thought he was going to turn and run away, he aimed the knife at Chessie's throat and lunged. She stepped to the side and walloped him with her bag of stones, right across his face. She hit him so hard a sharp *crack* sounded. His hat flew off and he let out a howl of agony and fell over, landing on his side in the sun-dappled sand.

He writhed back and forth with his hands over his face, groaning and moaning as ribbons of blood oozed from between his fingers.

'Let's go!' Nadine said, grabbing the blanket and taking hold of my arm.

We raced down the path, around a pile of canoes, and headed for the car. Oletta and Chessie thundered behind us, the panting of their breath loud in my ears. Everyone piled into the car as Nadine fired up the engine, and when we reached the highway, she was driving so fast my eyes began to water.

Oletta called out through the buffeting wind, 'Nadine, stop at a gas station so we can call the police.'

'What do you think the police will do?' Nadine yelled through the wind. 'You think they'll take the word of three colored women over the word of a white man?' Her jaw hardened as she tromped on the gas pedal and rocketed down the road.

Chessie turned in her seat. 'Nadine's right. Ain't no justice to be done.'

Oletta nodded and put her arm around my shoulders. I sunk low into the seat and watched the landscape spin into a blur. My stomach was in knots, and I closed my eyes, leaned against Oletta, and hoped I wouldn't get sick.

When we arrived at Aunt Tootie's house, Oletta ran to unlock the back door so Nadine could phone her husband at work, while Chessie and I unloaded the trunk in slow, foggy movements. As we carried the cooler toward the house, I couldn't wipe the image of the man's face from my mind – how his lips curled when he'd sneered at Nadine, and how his eyes had narrowed to slits of pure hatred. I thought about all the scary stories I'd read where evil-eyed villains left me paralyzed with fear in the wee hours of the night. Yet, no matter what they did or threatened to do, I always knew I could close the book and make them go away. But the man at Tybee Island was real, and what he did had changed my view of the world. Forever.

The four of us gathered at the kitchen table. Nobody said much, but as I went down the hall to use the bathroom, I heard Nadine say, 'That son of a bitch deserved a whole lot worse than a broken nose.'

'Devil's spawn,' Chessie said. 'That's what he is.'

What they said after that, I don't know. The minute I closed the bathroom door, I got down on my knees and clutched the toilet bowl, retching until my eyes watered. I flushed the toilet and curled up on the cool tile floor, feeling my pulse throb at the base of my throat.

Oletta rapped on the door. 'Cecelia? Child, are you all right?'

I sat up and wiped sweat from my face. 'Yes, ma'am. I'll be out in a minute.'

After washing my face with cold water and rinsing my mouth, I returned to the kitchen and sat next to Oletta. Nadine sat slumped in a chair, arms crossed over her chest as she stared out the window. 'That bastard stole my diamond necklace,' she said, angrily. 'My gold watch too.'

Chessie reached out and rested her hand on Nadine's shoulder. 'His judgment day is comin', sistah.' She leaned close to Nadine and shook her head. 'Look what he done to you. That chain cut into your skin.'

That's when I saw a bright red mark on the back of her neck.

Oletta went into the pantry and returned with a small bottle of iodine. She dabbed it along the wound, her lips pressed together, a scowl on her face.

The *toot* of a horn sounded from the street and Nadine turned from the window. 'I'd know the sound of that horn anywhere. That's Taye.'

We all filed down the hallway toward the front door, and before Chessie descended the steps, I reached out and touched her arm. She covered my hand with hers and looked deep into my eyes. As I watched her lumber down the steps, her sack of stones hanging heavy from her fingers, I thanked God that her name had been written in my Life Book.

Minute by slow minute, the afternoon light faded into the long shadows of evening. Though Oletta kept me busy, washing out the cooler and vacuuming sand from inside Aunt Tootie's car, I couldn't stop thinking about the man at Tybee Island. He had ignited a dark, unnameable fear that burned deep into my bones. Every sharp sound made me jump, and it felt unbearable when Oletta moved out of my sight. When she used the bathroom, I stood outside the door, breathing in small puffs of air while my stomach churned.

After a cold supper of leftovers, of which neither of us ate much, we sat outside on the porch glider. I curled up close to Oletta and rested my head in her lap. As she rocked her foot from heel to toe, sending the glider into an easy rhythmic movement, I turned and looked up at her. 'Oletta, are we safe?'

'Yes, child, we're safe.'

'What about Aunt Tootie, will she be able to help get Nadine's jewelry back?'

'I don't know. But when she gets home, I'll tell her what happened and see what she thinks we should do.' Oletta then closed her eyes and started humming a song.

When it was time for bed, I clung to Oletta like lint to a wool sock as she went through the house, locking the doors and securing the windows. Slowly we climbed the stairs, and as we reached the doorway of her bedroom, she stopped and pulled me close. 'These legs of mine are tired, but before we go to bed I've got something to say. Now, I want you to listen. Will you do that?'

I nodded.

'What happened today was a terrible thing, but I believe with all my heart that the Good Lord is holdin' all of us in His arms. That man don't know who we are or where we live, and he ain't gonna find out. We all need to be careful in this world, but I promise you, for every bad person on this earth there's a hundred good ones.'

I buried my face into her soft bosom. Though I wanted to ask if I could sleep in her room, I didn't want her to think I was a big baby.

'Everything will be all right, child. The house is locked up nice 'n tight, so you go on up to bed and get some sleep. I'll be right here if you need me. I'll leave the door open.' She patted my arm, said good night, and shuffled into the bedroom.

For hours I lay on my bed, fully dressed, eyes pressed wide against the darkness. When the grandfather clock sent eleven slow *bongs* into the night, I slid off my bed. With my pillow and blanket tucked in my arms, I crept down the stairs. The rugs felt cool and smooth against my bare feet as I moved down the shadowy hall. I stopped at the doorway of Oletta's bedroom and peeked in. The moonlight filtered through the window blinds and fell across her face in pale stripes of blue. She was sleeping on her side, covered lightly by a sheet. One of her arms was dangling over the side of the bed.

Careful not to make a sound, I tiptoed across the room, set the pillow on the floor next to the bed, and lay down. Being close to Oletta calmed my mind, and soon my breathing fell into rhythm with hers.

Though I closed my eyes and tried to sleep, my thoughts were pierced by images of the man at Tybee Island: the hatred in his eyes, the icy glint that flashed from the blade of his knife, his sneer. The horror of it crawled like a living thing beneath my skin.

I thought about the terror Omu experienced when she was ripped from the sandy beach of her homeland. And now, all these years later, her magic stones had saved us from harm on what we thought was a safe beach.

I thought about how Oletta, Chessie, and Nadine were too scared to call the police for no other reason but the color of their skin. Though nearly two hundred years had passed since Omu's life had been destroyed, I realized that in some ways things really hadn't changed all that much for colored folks. I thought about that for a long time.

As I watched a slant of moonlight glide across the flowery wallpaper, I reached up and took hold of Oletta's hand.

Sixteen

The day following the attack at Tybee Island left me raw with fear. I wouldn't even go out on the porch in broad daylight unless Oletta was with me. No matter what she was doing, I'd hover close, but she didn't seem to mind. Even when I got underfoot, she'd give me a squeeze and tell me everything was all right.

After we did laundry, I helped Oletta make a cherry pie. When she pulled it from the oven and turned to set it on the counter, she nearly fell over me. The bubbling hot juice splashed over the edge of the pot holders and burned her fingers. Though she didn't scold me, she sat me down at the kitchen table for a long talk.

'I know you're scared,' she said, smoothing an ice cube over her blistering fingers, 'but you gotta grab hold of yourself. Every time you give in to your fears, you're lettin' that man win. And every time you do that, he gets stronger while you get weaker. Givin' in to your fears will rob you blind. You'll end up a prisoner to that man for the rest of your life.'

I sat quietly and listened to all she said. Deep down I had the feeling that Oletta most likely knew all that was worth knowing, not in book-learning ways, but in the ways that really mattered, ways that let you hum songs during the day and sleep peacefully at night. I knew she was right about me needing to take hold of myself, but I was at a loss as to how to go about it. No sooner did I wonder about that than Oletta rose from the chair. 'C'mon, today's the day – you've got to reclaim your power.'

She took Aunt Tootie's floral snips and wicker basket from the shelf in the hall, handed them to me, and opened the back door. When we stepped onto the porch, she said, 'Now I want you to go on over to the garden and cut me a nice bouquet. Keep the stems long enough to put in water. I'm gonna stand right here and watch. Nothing bad is gonna happen to you.'

The thought of being so far from Oletta was unbearable, but I took a deep breath and did as I was told, the whole time chewing the inside of my lip. When I reached the far edge of the garden, I spun around and was relieved to see her standing in a shaft of sunlight, watching me.

'Okay, now go ahead and cut me some flowers,' she called out.

After I cut enough for a good-size bouquet, Oletta said, 'Now take the basket and go over to the side of the house. Cut me some roses.'

Going to the rose garden meant Oletta would be out of my sight. 'But . . . but, will you go with me?'

'It's all right, child,' she called out. 'Go on now, cut me some pretty roses. I like the red ones with the pink centers. I'll be waitin' right here.'

I knew I had to do it, so I wrenched my feet free from the earth and headed for the side of the house, turning twice to make certain Oletta was still on the porch. Quickly I snipped a handful of roses, never once caring that I pricked my fingers till they bled. I raced to the back of the house and looked for

Oletta. And there she was, standing on the porch, just as she'd promised.

'Now c'mon and walk back to me, but take your time and do it nice and slow. Hold your head proud. Walk like you ain't afraid of a thing.'

I tried real hard not to run, but when I reached the patio I propelled myself up the steps at a preposterous speed.

Oletta held me close. 'See, that wasn't so bad, was it? Every day you'll get stronger and stronger.' She stepped back, held me at arm's length, and looked deep into my eyes. 'Just remember what I told you. Don't let *nobody* rob you of your freedom. Now let's go inside and get the flowers in some water.'

As Oletta stood at the counter and arranged the flowers in a vase, the doorbell sounded. I followed her down the hallway, still her shadow, still fearful of what might happen if she got out of my sight. When she opened the door, Nadine all but shoved Chessie into the foy-yay and said, 'Oletta, did you see the morning paper?'

When Chessie saw me standing behind Oletta, she reached back, grabbed Nadine's arm, and flashed her a warning look.

Nadine forced a smile. 'Well, hello, Cecelia. How're you doing today?'

'Fine,' I answered thinly, immediately sensing something was wrong.

'Oletta, can we talk to you for a few minutes?' Chessie said.

Though Chessie and Nadine tried to act casual, I saw the look that telegraphed between them, and there was nothing casual about it.

Oletta's face eclipsed from surprise to concern as she closed the door and turned the bolt. 'Cecelia, go on up to your bedroom and stay there till I call you.'

'But . . . but I don't want to be alone. And—'

169

Oletta raised her eyebrows. 'Did you already forget what we talked about today?'

I looked down and shook my head.

'All right, now you go on and do as I say. I won't be long.'

'Yes, ma'am.'

I climbed the stairs as the three of them headed toward the kitchen. When I reached the second floor, I stopped and leaned over the railing. Oletta's voice boomed up the stairs, 'What did I just tell you?' She put her hands on her hips and gave me a warning look. 'When I ask you to do something, you do it. Understand?'

I nodded and walked to the door of the third floor. But instead of going to my bedroom, I stopped and waited a moment. Slowly I inched my way down the hall. I tried to hear what was going on, but the texture of their voices was low, as if they were conducting some sort of serious tribunal. I pulled off my sneakers and tiptoed down the steps. But I still couldn't hear their words. Though I knew disobeying Oletta was the absolute worst thing I could do, I couldn't stop myself from darting down the hallway. If I couldn't see her, knowing she was close was the next best thing. I crouched beside the china cupboard that stood outside the kitchen door and listened.

Oletta let out a moan, and I heard the rustle of paper. 'I can't believe it. What's he tryin' to pull?'

Nadine's voice was bitter. 'He's tryin' to frame us is what. I just hope nobody saw us.'

'Royal Watson knows we was there.'

'Oh, shit, that's right. But she's so stupid she don't count.'

'And don't forget, Miz Tootie knows too. She let us take her car.'

'When's she comin' back?' Chessie asked.

'Not for a few more days.'

'Good, maybe by that time things'll quiet down. Just make sure you throw out the newspaper so she don't see it.'

'She'll hear about it no matter if she sees the paper or not,' Oletta said. 'When she gets home, I'll tell her about it myself.'

'No, you can't!' Nadine said.

'You don't know what's been goin' on here. Cecelia is scared half outta her mind. When Miz Tootie comes home, I'll tell her what happened. She'll go to the police and tell them the truth.'

Nadine's voice shot up. 'Oletta Jones, what's *wrong* with you? Have you lost your mind? You know it don't matter what the *truth* is. This is a setup, plain as day.'

'Nadine's right,' Chessie said. 'He hates coloreds. It's a hate I ain't seen in a long, long time.'

Her words sent chills racing up my arms.

Nadine's voice was filled with fear. 'You wouldn't be talkin' about goin' to the police if you'd seen his face when he pulled that knife. He wanted to slit my throat just for the fun of it.'

'But Miz Tootie will help us if—'

'Oletta, don't you get it? He robbed me and ended up getting his ass shellacked by Chessie. Now he's spittin' mad. He's tryin' to flesh us out. He *wants* us to go to the police so he can find out who we are! Me, Taye, and Chessie stayed up half the night talkin' about it. Taye says if we go to the police, it'd be the same as diggin' our own graves. That son of a bitch is connected to the Klan. He had a tattoo of a red circle with a black cross on the inside of his arm. I saw it with my own eyes!'

'Hush, Nadine,' Chessie said. 'Keep your voice down.'

'You can't tell Miz Tootie about this,' Nadine whispered. 'It won't matter to the police who Miz Tootie is or what she says – *she wasn't there*. It's our word against his. I said it yesterday and I'll say it again: ain't nobody gonna take the word of three colored women.'

171

After a long pause, Oletta sighed. 'I have to tell her, for the child's sake.'

Nadine's voice was filled with fear. 'Oletta, we been friends for over thirty years. I'm beggin' you not to tell Miz Tootie. You've got to give us your *word*.'

There was a long moment of silence, then Chessie said, 'Oletta, you gotta to do what you feel is right. Nobody in this room is in trouble but me. I'm the one who hit that man in the head. And I don't regret it, neither. Good thing I was wearin' them overalls, at least he thinks I was a man. That'll throw the police off. Lord, they'll be roundin' up every big darky from here to Mississippi.'

'There's nothin' we can do about it now, but pray,' Oletta said. 'So, c'mon, let's pull ourselves together and give this up to the Lord.'

Afraid they were about to walk out of the kitchen, I flattened myself against the wall and held my breath.

The sound of chairs scraping across the floor was followed by a long moment of silence. Oletta then spoke, in a soft but powerful voice. 'O Mighty Father, we come to you today in need . . . '

I crawled around the cabinet on my hands and knees and peeked into the kitchen. They were sitting at the table, heads bowed and eyes closed. They held hands across the table, making a circle with their brown arms. The image of them was a sight to behold: Chessie in a baggy plaid dress, Nadine in a flowery halter top and jeans rolled up to her knees, and Oletta in her white apron stained with cherry juice.

'Have mercy on us, Lord. Hold us close and guide us . . . '

I knew I had to get out of there, and fast. I pushed myself up from the floor and darted down the hall.

After supper, Oletta and I took glasses of sweet tea outside and sat on the porch – she mending a torn pocket on one of her aprons, me munching an apple and reading a book. Throughout dinner Oletta had been quieter than usual, and now she had fallen so silent that she wasn't even humming a song like she usually did.

When I went into the house to throw away the apple core, I noticed the edge of a newspaper shoved deep inside the wastebasket. There was no doubt in my mind that it was the paper Nadine and Chessie had brought for Oletta to see. Quietly, slowly, I dug it out and brushed off bread crumbs. I needed time to examine it, so I tiptoed across the kitchen and peeked out the window. Oletta was still absorbed in her sewing, so I took the newspaper into the bathroom and locked the door. I sat on the floor and smoothed out the wrinkles, but there was nothing of interest on the front page. I turned to the second page and scanned the columns, and when I got halfway down, I drew in a quick breath.

MAN ATTACKED AND ROBBED
AT TYBEE ISLAND

In a secluded beach area of Tybee Island, Lucas Slade, age 34, was attacked yesterday afternoon by three Negroes – one man and two women. As a young white girl watched, the women demanded that Slade hand over his wallet and wrist-watch. After Slade complied, the man knocked him to the ground and beat him in the head. Slade suffered a broken nose and fractured cheekbone. Anyone with information is asked to call Detective Beauford . . .

So *this* was what Nadine meant when she'd used the word 'framed.' As the vision of what had really happened flashed through my mind, a blistering heat rose from my belly. The fear I had been feeling was replaced with an anger so powerful that my hands shook.

After reading the article one last time, I crumpled the newspaper into a tight ball and returned to the kitchen. Careful not to make a sound, I shoved it deep into the wastebasket.

As I stepped toward the screen door, I heard Oletta mutter to herself, 'Lord, Lord, we're in a warehouse full of trouble . . .'

I waited a moment, then pushed the door open. Oletta stopped talking and glanced up. 'I was just about to go in and see what you was doin'.' She put down her mending and looked at me closely. 'Your face is flushed,' she said, reaching out and pressing her palm to my cheek. 'You're warm. Do you feel all right?'

'I'm okay.'

'Must be from all that sun you got yesterday,' she said, touching my cheek one last time.

I nodded and sat in the rocker while she returned to her mending.

For a long time I stared across the garden. The flush on my face had nothing to do with sun. It was the heat of my awareness that Nadine was right: Lucas Slade was trying to pull something. Something really bad.

Mrs. Odell once said that God watched out for us. But if that was really true, then why did He allow bad things to happen? Supposedly He had all the power; people prayed to him, built churches in His honor, and turned to Him in times of need. So why didn't He bother to take a look now and then and help people?

I turned and watched Oletta; each stitch she made was so tiny and precise it became invisible when she tightened the thread. I wondered why God couldn't do the same thing – why couldn't he mend things when they needed mending? As far as I could tell, God just left us down here to figure things out all on our own.

After she finished repairing her apron, Oletta asked me to help her water the gardens before it got dark. I plucked dead blooms from a few potted plants as she uncoiled the garden hose. While spraying the flower beds, she looked at me and said, 'You feelin' all right?'

I smiled up at her and nodded. 'I'm fine now. You were right, Oletta. Starting today, that man doesn't have any power over me.'

Whether it was the newfound strength in my voice or the way I had peered into her eyes, I didn't know. But whatever it was, Oletta's shoulders stiffened, and the look on her face slammed me broadside. With equal measure of wonder and dread, I watched her psychic barometer rise to the danger zone. How she knew I had disobeyed and eavesdropped on her conversation with Nadine and Chessie is something I'll never understand, but she knew.

She lifted her chin and pressed her lips together till they thinned to pale blades. Thunder rolled across her face. Never had I seen anyone look so angry. But there was fear in her eyes too. It was just a flicker, but I saw it as plain as day.

Agony gnawed at my bones as I held her gaze, but there was no turning back. I stood tall and squared my shoulders. 'He's evil and he's a liar. Nadine and Chessie are right. He's trying to set us up. We can't tell the police and we can't tell Aunt Tootie because she'll *go* to the police. I know she will. There's nothing more I have to say about it. Not to anyone. Not ever.'

Oletta never blinked, never moved a muscle. The storm in her eyes flickered one more time and then vanished as quickly as it had come. With a single, nearly imperceptible nod, she slowly turned away and began to hose down the patio.

175

Seventeen

As she had done every morning since leaving for Raleigh, Aunt Tootie called to see how Oletta and I were doing. Oletta cradled the phone in the crook of her shoulder as she whipped eggs and cream in a bowl. All Oletta said was the occasional 'Um-hm' and 'Yes' and 'That'll be fine.' After a minute of that one-sided conversation, Oletta handed me the phone. Aunt Tootie said she'd be gone for a few days longer than expected, but was quick to assure me that Oletta was happy to stay at the house until she got back.

When our conversation ended, Oletta began cooking omelets while I set the table out on the porch. The clock above the stove read 8:40, and already the humidity was pressing down through the moss-covered trees. Oletta set our plates on the table and eased herself into a chair. After saying grace, she glanced into the sky and shook her head. 'Weatherman on the radio said it's gonna hit ninety degrees today. I hate to ride the bus when it's this hot.'

'Ride the bus?'

'Um-hmm. Every other Saturday I go visit my Aunt Sapphire. So, after I frost the brownies I baked last night, I've gotta get ready and catch the ten-twenty bus. But don't you worry, Nadine's gonna drive over and stay with you till I get back.'

I put down my fork and looked at her. 'Can't I go with you?'

'No, child. It's a long ride, and you wouldn't much like it once you got there. Just lots of old folks waitin' for the Lord to call them home. You're better off stayin' here. Nadine said she'd bring her playin' cards and teach you gin rummy. She loves that game. But make sure you pay attention,' Oletta said with a chuckle. 'Nadine cheats.'

I leaned back in the chair. 'Please take me with you.'

'You sure you don't want to stay here and learn to play cards? Nadine said she'd bring over her jewelry-makin' box, too. Said she'd make you a necklace.'

'I really want to go with you, Oletta.'

She was quiet for a moment, then looked at me thoughtfully. 'Child, I been doin' a lot of thinkin'. I know you's scared 'cause of what that man did. It scared me too. I think it's best we sit down with Miz Tootie when she gets home and tell her about—'

'No, Oletta.' The force of my words surprised me. I think it surprised Oletta too. 'I'm not asking to go with you because I'm scared. I'm asking because I want to be with you. That's all.'

She looked down at her plate and didn't say anything more about it. We finished our breakfast, and after we did the dishes, she dried her hands and looked at me. 'I'm tellin' you, it'll be hot as blazes on that bus. But if you wanna go, then you better put on the coolest sundress you got.'

I grinned. 'Thank you, Oletta. I'll go do it right now.' As I trotted down the hallway, Oletta called Nadine to tell her about the change in plans.

Oletta sure was right about the bus ride. It was so long and hot that the brownies she held in a plastic container melted to

177

a lumpy, sweet-smelling mud. 'Sapphire's gonna need a spoon to eat these,' Oletta said, shaking her head.

Finally the bus rolled to a stop and we climbed off, fanning away a cloud of engine fumes as it pulled away. Shoved into the earth at the side of a long gravel driveway was a wooden sign. Green Hills Home was what it said, but I didn't see any hills, and the only thing even close to the color green was a scraggly pine tree off in the distance.

'Well,' Oletta said, hoisting her handbag over her shoulder, 'let's go see how Sapphire is doin' today.'

We trooped down the driveway, maneuvering over gravel the size of redskin potatoes. The white-hot sun beat down, searching for one more blade of grass to burn, one more flower to shrivel. A lone crow flew overhead, and I watched his shadow skitter over the parched earth like the remnant of a runaway dream. We walked around a bend, passed a dried-up pond, and then a two-story brick building came into view. Oletta told me it had once been a fine mansion surrounded by a pecan grove. A gentleman's farm is what she called it. But that was a long time ago, and it now was a home for the aged.

The long, saggy front porch was dotted with people sitting in chairs. A spindly old man shuffled forward as we climbed the steps. He looked at Oletta with wide, hopeful eyes. 'Mabel, I been waitin' on you all day.'

Oletta patted his shoulder. 'How you doin', Mr. Higgins? Remember me? I'm Oletta. You know, Sapphire's kin.'

His face collapsed into deep folds of sadness, and he turned away and whimpered, 'You're a mean woman, Mabel. Got the heart of a stone.'

An old woman reached out and shooed him away. 'Now, you hush up,' she scolded. 'You'll wake the baby.'

But there was no baby.

I followed Oletta inside the building, feeling glad to be out of the sun. We walked through a room filled with lumpy-looking sofas and all sorts of mismatched chairs, then headed into an alcove where there was a drinking fountain. After taking long, cool drinks of water, she turned and led me down a dimly lit hallway.

A bare lightbulb flickered and buzzed near the ceiling, and the odors of old age and despair spilled from the open doorways. Though I tried to keep my eyes set on the floor in front of me, I couldn't help taking a sideways glance into some of the rooms. One old lady with deep-suffering eyes reached her hand through the metal rails surrounding her bed, spread her bony fingers, and begged me to take her home. It was the saddest five seconds of my life.

We entered a room where two narrow beds sat side by side, neatly made up with pale yellow chenille bedspreads that were so old the tufts were worn smooth. In the window a rickety fan oscillated, sending a stream of air across the shadowy room. I stood in front of the fan for a minute and dried the sweat off my forehead.

'How old is your aunt?'

'Sapphire's ninety-one,' Oletta said, setting the container of melted brownies on top of a chest of drawers and peering out the window. 'She must be out back.'

We exited the room as a tiny, bow-legged woman in a floral housedress shuffled from the doorway across the hall. A strand of plastic pop beads hung around her neck, and rhinestone earrings as big as quarters tugged at her thin earlobes. 'Y'all better hurry,' she said with a wide, denture-clicking smile. 'Louis Armstrong is here. We're gonna sing a duet together in the dinin' room.'

Oletta nodded. 'Thank you kindly for tellin' us, Miz Pearson. We'll be along shortly.'

As the woman scuttled down the hall in a pair of green terrycloth slippers, I turned to Oletta. 'Wow. Louis Armstrong is here? Mrs. Odell and I saw him on TV. Can we listen to him sing?'

Oletta leaned close and whispered, 'Louis Armstrong ain't here. He's only here in poor Miz Pearson's mind. But the nurses let her believe he's here 'cause that's the only way they can get her to take a bath.'

I followed Oletta to the end of the hallway, where she pushed open a screen door and stepped onto a low-roofed porch. Sitting around a small table were two women and one painfully frail-looking man. In the center of the table was a Chinese checkers game.

The smaller woman scowled at the man sitting across from her. 'Well, Virgil, maybe you'd rather play pin the tail on the jackass.'

A look of utter insult registered on the old man's face. He rose from the table, and with a refined, gentlemanly gesture, he tipped his misshapen straw hat and spoke in a slow, dignified tone. 'All right, Sapphire. I'll go see if I can find me a pin, and when you's ready to wear your tail, you just let me know.'

The old woman's eyes grew huge behind the lenses of her glasses. 'Don't you talk like that to *me*. Who's callin' *who* a jackass?' With fingers knotted like the roots of ancient trees, she picked up a marble and threw it, hitting the old man in the center of his back. As he shuffled away with a wry smile on his face, the other old woman at the table grabbed a marble from the game board and dropped it down the front of her baggy floral dress.

Oletta turned toward the woman who had pilfered the marble. 'How you doin' today, Miz Obee? That dress you're wearin' sure is pretty.'

The old lady, who had round dumpling cheeks, offered a shy

smile. Sapphire, who was a tiny bucket of bones with wild gray hair that resembled full-blown dandelion fuzz, turned toward us. The instant she laid eyes on me, her eyes sparked. 'Who the Sam Hill are *you*?'

Oletta put her arm around my shoulders. 'This here child is Cecelia Honeycutt, and she's—'

'*White!* Why'd you bring a white girl here?'

I thought Oletta's eyes would pop clean out of her head. 'Sapphire June Wilson! Where on *earth* are your manners? Now, you apologize.'

A nearly imperceptible smile flashed across Sapphire's lips as she leaned back in her chair. 'Apologize? For what? Ain't my fault she's white.'

Oletta was appalled, but I laughed out loud. Though Sapphire continued to scald me with her stare, she pointed a bony finger at a chair and said, 'Lawd, you're white. But if you've gotta be here, then sit in the shade so you don't hurt my eyes.'

I sat next to the angelic-faced Miz Obee, while Oletta dragged over a chair from the far side of the porch and lowered herself down. She inquired how Sapphire was doing and if she needed anything.

Sapphire wouldn't take her eyes off me. 'I'm doin' just fine. But I want to know who *she* is and why you brought her here.'

Miz Obee watched me with the inquisitive eyes of a child, but she never uttered a word.

Oletta explained that I was kin of Aunt Tootie's and had come to live in Savannah because my mother unexpectedly passed away. Miz Obee's face grew sad, and she looked down at her hands, but Sapphire continued to give me the evil eye and interrupted Oletta by saying, 'I don't want to hear any of that boo-hoo stuff. Death don't mean a bag o' beans to me. People dyin' every day, so what?'

Sapphire leaned toward me and narrowed her eyes, but her voice was full of mischief when she said, 'What I want to know is, can she play Chinese checkers?'

I grinned. 'Yes, ma'am. Mrs. Odell taught me.'

She slapped the table and squawked, 'I don't give a chicken's sorry ass who taught you. I just want to play.'

Oletta flashed Sapphire a dangerous look, but Sapphire ignored her, leaned back in her chair, and pointed to the game board. 'Well, don't just sit there starin' at me like you ain't got nuthin' but cotton between your ears. Rack 'em up.'

I tried not to smile as I gathered the marbles. After counting them out by color and placing them into the holes, I looked at Sapphire and shrugged. 'There aren't enough.'

Miz Obee's faced tensed, but Sapphire looked at her friend kindly, patted the table, and said, 'Just set up the board as best you can. We'll play with whatever we got.'

I thought that was one of the wisest things I'd ever heard anyone say.

Through an open window the scratchy sound of a worn-out record began, and a moment later Louis Armstrong, accompanied by Miz Pearson, began singing 'What a Wonderful World.'

Sapphire, Miz Obee, and Oletta swayed in their chairs, each with a smile blooming on her face. I couldn't help but smile myself. And as I leaned back in the chair and looked into the sky, I thought, *Yes, this really is a wonderful world.*

When the song ended, Miz Pearson shuffled out to the porch, blowing kisses like a celebrity. 'How'd I sound?' she asked.

'Olive, you was great,' Sapphire said. 'Ella Fitzgerald ain't got nothin' on you.'

Miz Pearson beamed, we all clapped, and then a nurse came and gently led her back inside.

It was such a small thing, letting Miz Pearson sing along to an old record. It caused no harm and made her so happy. I thought about Momma, how she was happiest when she could live in her imaginary world of beauty pageants. And as crazy as that world was, I knew that if my father would have listened to me and taken her to a special hospital, she'd still be alive.

Oletta went inside and returned with an armful of Sapphire's clothes that needed mending. She sat quietly and stitched a torn hem, while Sapphire and I played a game that, as far as I could tell, didn't have any rules. It pretty much goes without saying that Sapphire always won. When Miz Obee thought nobody was looking, she'd sneak a marble off the board and drop it down the front of her dress. After a while, she had more marbles in her dress than we had on the board.

Sapphire knew full well what Miz Obee was doing, but she always looked at her friend with tenderness in her eyes and pretended not to notice. As I watched this silent exchange between Sapphire and Miz Obee, it occurred to me that that's what friends should do: cherish the good and pretend not to notice the harmless rest.

'Well, Sapphire,' Oletta said, returning her needle and thread to her handbag and pulling out a bottle of bright red nail polish, 'now that I've got your mendin' done, how 'bout I paint your nails? I've got a brand-new color here. They call it Flames of Passion.'

Sapphire grinned like a schoolgirl, and when she placed her gnarled old hands on the table, I could see the gray shadow of her bones through her tissue-thin skin.

Oletta shook the bottle of polish and said, 'Miz Obee, I bet Cecelia would like to see your secrets.'

Miz Obee's face lit up like a 300-watt bulb. She pushed herself up from the chair and motioned for me to join her. As I followed her down the porch steps and around the side of the building, it occurred to me that Miz Obee hadn't uttered a single word since we'd arrived.

Her pace quickened when a small patch of sunflowers came into view. Dozens of tall stalks topped with heavy golden flower heads swayed in the hot breeze. From a distance they looked like a group of ladies with their heads hung low, as if embarrassed that they'd arrived at a party wearing identical hats.

Miz Obee led me beyond the sunflowers toward a beat-up old car that sat low to the ground. Dappled with rust and stripped of its tires, it was little more than a shell. Even the seats and the steering wheel were missing. But all of its windows were sparkling clean and had been lowered halfway down. A sharp, rusty squeak sounded when Miz Obee pulled open a door and gestured for me to look inside.

For a moment I was dumbstruck. The interior of the car was filled with orchids – each one more dazzling than the one before it. There were yellow ones splashed with bright orange dots, purple and pale green ones striped like zebras, and red ones tinged with delicate pink. There must have been at least twenty pots of orchids in all.

I leaned farther into the car. 'Wow. You grow these? They're the most amazing flowers I've ever seen.' From over my shoulder I looked at Miz Obee and grinned. 'So this old car is like a greenhouse. Rolling the windows up and down is how you control the humidity, right?'

She nodded furiously, seeming beside herself with joy that I understood the valuable use of the old car. She went from one side to the other, opening the doors and showing me her living treasures. I took my time and admired each one. Gently I touched a petal of a vivid purple bloom that had a speckled yellow throat, then I turned to Miz Obee. 'I have a friend, her name's Mrs. Odell. She always had an orchid on her windowsill back in Ohio, but she never had anything like these. I sure wish she was here to see them. They're the most beautiful flowers I've ever seen.'

Miz Obee clasped her hands beneath her chin and nodded with pleasure. She reached inside the car and reverently lifted out a small clay pot. Sprouting along a slender curved stem were seven delicate orchid blooms. They looked like little dollops of whipped cream. The petals fluttered in the breeze and the image of Omu's seven tiny white birds came to mind.

I examined the plant closely and whispered, 'Oh, Miz Obee, I think I like this one best of all.'

She pressed the pot into my hands and smiled.

'She's wants you to have it – as a gift,' someone said in a gravelly voice.

I turned to see a face embroidered with a web of deep lines peek out from behind the sunflowers. A threadbare ankle-length slip hung loosely from her thin frame, and tossed over her shoulders was a blue plaid lumberjack shirt, at least four sizes too big. I wondered what it was she had on her head, and when she took a few steps forward, I realized it was a pink plastic shower cap. Why she was wearing a shower cap on a hot summer's day I couldn't imagine, but, in all truthfulness, I have to say it suited her. In her hand was a crooked walking stick, and crouched by her feet was a gray tabby cat with a wide scar across his nose.

'Miz Obee can't talk – had her voice box removed 'cause of cancer. But she wants you to have those flowers.'

Miz Obee nodded and patted my hand, and when she did, a marble fell from her dress and rolled to a stop by the toe of my shoe.

I looked at her kindly and pretended not to notice.

The woman wearing the shower cap grinned. 'My name's

Faustina – Faustina Woodlow. But everyone calls me Flossy. And this here is Mistah Moe. Did you know he's the best mouser in all of Georgia?'

'No, I didn't know that,' I said, bending down to scratch the cat behind his ears. 'I'm CeeCee Honeycutt. I'm here with Oletta. Do you know her?'

'Oh, good heavens, yes. I've known Oletta for years. Is she up at the house with Sapphire?'

'Yes, ma'am.'

'Well, let's go on up,' Flossy said, shaking her cane in the direction of the house. 'I'd like to say hello.'

Miz Obee closed the car door, and we headed back to the house – me with my orchid held carefully in my hands, Flossy with her tattered slip flapping in the wind, and Miz Obee with the occasional marble falling out of her dress. Mistah Moe lagged behind, chasing a runaway marble across a patch of dirt.

Just when we stepped onto the porch, a low rumble sounded and a flurry of starlings burst from the field, lifting high in the air, as thick as a storm cloud. Everyone stopped what they were doing and listened. The rumble grew louder, and a moment later a man driving an orange tractor with a flatbed wagon in tow came into view. The tractor chugged along a bumpy path, belching up clouds of gray smoke. The driver waved and pulled to a stop just beyond the sunflower patch.

'Lawd, will you look at that,' Sapphire said, rising from her chair more spryly than a ninety-one-year-old had a right to. 'It's Jeb Cummins, and he's got strawberries. I bet it's the last pick of the season.'

Miz Obee clapped her hands, and Flossy waved her cane in the air and did a stiff little dance. 'We'll have to bribe Tilly-Jo into makin' us some shortcake tonight.'

Next thing I knew the three of them took off toward the

wagon as fast as their old legs would go. It was only then that I noticed Sapphire had her dress on backward.

They tottered away, kicking up small clouds of dust in their wake. My bet was that Sapphire would be the one to break free from the pack and reach the strawberry wagon first.

Eighteen

When Oletta and I stepped off the bus from our day at Green Hills Home, a mirage of heat waves shimmered across the pavement. I noticed an adventuresome earthworm that had made a wrong turn and wandered onto the sidewalk – it lay there sizzled up like a forgotten sausage on a grill. And poor Oletta – the heat had caused her feet to swell like muffins over the tops of her shoes.

We hadn't been inside the house for two minutes when the phone rang. Oletta answered while I dropped ice cubes into two glasses and opened a bottle of Coke. I listened to the fizzing sound, slurping off the foam and not paying much attention to Oletta's conversation.

When she hung up, she took a slow drink of her Coke. 'Oh, that sure tastes good.'

'Who called?'

'Miz Goodpepper. She's goin' to a wedding reception and needs me to stitch a tear in her dress. She said she'd be right over.'

I licked the foam from the side of my glass, then took a sip. 'I had so much fun today. I like your aunt Sapphire.'

Oletta pulled out a chair and lowered herself down with a

tired groan. 'She sure is somethin'. Lord, you should have seen her in her day. Her momma shoulda named her Spitfire instead of Sapphire.'

Footsteps sounded on the porch steps, and in a flutter of green chiffon, Miz Goodpepper walked into the kitchen. 'Oletta, I can't thank you enough,' she said, pointing to the plunging neckline of her dress. 'See, it's just a small rip, right here in the center. But you know I can't even thread a needle.'

Oletta rose from the table for a closer look. 'That'll only take a minute,' she said, heading into the pantry. 'Hope I got the right color thread is all.'

Miz Goodpepper's dress skimmed the floor and was cut so low in back that it made me blush. She was wearing a pin with a big blue stone. It looked like a piece of summer sky had fallen onto her shoulder.

'You look beautiful,' I said.

'Thank you, darling.' She smoothed her hands over her hips. 'Do you like this color on me?'

I nodded. 'You look like a lime Popsicle.' After saying those words, I realized how strange they sounded. But Miz Goodpepper smiled, seeming to understand exactly what I meant.

'We're in luck,' Oletta said, returning from the pantry. 'Got the thread I need right here.' She flicked the switch of the overhead light. 'Now, come over here by the table so I can see what I'm doin'.'

Miz Goodpepper stood motionless while Oletta began stitching the tear. When Oletta slid her fingers beneath between the fabric and Miz Goodpepper's skin, her eyebrows shot up. 'What in the world you got under here?'

'Duct tape,' Miz Goodpepper said with a chuckle. 'There's no way to wear a bra under this dress,' she said, cupping her hands beneath her breasts. 'But I wanted my girls to look ... well,

189

perkier than they actually are. So I scrounged around in the basement and found a roll of duct tape. And let me tell you, it works like a charm.'

I didn't know what to say, but Oletta laughed so hard her eyes watered. 'Well, that's it. I might as well go pick out my coffin, 'cause now I've heard it all. But what you gonna do when you try and pull that tape off? You know half your skin is gonna come right off with it.'

Miz Goodpepper shrugged her shoulders. 'You're probably right. But it'll be worth it. I haven't looked this good in a backless dress in fifteen years.'

Oletta shook her head and went back to her sewing. 'So who you goin' to the reception with? He must be mighty special for you to go through all *this* trouble.'

'Well, Travis Davidson asked me, and I said yes. But then, when Clayton Brewster called and asked me too, I just had to accept.'

'Oh, my holy Christmas. Clayton Brewster? I thought you was done with him.'

Miz Goodpepper blushed. 'Oh, now, don't be mad at me. I know he's a scoundrel, but he's deliciously entertaining and the best dancer I've ever known.'

'What you gonna do when Mr. Travis sees you with Mr. Brewster?'

'I have no idea,' Miz Goodpepper said with a throaty laugh. 'It was a terrible thing for me to do. I deserve to be electrocuted.'

In just a few minutes, Miz Goodpepper's dress was repaired. Oletta snipped the end of the thread and stepped back to look at her work. 'Perfect,' she said proudly. 'Nobody'd ever know.'

'Oletta, I can't thank you enough.'

'Glad I could help.'

'All right, I'm off to dance the night away with Clayton,' Miz Goodpepper said, heading for the door.

'Don't be callin' me when you can't get that tape off.'

Miz Goodpepper laughed and disappeared.

The long bus ride and the heat had left Oletta and me feeling grimy, so we headed upstairs to take showers. With my hair still wet, I returned to the kitchen wearing white eyelet shorty pajamas that I loved too much for words. Oletta was standing at the counter in a brightly patterned floral housedress. While she piled two plates high with cottage cheese and slices of cool, sweet strawberries, I stood at the window and watched a pair of speckled moths splay themselves across the screen like tiny lost kites hoping for wind. It was so hot even the June bugs looked forlorn.

We took our supper to the back porch and ate with our plates in our laps, not saying too much, just enjoying the quiet and thinking our private thoughts. After we'd finished, Oletta relaxed and rocked in the chair, while I cleaned up and did the dishes.

'Listen. Can you hear that rumbling?' she said when I returned to the porch. 'Must be the high school band practicin' for the Labor Day parade. It's a big deal around these parts. Do you like parades?'

I shook my head.

Oletta took a sip of iced tea. 'No? I thought all young'uns liked parades.'

'Well, not me. Not anymore.'

'Why is that?'

The memory rose up in my mind, as bright as Technicolor on a silver screen. I plunked down in the chair and told Oletta the story.

Every summer our town had a Fourth of July parade. It was a much-anticipated event, and preparations began a week in advance. The fire department showed off their gleaming hook-and-ladder truck as they strung miles of crepe paper streamers from one light pole to the next, all the way up Euclid Avenue. American flags were hung in shop windows, and huge bouquets of red, white, and blue helium balloons bobbed from long strings tied to the columns of the town's gazebo.

Early in the day, the residents began hauling folding chairs down to the sidewalks, each one staking their claim for the best view. Even some frail old folks were wheeled out to the porch of the nursing home, wrapped in blankets like cocoons as they waited to see the parade go by.

I found a spot where I could stand, camouflaged by the foliage of a tall lilac bush. I was eleven years old at the time and enduring the height of all the teasing about my mother, so I wanted to be as inconspicuous as possible.

The parade began with a drumroll and the crash of brass cymbals as the marching band rounded the corner. The drum major led them through the center of town, strutting to a deafening rendition of 'The Stars and Stripes Forever.' Behind him, a row of pink-cheeked majorettes grinned at the crowd, their silver batons twirling so fast they looked like lit sparklers. They turned their heads from left to right in perfectly choreographed unison. It was the same old parade year after year, and the only reason I kept going was to see Mr. Kronsky.

After the American Legion marched past, a roar of cheers and whistles lifted high into the air. And sure enough, rounding the corner came good old Mr. Kronsky wearing his famous Uncle Sam costume: an oversize red-and-white-striped top hat splashed with glittery stars, a blue coat with tails, and red-white-and-blue-striped pants. Glued to his chin and slightly askew was a white goatee that was so old it looked like matted wool.

It wasn't his outfit that made the crowd go wild; it was the fact that he was more than seventy years old and was riding a unicycle – a very tall unicycle – so tall that his feet were at least six feet off the ground.

Everyone watched the old circus performer pedal his unicycle through the center of town, with his arms spread as he groped for balance and a look of astonishment on his face. I think he was more amazed that he could still do such a thing than the crowd of onlookers was.

Bringing up the end of the parade was a shiny red pickup truck pulling a small flatbed wagon that was smothered in white tissue paper flowers. Cardboard signs that read LITTLE MISS WILLOUGHBY were taped to both its sides. Sitting in the wagon was a blonde-haired girl dressed in a flouncy blue dress. Even from a distance I recognized her. She was Francine Fillmore, one of the girls from my class who derived immeasurable pleasure from poking fun at me about my mother. I hated her guts.

While Francine waved and threw paper-wrapped taffy to the outstretched hands of the onlookers, I slunk into the shadows. After her stupid float had finally passed, I stepped onto the sidewalk and was heading home when an explosion of pink burst from the crowd. I stood, horrified, as Momma barreled down the street in a satin party dress.

'Wait for me!' she cried, chasing behind Little Miss Willoughby's flower-studded float. Flapping across her chest was her prized green-silk sash with the words 1951 VIDALIA ONION QUEEN shimmering in the sunlight.

The crowd erupted into gales of laughter, but Momma kept right on running. When she reached the float, she took a flying leap in an attempt to join the wide-eyed Francine, but Momma's hands slipped from the back of the wagon and she landed face-down on the pavement. The back of her dress flipped up, and, to my eye-popping horror, she didn't have any underpants on.

Time slowed and there was a dreadful silence as, one by one, the crowd turned and looked at me. I thought I'd die. I wanted to die. Momma crawled to her knees, and I was thankful that her dress fell over her bare rear end. A hailstorm of laughter pummeled me as I walked into the street and helped her up. I couldn't have hurt more had someone hauled off and walloped me with a sledgehammer.

'So, anyway,' I said, looking at Oletta, 'I hope I never see a parade again.'

She reached over and took hold of my hand. She didn't say a word; all she did was gently squeeze my fingers. We sat like that until the sound of the marching band faded and the night sky turned from violet to a deep indigo blue.

I rested my head against the back of the chair and listened to a chorus of crickets while the hot breeze stroked the leaves on the trees. A long, thin white cloud moved across the sky, looking like the windblown veil of a runaway bride.

Since moving to Savannah, I'd become more awake to nature — to the sounds, smells, and sights of the world around me. I was constantly surprised by the things that waited to be discovered beyond the pages of the books I'd always kept in front of my nose. Even the moon looked rounder and fatter than I'd ever remembered, and as it pushed higher into the sky, it lit the surface of Miz Hobbs's swimming pool into a shimmering skin of silver.

I glanced over at Oletta. Her head was relaxed against the back of the chair and her eyes were closed. She looked so peaceful I thought she'd fallen asleep, but then she waved away a mosquito from her face.

'Oletta. When we were at the ocean, you told me it was impossible to learn to swim in the waves.'

'That's right. You need calm water to learn.'

'Well, Miz Hobbs is still in the hospital, so how about we sneak into her backyard and use her pool?'

Oletta opened her eyes and looked at me. 'Child, colored folks don't swim in white folks' pools. If Miz Hobbs ever got wind of it, she'd pitch a fit from here to Sunday.'

'But she'd never know. Nobody would even see us. There's an opening in the hedge by Miz Goodpepper's roses. We can get in that way.'

Oletta shook her head. 'Even if we did go over there, it takes a whole lot more than one time to learn to swim.'

I couldn't stop gazing at the shimmering pool. Seeing it sit there without being used seemed like a big waste of water. I began to rock in my chair and said, 'Miz Goodpepper told me about Miz Hobbs murdering the magnolia tree. She said Miz Hobbs was a witch.'

'It'd be fine with me if I never laid eyes on Miz Hobbs again. She's always been real uppity, and she sure don't like colored folks – looks at us like we're stains on this earth. Her last cook, Betty, was real easygoin'. But after a while even she couldn't take Miz Hobbs's big mouth. Betty got so fed up that she walked out in the middle of cookin' supper.' Oletta laughed. 'Left the pots burning on the stove.'

'Ha! Good for her.'

'When Miz Tootie ain't around, Miz Hobbs talks to me like I ain't nothin' more'n dirt on them fancy shoes she wears.' Oletta's eyes narrowed when she turned to me. 'You know what I heard her call me?'

'What?'

'Miz Tootie's nigger.'

My jaw dropped. 'She called you that word?'

Oletta nodded. 'More'n once. Heard her with my own ears.'

I sat stock-still, feeling the caustic burn of hatred in my throat. 'That's terrible, Oletta. One of the boys in my class said that word, and the teacher dragged him from his desk and made him stand in the corner with a bar of soap in his mouth till the bell rang.'

Oletta let out a *hmpf*. 'It'd take a whole lot more than a bar of soap to clean up that woman's mouth. She's sure got herself some highfalutin' attitude. She claims she was raised in some mansion up in Charleston, but that ain't true,' Oletta said, shaking her head. 'Truth is, she grew up in a poor town in Mississippi, but now she pretends she's the belle of the South.'

'All the more reason to swim in her pool.'

Oletta's words were edged with longing when she said, 'I've never been in a swimming pool. Always wondered what it'd be like to swim in clean, clear water. The swimmin' hole we had when I was a child was muddy, and sometimes the fish would come up and nip our toes. Lord, how we'd squeal. But we sure had fun in them days. On nights when we couldn't sleep, me and my sister, Geneva, would light an oil lantern and hang it from a tree. Then we'd take off our nightgowns and go skinny-dippin'. Too bad your folks never taught you to swim. It's one of the joys of bein' young.'

'They never taught me anything.'

She gave me a sad look and pushed herself up from the chair. 'I'm goin' in to get more iced tea. You want anything?'

'No, thank you.' I closed my eyes and began to rock, enjoying the way the chair creaked in a soothing rhythm across the floorboards of the porch.

A few minutes later the screen door opened. I looked up to see Oletta standing in a slant of pale-blue moonlight. In her arms was a stack of towels and a flashlight. 'Well, don't just sit there bein' a lazybones. C'mon, let's go swimmin'.'

I sat up so fast that the chair nearly bucked me out of my seat. 'Oh, my gosh. Are you serious?'

'I am right now. So hurry up 'fore I change my mind.'

'But what should I wear? I don't have a bathing suit.'

'Neither do I. We're goin' skinny-dippin'. So quit flappin' your jaws, and let's go.'

I jumped to my feet and took the towels from Oletta's arms. She turned on the flashlight and led the way down the steps and across the garden, keeping the beam low as we moved into the cool, velvety shadows of Miz Goodpepper's backyard.

'So where's that hole in the hedge you talked about?' she whispered, picking her way around a flower bed.

I put my hand on the flashlight and aimed it toward the far side of the garden. 'Right there. See it?'

Oletta grumbled, 'I can't fit through that.'

I urged her forward. 'Yes, you can. It'll be okay.'

Well, poor Oletta got her bare arms scratched up in the process, but she finally squeezed through the hedge. We moved across Miz Hobbs's lawn and onto the brick patio that surrounded the pool. Oletta kicked off her shoes and whispered, 'Turn around while I pull off my dress and get in the pool. I want to see how deep it is.'

'Can I take off my pajamas?' I asked.

'Wouldn't be skinny-dippin' if you didn't.'

While pulling off my pajamas, I heard a splash.

'Ahhh, this water is just right. Okay, now c'mon in. Take hold of that handrail and walk down the steps real slow. I'm right here.'

I scampered across the warm bricks and stepped into the water.

'Here, child, take my hand.'

The water slapped against my bare chest and sent shivers up

my spine. I let out a giggle as we walked from one side of the pool to the other, bobbing like two happy corks. Oletta kept hold of my hand, but I wasn't scared at all. I dunked my face into the water, and before long I began to dog-paddle all on my own.

When I grew tired, we leaned against the side of the pool and gazed into the sky. The stars looked so close I longed to reach up, pluck the brightest one, and give it to Oletta. I wanted to tell her how much I loved her. I wanted to taste the words on my tongue and sing them into the night air. And I wanted, more than anything, to hear her say she loved me too.

Over and over I practiced saying the words in my mind: *I love you, Oletta. I love you.* But when I gathered the courage to say them out loud, the words that popped out were, 'Oletta, if you and I had met when we were both kids, would you have liked me?'

That question seemed to surprise her as much as it did me. Even in the darkness I could see her eyes crinkle up when she smiled. 'Oh, yes, I'da liked you just fine, but I'd probably been a little scared of you too.'

'Scared? Why?'

'Because you're so smart and pretty. Sometimes them two things in one person can mean a whole lot of trouble.'

My voice squeaked when I said, 'Pretty?'

'Ain't nobody ever tell you that? You got the prettiest skin and eyes I ever seen.'

I smoothed my fingertips over my cheek.

'Oletta, what were you like when you were my age?'

She leaned her head back and said, 'When I was your age, I was full of dreams. My momma used to say if she had a drop of water for every dream I had, we'd be livin' on a houseboat in the middle of a clear blue lake. I loved to sew and got it in my head that I wanted to make wedding dresses. By the time I was thirteen, I could sew just about anything. I'll never forget the Christmas of 1924. My sweet momma went out and bought me a used sewing machine, the kind with the foot treadle. I cleaned it up and oiled it real good. Lord, I'd have that machine goin' so fast it'd send out a breeze. Then I got it in my mind that I wanted to be a gospel singer. I'd stand on the porch and sing my heart out when I ironed clothes.'

'Did you sing in the school choir?'

'I did when I was real young, but my momma had to get a job when my pappy died. So I quit school and stayed home to take care of my sisters.' Oletta fluttered her feet in the water and looked into the sky. 'But there's a blessing in everything if we open our eyes. That's the reason why I'm a good cook. I been workin' in the kitchen my whole life. I wish I could have finished school, but there's no sense in feelin' sorry for myself. Life is what it is. When I was seventeen, I got a job cookin' in a restaurant. I worked there for years.

'Then one day I heard about a lady over on Gaston Street who was lookin' for a cook. I did some checkin' and found out which house she lived in. I made up my mind I was gonna have that job. When I got off work that afternoon, I went home and cooked up my fried chicken. I put on my best Sunday dress and took the bus to Miz Tootie's house with a plate of hot fried chicken in my hands.

'I'll never forget it. I rang the doorbell, and it was Mr. Taylor who answered. I said, "My name is Oletta Jones, and I'm the best cook in all of Savannah – brought my secret recipe fried chicken to prove it."'

Oletta let out a hearty laugh. 'I sure was bold in them days. Mr. Taylor looked at me kinda funny and said, "Is that right? So what's the secret?" I looked him in the eye and said, "If I told you, then it wouldn't be a secret no more." Oh, how that man laughed. He took a piece of my chicken and ate it, standing right there at the front door. He asked me to come inside and then he called down the hall, "Tootie, your new cook is here." They hired me on the spot, and Mr. Taylor offered to drive me home if I'd leave him the plate of chicken.'

I threw back my head and laughed. 'He did?'

'Um-hm. That was the luckiest day of my life. Sometimes I feel bad about not finishing school, but I have it a whole lot better than my momma did. I wish I could read better, but I sure like it when you read to me. My daughter, Jewel, used to read to me while I was makin' supper. I remember she loved some story about an old frog that was always gettin' himself into all kinds of trouble. Lord, she musta read it a hundred times.'

Oletta fell quiet, and though the moonlight was slim, I could see the sadness in her face. I knew she was lost in her memories of Jewel. And just as she'd done for me earlier in the evening, I reached over and took hold of her hand.

We floated and gazed into the sky until Oletta said, 'Your toes is probably shriveled up like raisins. You better get out and dry off. This might be my first and last time in a pool, so I'm gonna swim for a few minutes. Then we'll go home.'

I climbed out of the pool and dried off. After pulling on my pajamas, I sat in a lounge chair and watched Oletta swim from one end to the other. Gone was the lumbering, swollen-kneed woman, and in her place was a graceful creature. Leaving only a silent ripple behind, Oletta plunged deep into the water, her wavy reflection moving like a shadowy dream along the bottom of the pool. She rose to the surface at the far end and floated weightlessly in the moonlit water. From a distance she looked like a blissfully content manatee.

While rubbing a towel over my hair, I noticed something lying in the bushes on the side of Miz Hobbs's back porch. I grabbed the flashlight, crept through the shadows, and aimed the beam. When I realized what it was, I pushed my hand through a thorny bush and pulled out Miz Hobbs's brassiere. I laughed to myself as I recalled how Earl Jenkins had spun it in the air and let it sail off into the night.

For some demented reason, I took the brassiere and wrapped it in a towel so Oletta wouldn't see it. What I thought I'd do with it I couldn't have said, but I wanted it just the same. Later that night I hid it on the shelf in my closet, feeling smug and not knowing why.

Nineteen

Aunt Tootie breezed in through the door from her trip to Raleigh, full of chatter and bearing gifts – a green scarf for Oletta, and a yellow jumper for me. 'Oh, sugar, I missed you so much,' she said, wrapping me in her arms. 'Come upstairs and talk to me. I want to hear all about your day at Tybee Island.'

Oletta's eyes met mine, then I turned and followed my aunt upstairs.

I sat on the bed and we talked while she unpacked her suitcase. 'So how was your picnic with Oletta and her friends? Did you have fun?'

'Yes, ma'am.' My cheeks heated up from the secret that stirred inside of me. I looked down and picked at the toe of my shoe, searching for a way to change the subject.

'Tell me about it, sugar,' my aunt said, dropping an armful of clothes into a laundry basket. 'I see you got some sun.'

I grinned up at her, but my tongue turned thick. *For Pete's sake, say something, CeeCee. Act normal.* Words tumbled from my lips so fast they bumped into one another. 'Well, I liked the ocean a lot. Nadine made me a bracelet, and we ate a ton of food. That's about it.'

'Taylor and I used to go to Tybee now and then. He liked to

crumble up bread and throw handfuls to the gulls. We always had so much fun . . .'

She finished emptying her suitcase and clicked it shut. 'All right, now that I've got that out of the way, how about going for a little drive with me to the market? I'm just about out of shampoo and aspirin. I think Oletta might want me to pick up a few things too. Why don't you run downstairs and ask her?'

'Sure,' I said, practically springing off the bed with relief that the subject of Tybee Island had come to an end.

When we arrived at the market, Aunt Tootie pushed the cart down an aisle as I read from the shopping list, checking off each item as she put it into the cart. While heading for the checkout, we bumped into Miz Goodpepper. In her cart were eight large bottles of carrot juice, a tin of sea salt, and a tube of Preparation H.

While the three of us talked, Aunt Tootie kept glancing into Miz Goodpepper's cart with a furrowed brow. 'Thelma, honey, are you all right?'

Miz Goodpepper chuckled. 'I read an article about detoxifying the body. It said to pour the carrot juice and sea salt into a bathtub filled with hot water. After soaking for twenty minutes, you're to get out, take a steamy shower, and scrub with a loofah. Have you ever heard of it, Tootie?'

'No, I can't say that I have.'

When the cashier started wringing up our groceries, Miz Goodpepper said, 'Oh, and the Preparation H is for my skin. I was having my hair trimmed the other day, and everyone in the beauty shop was talking about how it smooths the skin and tightens the bags under the eyes.'

I had to look away. Between the duct tape she'd used on her breasts and now the Preparation H and the carrot juice, it was all I could do not to burst out laughing.

'Well, Thelma,' Aunt Tootie said with a crooked smile,

'you've always been willing to try new things, bless your heart. You'll have to let me know how it all works out.'

As we headed to the parking lot, Miz Goodpepper said, 'I ran into Minnie Hayes yesterday. Isn't she the sweetest thing?'

'She sure is. I haven't seen her since Easter, but we talked on the phone awhile back and made plans to have lunch together. If I remember right, I believe it's next Tuesday.'

Miz Goodpepper unlocked the trunk of her car and turned to my aunt. 'Well, I've got a little bit of gossip. Minnie told me that two police cars were parked in front of her neighbor's house a few days ago. And then a detective went door-to-door all the way down the street, asking questions and taking notes. Minnie didn't have many details, but her neighbors are Augustus and Marilee Slade. Apparently something's happened to their son. Do you know them, Tootie?'

'No, I don't. I remember meeting them at a party years ago, but we've never socialized.'

Oh, my God! They're talking about Lucas Slade's parents. I took in a gulp of air and stepped back.

'Did Minnie say what happened?'

'She didn't know,' Miz Goodpepper said, lifting her bags into the trunk. 'But she said something peculiar is going on. She tried to call Marilee several times, but Marilee didn't answer. Maybe Minnie will know more when you have lunch. Anyway, that's all the news I have to report. Glad to have you back in town, Tootie. I'm heading home to try my carrot juice detoxification,' she said with a laugh.

I forced a smile and tried to act casual. Aunt Tootie waved good-bye, and called out, 'Have fun, darlin'.'

My stomach churned as we drove home, and I set my gaze out the windshield and thought to myself, *Stay quiet, CeeCee. It'll be okay. Just hold on to the secret.*

When we arrived home, Oletta was ironing in the kitchen. The warm smell of starched linen lingered in the air. Aunt Tootie headed upstairs with her shampoo and aspirin while I put away the groceries. I hovered in the kitchen, wondering if I should pull Oletta aside and tell her what Miz Goodpepper had said about Lucas Slade.

I chewed my fingernails and wandered from the window to the kitchen counter, and back to the window again.

The iron let out a *hiss* when Oletta unplugged it. As she set a stack of pillowcases into a laundry basket, she looked at me. 'What's wrong, child, you got ants in your pants?'

'No, but ...' Words clotted in my throat. And it's a good thing, because right then Aunt Tootie came into the kitchen.

'Oletta, have you seen my address book?'

'Did you take it when you went to Raleigh?'

Aunt Tootie tapped her forehead. 'Well, of course I did. Now I remember, it's in my handbag,' she said, heading out of the room.

Knowing this wasn't the time to talk to Oletta, I went outside and sat on the porch steps.

Later that afternoon, while Aunt Tootie was on the phone in the den, I followed Oletta into the pantry. She hung up her apron, and as she took hold of her handbag, I reached out and touched her arm. 'Oletta,' I whispered. 'I need to tell you something.'

Her eyes widened when I told her what Miz Goodpepper had said. I didn't know that colored people could pale, but Oletta's face turned ashy. 'Lord have mercy. Well, it's time to tell Miz Tootie.'

I shook my head. 'No, Oletta. Don't do that.'

For a long moment we stood by the window in a slant of sunlight, not moving a muscle, studying each other. From the hook on the door I removed her sweater and draped it over her arm. She let out a slow breath, turned, and left for home.

The following afternoon, I brought in the mail and set it on Aunt Tootie's desk. Among the magazines and bills was a letter from Mrs. Odell. I sat in a chair by the window and opened it, slowly deciphering her small, scratchy writing.

Dearest CeeCee,
I love the picture you sent me of the water lily. I've got it sitting on my bedside table. It's the first thing I see in the morning, and the last thing I see before going to sleep.
Have you met some nice people in Savannah? You have no idea how it brightens my day to receive your letters and pictures. Send more when you can.

I love you,
Mrs. O

I took her letter and trotted upstairs just as Aunt Tootie was on her way down. 'I got a letter from Mrs. Odell today. She liked the picture of the water lily.'

'I bet she did,' Aunt Tootie said, stopping to pat my shoulder. 'You're good with the camera, sugar.'

'Would it be okay if I went over to Forsyth Park? I'd like to take more pictures to send her.'

'Of course. Just don't be gone too long.'

I promised to be home within half an hour, and went to my bedroom to get my camera and sunglasses. I wanted to wear my hat too, and when I pulled it from the shelf, Miz Hobbs's brassiere came down with it. Why that brassiere held my fascination is something I honestly didn't know. I sat on the bed and examined it closely. It was white and so stiff the cups stood up like twin mountain peaks.

I thought about the comments Miz Hobbs had made about

my hair, how she'd murdered Miz Goodpepper's magnolia, and how she used those disgusting words to refer to Oletta – 'Miz Tootie's nigger.' And the more I thought about those things, the madder I got. I stared at the brassiere and wondered what kind of person could think such an ugly thing – much less say it out loud. A dark loathing rippled though me, and with it came an idea that bloomed in my mind like a thorny rose. Maybe Oletta couldn't get even with Miz Hobbs, but *I* would.

I folded the brassiere and shoved it into my pocket. With my hat on my head and my sunglasses in place, I grabbed the camera and headed out of the house.

On the corner of Gaston and Whitaker was the Georgia Historical Society; a stately, serious-looking building that evoked an abiding respect for the past. It was the perfect place to take a picture of something as ridiculous as Miz Hobbs's brassiere.

I waited until no one was in sight, then I flung the brassiere over the large bronze sign posted in the yard and took a picture. Quickly I stuffed the brassiere in my pocket and retreated into the shadows of the trees. When the picture developed I let out a squeal. It was a triumph.

And so began my first real hobby – the photo exposé of the unpredictable escapades of Miz Hobbs's remarkable traveling brassiere.

During the next few days, I wandered beyond the safe frontiers of Gaston Street and took Miz Hobbs's brassiere to visit the highlights of Savannah. Along shady sidewalks I went, smiling inwardly with it shoved deep inside my pocket. I took the brassiere to Chippewa Square, laid it out prettily – with its cups standing at full attention – at the base of General Oglethorpe's statue, and took a shot. I marched happily down Bull Street, where I secured the brassiere to a wooden Indian that stood outside the door of a tobacco shop, and quickly snapped a picture.

But my favorite picture came on a sun-sparked morning when I walked all the way to the Cotton Exchange on Bay Street.

The Cotton Exchange was a grand brick building that sat high on the banks above the Savannah River. In front of the Cotton Exchange was a regal, winged lion fountain that spewed a stream of water from its mouth. I climbed over the low iron fence, pulled myself onto the base of the lion, and hung the brassiere over one of its ears, making sure to keep the tips of the cups pointy. Laughter bubbled in my throat when I jumped down and took a picture.

Just as I climbed up to remove the brassiere, someone shouted, 'Hey. What do you think you're doing?'

I turned to see a policeman trotting toward me. I snatched the brassiere off the lion's ears, lobbed myself over the fence, and took off.

'You stop right now!' he bellowed.

I blitzed my way down Bay Street to Whitaker, never once looking back.

I arrived home sweaty and winded. I wasn't about to stop my chronicles of Miz Hobbs's brassiere, but I knew I had to be a lot more careful. Already I had several photographs in a manila envelope hidden beneath my bedroom rug, and when the timing was right, I'd launch my secret campaign to drive Miz Hobbs crazy.

Then came the day when I overheard Aunt Tootie tell Oletta that Miz Hobbs had returned home from the hospital. I grinned like a Cheshire cat: at last the time had come. I needed a pad of paper and envelopes, but I knew better than to use Aunt Tootie's fine stationery. So later that afternoon I walked to the five-and-dime and bought the plainest envelopes and paper they had. Then, when Aunt Tootie was out in the garden, I slid open her desk drawer, removed a page of stamps, and retreated to my bedroom.

The first picture I sent Miz Hobbs was the one of her brassiere lying at the base of General Oglethorpe's statue. I composed a short note and took my time printing it out. The note read:

Hi Violene,
> You and Earl left me hanging in the bushes.
> But finally I was rescued.
> I had my picture taken in Chippewa Square
> and thought you'd like to see it.

> Love from your brassiere

I tucked the note inside the envelope along with the picture, then skipped to the mailbox at the corner of the street and shoved it into the slot.

Every few days I wrote another note and sent it off with a corresponding picture. I'd have given anything to see Miz Hobbs's face when the mystery notes arrived. I imagined her lips tightening into a little red circle as she ripped open the envelope, and I could all but hear the shriek she'd let out when she saw her brassiere flaunting itself all over Savannah.

Whenever I went for a walk, I shoved Miz Hobbs's brassiere into my pocket in case the opportunity for a perfect picture presented itself. One day I was taking pictures of a flower garden on Habersham Street to send to Mrs. Odell when a police car came to a screeching stop at the curb. I froze when Earl, Miz Hobbs's married boyfriend, climbed out and adjusted his gun holster. And there I was, camera in hand and Miz Hobbs's brassiere in the pocket of my jumper.

Oh, my God. He knows it's me sending those notes!

But Earl never so much as glanced my way. He locked his cruiser, stepped onto the sidewalk, and headed for Dilly Ray's Café. As I watched him saunter inside, my fear fell away and I knew I had just struck gold. The picture I was about to take would bring a thunderclap to Miz Hobbs's world.

Trying to look breezy and carefree, I ambled down the sidewalk, cupped my hands around my eyes, and peered through the restaurant window. Earl was sitting at the counter, smoking a cigarette and reading the menu. I waited for a few people to walk by, and when the coast was clear, I dashed into the street and placed Miz Hobbs's brassiere on the rear bumper of his cruiser. Written across the trunk above the splayed-out brassiere was the single word I wanted to be in the picture: P–O–L–I–C–E.

I snapped the picture and hightailed it home, laughing the whole way.

Early the following morning I sat down at the writing desk in my bedroom and addressed an envelope to Miz Hobbs. After pressing a stamp in its corner, I pulled a pad of paper from the drawer and wrote:

Good Morning, Violene
  How's Earl these days?

  Love – your brassiere

I glanced at the clock and knew I'd be late for breakfast if I didn't hustle, so I left everything on the desk and ran into the bathroom to take a shower. While shampooing my hair, I wondered: *Is Miz Hobbs going crazy when she receives her mail? Who does she think is sending the photos and notes?*

I tingled with delight as I imagined the shocked look on her face when she opened my envelopes, and I laughed out loud as I toweled off and slipped into my robe. But when I padded out of the bathroom, my delight evaporated.

There, sitting on my bed with the note, photograph, and envelope in her hands, was Oletta. A dreadful silence seeped into the room. When she finally spoke, her voice was low and serious.

'So, this is your diploma of worth? You think this is something a fine young lady would do? I got worried when you didn't come down for breakfast, so I came all the way up here to check on you. And what do I find?' she said, looking down at the items in her hand. 'What are you doin' taking pictures of a brassiere and writin' notes to Miz Hobbs? What's all this about?'

My legs grew weak as I crossed the room and sat in the chair, facing her. With my hands clamped between my knees, I fessed up. I told Oletta about Miz Goodpepper and the flying slugs – how Earl, the married policeman, had danced around the porch in his Zorro mask and underpants while swinging Miz Hobbs's brassiere, and how, when Miz Hobbs ran down the steps, she slipped on a slug and cracked her head open. I finished my confession by telling Oletta I'd found the brassiere in the shrubs the night she and I had gone swimming.

Oletta shook her head. 'So, you've been doing this just for ugly's sake? Is that right?'

The look on her face was worse than if she'd raised her voice and scolded me. The way the corners of her mouth sagged was so awful that I crashed, fell right out of the sky of our friendship and watched myself go up in flames.

She rose to her feet, slid the note and photograph inside the envelope, and pushed it deep into her apron pocket. Her voice was barely audible when she leveled her eyes on me. 'You got any more pictures?'

I knew better than to lie, so I got down on my knees, flipped over the edge of the rug, and handed her the envelope. Oletta pulled out the one remaining photograph: the one of the brassiere looped over the lion's ear at the Cotton Exchange. It was my favorite picture of all, and I had been saving it for last. In fact, I loved it so much I'd been contemplating keeping it for myself.

She shoved the picture into her apron pocket. 'Where's the brassiere?'

Unable to speak, I headed toward the closet, wading waist-deep in shame. Slowly I opened the door, pulled the brassiere from beneath my hat, and handed it over.

'Get dressed and come downstairs.'

That was it. That was all she said. But it was the way her shoulders slumped when she turned and shuffled out the door that blew a hole into my world. I sat on the bed and studied my reflection in the cheval mirror, amazed at the damage I'd caused. How I'd begin to repair it was something I simply didn't know.

Oletta didn't so much as glance my way when I got to the kitchen. She took my plate into the breakfast room, set it on the table, and went about her business. But her silence was like the ticking of a bomb.

The day stretched on, minute by agonizing minute, and still she said nothing. I had been exiled from the warmth of her touch and the delight of her laughter, and it was killing me. I figured it was best if I stayed out of sight, so I spent the majority of the day in my bedroom, reading. When I went downstairs in the afternoon to get something fresh to drink, Oletta was standing at the counter chopping onions.

I walked to her side, hoping she'd look at me. But she didn't.

I took in a breath for courage and said, 'Oletta, I know what I did was wrong. It's just . . . just that I got so mad when you told me what Miz Hobbs called you. I hate that word.'

She stopped chopping the onions and put down the knife. 'You can't run around town tryin' to get even with every person who done you wrong. Ain't enough hours in the day to do that. Besides, two wrongs don't make a right. Understand?'

I hung my head and nodded. 'Please don't be mad at me.'

'I ain't mad. I'm disappointed is all. Since the first day you came here, I been thinkin' you was one of the nicest young people I ever did know. Didn't think you had a mean bone in your body.'

'I'm sorry, Oletta. Will you forgive me?'

'Don't worry. I forgive you. We all do things we ain't proud of. That's human nature.'

'So . . . so, I'm not in trouble?'

She raised her eyebrows and peered down at me. 'I said I forgive you. I never said you wasn't in trouble. Them's two entirely different things. You're in trouble plenty.'

I leaned against the counter and fidgeted with a button on my blouse. 'What kind of trouble?'

She picked up the knife and went back to chopping onions. 'I ain't figured that out just yet.'

The tone in her voice made it clear that our conversation was over. I pushed myself away from the counter and glanced at the clock above the stove. It was three-thirty. I knew I'd crumble if Oletta left at four o'clock and didn't hug me good-bye like she always did, so I decided to go feed the birds at Forsyth Park and stay out of sight until she went home for the weekend.

I wandered into the pantry, and while stuffing my pockets with sunflower seeds, I noticed Oletta's purse hanging on a hook on the back of the door. Sticking out of one of the side pockets was the envelope I'd addressed to Miz Hobbs. I felt sick to my stomach. Aunt Tootie would be home any minute, and I knew Oletta would give it to her. The envelope wasn't sealed, and I silently slid my fingers inside to see if the note and picture were still there. They were. I was doomed. Not only had I lost my best friend but I was about to fall out of Aunt Tootie's favor with a big bang.

I slipped out of the house and headed toward the park.

While I was sitting on a bench throwing sunflower seeds to a chickadee, two girls pedaled toward me on bikes. One was wearing a floppy straw hat, and the other had a pink sun visor shading her eyes. They were riding one-handed while licking ice cream cones. Perfect little belles – that's what they were. I was certain they'd never had a single worry in their lives. All they had to do all day was have fun, eat ice cream, and be their darling little peaches-and-cream selves. I looked away as they passed me by, the spokes of their bikes whirring and their laughter flowing behind them.

After throwing the remaining seeds into the grass, I decided to take the long way home. I walked around the massive fountain and took a narrow path that spit me out on Drayton Street. As I approached Gaston, I saw Oletta. She was shuffling down the sidewalk on her way to the bus stop. I thought I'd die if she didn't look my way and speak to me, but then I thought I'd die if she did. Deciding it was in my best interest to stay out of sight, I plastered myself against a tree and peeked around the trunk.

She stopped at the corner, and from her handbag she removed the envelope I'd addressed to Miz Hobbs. I could hardly believe my eyes when she licked it closed. Then she let out a laugh and shoved it into the mailbox. A moment later the hiss of air brakes sounded as the bus rolled to a stop. Oletta pulled herself up the steps, and I heard the *clinkety-clink* as she dropped coins into the receptacle. Relief flowed over me like a fresh breeze. Oletta had changed her mind. I wasn't in trouble after all. When the bus pulled away from the curb, I leaned my forehead against the tree trunk and let out a sigh of pure relief.

Monday morning arrived, and I went down to the kitchen for breakfast, wondering how Oletta would be. When she saw me in the doorway, she smiled her usual smile. Never once did she mention anything about my chronicles of Miz Hobbs's traveling brassiere. And believe me, neither did I. Nor did I tell Oletta that I'd seen her mail the envelope. We took up our friendship as if nothing had happened.

Late Wednesday afternoon, I was lounging in the den with the newest issue of *National Geographic* when Aunt Tootie arrived home. I overheard her talking with Oletta about Miz Hobbs, so I put down the magazine and walked into the kitchen as Oletta pulled a covered dish from the oven.

'Oletta, thank you for making that ham and cheese casserole for Violene. I know she's a thorn in your side. Mine too. But maybe that fall she took has knocked some sense into her. We can always hope.'

Oletta let out a grunt as she wrapped the casserole in a dish towel and placed it in a basket along with a loaf of her homemade bread and a jar of preserves.

Aunt Tootie tied a ribbon on the basket handle, and while making a bow, she said, 'I'll go over and drop this off right now while the casserole is still nice and hot.'

When Oletta saw me standing in the doorway, she turned to Aunt Tootie and smiled. 'Cecelia asked if *she* could take the get-well basket over to Miz Hobbs. Would that be all right with you?'

What! Is she crazy? Why would she say that?

I wanted to see Miz Hobbs about as much as I wanted to set

215

my hair on fire. My mouth dropped open in protest, but I quickly clamped it shut when Aunt Tootie turned and looked at me with surprise. 'That's so thoughtful of you, Cecelia. Bless your heart. It'll brighten Violene's day to have you deliver this basket. I'm sure she'll be thrilled. I've got some flowers too,' she said, walking into the pantry and returning with a small vase filled with roses.

'Now, you know how Violene is, so no matter what she says or how annoying she gets, just do your best to be real sweet. If she talks for more than an hour, then just be polite and excuse yourself. Tell her you have to come home and help me do some work in the garden.'

If she talks for more than an hour!

I slouched against the doorjamb and telegraphed a look to Oletta that said, *How could you do this to me?*

A devilish twinkle sparked in Oletta's eyes when she handed me the basket and said, 'Miz Hobbs sure will be glad to see you.'

So *this* was my punishment. The black boomerang of karma had circled through the sky and was about to land at my feet, and there wasn't a darn thing I could do about it. With the basket in one hand and the vase of flowers in the other, I headed out the door. From the open kitchen window, I heard Oletta laugh.

Around the side of the house I went, muttering about the cruelty of my punishment. Had I walked any slower to Miz Hobbs's house, I would have fallen over. I even stopped a few times to tie and retie my shoes.

Just as I reached up to knock on her door, it swung wide open. Miz Hobbs stood there with a gauze bandage wrapped around her head, grinning like we were best friends.

'Well, what a treat *this* is!' she trilled. 'I was on the sofa just startin' to doze off when I saw you comin' down the sidewalk with that basket and flowers. I wondered if they were for me.'

'Yes, ma'am. I don't want to interrupt your nap,' I said, pushing the vase of roses into her hands. As I leaned over and shoved the basket inside the door with the intent of a quick escape, she took hold of my arm and yanked me inside.

'Come in and keep me company!' she said, pushing the door closed so fast I had to jump out of the way. 'My neck and shoulders ache somethin' awful, so while we're talkin', you can rub them for me.'

My insides sputtered like spit on a griddle as she ushered me into her living room. In my mind I envisioned Oletta tidying the kitchen before she went home. There was no missing the smile on her face.

Twenty

It was a dismal, rainy afternoon. I was sitting at the kitchen table working on a crossword puzzle while Oletta stood at the counter, peeling potatoes. The radio was turned down low, and predictions of strong winds and flood warnings for low-lying areas crowded the airwaves. When the lights flickered and the radio began to crackle, Oletta turned it off and looked out the window. 'Big storm's comin'. I hope we don't lose power before I get these scalloped potatoes in the oven.'

'I love scalloped potatoes. I made them a few times with Mrs. Odell,' I said, glancing at all the ingredients on the counter. 'But what's the brown sugar for?'

'I sprinkle it on the potatoes after I pour in the cream.'

'Sugar on potatoes?'

'Where you been, child?' Oletta said with a laugh. 'Don't you know that sugar is food's best friend?'

Just then the back door swung open with a windy *bang*, followed by the sound of Tootie's footsteps. 'It's miserable out there,' she said, shaking off her raincoat and hanging her umbrella on a hook in the hall. 'I wish this rain would let up. If I don't do some work in the garden soon, it'll turn into a jungle.'

'You won't be doin' no gardening for a few days,' Oletta said, pushing the potato peels into a paper bag. 'Weatherman says it's gonna rain till Saturday.'

'Saturday? We'll all float away by then, so I guess it won't matter what the garden looks like.' Aunt Tootie stepped across the kitchen and gave me a kiss on the cheek. 'How's your puzzle going?'

I looked up and shrugged. 'I'm stumped.'

She rested her hand on my back and leaned over my shoulder. 'What's the clue?'

'English explorer and the first European to reach Lake Victoria. His last name is five letters long and begins with an *S*.'

She furrowed her brow and thought for a moment. 'I have no idea. Sorry, honey.' She walked across the kitchen and lifted the kettle from the stove. While filling it with water, she said to Oletta, 'I had lunch with Minnie Hayes today. She wanted me to be sure to give you her best.'

'I haven't seen her in ages. How's she doin'?'

'She's fine, busy as ever. She's a grandmother now. Her eldest daughter just had a baby girl. They named her Doric Bree. Isn't that precious?'

Oletta smiled and nodded, but I kept my mouth shut. I thought it sounded like the name of a tugboat.

Aunt Tootie returned the kettle to the stove and switched on the burner. Blue flames shot up and licked its sides. 'After we got caught up on family talk, Minnie told me the strangest story. Her neighbor's son claims he was attacked by Negroes over on Tybee. Did you hear anything about that?'

Oletta and I exchanged a brief, paralyzing glance. Her lips barely moved when she said, 'Yes, ma'am. I heard some about it.'

'Well, wait till you hear this. His name is Lucas Slade, and Minnie said when he was a teenager, he got mixed up with the wrong crowd and started getting into trouble – stealing cars,

219

drinking, and then taking drugs. His parents got so tired of bailing him out of juvenile court and paying lawyers that they all but disowned him. His daddy sent him off to some sort of military school, hoping they'd straighten him out, but Lucas got himself expelled. He left home when he was seventeen and never came back.

'Out of the blue, he showed up at his youngest sister's house a few weeks ago and demanded money. When she refused, he beat her up something terrible and left with all her jewelry and her wallet. His own sister! Isn't that dreadful?'

Beads of perspiration bloomed on Oletta's forehead. 'Yes, it surely is,' she said, avoiding my aunt's eyes as she closed the bag of potato peels, one slow fold at a time.

'Now, here's where it really gets interesting. It was that very same day that Lucas went to the hospital and claimed that *he* was attacked at Tybee. Well, Minnie said when a detective went to the hospital and started questioning him, his story just didn't add up. One thing led to another and apparently Lucas up and snapped. He went after the detective's throat with his bare hands! He was hauled off to jail and the police got a search warrant for the apartment he lived in. When they went there, guess what they found?'

I stiffened. Oletta kept her eyes on the counter, rubbing the same spot with a paper towel, over and over. 'What'd they find?'

'Drugs! They found a bag full of jewelry and several guns too. Remember that man who owned the watch shop over on Liberty Street – you know, the one who got shot in a robbery this past spring?'

Oletta nodded. 'I remember.'

Well, Minnie's son-in-law, Wade, works over at the courthouse, and he said the police found evidence that it was Lucas who robbed and shot that poor man. Wade told Minnie that Lucas Slade will most likely be in jail for a long, long time.'

'Sure hope so,' Oletta said, and I could see her shoulders sag with relief.

'I can't imagine how devastated and shamed his parents must be. I feel sorry for them. But as far as I'm concerned,' my aunt said with a sniff, 'Lucas Slade got his comeuppance, and not a day too soon.'

Aunt Tootie turned her full attention to me. 'Cecelia Rose, whole families can be ripped apart by drugs. It's happening more and more these days, and it scares me something awful. If anyone *ever* tries to get you to take drugs, I want you to promise that you won't do it. Not ever.'

I swallowed hard and said, 'I promise.'

The kettle whistled, and Aunt Tootie lifted it from the burner and poured water into her cup. 'This just goes to show that even with fine, upstanding parents and the best educational opportunities available, some children fall to ruin. Well,' she said, dunking the tea bag up and down, 'I think I'll go into the den and take a look at the mail. Oh, and Oletta, I don't want you standing at the bus stop in this downpour. When you're ready to go home, I'll drive you.'

'Thank you. That'd be nice.'

'You're welcome.' Aunt Tootie took her tea and headed out the door.

Oletta and I looked at each other, and when the sound of my aunt's footsteps faded, I rose from the chair. Oletta opened her arms, I opened mine, and we met each other like two puzzle pieces sliding into place.

'Praise the Good Lord,' she whispered into my hair.

And I whispered back, 'Amen.'

Twenty-one

From the day Aunt Tootie delivered the news of Lucas Slade's fate, Oletta began talking to Jesus as if he were sitting right there in the kitchen. One morning I came down for breakfast and heard her say, 'Thank you for answering my prayers. I'll never doubt you again, sweet Jesus. No, I surely won't.'

It got to the point where I wouldn't have been surprised to see her whipping up an extra serving of scrambled eggs and adding another place setting to the table so Jesus could have himself a feast. She was so happy, she'd tune in the radio to a gospel station and sing her heart out while she washed dishes.

Besides talking to Jesus on a regular basis, Oletta also began wearing the hat pin she'd found at Tybee Island – sometimes in the back of her headscarf, sometimes at the side above her ear. When Aunt Tootie asked her about it, Oletta said it was some old thing she'd found. But I figured she viewed it as a symbol of prayers answered.

One day I passed Oletta on the stairs. She was carrying a stack of fresh laundry in her arms, her hat pin bobbing with each step she took. She grinned broadly and said, 'Don't forget to show the Lord your grateful heart today.'

I smiled and said, 'Yes, ma'am.'

After gathering a basket and a pair of Aunt Tootie's old gardening gloves, I headed outside, and from the open windows I heard Oletta's powerful voice belt out the words to 'Amazing Grace.'

The soil was still damp from all the rain, and the weeds I pulled slid from the earth with nothing more than a light tug. In no time I had worked my way through Aunt Tootie's perennial garden, so I decided to go ahead and weed her herb patch too.

I was on my knees, enjoying the fresh breeze and birdsong, when the sound of tinkling bells floated through the air. I rocked back on my heels and listened. The tinkling came again, as light and happy as laughter, but from where I didn't know. I pulled a few more weeds and threw them into the basket. Just as I moved to the next row, I heard Miz Goodpepper's throaty laugh.

'Hello, Miss CeeCee,' she said, appearing through the opening in the hedge.

'Hi.'

It was impossible not to gawk at her outfit. Like bread dough rising in a warm pan, her milky-white breasts overflowed from a purple bikini top. Tied at her waist was a filmy red scarf that floated over black cigarette pants. Looped over her middle fingers and thumbs were little golden disks. She tapped them together, sending the happy sound of tiny bells into the air.

'What are those?'

'Zills, though some people call them finger cymbals. I just love them. Their chime is so delightful, don't you think?' she said, tapping them again. 'I found them at an estate sale. And I found a treasure for you too.'

I rose to my feet. 'For me? What kind of treasure?'

'Come see,' she said, her laughter luring me from the garden like the Pied Piper.

I pulled off my gloves, tossed them into the basket, and ran after her.

Across her yard, through the kitchen, and down the hall she led me, her red scarf flowing around her legs with each step she took. We entered the living room, where a cardboard box sat on a silky Oriental rug.

Miz Goodpepper lowered herself down on the floor and removed her zills. 'So many wonderful treasures I have here.'

I sat across from her, flushed with excitement as I peered into the box.

She reached inside and pulled out a silver brush and comb set. 'No, these aren't for you,' she said in a teasing tone. Again she reached inside the box, removing a compact that was shaped like a fan. 'This beauty is crafted from malachite and enamel,' she said in breathy amazement. 'It was made in France and signed by the artisan. See the date on the back?' she said, handing it to me.

'Wow, 1884. It sure is old.' I smoothed my fingertips over its cool surface and held it to the light. 'It's beautiful,' I said, handing it back to Miz Goodpepper.

'Buck bought it for me. He's so generous.'

'Who's he?

'Buck Preston is a friend of mine. He lives in Texas, but whenever he's up here on business, we'll go to dinner and the occasional estate sale.'

There was no mistaking the fondness that glowed in her eyes, but whether it was for the compact or the man named Buck, I couldn't tell.

'Is he your boyfriend?'

Miz Goodpepper let out a brief laugh. 'Oh, I enjoy Buck immensely, but I wouldn't say he's my boyfriend. I swear that man could charm the fangs right out of a rattlesnake's mouth. Once, when I caught him in an outright lie, I was so angry I told him I never wanted to see him again. Well, he looked at me from the shadow of that ten-gallon hat he always wears and said, "Thelma Rae, c'mon now, honey, don't be mad at me. I don't mean to lie, I just remember big."'

Miz Goodpepper and I laughed.

'But lately,' she said, wiggling her bare toes, 'I find all men to be very much like wearing high-heeled shoes – I love how pretty they make me feel, but by the end of the night I can't wait to get rid of them.'

She set the compact aside and winked. 'All right, I believe there's a treasure for you somewhere in the box.' She dug through wads of newspaper and removed a tissue-wrapped package. 'For you, darling.'

By this time the anticipation was killing me. I ripped off the wrapping with abandon to reveal an old book. Bound in deep plum-colored leather, its title was *The Eugene Field Book.* Carefully I opened it; the pages were dry to the touch and had a faint odor of mildew. The first page read:

VERSES, STORIES AND LETTERS
FOR SCHOOL READING

At the bottom of the page was the publication date: 1898. I leafed through the stiff yellowing pages, then looked at Miz Goodpepper. 'Thank you.'

'It's a first edition and quite rare,' she said, sliding the book from my fingers. 'I adore Eugene Field. He was a masterful poet and storyteller for children. But I find his works can be read on many levels. He was wonderfully eccentric. Look at this,' she said, turning to a photograph in the book. 'This is his doll collection.'

I moved closer and peered down at the picture. 'I've never heard of a man collecting dolls.'

She handed me the book and nodded. 'Eugene Field had marvelous dolls – toys too. His collection is displayed in his old house in Missouri. My grandmother introduced me to his writing when I was a little girl, and I've loved him ever since. Grandmother adored books, especially those written for children. She said something to me when I was about your age, and those words have been my daily mantra ever since.'

Miz Goodpepper leaned forward and looked deep into my eyes. 'My grandmother said, "Don't grow up too fast, darling. Age is inevitable, but if you nurture a childlike heart, you'll never *ever* grow old."'

I hugged the book to my chest and whispered, 'Thank you.'

'Now, how about some refreshments?' she said, grabbing her zills off the floor and rising to her feet.

I took my book and followed her into the kitchen. After setting out a plate of ginger cookies, she poured me a glass of orange soda, then pulled a bottle of wine from the cupboard, removing the cork with a *pop*.

'My grandmother was so creative. I'll never forget the day she and I painted the top of her dining table white. We used plain old house paint and just slopped it all over the beautiful mahogany. When my grandfather saw what we'd done he pitched a fit. But Grandmother just laughed.

'Then, every time they entertained dinner guests, she'd place a pencil next to the silverware. Guests were asked to write something or sign their names on the tabletop. When it was full of all sorts of clever sayings and signatures, my grandmother varnished it.'

I wasn't sure what to say. Though it sure sounded interesting, it also seemed a little crazy.

Miz Goodpepper poured wine into a goblet and took a drink. 'But after a few years the pencil marks faded and the varnish cracked, so my grandfather had the table stripped and refinished.'

'Too bad your grandmother didn't give those people Magic Markers instead of pencils.'

'Well, had there been markers back in those days, that table would be worth a fortune. Will Rogers signed that table, so did Ethel Merman. Oh, Cecelia, you would have loved my grand-mother,' Miz Goodpepper said, dunking a cookie into her glass of wine. 'She was so alive and full of original ideas, especially for that era. While other women were busy being *proper*, she was busy cultivating her spirit.'

Miz Goodpepper bit into the wine-soaked cookie and let out a small moan of pleasure. 'I can't tell you how many times my grandmother and I danced barefoot in the rain. She was so much fun.'

I smiled up at Miz Goodpepper. 'Are you a lot like her?'

'I hope so,' she said, slipping her fingers through the loops on her zills and admiring them. 'Grandmother would have adored these.'

While I finished the last of my cookies, I thought about Momma, how she twirled through the house in her red shoes, singing at the top of her lungs, and how delighted she was to wave and blow kisses to her imaginary admirers. And I thought about Eugene Field's doll collection, and how Miz Goodpepper's grand-mother had danced in the rain.

I licked crumbs from my fingers and looked at Miz Goodpepper thoughtfully. 'What's the difference between eccen-tric and crazy?'

She lifted her hands above her head, tapped her zills together, and danced out the door. From over her shoulder she laughed and called out, 'Nobody knows!'

Twenty-two

Aunt Tootie was drinking coffee and reading the Sunday newspaper on the porch. From the open window I heard the pages rustling and the clink of her cup meeting the saucer. As I dried the last of our breakfast dishes, she walked into the kitchen and said, 'Cecelia, let's go for a drive in the country. There's a farmer over in Tattnall County who has wonderful produce. Oletta's had an itch to put up preserves and she's always favored Mr. Dooley's peaches.'

'Okay,' I said, drying my hands. We put on our hats and off we went.

As we walked into the garage, I thought of how much fun it was when Nadine had put the top down, how the world looked bigger and brighter, and how the wind tickled my face. I helped Aunt Tootie push open the big doors, and when we climbed into the car, I looked at her and said, 'Could we put the top down?'

She was quiet for a moment, and I figured she'd say no, but when she started the engine, she let out a little laugh. 'Oh, why not?' She backed the car into the alley and pressed the switch. As the top folded into place, she grinned and looked into the sky. 'Cecelia, this was such a good idea. Thank you for suggesting it. This would please Taylor no end. All right, here we go.'

As was her custom, Aunt Tootie talked a mile a minute as we headed out of town. 'That dress is precious. I think pink-and-white checks are happy, don't you?'

I smoothed my hands along the crisp cotton fabric and nodded. 'Yes, ma'am. I love all the clothes you've given me. Thank you.'

'You're very welcome. Now, I'd like to talk with you about a few things that are important.'

'Okay,' I said, shifting in the seat to face her.

'I've had several conversations with your father, and I've asked him to give me full custody of you. Last week he agreed to sign the papers. It takes awhile to go through the courts, but I've got my attorney working on it.'

'Really? Does that mean I'd belong to you, like real family?'

'You *are* real family, honey. And yes, the legal papers would mean that we belong to each other. Your father wants the best for you.'

I lowered my eyes and mumbled, 'No, he doesn't.'

How can she think he wants the best for me? Why can't she see the truth? Why can't she see that he's a no-good liar who doesn't care about anyone but himself?

'Cecelia Rose, your father didn't agree to give me custody because he doesn't love you. I believe he agreed because he *does*. Now, I know he's made some terrible mistakes, and he wasn't there when you and your mother needed him most. But as flawed as he is, I know he loves you.'

This was one of those times when Aunt Tootie's eternal optimism grated on my nerves. She was always so chronically cheery and chirpy, so willing to look at the good in people that she ignored the bad parts – the parts that were unforgivable, the parts that were so raw they would never heal.

I looked at her and bleated, 'He *doesn't* care about me one bit. He never did.'

229

'People are aware of their shortcomings, though most times they don't want to admit it. Your father knows he made a mess of things, and I believe this is his way of trying to do right by you. I really do.'

Barbed words formed on my tongue, and I couldn't stop them from leaping from my mouth like spiny toads. 'I hate him!'

Aunt Tootie reached for my hand. 'Cecelia, no. Please don't hate. Don't ever hate.'

I yanked my hand away, anger flaring on my cheeks. 'He has a girlfriend in Detroit. That's where he was all those years when he left me alone to take care of Momma.'

'Oh, honey, I'm sure that's just a terrible rumor. Taylor traveled a great deal because of his business, and there were times when he'd be gone for over a week. Believe me, I know certain people questioned it. Small-minded people can be so vicious and—'

'No. He *told* me so. He admitted it the day he brought my books.'

'What?' Aunt Tootie's eyebrows shot up so high I could see them arch above her sunglasses. She pursed her lips and tightened her grip on the steering wheel.

'His girlfriend even called the house. I think Momma knew he had a girlfriend too.'

Aunt Tootie shook her head. 'Oh, no.'

I looked down at my hands and picked at my cuticles. Before I knew it, the story spilled from my lips.

It happened the winter before Momma died. I had bundled up and walked to the grocery store to buy some things for dinner. The wind had blown the snow into great white drifts, and the sound of shovels scraping across the sidewalks filled the crisp, biting air. When I arrived home, I heard Momma talking. She sounded angry. I put down the bag of groceries, peeled off my coat and boots, and headed up the stairs.

As I moved down the hallway, I heard her say, 'How dare you tell *me* what to do. I'll show you. You no-good Yankee bastard.'

I peered into my mother's bedroom. She was sitting on her vanity bench wearing a faded flannel nightgown and her red high-heeled shoes. Draped over her lap was a pair of my dad's pants.

An angry scowl tightened her face as she dabbed something gooey over the zipper. 'Pig-faced liar,' she said, furiously rubbing her fingers over the metal teeth.

I walked to the doorway. 'Momma, who are you talking to?'

'Your father,' she said.

'But he's not here.'

She shrugged. 'Here, not here, what difference does it make?'

'What are you doing?' I asked, stepping into the room.

'Giving him a nice little surprise. He had the audacity to call and tell me to press his good suit so he could stop by and pick it up. Stop by? *Stop by!*'

She squeezed more gooey stuff from a tube and smeared it on the underside of the zipper. 'He said he has to drive to Detroit for a big meeting on Saturday night – that he won't be home all weekend. Well, *I* know better. That conniving, cheating, liar.'

She was so mad her pulse throbbed at the side of her neck. I reached out, picked up the tube, and held it beneath the lamp-light. 'Momma, this is glue!'

Slowly she turned and looked at me. And what began as a tight-lipped frown transformed into the biggest, brightest smile I'd seen in years. 'Yes, it is.'

Aunt Tootie's face turned pale. 'Oh, Cecelia. I'm so sorry. Well, all I can say is shame on your father, just *shame* on him. Your poor, poor mother.'

She fell quiet, and as the wind whipped around us, I wondered what she was thinking. Maybe now she'd understand why I felt the way I did.

After driving in silence for several miles, she glanced at me and said, 'Tell you what, sugar. Go ahead and hate your father for a little while. Not too long, but for a while. I believe I'll hate him for a while myself.'

Then she reached out for my hand again, only this time I didn't pull it away.

As we drove deeper into the countryside, the red dirt road unfurled ahead of us for as far as I could see. Occasionally a farmhouse and a barn would pop into view, but mostly it was an endless, sweeping vista of crop fields and orchards.

'Cecelia Rose, I know you're hurt and angry, and you have every right to be. I'd like to help you sort through your feelings. Talk to me, honey.'

I looked away and mumbled, 'I just want to have a happy day. That's all.'

Aunt Tootie let out a heavy sigh. 'All right, tell you what. Today *will* be a happy day. We'll enjoy the beautiful weather, get ourselves some peaches, and then tonight we'll go out to supper and a movie. But tomorrow we're going to sit down together and talk. Will you promise me?'

I studied a squashed bug on the windshield and nodded.

'All right, since this day has been declared a happy day, I have something happy to tell you,' she said, relaxing against the seat. 'I spoke to the principal of your school back in Willoughby, and he mailed me all your records. They arrived last week, and I sat down and went through them. Cecelia Rose, you are a *very* bright young lady. I knew you were smart as a whip, but I had no idea what an exemplary student you've been. I'm so proud of you.'

'Thank you,' I said, glad to be off the subject of my father.

'So, I have an offer I'd like to make. There's a fine private school that has a wonderful curriculum. It's called the Rosemont School for Girls. It's small, only for grades seven through twelve.

Iris Fontaine is the headmistress, and she's an acquaintance of mine. I went to see her yesterday and showed her your school records. And guess what she said?'

'What?'

Aunt Tootie winked. 'She said you're a perfect candidate for Rosemont. So, how would you like to take a look at the school and see what you think? Iris would love to meet you. The school year will be starting up in no time and we've got to decide where you're going.'

School. I have to go to school.

I'd spent the summer living in a breezy, flower-scented fairy tale, a world that had swept me so high above normal life that I'd forgotten about school altogether. But girls from rich families were sent away to boarding schools. I knew that for a fact. On the outskirts of Willoughby there had been just such a school. Every September the students arrived, driven to the front door in fancy cars. When June came, the cars lined up along the shady driveway and took the girls away.

I chewed my lip and looked at Aunt Tootie. 'Is it a boarding school where I'd have to move away from you and Oletta?'

'Oh, no, honey. You'd keep right on living at home with me. Rosemont is just a short walk from our house. I thought I'd call Iris first thing Monday morning and make an appointment to show you the school. Would you like that?'

Relieved, I looked at her and smiled. 'Yes, ma'am.'

'Wonderful,' she said, turning down a bumpy dirt road and almost losing her hat in the process.

The miles rolled by, and just when I wondered how far this trip to get peaches was going to be, she slammed on the brakes so hard I slid from the seat and nearly smacked my head on the dashboard.

'Oh, good heavens, Cecelia, are you all right?'

I pulled myself back onto the seat. 'I'm okay.'

'I've been here dozens of times and still forget where the driveway is.'

Up ahead to the right was a pale yellow farmhouse with a wide front porch, and to the left sat a saggy red barn surrounded by all sorts of outbuildings. We stepped out of the car, and three tail-wagging dogs greeted us with whimpers and squeals, acting like they knew us well, had missed us terribly, and were sick with happiness to have us back. While I loved up the dogs, nearly getting knocked to the ground by their nuzzling and rubbing, Aunt Tootie headed for the barn. 'The peach coolers are in here,' she called over her shoulder.

When the dogs calmed down and loped off through the tall grass, I brushed their dusty paw prints from my dress and looked around. Beyond the barn was a small pond, the water so still the blue sky reflected on its surface like a mirror. Butterflies sailed across the open field, and the air was tinged with the sweet smell of peaches and warm earth. I closed my eyes and breathed in deeply, letting the scents travel through my body. I was in the middle of an accidental kind of happiness that made me grateful for having a nose.

'Want a peach?'

I turned to see a boy, no more than five years old, standing at the side of the car. His skin was honey-dipped from the sun. In his hands he held a basket of peaches.

'Best peaches in Georgia,' he said, holding up the basket. 'Go ahead, take one.'

I selected a peach and thanked him.

'Gotta go now. Pa needs me to help sort today's pick.' His bare feet made tiny imprints in the dusty driveway as he trotted toward the barn.

The peach was warm and fuzzy, as if a small animal had

curled up in my hand and fallen asleep, and when I held it beneath my nose and took a deep breath, it smelled more wonderful than anything had a right to. With my thumbnail I pierced the top, peeled back a piece of its skin, and took a bite. Juice ran down my chin, and I quickly licked it away so it wouldn't stain my dress. I was about to take another bite when I glanced toward the farmhouse, and that's when I saw her.

She was standing in a patch of sunlight hanging laundry on the line. Her shiny brown hair was pinned at the nape of her neck, and her apron billowed in the warm breeze. On a patchwork quilt in the shade of a tree sat a baby with a pink bonnet on her head. The woman shook out a pillowcase, hung it on the line, and said something sweet to the baby. As the baby laughed and clapped her hands, the mother bent down, picked her up, and twirled her in a circle.

The vision of them was like a gunshot to my chest. I tried to close my eyes, but they were pressed wide on the image of the mother and her baby girl.

A low hum vibrated in my ears, and I started to shrink, to fold in on myself, until I was the baby and it was Momma holding me. 'You're my one and only honey-bunny,' my mother cooed. She twirled me in circle after circle, and soon the leaves on the trees became a blur of green. 'You can never leave me, Cecelia. Promise you'll never leave me.' She pressed her nose to mine and looked into my eyes. 'No matter what happens, we'll always have each other.'

My hands began to tremble, and, like a slow-motion clip from a movie, I watched the peach fall from my fingers, sending droplets of juice whirling in the air as it spun toward the ground. I hurt way down deep, in a place I never knew existed.

And then the unspeakable truth of Momma's last day spread out before my eyes.

I was lying on my bed, absorbed in *The Swiss Family Robinson*, when I heard my mother's footsteps in the hall. I glanced up to see her standing in the doorway. Black eyeliner circled wild blue eyes that revealed the fragmented radiance of her madness. Red shoes. White dress. Tiara in her hand. Her mouth was a smear of pink lipstick.

'Let's go shopping,' she said. 'I need a new gown for tonight's pageant.'

I rolled my eyes in disgust. 'Stop it, Momma. There is no pageant. Not tonight, not tomorrow, not next week or next year.'

'Of course there is,' she said, walking to the mirror and adjusting her tiara. 'I want to buy you a pretty party dress too. I'm signing us up for the Mother–Daughter Beauty Pageant.'

Mother-Daughter Beauty Pageant!

Momma giggled. 'It'll be so much fun. I can't wait to see you all dressed up. We need to wear the same color. What about pink?'

When I didn't answer, she turned and looked at me. 'C'mon, CeeCee, let's pick out dresses.'

I glared at her, and not for the first time I wished her dead. 'No. I can't take it anymore. I'm not going to wear a party dress, I'm not going to be in any stupid beauty pageant, and I'm *not* going to be like you!'

'Fine!' she snipped, walking across the room. 'If you're *that* jealous then I'll go alone.'

I called after her, 'Don't buy me a dress. I mean it, Momma!'

There was no mistaking the hurt in her voice when she called back, 'You'll be sorry if you don't go.'

The screen door slapped closed and a moment later the sharp clicking of her high heels sounded on the sidewalk. My eyes narrowed as I pushed myself up on my elbows and glanced out the window. I watched her walk away, swinging her arms like she didn't have a care in the world – like she was as normal as could be with that ridiculous tiara on her head. The thought of another summer of her escapades was more than I could bear. I flipped over on my back and stared at the ceiling, hating her, her illness, her party dresses, her red shoes – hating all of it – hating the shame she brought me every day of my life.

'Just keep on walking, Momma. Walk yourself to China for all I care. I hope you never come back,' I said, tasting the acid bite those words left on my tongue.

But I knew she'd come back sooner or later – she always did.

The sound of a furious wind howled deep inside me. I heard the sickening sound of a dull *thud,* and in my mind I saw Momma's feet leave her shoes as she soared through the air, landing on the pavement in a brutal twist of broken limbs and blood-spattered chiffon. Eyes wide open. Lips parted. Fingers twitching as if typing out her final good-bye on the hot surface of the road. It was as real as if I'd been there, as if I'd witnessed the entire thing.

Over and over, my mother's voice echoed around me, *'You'll be sorry if you don't go . . . you'll be sorry . . . you'll be sorry . . . '*

I reached for the handle of the car door, my insides blistered with guilt. I crawled onto the seat, tucked my knees to my chest, and clamped my hands over my head. But the sound of her voice and the vision of her lying dead in the street stayed with me. Sweat poured off my forehead. I was burning up.

Then, like sugar in the rain, the image of my mother melted away. And she was gone, just gone.

In the distance I heard the jangle of keys. The trunk was opened then closed, and Aunt Tootie's voice floated over my head: 'I got some beautiful peaches. Oletta will be so happy. Just wait till – Cecelia? What's wrong?'

I felt her hand on my back. 'What is it? Cecelia, talk to me.'

Then everything went black.

Twenty-three

I woke to the chirping of birds and the fresh scent of cool morning air. My eyelids felt like they'd been sewn shut, and when I forced them open, something wavy and dark floated in front of me. Once my vision came into focus, I recognized Oletta's face.

She leaned close and smoothed her hand over my head. 'Well, look at this. It's about time you woke up. I told you a long time ago that I ain't got time for no lazybones.'

I looked around the room, feeling confused. I was lying in the four-poster bed in the bedroom Aunt Tootie had referred to as the Snowflake Room. I pushed against my elbows and tried to sit up, but my head flopped back on the pillow.

Footsteps sounded in the hallway, and a moment later Aunt Tootie's face appeared next to Oletta's. 'Oh, Cecelia, it's so good to see you awake.'

Oletta smiled. 'I've got to check on the bread in the oven. I'll be back a little later and bring you some nice apple-butter toast.'

As Oletta left the room, Aunt Tootie sat on the edge of the bed and brushed my bangs off my forehead. 'You just rest and let us take care of you.'

My throat felt scraped and raw, and my voice sounded raspy when I said, 'What happened?'

She lifted a glass from the bedside table and held a straw to my lips. 'Take a sip of this lemon and honey water. It'll make you feel better.' After I took a long drink, she set down the glass and patted my hand. 'You're a little groggy, don't let it scare you. Last night Dr. O'Connor gave you a shot to help you sleep for a while. I'm right here with you. I'm not going anywhere.'

'But . . . what happened?'

She rubbed my arm and a shadow moved across her face when she said, 'We'll talk about it later. For now I think it's best that you rest.'

'How long have I been in this bed?'

'Not all that long – just since yesterday afternoon.'

A surge of panic washed over me. *Is this the beginning? Am I losing my mind like Momma did?*

'Please, Aunt Tootie, I need to know. What happened?'

She nodded and squeezed my fingers. 'All right. Why don't you tell me what you remember and we'll see if we can piece things together from there.'

'We went to the peach farm. I was petting the dogs, and then . . . ' Words clumped in my throat. I looked away and chewed my lip. I ached everywhere, as if I'd been beaten up on the inside.

'What is it, Cecelia?'

'I saw things . . . bad things. They came at me like a storm. But now I'm here. How? How did that happen?'

'It's all right,' she said, rubbing my arm. 'I brought you home from the peach farm.'

I looked around the room. 'But how did I get in this bed?'

Aunt Tootie tilted her head. 'You and I did it together, honey. We climbed the stairs and I got you into bed. Now, tell me, what did you see?'

I closed my eyes and said, 'I saw the day Momma died. It was

239

like watching a movie. When she got hit by the truck there was a terrible thud, and then I saw her lying in the road. It made me hurt . . . everywhere. Then I fell into a black hole. That's all I remember.'

Aunt Tootie gasped, and her hand flew to her mouth. 'Oh, my Lord. Cecelia, are you saying that you were *with* your mother when she died?'

I swallowed hard and shook my head. 'No, I wasn't with her. I was at home. But in my mind I saw things as if I *was* there. And the sound of that thud, I never heard it with my own ears, but it echoed in my mind as if I did.'

Tears burned my eyes. 'It's my fault. She wanted me to go to the Goodwill store, but I said no. And I said mean things to her too.'

'Oh, honey. Is that what this is about?' Aunt Tootie tucked the covers around me and took hold of my hand. 'Your mother's death had nothing to do with you, Cecelia. I promise it didn't. The human mind is an amazing thing. It protects us when we can't protect ourselves. Sometimes when we're holding pain and it gets to be too heavy or goes too deep, we have to give in to it, let it knock us over and pull us all the way down. Once we hit bottom, we rest in a quiet place for a while. Then, when the pain eases and we're ready to face the world again, we come right back up.'

She leaned down, wrapped me in her arms, and held me for a long moment. When she sat up, she searched my face. 'I called Gertrude last night. We had a long talk.'

'Mrs. Odell? You talked to Mrs. Odell?'

'Yes. I called to see if she knew anything about your medical records. I had asked your father to get them for me, but I guess he either forgot or hadn't gotten around to it yet. Gertrude was so kind and helpful. She loves you very much, Cecelia. She said you'd always been healthy as a horse but that you had a tendency to hold things in.' Aunt Tootie looked deep into my eyes. 'Gertrude gave me a clearer picture of what you went through with your mother. Oh, honey, I'm so sorry. I had no idea how ill she was.'

I was mortified. That old familiar heat of embarrassment burned my cheeks. I looked away and covered my face with my hands. *What had Mrs. Odell told Aunt Tootie? How could she do this to me?*

'Cecelia Rose, please look at me,' my aunt said, gently pulling my hands away from my face. 'Will you do that? I want you to know something. Gertrude didn't tell me about your mother's problems to hurt you. She told me so I'd know more of your history, so I could understand and help you.'

Is Aunt Tootie sorry she'd taken me? Is she worried that one day she'll look out the window to see me parading down the sidewalk in some raggedy old prom dress?

It seemed that no matter how far away I moved or how hard I tried to forget about all that had happened, my past would always be lurking in the shadows, waiting to drag me down. I rolled on my side and buried my face in the pillow.

'Let me tell you a story,' Aunt Tootie said, stroking her hand across my back. 'One afternoon I went to the grocery market. Taylor had been gone a little over a year, and though I was still grieving, I was doing a pretty good job of holding myself together. Or so I thought.

'I was standing in the checkout line and glanced down at my basket. And there on top of my groceries was a carton of Taylor's favorite ice cream – Strawberry Surprise. I used to buy him a carton every week, and he loved it so much it'd be gone in three or four days. I never cared for strawberry ice cream, and I'd have never bought it for myself. Now, I can assure you I had no recollection of putting that ice cream into the basket, but I knew I must have – how else would it have gotten there? I stared at that ice cream for the longest time, and then a horrible pain took hold of me. It was so awful I couldn't breathe. Next thing I knew, I dropped the basket and ran from the store.

'That's all I remember of that day. How I drove home is something I'll never know. It was Oletta who found me on the floor of my bedroom the following morning. I was so out of sorts I couldn't even talk. But with some rest and Oletta's care, I eventually came around. Before too long I was back in the middle of my life, doing things and going places with my friends. But I had to plunge deep into my pain and grief before I could move on.'

I rolled on my back and rubbed my eyes. 'But, Aunt Tootie, I never even cried the day Momma died. I tried, but I couldn't. And I feel terrible because all she ever talked about was moving back to Georgia – it was her dream. But now I'm here instead of her. And I'm scared.'

Aunt Tootie furrowed her brow and looked at me thought-fully. 'Why, honey? What are you scared of?'

I stared at the ceiling. Visions of Momma swam through my mind. I could see her standing at the bathroom mirror, wearing a slip and her red shoes, screaming at my father who wasn't even there. And I smelled the sour scent of her when she was so far gone that she hadn't bathed for days.

I couldn't even look at Aunt Tootie. It was as if I were stand-ing outside myself. Watching. Waiting. Wondering who that girl in the bed really was, and what would become of her.

'Talk to me, sugar. Please. I need to know why you're so afraid.'

It wasn't until my aunt squeezed my hand that I opened my mouth and the truth fell from my lips. 'I'm scared that no matter where I go, how many books I read, or how hard I study, I'll never have a normal life because I'm *not* normal – I'm *her* daughter. I'll end up going insane just like she did.' I let out a raspy sob. 'And what happened at the peach farm proves it. I'm already starting to go crazy.'

Aunt Tootie pulled a handkerchief from her dress pocket and pressed it into my hand. 'Cecelia Rose, it's not your fault that your mother died. And whatever was wrong with her isn't something she passed down to you. We'll never fully understand what all happened, but as sure as I'm sitting here on this bed, I know that whatever it was that went haywire in your mother's mind *isn't* going to happen to you.'

'But how?' I squeaked. 'How do you know that?'

She took hold of my hand and kissed it, leaving a pale tattoo of red lipstick behind. 'Because I just *do*. This isn't something I think in my brain – it's something I *feel* in my heart, and there's a mighty big difference between the two. It's our hearts that tell us the truth of things, honey, and my heart has never betrayed me. Not ever.'

'But I looked up *psychosis* in the dictionary, and it said that sometimes mental illness is passed down. And—'

Aunt Tootie's voice was so firm it shocked me. 'Cecelia Rose Honeycutt, you are *not* going to lose your mind.' She leaned close and her voice softened when she said, 'Now, here's something else I know. You might not think you're grieving, but grief comes in all sorts of ways. There's the kind of grief that leaves you numb, and the kind of grief that rips your world in half. And then there's another kind of grief that doesn't feel like grief at all. It's like a tiny splinter you don't even know you have until it festers so deep it has nowhere left to go but into your soul. I think that's the hardest kind of grief there is because you know you're hurting but you don't know why.'

I closed my eyes and shook my head.

'You know what else I think?'

I didn't want to hear another word, but I didn't want to be rude, either, so I let out a tired sigh and said, 'What?'

'I think while your mother was alive you held tight to the hope that one day you'd wake up and she'd be healthy – behave like a *real* mother. Then you'd be able live your life the way children are supposed to. But that day never came. Oh, honey, you've held so much inside for such a long time. You've been very brave.' She pressed her palm to my cheek and tilted her head. 'But even the bravest among us can't hold that much hurt inside. I believe you're not only hurting but you're grieving too. Not only for the mother you had but for the mother and the childhood you didn't.'

For the next few days I stayed in bed and slept a lot, but during the hushed hours of the night, I'd get up and switch on the bathroom light. Rising on my tiptoes, I'd lean close to the mirror and look deep into my eyes. I knew what happened when people lost their minds – for years I had watched my mother's eyes dilate until they became round black voids. Whenever that happened, I knew the storm would soon follow. I promised myself that if I saw even so much as a hint of that void in my own eyes, I'd run to the nearest bridge and heave myself over the side.

I'd stare into the bathroom mirror until I was sure my eyes looked normal, then I'd go back to bed. But I would lie awake and think about all that had happened to me in the first twelve years of my life – years that now collapsed around me, as lifeless and flat as the bedsheets.

I felt small and lost in the big bed, so one night I took my blanket and pillow and made a nest for myself on the window seat. With my knees tucked close to my chest, I rested my head against the pillow. A light rain began to fall, and as I listened to the roll of thunder far off in the distance, I thought about the upcoming school year and wondered how I'd find a way to fit in. Though I could spell words from *archipelago* to *zibeline* and tell you what they meant, I had no idea how to interact with girls my own age.

As I watched raindrops glide down the windowpane, I thought about Momma and all the crazy things she did and said. Though I didn't want to admit it, a part of me missed her. Not the way she was before she died, but the way she was before she got sick.

I had been ashamed of her for so long that any good memories had been distorted and smudged by her illness. I'd forgotten how much fun she was when I was real little, how she'd tell me bedtime stories about fairies who used daisies as umbrellas, how she'd buy me coloring books and sit at the table and help me pick out what crayons I should use. And then I remembered something that happened on a cold winter's morning when I couldn't have been much more than three years old.

Momma came into my bedroom and woke me. Her eyes shone bright in the violet tint of predawn light. 'There's magic outside,' she said, scooping me into her arms. 'Come see.' Her robe was soft against my cheek as she carried me down the stairs.

'Look,' she said, holding me in front of the living room window. 'See what the angels did? Isn't it pretty? They came last night when you were asleep and scattered sugar from the sky. Cecelia, look at the trees. Aren't they the most beautiful things you've ever seen?'

'That's snow,' I said, rubbing my eyes.

'No, look again. See all the sparkles way up in the tree branches? That's sugar.'

I looked out the window, feeling confused, but then decided she was right – it *was* sugar. 'Why, Momma? Why did the angels do that?'

She pressed her nose to mine and looked deep into my eyes. 'Because you're the sweetest little girl in the world.'

Now, as the rain came harder, I lifted my finger and traced the trail of a raindrop as it slid down the windowpane. My chest ached when I remembered how often she had said, 'Promise you'll never leave me.'

I could smell her Shalimar perfume, and I could feel the gentleness of her kiss on my cheek.

And then they came. Tears. Hot and stinging.

Not tears for me, for my shame, or for all the things I feared about the future. They were tears for Momma: the haunting sadness she felt – the years her illness had slashed out of her life – her tragic death.

I burrowed deeper under the blanket, and as the rain beat against the window and thunder rolled over the house, I closed my eyes, let go, and fell into the depths of my sadness. And as I fell, I accepted the truth I had fought for so long – I missed my mother.

I woke to the sound of the door opening and the spicy, warm aroma of Oletta's famous cinnamon rolls, her tried-and-true antidote for sadness, gloom, and all that ailed one. She set the breakfast tray on the bed and came to sit next to me on the window seat.

Her eyelids sagged like the roof of an old porch when she took hold of my hand. 'Child, child. You're too young to have all that sadness in your eyes. I was thinkin' this morning that you ain't read me that book like you promised. You know, the next Nancy Drew you talked about?'

'I've tried to read, but sometimes the words look like a string of little black bugs creeping across the page. Aunt Tootie says I should just rest and give myself time. But what if I never get better? What if the words never stop moving?'

Oletta gazed out the window, her eyes shining like wet stones. 'Maybe them words keep moving 'cause they're tryin' to show you something.'

'What do you mean?'

'Look out the window. Can you see it?'

I leaned forward and pressed my nose to the glass. 'What? What do you want me to see?'

She reached over and pushed up the window. A rain-freshened breeze rolled in like an unexpected gift.

'Look,' she said, smiling out at the trees, the sky, and the birds flying by. 'That's life out there. See how it's movin'? Even the leaves on the trees is movin'. Life don't wait for nobody, and even as special as you are, it ain't gonna wait for you, neither. So it's time to make up your mind that you're gonna join it.'

I looked out the window and thought about what she said. And for the first time in days I felt a smile curve the corner of my lips.

Before leaving the room, Oletta told me she loved me. Well, not the exact words *I love you*, but what she said was, 'Ain't no sun in the kitchen without your face lookin' up at me.'

That was the finest thing anyone could have said.

Dr. O'Connor, who smelled of pipe tobacco and looked a lot like Jack Benny, came to see me every day. He'd press a cold stethoscope to my chest, take my pulse, and talk with me about how I felt. Then, on a crystal-blue Thursday morning, Dr. O'Connor examined me from head to toe. He zipped closed his brown leather bag and announced to Aunt Tootie, 'Your girl doesn't need the likes of me. All she needs is some exercise and sunshine.' He gave me a wink, gently pinched my toes, and left.

The Snowflake Room was too big and too fancy and definitely too white. I felt like I'd been held captive in the middle of a perpetual wedding. I missed my little tree-house bedroom with its happy colors and views of the ever-changing sky, and I was glad when Aunt Tootie said I was well enough to return to the third floor.

My legs felt weak as I climbed the stairs, but it felt good to be up and walking. After showering and washing my hair, I got dressed. From the bookshelf next to my bed, I removed *The Clue of the Broken Locket* and made my way down the stairs.

Oletta was busy in the pantry and didn't see me walk into the kitchen. I pulled myself onto the stool by the chopping block and waited. Oletta didn't notice me when she stepped out of the pantry with a sack of flour in her arms, and she still didn't notice me when she set it on the counter and shuffled to the oven to check on the bread she was baking.

I opened the book to the first chapter and began reading aloud, "'The light from the bull's-eye window began to flash on and off. Surely this must be a signal . . .'"

Twenty-four

The days passed, and I grew stronger. Oletta made my favorite foods – grilled cheese sandwiches, banana bread, and thick buttermilk pancakes. She even spent an entire Monday afternoon making a seven-layer chocolate cream cake from scratch. Aunt Tootie, who had rarely left the house while I was recuperating, resumed her hectic schedule of saving houses from the wrecking ball. But she always spent time with me after dinner, and we'd talk, go for a walk, or watch TV together.

When I went to bed at night, I no longer lay awake in fear that Momma's illness had been passed down to me. In some ways my life in Willoughby had begun to fade, much the same way a nightmare loses its grip when you find the courage to reach out in the darkness and turn on the light. I was still a little nervous about going to school and meeting my classmates, but whenever those worries grabbed hold of me, I envisioned the strength in Oletta's eyes when she lifted her chin and said: 'Today's the day – you've got to reclaim your power.'

One evening during dinner Aunt Tootie announced we'd be going to visit the Rosemont School for Girls the following morning. I went to bed tingling with both excitement and fear and woke early the next morning wondering what lay ahead.

After breakfast I spent an absurd amount of time pulling dresses from my closet and holding them up in front of me, eventually deciding on a pink jumper and white blouse. I tied a ribbon around my ponytail, buckled my shoes, and went downstairs to the living room.

A moment later Aunt Tootie came down the stairs in a blue linen suit and matching hat. 'Oh, Cecelia, you look so pretty. Are you ready to go see the school?'

I nodded but was too nervous too speak. When we headed for the garage, I had one of those strange moments where you're so wide-awake and fully open that the air sparks when you move though it.

The Rosemont School for Girls was a three-story brick building with tall windows and a green-painted front door. A thick hedge ran along the perimeter of the property, framing a perfectly clipped lawn. As we got out of the car, Aunt Tootie said, 'Well, Cecelia Rose, this is your big day.'

I could hardly breathe as we approached the front door. My aunt stopped and looked up at the building. 'Isn't this lovely? It used to be a private residence. I know from the front it looks too small to be a school, but there's a big addition in the back. You'll see it when we take the tour. So let's go in and see what you think.' She took hold of my hand and pushed open the door.

It certainly didn't look like a school – not with its high ceilings, mahogany moldings, and gleaming leaded-glass windows. Since moving to Savannah, I'd begun to recognize the aroma of wealth, and from the walls of this school there oozed the unmistakable scent of prosperity. Though the idea of attending a private school had originally sounded wonderful, I now wasn't so sure. Clearly the Rosemont School for Girls was for the best of the best, the smartest of the smart, and the richest of the rich.

If I go to school here, will the other girls think I don't belong?

Before that thought could drag me down, Aunt Tootie whisked me into a small, brightly lit waiting room.

A white-haired, rosy-cheeked woman opened an interior door. She smiled, looking as happy and plump as a July toad. 'Well, good morning, Tootie. What a fine day this is.'

Aunt Tootie shook the woman's outstretched hand. 'It's so pleasant now that the humidity has let up. Iris, I'd like you to meet my grandniece, Cecelia Rose Honeycutt. And Cecelia, this is Mrs. Iris Fontaine, the headmistress of this lovely school.'

Mrs. Fontaine grinned and took my hand. 'Cecelia, welcome to Rosemont. I can't tell you how much I've been looking forward to meeting you.'

My cheeks colored up, and when I opened my mouth to speak, the words *Thank you, ma'am* came out as an unintelligible 'Tat Hayo, man.'

I wanted to die.

Aunt Tootie looked at me kinda strange, but Mrs. Fontaine just smiled and said, 'Please, come into my office so we can relax and chat.'

From a gray cardigan draped around her shoulders, I detected the faint scent of mothballs as she led us into a mahogany-paneled room that had a big desk plunked in the center. After listening to her give us a proud history of the school and its many virtues, she nodded toward the door. 'I'd love to show you what we have to offer, Cecelia. Would you like a tour?'

'Yes, ma'am.'

Aunt Tootie gave me a quick wink as we followed Mrs. Fontaine out the door.

Lining the walls of the first-floor hallway were framed photographs of the students, all of them wearing plaid kilts and blazers that had a crest on the chest pocket.

Perfect little Southern belles.

I stood on my tiptoes and scanned their faces. They were the kind of girls who played croquet on perfectly manicured lawns, their faces glowing with that luminous light of carefree privilege. I touched my cheek and wondered what it would take for me to obtain that same kind of radiance. How long I examined the pictures of those fresh-faced girls I don't know, but I was startled when Aunt Tootie called from the other end of the hallway. 'Cecelia Rose, c'mon, honey, we're heading upstairs.'

After we toured the classrooms and the art department, Mrs. Fontaine showed us the new library, which was so wonderful I was left speechless.

'This was just completed in March,' Mrs. Fontaine said, gesturing to the massive bookcases and rows of study tables. 'We're quite proud of it.'

Aunt Tootie smoothed her hand over the side of a polished bookshelf. 'You certainly should be, Iris. It's just lovely.'

'You have three sets of encyclopedias?' I said, scanning a case full of research books.

Mrs. Fontaine nodded. 'Yes, and we have an entire section dedicated to the American masters of literature and art.'

'Isn't it wonderful, Cecelia?' Aunt Tootie said. Then she turned to Mrs. Fontaine. 'Iris, where's the powder room?'

'Down the hall to your left.'

'Thank you.' She looked at me and said, 'I'll be right back, honey.'

I didn't want her to leave, but I knew I'd look like a big baby if I followed her. My throat tightened as I watched her disappear.

Though Mrs. Fontaine smiled, I couldn't help but wonder if she'd sized me up and found me lacking. She folded her hands and looked at me thoughtfully. 'Cecelia Rose, when I went through your transcripts, I was quite surprised. Pleasantly so. It's rare for a student to consistently excel in such a broad range of subjects.'

I let out a breath and relaxed a little. 'Thank you, ma'am.'

Mrs. Fontaine pulled out a chair and sat down. She gestured to the chair next to her, and I sat, clamping my hands between my knees so she wouldn't see them shake. We were so close I could smell the mothballs again.

'When I went over your transcripts, I was particularly impressed with your English scores.'

Her compliment made my cheeks color up, and I fiddled with the hem of my jumper. 'I love English. It's my favorite subject.'

Mrs. Fontaine smiled. 'We're kindred spirits in that regard. It was my favorite subject too. So tell me, Cecelia, what are some of your favorite books?'

'Well, I like anything by Agatha Christie, and I love Nancy Drew.' I looked around the library and tried to imagine what it would be like to study in such a beautiful room. 'Are ... are all these books just to read here in the library, or can they be checked out?'

'With the exception of the research books, everything can be taken home. We have a librarian who keeps track of everything.'

Just then the door opened and Aunt Tootie walked in. 'The powder room is charming, Iris. I just love those tiny hexagon tiles and the pink wallpaper.'

'We tried to keep the new addition in keeping with the original house. I'm so glad you approve.' Mrs. Fontaine stood and rested her hand on my shoulder. 'Well, I'll let you two talk in private. If you have any questions, please stop by my office.'

Aunt Tootie took Mrs. Fontaine's hand and shook it. 'Thank you so much.'

'It's been a pleasure.'

When the sound of Mrs. Fontaine's footsteps faded, Aunt Tootie leaned her hip against a study table and scanned my face.

'Well, sugar, I think this school is full of lots of wonderful possibilities. But what I think isn't important. What matters is what *you* think.'

I chewed my bottom lip and glanced at the pictures of honor students that hung above the door. They peered down at me, as if waiting to hear what I had to say. I took a breath and looked into Aunt Tootie's eyes. 'I love this school, but . . . but do you think I'd fit in, being a Northerner and all? Do you think the girls would like me?'

She smiled and nodded. 'I believe the girls would like you just fine. There's a whole lot about you to like.'

I picked at my cuticles for a moment, feeling a wave of anxiety move through me.

'What is it, honey?'

'If someone asks me about, well . . . about Momma or Dad, what should I say?'

Aunt Tootie sat down next to me. 'Cecelia Rose. People are, by nature, curious. And as you go through life, many people will ask questions about your past. And when they do, you just say the truth, plain and simple – your mother passed away and your father travels for his work, so you came to live with me. That's all you ever have to say, honey. Everything will be just fine, as long as *you* make it fine. Now, there's something I want you to think about. Something important. And I promise you, it will serve you well throughout your life. I'm going to tell you something that my mother said to me a long time ago.'

My aunt's face was so serious I couldn't imagine what she was going to say.

She took hold of my hand and looked into my eyes. 'It's what we believe about ourselves that determines how others see us.'

I considered her words as we sat knee-to-knee, looking at each other. 'You make it sound so easy.'

'You know what, sugar? Once you set your mind to it, it *is* easy. So, is this where you'd like to go to school?'

I took a deep breath. 'Yes, ma'am.'

She stood and tilted her head toward the door. 'Well, then, shall we go tell Mrs. Fontaine you'll be her newest student?'

I was so happy, I all but jumped out of the chair.

Mrs. Fontaine was thrilled and assured Aunt Tootie and me that neither of us would be disappointed. 'Let's get you measured so I can order your new uniform,' she said, pulling a measuring tape from her desk.

After my measurements had been recorded, Aunt Tootie filled out a few forms and signed some papers. As we were about to leave, a man dressed in a suit and tie stepped through the open door. Beside him stood a girl about my height with startling green eyes framed by a pair of gold-rimmed granny-style glasses. A mop of curly, reddish-brown hair fell to her shoulders, and splashed across her nose and cheeks was a handful of pale freckles. Her face was round and full of questions.

'Excuse me,' the man said. 'When I saw the door open—'

'Oh, please, come in,' Mrs. Fontaine said, stepping across the room. She shook the man's hand and made introductions. His name was Howard McAllister, and the girl was his daughter, Dixie Lee.

Mrs. Fontaine grinned. 'Dixie, Cecelia will be in your class.'

Dixie's eyebrows arched and her eyes widened. A bolt of fear shot through me when I saw the look on her face.

Oh, no. What does she see in me?

Dixie chirped, 'You are? That's great. Where do you live?'

I was so stunned by her words that it took me a moment to respond. I swallowed and glanced up at Aunt Tootie with pride. 'I live on Gaston Street.'

'We're almost neighbors. I live on West Jones.'

Mrs. Fontaine, who at this point was all puffed up like a proud Mother Goose, said, 'Dixie, you and Cecelia have a great deal in common. Cecelia loves English, and I understand she enjoys reading as much as you do.'

'Did you see the new library?' Dixie asked.

I nodded, and the next thing I knew, the adults began talking and Dixie led me out of the office, down the hall, and out the front door. She told me about her new kitten and how she'd begun taking tap dance lessons. We walked side by side as Dixie jabbered like we'd known each other for years. And me? I was tongue-tied and dumbstruck by this gregarious green-eyed girl. And as we strolled along a shady brick path that surrounded the school, I don't think my feet ever fully touched the ground.

'We're leaving tomorrow to visit my grandmother in Louisiana,' Dixie said, trotting to her father's car. 'But we'll be back a few days before school starts.' She pulled a notepad and pen from the glove box. 'Let's walk to school together.'

I wanted it so badly my voice squeaked when I answered, 'Okay.' And when we exchanged addresses, I felt happier than a dog with a brand-new bone.

'I'll be at your house at seven forty-five,' she said, folding the paper and sliding it deep into her sock. 'Gosh, I'm so glad we met, Cecelia. I was real scared to switch schools.' She laughed and said, 'But not anymore.'

Her laughter was a wondrous, liquid thing that splashed across my face, over the toes of my shoes, and into the grass.

'I'm glad we met too. If you want, you can call me CeeCee.'

The front door of the school opened, and we turned to see Aunt Tootie and Dixie's father walk out. They waved good-bye to Mrs. Fontaine and headed toward the parking lot.

'Well, looks like I've gotta go now,' Dixie said with a shrug.

She climbed into a green convertible sports car with her dad and waved as they headed down the driveway.

I prayed the name Dixie McAllister was written in my Life Book.

Just before the car turned into the street, Dixie jumped up in her seat and called out, 'I promise I'll be waiting for you, CeeCee!' Her father reached up, grabbed the hem of her dress, and pulled her down.

As I stood in a pool of bright lemon light and watched the car disappear into a tunnel of shady trees, I believed Dixie McAllister. I believed her with all my heart.

Twenty-five

Three days following my visit to Rosemont School a box arrived in the mail. It was a small box, not much bigger than my hand. The neatly typed label was addressed to Miss Cecelia Rose Honeycutt in care of Mrs. Tallulah Caldwell. There was no return address.

Positive it was something special from my new school, I set the rest of the mail on Aunt Tootie's desk and took the box upstairs.

I sat on my bed and ripped away the tape. *What can this be? Oh, my gosh, maybe it's a school pin.*

After opening the box, I pulled out a square of cotton. I sucked in a breath of air when I saw the silky pink pouch. I knew what was inside.

Momma's pearls.

Slowly I opened the pouch and slid the necklace into my hand. It was cool and smooth to the touch, just as I remembered. I closed my fingers and held it for a long time, feeling so many emotions I couldn't move. I might have stayed like that for hours, sitting frozen on my bed, had the box not slipped off my lap and tumbled to the floor. A small piece of paper fell out, and when I picked it up and opened it, I recognized my father's writing.

Dear CeeCee,

I thought you should have your mother's pearls. If I remember right, her mother gave them to her when she graduated from high school.

Love,
Dad

I put the note aside and looked down at my mother's necklace. Gently I began rubbing a single pearl between my thumb and forefinger, feeling myself slip backward in time.

I remembered a rainy day when Momma and I were in her bedroom, playing dress-up. After dabbing rouge on my cheeks, she pulled her favorite pink sweater over my head and slid her pearl necklace from its pouch.

'Nothing brings light to a woman's face like pearls,' she said, clasping the strand around my neck. 'If you want to glow like you're lit from within, CeeCee, wear pearls and a pale pink sweater.' She lifted me onto her vanity bench and smiled. 'See how pretty you look?'

I grinned at my reflection.

She put her arms around me. 'Do you know how pearls are made?'

'No, Momma.'

'Well, let me tell you the story. One day an oyster was just sittin' at the bottom the ocean, all happy and minding its own business. Then, when it was time to take an afternoon nap, the oyster yawned and a little grain of sand floated into its mouth. That grain of sand irritated the oyster something awful, but no matter how it tried, the oyster couldn't spit it out. Six long years went by and the oyster kept rolling that piece of sand around in its mouth. The grain of sand got bigger and bigger, and then one day the oyster felt a lump under its tongue. Well, the oyster mustered all of its strength, opened its mouth, and spit it out. But it wasn't a piece of sand anymore. It was a beautiful pearl.'

I looked up at her, amazed. 'Really?'

She sat on the bed and nodded. 'Oysters are a lot like women. It's how we survive the hurts in life that brings us strength and gives us our beauty.' She fell silent for a moment and gazed out the window. 'They say there's no such thing as a perfect pearl – that nothing from nature can ever be truly perfect.'

Abruptly she turned to me, and the look in her eyes was fierce. 'But they're wrong,' she said, pulling me close. 'You, Cecelia Rose, are a perfect pearl. *My* perfect little pearl.'

When the memory faded, I slid the necklace back inside the pouch and placed it in the drawer of my night chest.

Later that afternoon, Aunt Tootie and I drove to the hardware store in search of a new garden rake. She found the kind she wanted, and some other things too – a dirt sifter and an odd-looking contraption for planting bulbs.

After loading everything into the trunk, we climbed into the car, and to my surprise, Aunt Tootie put the top down. The afternoon sunlight sparked off the tips of Delilah's wings as we drove back to town. I leaned my head against the seat, enjoying how the wind pushed through my hair.

'I bought that bulb planter because I want to do something different at the front of the house,' Aunt Tootie said, glancing over at me. 'Last week I ordered two hundred tulip bulbs and a thousand grape hyacinths.'

'A *thousand*? Holy cow! It'll take us forever to plant that many.'

She laughed. 'I hired a gardener to do the autumn planting. But you and I will lay everything out. Half the tulips are pink and the others are yellow. We'll surround them with all those gorgeous purple grape hyacinths. Won't that be pretty?'

I nodded. 'But I like to plant bulbs. We could do it together, couldn't we?'

'Honey, I hate to admit it, but I'm getting old. My back aches something awful when I bend over for too long. And come November, when the bulbs arrive and planting season begins, you'll be busy with school and all sorts of fun activities. But we can plant some things in the side yard,' she said with a wink.

Aunt Tootie threaded her way through town, but when we got to our street, she sailed right by. When I asked her where we were going, she just smiled and said, 'You'll see.'

A few minutes later we rolled to a stop in front of the house that was saved from the wrecking ball. My jaw dropped. Gone were the saggy roof and dilapidated front steps. A web of scaffolding surrounded the house, and workmen were busy scraping and sanding old paint from the arched windows.

'Oh, my gosh,' I said, climbing out of the car. 'It looks so different.'

'Just wait till you see the inside.'

We walked under the scaffolding and in through the open front door. 'Hi, Jake,' Aunt Tootie said to a man who was up on a ladder, painting a wall in the living room.

'Afta-noon, Miz Caldwell. So how's she look?'

'She looks beautiful. You're doing a fine job. Was it hard to get all that old wallpaper off?'

The man laughed. 'About killed me.'

'I'm here to show my grandniece around.'

'Sure thing,' he said, going back to his painting. 'But don't go up the stairs, they were just stained this morning.'

Aunt Tootie led me into the dining room. 'Look, Cecelia. Remember this?' she said, flicking a switch.

The chandelier exploded with light, and all the icy crystal prisms came to life. It was so dazzling all I could say was, 'Wow.'

'And come see this,' she said, heading down the hall. I followed, walking over smooth refinished floors that glowed from beneath layers of new varnish.

Taped to a length of rope that had been stretched across a doorway was a piece of cardboard. Printed in bold red marker were the words STOP! HISTORICAL PRESERVATION AREA. DO NOT ENTER!

Aunt Tootie and I ducked beneath the rope, then she turned on an overhead light. 'Cecelia, look,' she said with wonder.

On the wall opposite the windows was something the likes of which I'd never seen. A painting filled the entire wall from floor to ceiling, yet it was far more than a painting – it was like stumbling upon the entrance to a secret garden. Beneath a blue sky filled with pink-tinted clouds was a scene so real I had the urge to step right into it. Flowers lined a stone path that wound its way toward a reflection pool that looked so cool and wet I wanted to dip my fingers into its shimmering surface. Birds in flight seemed to lift from the walls, and a ladybug crawled along the branch of a tree – its green leaves so real they all but rustled in a breeze.

'When the workmen removed all that nasty wallpaper, they found this beneath. The technique is called trompe l'oeil; that's French for "tricks the eye." It's the ultimate in artistic optical illusion. This is a masterpiece.'

We stood side by side, our lips parted in wonderment as if we were gazing at the ceiling of the Sistine Chapel.

'It doesn't appear to be signed anywhere, but we're going to try to find out who painted it, and when. The house was built in 1859, and I suspect it was painted shortly thereafter. Oh, Cecelia, this house was once dearly loved. It's been an honor to save it from destruction.'

I watched her. Studied her. She was still the aunt I had come to love, yet there was something else, something I became aware of for the first time. I could see it in her eyes, hear it in her voice, and I could feel it radiating from her body.

It was her fire.

And it was real.

As I followed her down the hall toward the front door, I stopped for a moment and looked down at my feet. And as sure as my name is Cecelia Rose Honeycutt, I felt the life of that old house humming through the soles of my shoes.

Twenty-six

My new life had begun to bloom as sweetly as a Georgia peach. Just when I thought things couldn't possibly get better, Oletta walked into the kitchen and set a stack of mail on the counter. 'You got a letter from your friend in Ohio.'

I stopped stirring a bowl of brownie batter and ripped open the envelope.

'Now, wait a minute,' Oletta said, propping her hands on her hips. 'You can't just stop stirring the brownies like that. They got to be mixed real good.'

I pulled out a kitchen chair and plopped down at the table. 'I did.'

She shook her head, gave the batter a few quick stirs, and shot me a look that said, *Oh, no, you didn't.*

I unfolded the letter and read:

Dearest CeeCee,

You'll never believe what has happened. I called a realty company to sell my house. When the agent came to see it, he bought it as a wedding gift for his daughter and her new husband.

I'm taking the bus and moving to Kissimmee, Florida, to

*live with my cousin Adele. I called your aunt Tallulah and
asked if I could stop by and see you for a few days, and she
invited me to stay for as long as I wanted. So I've decided to
come for two weeks.*

I can't wait to see you.

*All my love,
Mrs. O*

I jumped from my chair and yelped, 'Oh, my gosh!'

Oletta jolted. 'You about scared me to death. What are you
all whipped up about?'

'Mrs. Odell is coming to Savannah.' I pressed her letter to my
chest and danced in a circle.

On the morning of Mrs. Odell's arrival, I woke to the steady
growl of a lawnmower. When I came down the stairs and stepped
into the second-floor hallway, Oletta was making the bed in one
of the guest rooms. The faint scent of lavender linen water – lav-
ishly sprinkled on the sheets at the time they were ironed –
floated in the upstairs hallway like a half-remembered dream.

'Good morning,' I said, walking in to help her.

'Well, if it ain't Miz Lazybones. It's half past nine.'

Knowing how much it annoyed her if I wasn't dressed and
ready for breakfast by eight-thirty, I looked at her sheepishly.
'I'm sorry, Oletta.'

'That's okay. Give me a minute to finish up, and I'll make you
some French toast.'

'Thanks, but I'm not very hungry. I think I'll just have some
fruit.' I tucked a pillow into its case and fluffed it up. 'I can't wait
to see Mrs. Odell. It feels like I haven't seen her in years.'

'That's how it is when you love someone. I'm sure she's as
excited as you are.'

After straightening the coverlet, we headed down the stairs.

While I sat at the kitchen table and peeled an orange, I looked out the window and watched Aunt Tootie. She was bent over with her rear to the sky, cutting flowers. The vision took me back to the memories I had of Mrs. Odell working in her garden, and the thought of seeing my old friend in just a few hours made me so happy I thought I'd burst.

We arrived at the terminal a half hour before Mrs. Odell's bus was scheduled to arrive, Aunt Tootie in a soft yellow linen dress and a straw hat and me in a periwinkle blue sundress and white, ballet-style leather shoes. From a bench by a window we sat and watched weary travelers waiting for their suitcases to be pulled from the bellies of buses that were lined up in the parking lot.

I was so excited, I kept banging my knees together. 'How will we know which bus is hers?' I asked.

'I believe her bus number is eighty-three.' Aunt Tootie pulled a paper from her handbag and squinted. 'Yes, that's it. Eighty-three.' She slipped the paper back inside her handbag and patted my knee. 'Guess what, sugar? I've got a special event planned for Thursday. Several of my friends are opening their gardens in honor of Gertrude's visit. Isn't that sweet of them? We'll start with a luncheon at our house, then we'll visit the other gardens and finish up at Thelma Rae's for desserts and refreshments.'

'Look! I think she's here.' I jumped from the bench and ran to the window as a bus rolled into the parking lot. 'She is! It's bus number eighty-three.'

Aunt Tootie stood. 'All right, let's go out. But don't run toward the bus. Just wait till everyone gets off.'

'Okay,' I said, tugging at her arm.

A handful of tired-looking travelers climbed off the bus, gathered their suitcases, and headed for the terminal, but Mrs. Odell wasn't among them. 'Oh, dear, I wonder what happened,' my aunt said. 'I'd better go in and see if I made a mistake when I wrote down the information.'

Just then the bus driver climbed back onto the bus. My heart rolled over as I watched him help Mrs. Odell down the steps, one slow movement at a time. I waved my arms and called out, 'Mrs. Odell. Mrs. Odell!'

When she looked up and saw me, she smiled the smile I had loved for all my life. I took off running and made a beeline across the parking lot. Mrs. Odell opened her arms, and I soared right into them. I buried my face in her shoulder and breathed her in. She smelled of freshly ironed cotton, exactly as I remembered.

'Oh, it's good to hold my little pal again. I've missed you so much, Cecelia.'

Hardly believing this moment was real, I leaned back to look at her face. A runaway tear traveled along Mrs. Odell's chin. It ran down her neck and disappeared behind the slightly frayed collar of her thin cotton dress – a dress that surely began its life long before I was born.

The first few days of Mrs. Odell's stay in Savannah were filled with morning sightseeing tours followed by lunches out on the back porch. One afternoon three friends of Aunt Tootie's stopped by to meet Mrs. Odell. The first was Estelle Trent, whom I'd met, and coming up the walk right behind her were two women I didn't recognize. Aunt Tootie introduced them as Agnes White and Lottie Donahue, both members of the Historic Savannah Foundation. All three ladies arrived with gifts in hand: Estelle with a vase of fresh-cut flowers, Agnes with a jar of homemade jam with a ribbon tied around the top, and Lottie with a loaf of bread, still fragrant with yeast and warm from the oven.

As I watched all the comings and goings and listened to the charming 'Welcome to Savannah's' and the heartfelt 'I'm so pleased to meet you's' that dripped like honey from these women's lips, I realized that Southern hospitality not only came from the heart but was a practiced social art that had been passed down from one generation to the next — like fine silverware or china. Southerners had a way of doing things that made you feel special, and Mrs. Odell soaked in every drop of the kindness.

The luncheon Aunt Tootie had arranged was a huge success, and before beginning the garden tour, Mrs. Odell was presented with an official Ladies of Savannah Garden Club hat. The hat, which was the size of a turkey platter and crafted from finely woven straw, had a cluster of white silk flowers pinned to the garden club's signature pink-grosgrain band. All the women clapped when Mrs. Odell put it on her head, and to see Mrs. Odell wear that hat as she strolled through the lush private gardens, well, my heart puffed up like a cherry popover is all I can say.

Mrs. Odell liked the hat so much she took to wearing it every day. And once, when I walked by her room just before bed, I saw her sitting on the chair reading a magazine, wearing a nightgown with the hat on her head. Her feet were propped on a footstool, and stuck to the sole of one of her slippers was a price tag that read: SALE 75¢.

It was an image I would carry with me for the rest of my life.

One afternoon while Aunt Tootie and Mrs. Odell were sitting in the living room talking, I wandered to the back porch to read for a while. When I stepped out the door, I was startled when something flew in front of my face. I jumped back to see a huge dusty cobweb hanging from the porch ceiling like an old fishing net.

From the pantry I gathered a broom and stepstool. While

brushing the web away, I heard music weaving through the tree branches. I smiled to myself and wondered if one of Miz Goodpepper's plants was feeling poorly.

A few minutes later Miz Goodpepper appeared on the far side of the patio. She was wearing a long, filmy white cocoon of a dress. The fabric was so gauzy I could see the shadowed outline of her body beneath. As I watched her approach, I felt that same magnetic pull and strange fascination I had experienced when I first laid eyes on her.

'Hello, darling,' she said, smiling her ever-knowing, catlike smile as she climbed the steps. 'What are you doing?'

'Cleaning cobwebs.'

Her eyes widened. 'You're not killing any spiders, are you?'

'No, ma'am,' I said, stepping down from the stool.

'Good. Spiders are such wonderful, misunderstood creatures. It's terrible how they've been demonized over the years. Did I ever introduce you to Matilda?'

'Who's that?'

She sat in one of the chairs and crossed her legs. 'Matilda's a beautiful yellow garden spider who's taken up residence in my jasmine trellis. She's been with me for two years. I'm enormously fond of her. Last week she spun a new web that spans from the trellis to my statue of Persephone. When the afternoon sun hits it just right, the web looks like lace that's been made from strands of silver light. You'll have to come see it. Matilda is a true artist – a highly advanced spirit in the spider kingdom.'

I looked at the dusty cobwebs that covered the broom in my hand, and tried to think of something to say.

'The other day I was playing a violin concerto for my dogwood tree and noticed that Matilda was weaving her web in tune to the music. She never missed a single nuance. I wouldn't be at all surprised if she reincarnates as a fine musician. I can picture her poised at a grand piano, her nimble fingers blazing through a Mozart sonata. It was such a splendid moment that I believe I had a tiny glimpse at nirvana.'

I leaned against the porch rail. 'Did you know there's a place called nirvana in Idaho?'

'Idaho!' She fell back in the chair, all laughter and legs. 'Oh, Cecelia, you never cease to delight me.'

'Well, there is. I brought in the mail the other day, and on the cover of one of Aunt Tootie's magazines it said there was a place in Idaho called Serenity Gardens. And they have some kind of water garden that's named Little Nirvana. So I figured that's where it was.'

'Well, nirvana *is* a place of serenity, but it's not an external place. It's a state of perfect calm and acceptance where we join the eternal rhythm. Nirvana represents the final goal of Buddhism.' Miz Goodpepper looked into the sky. 'But it takes many, many lifetimes to get there.'

'Well, too bad it's not in Idaho; then you could go there right away.'

She laughed and shook her head. 'Cecelia, you always brighten my day. I wish you'd come over and spend more time with me.'

I picked cobwebs from the broom bristles and flicked them over the porch rail. 'I will, after Mrs. Odell goes to Florida.'

'Oh,' she said, rising to her feet, 'I got so lost in our conversation, I almost forgot. I have a little something for Gertrude. Is she here?'

I escorted Miz Goodpepper into the house and led her down the hallway to the living room. She reached into the pocket of her dress and pulled out a small narrow box tied with a blue ribbon. 'For you, Gertrude.'

Inside was a silver bookmark. Mrs. Odell smoothed her

fingers over its surface and smiled. 'It's just beautiful, Thelma. Thank you.'

Miz Goodpepper reclined on the sofa. 'When we all got together after the garden tour, Cecelia mentioned how much you loved to read.'

'Yes, I do. But I've never had such a lovely bookmark.'

'It's quite old; my guess is that it was probably made during the 1880s.'

'So was I,' Mrs. Odell said with a chuckle.

'I'm fascinated with antiques,' Miz Goodpepper said, bathing in a pool of soft light from the window. 'I find there's a sweet sorrow in objects that have slipped away from their original owners. Years ago I began to collect antique perfume bottles. I'd scour estate sales and antique shops, and every time I'd find one and bring it home, I'd wonder whose fingers had first wrapped around it, what she dreamed about, what she looked like . . . if she was happy.'

There was a thoughtful stillness about Miz Goodpepper as she gazed out the window. 'Once, when I was holding one of those beautiful bottles in my hand, I got a fleeting glimpse of the woman who owned it. It was like the fringed edge of a fading dream. Anyway,' she said, fluffing her dress, 'when I was browsing through that darling shop over on Tattnall yesterday, I saw the bookmark and thought you might like it.'

'Oh, I do,' Mrs. Odell said, smoothing her fingers over its surface. 'I'll cherish it.'

Not ten minutes after she excused herself and left for home, Miz Hobbs blew in through the back door without so much as knocking. She was wearing a frightful green floral dress, and in her hands she held a gift box of sugar-coated pecans.

'I just hate bein' the last one to meet your friend,' she said, tugging at her dress, 'but I've been havin' such awful headaches lately. The doctor said they'd go away once the swelling in my brain went all the way down.' She laughed and patted my shoulder. 'Who knew a brain could swell? Do you suppose I'll get any smarter?'

I pretended to laugh.

'So where's your friend?'

'In the living room with Aunt Tootie.'

I was about to lead her down the hall when she turned and left the kitchen without me. Her hat didn't cover the bald spot on the back of her head from where she'd gotten stitches, and her scar looked like a pink zipper. The sight of it made me feel bad, but not bad enough to go and join her in the living room.

All these visitors made me remember something Momma had said several years ago. She'd been more distraught than usual about her life in Ohio and was on a rampage when I got home from school. After smashing a coffee mug against the refrigerator, she looked at me and cried, 'Being in the North isn't living – it's absolute hell. Northerners have no idea what *real* living means, and they don't know a damn thing about etiquette or hospitality.'

What triggered that outburst I'll never know, but as crazy as Momma sometimes was, I now recognized that her statement held more than a grain of truth.

During one of my visits to Miz Goodpepper's house, she had pointed out a camellia bush in her yard and told me it couldn't survive above the Mason–Dixon Line. She said camellias needed warmth to thrive and bloom. And now I wondered if my mother, Camille Sugarbaker Honeycutt, had been like her flowering namesake.

When my father plucked her from the warm Georgia soil and drove her to Ohio, did she begin to wither when they sped across the Mason–Dixon Line? Was she geographically doomed?

I wondered about it so much that one night, when Aunt Tootie and I were alone in the den, I asked her what she thought. She put down her cross-stitch and looked at me thoughtfully. She neither confirmed nor denied the possibility, but what she said was, 'There's no doubt in my mind that certain temperaments do better in some climates than others. And if, from now on, you happen to think of your mother when you see a camellia in bloom, well, I'm sure she'd be tickled pink.'

The first week of Mrs. Odell's visit melted into a blur of luncheons, teas, and visitors at the door. Everyone seemed to be enjoying her visit to Savannah. Well, everyone but Oletta.

Shortly after Mrs. Odell's arrival, I noticed Oletta had grown quiet. Though she shuffled around the kitchen making meals and baking like she always did, she didn't say much. If anyone asked her a question, she'd answer, but not once did she initiate a conversation.

One afternoon, Aunt Tootie, Mrs. Odell, and I were sitting on the back porch having lunch. Oletta had made a creamy chicken salad with walnuts, grapes, and slivers of crisp celery that she served on a pillow of fresh greens. When she came out to the porch to refill our water glasses, Mrs. Odell beamed up at her. 'Oletta, I've never tasted such wonderful chicken salad. Is there whipped cream in the dressing?'

Oletta nodded.

'Well, it's just heavenly. Would you mind sharing your recipe?'

Oletta never even looked at Mrs. Odell, and her voice was cold and flat when she said, 'I don't give my cookin' secrets away.'

Aunt Tootie's face flushed, and I sat slack-mouthed. But Mrs. Odell never missed a beat when she said, 'I don't blame you one bit, Oletta. Good cooks should protect their recipes. Forgive me. I shouldn't have asked.'

After we'd finished lunch, Oletta cleared the table while the rest of us wandered into the garden. The way Oletta banged the dishes together was something she'd never done before. Aunt Tootie glanced toward the house and furrowed her brow as she watched Oletta carelessly pile the dishes on a tray.

Mrs. Odell, who didn't seem to notice the racket, stood at the far side of the garden and fussed over some red flowers that had bright yellow centers. 'Oh, these have such happy little faces.'

Aunt Tootie grinned. 'Would you like a bouquet for your bedroom, Gertrude?'

'Oh, I would.'

'I'll get my snips.' As she headed to the house, Aunt Tootie put her arm around my shoulders and said, 'Come with me.'

When we were out of Mrs. Odell's earshot, Aunt Tootie slowed her stride and whispered, 'Oletta hasn't been herself, and I believe I've figured out why. Sugar, you've been spending all your time with Gertrude, and I have the suspicion that Oletta's been feeling a little shoved out.'

'But I love Oletta.'

My aunt smoothed her hand down my back and leaned close to my ear. 'I know you do, and she loves you too. Ever since you came to live here, the two of you have been like peas in a pod. You're every bit as important to Oletta as she is to you. Try to give her a little attention. It'll do her good.'

How could I have been so stupid? I haven't even read to Oletta since Mrs. Odell came to visit.

While Aunt Tootie gathered her basket and garden snips, I wandered into the kitchen. Oletta was washing dishes and didn't look up when I pulled a towel from the drawer and started drying. Though I was standing right next to her, she acted like I wasn't there. When the dishes had been dried, I put them away while Oletta tidied the kitchen.

With a wet sponge in hand and her lips pressed tight, she worked her arm in a furious circular motion as she scrubbed the counter. 'Why ain't you outside with your friend?'

'Because I want to be with you.'

'Suit yourself,' she grumbled, working the sponge so hard it began to shred. 'Don't make no never-mind to me one way or the other.'

I wasn't about to give up, so I sat at the table and leafed through the newspaper, hoping that when she was done she'd decide to talk to me. At the bottom of the third page I noticed an article about Martin Luther King. Knowing how much Oletta admired him, I cleared my throat and read aloud: '"Dr. Martin Luther King delivered a speech at the Southern Christian Leadership Conference last week . . ."'

As I read the article, Oletta stopped scrubbing the counter. She came and sat across from me, listening intently, occasionally nodding her head. When I finished reading, I folded the paper and looked at her. 'He sure sounds like a smart man.'

'Yes, he is. Thank you for readin' it to me.' She pushed herself up from the table. 'I got somethin' for you,' she said, pulling a covered tin from the top of the refrigerator and handing it to me. 'I made 'em this morning.'

I pried off the lid, and when I saw what was inside, I felt awful. While I all but ignored her and went for a morning stroll through Forsyth Park with Mrs. Odell, Oletta had made me chocolate chip cookies. I looked into her eyes and said, 'Thank you, Oletta.'

'I put walnuts in the batter too, just how you like.'

I took a big bite of a cookie and groaned. 'You're the best cook, Oletta,' I said with my mouth full. And when she smiled, I stood up from the table and hugged her. 'You're the best cook and the best friend I've ever had.'

Before leaving for home that afternoon, Oletta handed me a pad of paper and a pencil. 'Sit down and write something for me, will you?'

I did as she asked, poised with pencil in hand, wondering what she was up to.

Oletta crossed her arms over her chest and gazed out the kitchen window as she dictated: 'Cut up two boiled chicken breasts – no skin. Chop three stalks of celery, half a small sweet onion, and a handful of grapes. Put all that in a bowl and . . .'

I smiled to myself as I wrote out Oletta's chicken salad recipe. When I finished, I handed her the paper, and she placed it on the kitchen counter next to Mrs. Odell's saccharin bottle. She seemed enormously pleased with herself, and for the first time in more than a week I heard her humming a tune as she hung her apron in the pantry and gathered her handbag and sweater.

Together we walked out the front door, down the steps, and along the shady sidewalk to the bus stop. When the bus slowed to a stop and the door swung open, Oletta hoisted her handbag over her shoulder and said, 'See you tomorrow, child.'

Just as she planted her feet on the first step, I blurted, 'I love you, Oletta Jones.'

She stopped and turned. Her face was so serious I wondered if maybe I'd done something wrong to speak such a thing in public.

The corners of her mouth edged into a smile, and from her lips came the words I'd longed to hear. 'Oletta Jones loves you too.'

Twenty-seven

Mrs. Odell wandered into the kitchen. She had just risen from a nap, and the hair on the back of her head stood up like wisps of damaged feathers.

'Did you have a nice rest, Gertrude?' Aunt Tootie asked, walking out of the pantry.

'Yes, thank you, I did.' Mrs. Odell seemed a bit embarrassed when she glanced at the clock. 'Oh, my word, I slept for nearly two hours. I had no idea.' She looked at the basket of peaches on the table and said, 'Oletta, would you like some help?'

'That'd be nice, Gertrude. Thank you.'

Mrs. Odell slipped an apron over her head, not bothering to tie it closed behind her back. She pulled a knife from the drawer and eased herself down across the table from Oletta. 'I've always liked peeling peaches. When I was a young girl back on the farm, my grandmother would make pies and . . . '

While Mrs. Odell, Oletta, and Aunt Tootie talked about peach pies, what to add to the grocery list, and how quickly the summer was coming to an end, I sat quietly and listened as their chatter lifted into the air, gilding all four corners of the kitchen. And as the sweet aroma of the fresh peaches mingled with the sound of their voices, I folded the memory into myself, feeling a peace I'd never before known.

When Mrs. Odell finished slicing a bowl of peaches, she wiped her hands on a towel and said, 'Oletta, I'm sorry, but my arthritis is acting up. I have to give these old hands of mine a rest for a few minutes.'

Oletta nodded. 'I appreciate your help, Gertrude. Thank you.'

Mrs. Odell stood at the sink and washed her hands. 'Tootie, would it be all right if I used the telephone? I'd like to call my cousin Adele.'

'Of course,' Aunt Tootie said. 'Please feel free to use the one in the den.'

Mrs. Odell thanked her and headed out of the kitchen. I don't know how long she was on the phone, but when I closed my book and climbed down from the stool, it seemed like she'd been gone for a long time. I ate a peach, asked Aunt Tootie if she'd please add chocolate ice cream to the shopping list, and wandered down the hall. Mrs. Odell wasn't in the den, so I headed for the stairs to see if she'd gone to her bedroom.

As I stepped into the foy-yay, I saw her from the corner of my eye. She was standing in the living room looking out the front window. Her hands were clasped behind her back and a ray of sunlight revealed far more scalp than hair on her head.

'Mrs. Odell?'

When she didn't answer, I stepped around a chair so I could see her face. Her skin was pale.

'Mrs. Odell, what's wrong?'

'I have no place to go,' she whispered.

Her words and the look on her face frightened me. I touched her shoulder. 'What do you mean?'

A blue vein pulsed at the side of her temple. 'No house, no furniture, nothing.'

I helped her into a chair and covered her hands with mine. 'Just stay here. I'll be right back.'

I bolted down the hall and skidded into the kitchen. 'Hurry! Something's wrong with Mrs. Odell.'

Aunt Tootie, Oletta, and I rushed to the living room and huddled around Mrs. Odell. 'Gertrude, what is it?' Aunt Tootie said, taking hold of her quivering hands. 'Do you feel sick?'

Mrs. Odell shook her head, but her voice was pained and brittle when she told us what had happened.

'I called Adele to see if any of my mail had arrived, but her son, Roy, answered. He told me he'd stopped by to see his mother last Wednesday, and when she didn't come to the door, he let himself in.' Mrs. Odell looked from me to Oletta and then to Aunt Tootie. 'He found Adele in the living room, sitting in a chair in front of the TV. Dead.'

Aunt Tootie gasped. 'Oh, Gertrude!'

'The doctor told Roy it was a stroke. Roy knew I was here in Savannah, but he couldn't find where Adele had put your phone number.' A tear leaked from the corner of Mrs. Odell's eye. 'I can't even go to the funeral, she's already been buried.'

Aunt Tootie pulled up an ottoman, sat down, and rested her hand on Mrs. Odell's knee. 'Did Roy say anything else?'

'He said I was welcome to live in Adele's house if I wanted to.' Mrs. Odell absentmindedly kneaded the hem of her dress with the saddest expression I'd ever seen. 'I'm a foolish old woman,' she said, lowering her head. 'I never dreamed something like this would happen.'

Oletta let out a long sigh and eased herself into a chair. 'So what you gonna do, Miz Gertrude?'

'Roy is such a nice man. He offered to drive up here and get me. But I don't know a soul in Florida. When my stay here is through, I guess I'll take the bus back to Ohio.'

Aunt Tootie scooted closer. 'But with your home being sold, there's no reason for you to go back, is there?'

Mrs. Odell's lips quivered. 'I have to. That's the only place I know. There are some apartments for senior citizens in Willoughby. I'm sure I'll find something.'

Aunt Tootie turned and looked out the window. After a brief moment I saw her lips curve into a smile. It was the exact same smile I'd seen on the day she walked into my life.

'Gertrude, you *do* have a home,' she said, turning toward Mrs. Odell. 'And it's right here in Savannah. I'd love to have you live here with Cecelia and me.'

Mrs. Odell shook her head. 'I thank you for your kindness, Tootie, but I couldn't impose.'

'You most certainly wouldn't be imposing.'

'This here child sure does love you,' Oletta said. 'If you was here in Savannah, then everyone would be happy.'

Mrs. Odell looked stunned. 'I'll admit I've grown fond of Savannah. The warmer weather has been good for these old bones of mine. I don't have much, but I have the money from the sale of my house. Maybe you could help me find a little place to rent, something close by. Within walking distance.'

Aunt Tootie reached out and patted Mrs. Odell's hand. 'Now, why would you want to up and rent a place when you have a home right here?'

'Oh, Tootie, you're so generous. But my knees are riddled with arthritis. I don't know how much longer I'll be able to climb the stairs.'

My aunt glanced toward the staircase and thought for a moment. 'Well, you can climb them now, right?'

Mrs. Odell nodded.

'All right, then this is where you'll stay until your knees say otherwise.' She smiled at Mrs. Odell and said, 'We'll be like Scarlett O'Hara and worry about the rest tomorrow.'

'I don't want charity. I've never needed it before, and I don't want to start now. If I did live here, then I'd have to pay my way and—'

'Gertrude, it's all settled. You'll live here with Cecelia and me, and your rent will be overseeing the care of the gardens. I don't have the time to fuss with them like I used to, so I hired a nice man to do the heavy work. I'd be thrilled if you'd keep an eye on things.'

I knelt on the floor in front of Mrs. Odell. 'Oh, please, say yes.'

While Mrs. Odell fumbled with a tissue and tried to regain her composure, Oletta rose to her feet. 'C'mon, Miz Gertrude, dry them eyes. We've got one more peck of peaches waitin' to be peeled. Let's go get it done so we can make us some nice preserves.' She reached out and offered Mrs. Odell her hand.

Aunt Tootie stood and winked. 'Oletta runs this house, so we all better do as she says.'

Like birds coming to roost in a favorite tree, we filed down the hallway and into the kitchen, settling comfortably in our places. It was a moment so perfect I wished I could stop time. I thought about how we all had Life Books – Mrs. Odell, Aunt Tootie, Oletta, and me – and how someone, somewhere, had seen fit to write our names on one another's pages.

That evening after dinner, Aunt Tootie, Mrs. Odell, and I were relaxing on the porch when we heard Miz Goodpepper scream. 'Oh, no. You evil little bitch!'

'What in the world?' Aunt Tootie said, rising to her feet.

'I'll go see.' I bolted down the steps, across the patio, and cut through the opening in the hedge. Miz Goodpepper was standing by the jasmine trellis. 'What's the matter?' I asked, trotting toward her.

She pointed to a huge spider web. 'Just look at what Matilda has done. I'll never forgive her.'

When I saw what she was so upset about, the hair on my arms prickled. 'Oh, no. We've got to save it.'

'It's too late,' Miz Goodpepper said, burying her face in her hands.

Caught in the sticky, silvery strands of web was an emerald green hummingbird. The bird's needlelike beak gaped open as it hung suspended in the web, dying.

Behind me I heard Aunt Tootie and Mrs. Odell making their way across the lawn.

'Oh, Thelma, how awful.' Aunt Tootie leaned closer to the web and shook her head. 'That poor little thing.'

Mrs. Odell never said a word as she stepped forward. Slowly she reached out and pushed her hand through the web, cupping the hummingbird in her palm. As she pulled it free, long strands of web fluttered in the breeze.

'Thelma, can you get me tweezers and some tissue?' she said, holding the bird in her left hand while gently pulling the tangles of web away with her right.

Miz Goodpepper raced into the house and quickly returned. 'Oh, Gertrude, do you think you can save him?'

'I don't know,' Mrs. Odell said, wrapping tissue around her index finger. 'But if the spider didn't inject him with venom, maybe it's not too late.'

She gently wiped away the web, then took the tweezers and pulled a few of the stickiest strands free of the bird's delicate wings.

'Here, honey,' she said, handing me the tweezers. 'Your hands are steadier than mine. See those pieces of web wound around his neck? Take the tweezers and pull them away. But don't pinch him.'

I held my breath as I removed the remnants of web. The bird lay so still I was certain he'd never survive.

'Well, this little fellow is in shock,' Mrs. Odell said. 'There's nothing more we can do but wait and see.'

'Gertrude, you need to sit down,' Miz Goodpepper said, taking her arm and guiding her to the patio.

We all pulled up chairs and sat in a circle, looking at the bird in Mrs. Odell's hand. I felt sick to my stomach knowing he would probably die any minute.

Aunt Tootie clasped her hands beneath her chin. 'Oh, I hope he makes it.'

No sooner did those words leave her lips than the hummingbird tried to right himself. We sat at the edge of our seats as he flopped around in Mrs. Odell's hand. It was so sad I could hardly bear to watch, but at the same time I couldn't look away.

All of a sudden his tiny wings fluttered and he got himself to his feet.

'Go on, honey,' Mrs. Odell said. 'Fly away and be free.'

And that's exactly what the hummingbird did. He lifted himself up from Mrs. Odell's hand and rose into the warm evening air.

'Gertrude, you're a miracle worker,' Miz Goodpepper said as she watched the bird disappear. 'Thank you.'

When Mrs. Odell pushed herself up from the chair, Miz Goodpepper nearly knocked her over with a bear hug. 'Bless you, Gertrude. There's a special place in heaven for people like you.'

'Glad I could help, Thelma.'

'I'm going to brush the rest of that web down right now,' Miz Goodpepper said, heading for her porch.

'Aunt Tootie, can I stay and help?'

'Sure, you can.'

Aunt Tootie and Mrs. Odell headed for home while Miz Goodpepper retrieved a broom. 'I can't believe my ignorance,' she sputtered, poking through the jasmine with her broom. 'I had no idea a hummingbird could get caught in a spider's web.'

'Oh, my gosh, is that her?' I said, pointing to a huge yellow and black spider that was fearfully clinging to a wooden slat at the top of the trellis.

Miz Goodpepper came and stood behind me. 'Yes, that's her, wicked little witch that she is.'

I moved closer and studied Matilda. 'I've never seen a spider marked like that. She really is pretty.'

Miz Goodpepper raised the broom. 'Not anymore she's not!'

I was shocked speechless when she knocked Matilda to the ground. *Slap* went the broom as Miz Goodpepper lifted it over her head and brought it down on Matilda. *Slap. Slap. Slap.*

Poor Matilda was pulverized. I looked at Miz Goodpepper and gasped. 'You killed Matilda! Why? I thought you loved her.'

'Yes,' she said with sadness in her voice. 'I did love her. But this had to be done. There was no choice. Better to be killed by someone who loves you than a total stranger.'

To me, dead was dead no matter *who* did the deed. But I figured this wasn't the time to share that thought.

I looked at what was left of Matilda, then peered up at Miz Goodpepper. I couldn't stop myself from saying, 'Well, looks like you won't be reaching nirvana anytime soon.'

She pushed a stray lock of hair off her forehead and sniffed. 'Yes, I suppose that's true. I guess I'll just have to settle for a trip to Idaho.'

Twenty-eight

I was on my way down the stairs carrying a basket of laundry when Aunt Tootie came bustling through the front door with several large shopping bags. 'Hi, sugar,' she said, dropping them on the floor and setting her handbag on the hall chest. 'What a day this has been.' She removed her hat and fluffed her hair. 'Help me get these bags into the kitchen, will you?'

'Sure. What did you get?'

'I was shopping with a friend of mine and I found the most beautiful table linens. They're so festive and bright. Just wait till you see them.'

We hauled the bags into the kitchen, where Oletta was showing Mrs. Odell how to make a sweet potato pie. The ceiling fan sent the spicy aroma of nutmeg whirling through the air.

Aunt Tootie chattered up a storm as she showed us what all she'd bought. 'Every store we visited had an end-of-summer sale. The bargains were amazing,' she said, pulling out a stack of coral-colored tablecloths and dozens of floral napkins edged in yellow piping.

Mrs. Odell wandered over to have a look. 'Those are so lovely. I'm partial to that shade of coral.'

'Me too,' Oletta said.

I couldn't imagine why she needed that many napkins, especially because an entire cupboard in the pantry was devoted to stacks upon stacks of table linens.

I smoothed my hand over the napkins. 'They're real pretty, but why do you need so many?'

Aunt Tootie pinched my cheek. 'I have a big surprise. The reason I bought all these beautiful table linens is because on Sunday afternoon I'll be hosting a lovely, ladies-only garden party. I wanted to have a party when you first arrived, but Oletta encouraged me to give you time to adjust to your new surroundings, and, as usual, she was right.'

Oletta beamed proudly and nodded.

'And now that Gertrude's here,' Aunt Tootie gushed, 'it's the perfect time to have a party. Remember that beautiful white dress I bought you at the beginning of summer – the one with the petticoats and the pink sash?'

Remember? How could I forget?

Aunt Tootie was all lit up, waiting for me to say something.

'Yes, ma'am, that dress is hanging in my closet.'

She clasped her hands beneath her chin. 'Well, now you'll *finally* have the opportunity to wear it.'

My stomach dropped to my ankles, and my mind screamed, *NOOOOOO. Not that dress. Oh, please don't make me wear that dress.*

'I've invited some of the neighbors, all the garden club members, and my friends from the Foundation. Just a nice, small party – about forty women in all.'

My mouth dropped open. 'Forty?'

Aunt Tootie put her arm around my shoulder. 'Oh, forty is nothing. I often have sixty or so.'

'And don't forget that Christmas party you had back in '56,' Oletta said. 'We had over a hundred people that night. I'll always remember . . . '

While Mrs. Odell and Aunt Tootie listened to Oletta recount the culinary details and festive decorations of the Christmas party, I slipped out of the kitchen and went upstairs to my bedroom.

From the back of my closet I removed the white dress from its hiding place and hung it on a hook by the door. I thought about all the party dresses and gowns Momma had collected over the years. How much she loved them, how much shame they brought me, and how mad I'd get when she wore them in public.

For how long I don't know, but I stood and stared at the dress until I was startled by a knock at the door.

'May I come in?' Aunt Tootie said, peeking around the door.

'Sure,' I said, forcing a smile.

When she saw me standing in front of the open closet, she couldn't have looked more pleased. 'Oh, I can't tell you how this warms my heart. I wondered where you'd gone, and here you are, looking at your pretty dress.'

I kept my smile plastered on my face and nodded.

'While we were talking downstairs, I realized that Oletta might need to do some alterations before the party. So how about putting it on so I can have a look?'

What was I to do? Say no? Tell Aunt Tootie I couldn't bring myself to wear the dress because it was almost exactly like the one Momma was wearing when she died? I began chewing the inside of my lip, then quickly stopped before I drew blood.

Aunt Tootie tilted her head. 'Honey, are you all right?'

Knowing I couldn't live with myself if I hurt her feelings, I reached up and pulled the dress from the hook. 'Yes, ma'am, I'm fine. I'll try it on right now.'

'Take your time,' she said, sitting down in the chair by the window. 'I'll wait right here.'

I stepped into the bathroom and closed the door. Slowly I

stripped out of my clothes, unzipped the back of the dress, and lifted it over my head. The crinoline petticoats rustled as they fell into place, feeling scratchy against my bare legs. I zipped up the dress as best I could and walked into the bedroom.

Aunt Tootie's eyes widened. 'Oh, my. That dress looks like it was made for you – it couldn't possibly be more perfect. Here, let me tie the sash.'

I turned around so she could finish zipping up the dress and fuss with the bubblegum-pink sash, and as she did so I avoided my reflection in the mirror. I felt a little dizzy and sick to my stomach as Aunt Tootie went on and on about how precious I looked.

As she tied and retied the sash, trying to get it just so, she said, 'Cecilia Rose, you look so sweet, everyone at the party will want to take a bite out of you. There, now it's perfect,' she said, giving the sash a final tug and fluffing the petticoats. When I turned around to face her, I saw tears in her eyes. 'Look in the mirror, and tell me what you think.'

I could not, would not, destroy this moment for my aunt by refusing to look in the mirror. This was something I had to do. I had to love her enough to not only do it graciously but do it with a smile on my face – a believable smile. Though seeing myself in this dress would surely be baptism by fire, I set my eyes on the floor and stepped across the room. When I lifted my head and looked at my reflection, I was horrified.

I swallowed, forced the brightest smile I could muster, and turned to face her. 'It's very pretty. I . . . I love it.' Though my words rang false in my ears, Aunt Tootie never noticed.

'Oh, I'm thrilled you like it.' She walked toward me and pressed her palms to my cheeks. 'And I love your hair in that long braid. We could tie a ribbon in it for the party. Would you like that?'

I nodded, grateful that she didn't want me to wear my hair in some silly updo or, worse, have it curled.

'Now, where are those lace-top socks and black patent-leather shoes I got to go with your dress?'

'Right here,' I said, heading for the closet. I tried on the socks and shoes, then turned and faced my aunt.

Her eyes widened and her lips parted. 'Cecelia Rose!' she chirped. 'You look just like a Madame Alexander doll.'

It was all I could do not to throw up.

'Oh, and I was thinking,' my aunt said, fussing with the sash again, 'why don't you invite Dixie Lee McAllister to the party?'

I wanted Dixie to see me in this dress about as much as I wanted to eat a bag of dirt. 'Dixie went to visit her grandma in Louisiana,' I blurted. A statement that was true. And to completely close the door on the conversation, I lied and said, 'She told me that she won't be home till late Sunday afternoon.'

'Well, that's a shame. I'd hoped your new friend could be here.' Aunt Tootie stepped back and scanned me from head to toe. 'Are you sure those shoes are comfortable? You'll be wearing them all afternoon.'

I nodded, said they felt fine, and thanked her for everything she'd done for me. I was certain she had no idea how badly I wanted to crawl out of my own skin. Never had I been more grateful than when she untied the sash, unzipped the dress, and took it downstairs to be steamed.

On the morning of the party, I woke to Aunt Tootie's voice rising through my open windows. 'Right over there. Yes, that's perfect. Now, y'all be careful. Watch out. Don't step on my flowers!'

The clock on my night chest read 7:55. Wondering what was going on so early, I pushed back the covers and padded to the window. In the garden below, a group of men in matching uni-forms were erecting a yellow-and-white-striped canopy on a frame of steel posts. Aunt Tootie stood in the center of the patio wearing a blue seersucker robe and a mesh hairnet tied around a head full of curlers.

I threw on shorts and a T-shirt, slipped into my shoes, and headed down the stairs. As I entered the kitchen, Aunt Tootie walked through the back door, looking frazzled. 'Sorry about all the commotion. I about fainted when I came downstairs to put coffee on and the doorbell rang. I can't believe Miller's Party Rental showed up so early. I could've sworn I told them to come at nine o'clock. Oh, well,' she said, pulling a cup and saucer from the cupboard, 'early is always better than late.'

I stood at the window and watched a team of men pull the canopy into position. 'Why are they putting up a tent? It's not supposed to rain, is it?'

'I always have a canopy set up for an outdoor party. Keeps the birds from ruining things when they perch in the trees and do their business. Plus, it offers some nice shade for the tables.'

Mrs. Odell wandered into the kitchen. 'Good morning. That's a beautiful tent, Tootie, so festive.'

'Good morning, Gertrude. I apologize for the ruckus. I hope it didn't wake you.'

'Oh, heavens, no. I was up at seven. I always read a few pages in my Bible on Sunday mornings. Then I went through my clothes and tried to decide what I should wear for the party. I hope I don't embarrass you. I don't have anything dressy . . .'

While Aunt Tootie and Mrs. Odell chattered back and forth, I went out to the porch and watched the workmen. I'd never been to a party, and though I'd met many of the women who where invited, there were just as many I hadn't. I leaned against the railing and wondered, *What will it be like?*

Aunt Tootie came out the door and called to one of the workmen, 'Please, be careful of that planter.'

She put her arm around my shoulders. 'I'm sure they think I'm an old ninny, but a few times in the past they've bumped into things and stepped on my border flowers, so I like to keep an eye on them.'

'Having a garden party sure seems like a lot of work.'

'It is. But oh, how it's worth it.'

Later that morning, I took a shower and washed my hair. While toweling off, I heard lots of voices outside, so I stood on the toilet lid and peered out the window. The patio and gardens were swarming with workmen and women carrying vases of flowers. Mrs. Odell and Aunt Tootie were standing at the far side of the striped canopy directing the activity. I bounded down the stairs to join them, liking the feel of my wet hair slapping against my back.

A van with the words Leslie Faye Florist was parked in the alley by the garage. Two women scuttled about, smoothing coral tablecloths over each table, while four others worked at fitting the chairs with gauzy white slipcovers.

Aunt Tootie pointed out a vase of flowers. Along the stems were rows of delicate white blooms that looked like ribbons tied into bows. 'Those are my favorites,' she said. 'I love the scent.'

'What are they?' I asked.

'Tuberose. Aren't they lovely?'

Mrs. Odell let out a gasp and pretended to swoon as she inhaled their perfume.

When we walked back into the house, three women, all wearing identical gray dresses and crisp aprons, were working in the kitchen. The rubber soles of their shoes squeaked across the floor as they hustled about, making cucumber sandwiches, arranging a circle of crackers around something muddy-looking that was called *pâté,* and smoothing plastic wrap over trays of tiny cakes that Aunt Tootie had called *petit fours.*

I had no idea what hosting a garden party involved, and all I can say is the preparation alone left both Mrs. Odell and me dumbstruck. I didn't understand how anyone could own so many dishes and serving trays. I also didn't understand Oletta's absence. The kitchen was her domain, and it seemed odd that she wasn't supervising.

When Aunt Tootie finished talking with the florist and closed the screen door, I asked, 'Where's Oletta?'

'She'll be here, and knowing Oletta, she'll try to run the kitchen. But she's not coming to the party to work. She's coming as a guest, well, *more* than a guest – she'll be here as part of your new family. Isn't that wonderful? I suspect she'll be here any minute.' Aunt Tootie ran her hand down the length of my hair. 'Your hair is still wet. Why don't you go outside and sit in the sun for a few minutes?'

Deciding it was best to stay out of the way of all the hoopla in the backyard, I walked down the hallway and out the front door. While sitting on the steps and fluffing my hair, I heard the bus come to a stop at the corner. A woman wearing the craziest-looking hat I'd ever seen climbed off. Made of straw with an extra-wide brim, the hat was smothered in red, purple, and iridescent green feathers.

I watched her move along the sidewalk, and when she reached Aunt Tootie's house, she looked up and saw me. 'What're you doin' out here, child?'

I couldn't believe it. I ran down the steps and flung open the gate. Gone were Oletta's gray dress, headscarf, and boxy shoes. Instead, she was wearing a Creamsicle-orange dress that had two rows of ruffles at the hem. On her feet was a pair of orange flats that had peep-toes. And speaking of toes, Oletta's were painted bright cherry red. She was even wearing lipstick. And her hat? Well, what could I say?

I peered up at her in awe. 'Oletta. I didn't recognize you! You look beautiful.'

'I got all dressed up, just for you. What do you think of my hat?' she said, doing a slow pirouette. 'I made it myself.'

'You did? It's . . . it's the most amazing thing I've ever seen.'

'I think so too,' she said with a chuckle. 'Took me a whole two weeks to get it right. Had to keep goin' back to the store to buy more feathers. So, how are things goin' in *my* kitchen?' she asked as we climbed the front steps.

'Okay, I guess. There sure is a lot of food.'

Oletta marched down the hall and into the kitchen like she was the queen of the whole world. After making a few changes to the trays and talking with the caterer, she seemed satisfied. 'Well,' she said, scowling at my rumpled shorts, 'it's time you got ready. People will be here soon. Where's your dress?'

'In my closet.'

'C'mon, then, Miz Gertrude wants to braid your hair.'

Oletta and I went upstairs to find Mrs. Odell in her bedroom. She was standing in front of a mirror, adjusting her honorary garden club hat. She turned to greet us, smiling like a teenager about to go to a spring dance. Her dress was a silky floral print in shades of pink and pale lavender. Mrs. Odell beamed. 'Tootie's so kind. She let me borrow this dress for the party. But please tell me the truth – do you think it's too young? I'd hate to make a fool of myself.'

'You sure do look pretty,' Oletta said with an approving nod. 'That dress fits like it was yours all along.'

'I love that dress,' I chirped.

Mrs. Odell blushed, and I wondered when was the last time she'd heard someone say she looked pretty. She took another quick glance in the mirror and then turned to me. 'Are you ready to have your hair braided? I've got everything ready.'

I sat on the vanity bench while Oletta sat in the chair by the window and watched Mrs. Odell braid my hair. Her arthritic fingers moved slowly, and when she reached the end, she looked at Oletta. 'My fingers are stiff today. Would you mind putting in the rubber band?'

Oletta twisted it into place and tied the ribbon in a bow. 'It's almost one o'clock,' she said, patting my shoulders. 'Time to get dressed.'

'I'll go to see if Tootie needs any help,' Mrs. Odell said as we left the room.

'We'll be down shortly, Gertrude.'

My hands grew clammy and my stomach tightened when Oletta and I climbed the stairs to my bedroom. This was it. I had to put on that party dress and pretend to be happy about it.

Once I was all ready, black Mary Janes, lace-top socks, white dress, and all, Oletta took a step back, propped her hands on her hips, and looked at me. 'You sure do look a whole lot different than that ragamuffin child who showed up here at the beginning of summer.'

I turned and walked to the window. Already the backyard was filling up with Aunt Tootie's friends.

'It's time to go downstairs.'

'You go ahead, Oletta. I'll be down in a few minutes.'

She reached out and touched my shoulder. 'What's bothering you?'

'It's just, well, it's this dress.' I felt miserable admitting this to Oletta.

Her voice shot up several octaves. 'You don't like it?'

I shook my head.

'Why? In all my days, I've never seen a prettier dress.'

Without saying another word I walked to the bed, knelt down, and pulled Momma's scrapbook from beneath the mattress. Slowly I turned to the picture that was taken the moment she won the Vidalia Onion Queen pageant.

Oletta pursed her lips as she studied the picture, then eased herself down on the bed. 'I know what you see in that picture, and I've got somethin' I want to say.' She looked deep into my eyes. 'Don't lay claim to somethin' that don't belong to you. This picture is of your Momma – not you. And that dress she's wearin' ain't the dress *you're* wearin'.

'Your momma lost her mind, and that's a mighty sad truth. Ain't no words for me to say how sorry I am for all you've been through in your young life. But what happened to your momma has nothin' to do with you, and it sure don't have nothin' to do with that dress you're wearin'.'

Oletta patted the bed, and when I sat down beside her, she took hold of my hand. 'Take the gift Miz Tootie is givin' you and hold it tight. Don't go wastin' all them bright tomorrows you ain't even seen by hangin' on to what happened yesterday. Let go, child. Just breathe out and let go.'

I knotted up the corners of my mouth and nodded. 'You're so wise, Oletta.'

'People is wise 'cause they get out in the world and live. Wisdom comes from experience – from knowin' each day is a gift and accepting it with gladness. You read a whole lot of books, and readin' sure has made you smart, but ain't no book in the world gonna make you wise.'

Oletta rose to her feet. 'So, c'mon, lots of nice ladies is waitin' for you.'

Twenty-nine

Oletta held my hand as we stepped out the door and onto the back porch. Without her grounding force, I might have turned and run back inside the house. I wasn't prepared for this extravaganza of color and chatter; everywhere I looked women in chiffon dresses and flowery hats were clustered in groups like pastel nosegays.

Oletta leaned close to my ear and whispered, 'You'll be fine – all you gotta do is smile.'

When Aunt Tootie saw me, she walked across the patio with open arms. 'Here she is! I want y'all to meet my sweet grand-niece.'

The chatter faded as everyone turned and watched me walk down the steps. My knees turned rubbery, and my pulse quickened. Before I knew what had happened, Aunt Tootie took hold of my hand and swept me into the fragrant crowd.

I was passed from one group of women to the next. My cheeks were pinched and kissed, and I was fawned over and made to turn in circles so they could get a good look at my dress. After a while I felt like one of those ballerinas that spin inside music boxes. I was called 'darlin'' and 'sugar' and 'sweet peach' and 'precious.' My heart was blessed too many times to count.

An elderly woman with cream-puff hair and droopy eyelids shuffled toward me. Countless strands of pearls circled her neck. Perched on her shoulder like a well-trained parakeet was a huge yellow brooch that glittered in the sunlight. She reached out and patted my arm. 'I love your hair,' she said in a dry, papery voice. 'When I was a young girl, I had long hair too.'

I liked her immediately.

Another woman pulled me aside. 'Oh, my word. I can hardly believe it. You're the spittin' image of Bobbie-Lynn Calhoun when she was a young girl.'

I had no idea who she was talking about and didn't ask because I couldn't stop staring at the thick fringe of her false eyelashes.

Alone at a table beneath the striped canopy, looking as cool as the cucumber sandwich she was nibbling, sat Miz Goodpepper in a peachy-pink sundress. She winked at me and smiled. At the far end of the garden I noticed Louie the peacock standing in the shadows. He tilted his head from left to right, curiously watching the party from a safe distance.

Trays filled with all sorts of hors d'oeuvres were passed among the crowd, and a giant crystal punch bowl was filled with something called Long Island iced tea. The women flocked to that punch bowl like a 50 percent-off table at a department store. Whatever Long Island iced tea consisted of, it sure made these women happy. Even Oletta poured herself a glass of the golden elixir.

When I was finally able to sneak away from the crowd, I darted inside the house and went upstairs to my bedroom. After washing the gooey residue of kisses from my cheeks, I loaded my camera with a fresh pack of film and headed downstairs.

On the patio sat a long dessert table draped in a scalloped-edged lace tablecloth that skimmed the ground. Its entire surface was smothered with cookies, cakes, and tiny tarts that were art-fully arranged like a display in a bakeshop window. I put a lemon cookie and two petit fours on a napkin, then sat on a bench in a shady corner of the garden.

While I was savoring the treats in private, someone let out a joyous yelp. I turned to see Oletta throw her arms in the air and wave like she was flagging down a taxi.

In through the garden gate came Chessie and Nadine, dressed to the nines. To my stunned delight, shuffling behind them were Sapphire, Miz Obee, and Flossy. Cradled in each of Miz Obee's arms was a pot of orchids. I jumped from the bench and bolted through the garden. When they saw me coming, they smiled. Even ornery old Sapphire gave me a sly, crooked grin. One by one I embraced them, feeling my chest swell with gladness. Miz Obee nodded furiously at my dress, indicating her overwhelm-ing approval.

Aunt Tootie came up behind me, rested her hands on my shoulders, and thanked them all for coming. She took Sapphire by the arm and guided her to a table beneath the canopy. Within moments a server arrived with a tray of cool drinks. Miz Obee was puffed up with pride, smiling shyly when she presented Aunt Tootie with a pale pink orchid. Streaks of crimson, as thin as dental floss, disappeared into the flower's deep, yellow-speck-led throat. It was so beautiful it didn't look real. Aunt Tootie made a fuss over it and exclaimed it was the most gorgeous orchid she'd ever seen. I ran to pull Mrs. Odell from the crowd, led her back to the table, and introduced her to everyone. Miz Obee's cheeks flushed with pleasure when she offered a pot of yellow orchids to Mrs. Odell.

Mrs. Odell's eyes grew bright. 'Oh, thank you,' she said, lightly touching a petal. 'It's a living jewel.'

Before they settled at the table, I gathered everyone together so I could take a group picture. I blew on the photograph as I watched it develop in my hand. Within a minute or two, I was holding the finest picture I'd ever taken.

Aunt Tootie excused herself and headed for the house to check on things in the kitchen. I followed her, and when we stepped into the back hall, I reached for her arm and held her back. 'How did you know?'

'You mean about Sapphire and her friends?' She cupped her hand beneath my chin. 'I knew because Oletta told me. She said you were quite a hit with everyone at Green Hills Home.'

'I was?'

'Yes, you certainly were. So I asked Oletta if they'd like to come to your party, and they were delighted by the invitation. Chessie and Nadine are so kind and thoughtful, they offered to drive all the way out there and pick them up.'

Aunt Tootie looked into my eyes and smiled. 'Cecelia Rose, you are one *very* popular young lady. Everyone thinks you're so lovely. I can't tell you how proud you've made me.'

Her words swirled around me like stars. Could it be that I, Cecelia Rose Honeycutt, the outcast from Willoughby, Ohio, had become *popular*? I hugged Aunt Tootie, marveling at the thought of it. What a gallant woman she was, swooping into my life and opening her heart and home to me, and never once had she asked for a thing in return. What I did to deserve her kindness, I'd never know.

I was filling a plate with cookies for everyone at the table when in through the garden gate waltzed Miz Hobbs. She was wearing a black hat and a disturbing yellow sundress printed with large black and red circles. Her rear end looked just like a giant bull's-eye. When she saw me standing by the pastry table, she wiggled her way across the patio in those absurd itty-bitty steps she always took.

'Cecelia, I hardly recognized you all dressed up,' she said with exaggerated surprise, planting a kiss on my cheek. 'What a beautiful dress. You look like a vanilla cupcake! Tootie always did have impeccable taste. But I must say I'm surprised you *still* haven't gotten your hair cut. Remember what I told you about those awful hippies?'

'I'll tell Aunt Tootie you're here,' I said, wiping her lipstick from my cheek with a napkin.

As I started to walk away, Miz Hobbs turned to a woman in a yellow dress and said, 'What in the world are all those nigras doing here! Has Tootie lost her mind?'

I was so mad I wanted to rip her lips off.

I settled at the table next to Mrs. Odell and glared at Miz Hobbs. She shimmied her way through the clusters of women with a plate of food in one hand and a drink in the other, nodding and sending kisses through the air like she was a movie star. When she sat at the table next to ours, Miz Goodpepper let out a sniff and angled her chair so her back was to Miz Hobbs.

'I'm in love with the live oaks,' Mrs. Odell said. 'And I can't wait to see the magnolias bloom in the spring. How beautiful they must be.'

Miz Goodpepper, who was fanning herself with her hat, raised her voice. 'Oh, Gertrude, magnolia blossoms smell so delicious they'll make your heart ache. I had a gorgeous magnolia in my garden, but while I was out of town this past spring, my evil neighbor *murdered* it.'

Miz Obee's jaw dropped, Flossy scooted closer, and Sapphire looked at Miz Goodpepper like she'd lost her mind. Mrs. Odell swallowed a bite of cookie with a gulp. 'Murdered your tree?'

'Yes,' Miz Goodpepper hissed, narrowing her eyes to slashes of blue. 'She had it chopped down in cold blood.'

Miz Hobbs stiffened as Miz Goodpepper spewed out the

story of the murdered magnolia. Miz Goodpepper's voice was steeped in loathing when she said, 'My neighbor is not only a lowly tree murderer but she also performs a striptease for one lucky member of the local police department.'

Everyone gasped. Well, everyone except Sapphire. She laughed.

Fueled by far too many Long Island iced teas, Miz Goodpepper leaned back and spoke over her shoulder, 'So, tell us, Violene, how's Earl? He's about due for another spanking, isn't he?'

Miz Hobbs jumped from her chair, eyes blazing. '*You bitch,*' she screamed through a mouthful of pâté. 'So *you're* the one who sent all those disgusting pictures and clever little notes!'

Miz Goodpepper rolled her eyes in an exquisite look of distaste. 'I don't know what you're talking about, but I *do* know that Earl Jenkins sure does like it when you spank him, especially when you're wearing that ludicrous chicken outfit.'

Miz Hobbs's jowls shook with fury. She reached over, dragged her fingers through the pâté on her plate, and smeared it across Miz Goodpepper's cheek.

With a smile as brief and deadly as a flash of lightning, Miz Goodpepper wiped it away with her napkin. 'Well, Violene, this has just proved what I've known for twenty years. You can haul the girl out of the trash, but you can *never* haul the trash out of the girl.'

'You think you're so damned lily-white and such an upstanding citizen? Well, I've got news. You are a sick exhibitionist – out there naked in broad daylight every Sunday morning, splashin' around in that ridiculous outdoor bathtub of yours while the rest of us are getting ready for church.'

Miz Goodpepper smirked and rose to her feet. 'Screaming *"Oh, God!"* from your bed is the closest you have *ever* been to church.'

Aunt Tootie set off across the patio in a furious click of heels. 'Now, y'all mind your manners and stop this nonsense right now.'

Miz Goodpepper snatched Miz Hobbs's hat from her head and hurled it across the garden like a flower-studded Frisbee. Miz Hobbs lunged forward, grabbed a shoulder strap of Miz Goodpepper's sundress with one hand, and started walloping her butt with the other. They spun in circles as the words 'bitch' and 'tramp' and 'slut' exploded in the air like bottle rockets.

Everyone scrambled to get out of the way – well, everyone but Sapphire, who was enjoying the spectacle immensely. She stayed glued to her chair, cupped her old gnarled hands around her mouth, and hollered, 'Get her, Thelma. Whup her ass real good.'

Miz Hobbs and Miz Goodpepper spun across the patio like a chiffon tornado, slapping and spanking each other. I could hardly believe it when Miz Goodpepper took hold of Miz Hobbs's beaded necklace and attempted to strangle her, but the necklace broke in her hand and a clatter of glass beads rained down on the patio.

They shrieked like murder as they careened into the dessert table. Silver trays filled with cookies and petit fours flew into the air like birds fleeing a gunshot while Miz Goodpepper and Miz Hobbs tumbled to the ground.

Everyone stood, wide-eyed and speechless, as the two of them lay in a heap of crushed cookies and torn dresses. Aunt Tootie lifted a jagged piece of a broken cake plate from the ground and cried, 'This belonged to Taylor's mother!'

Miz Hobbs let out a painful groan and rolled on her back. She looked like she'd stepped on a land mine. Miz Goodpepper sat up, took one look at Miz Hobbs, and began to laugh. I was stupefied when she pulled herself up from the bricks, reached out, and offered to help Miz Hobbs get up. Miz Hobbs was so angry she slapped her hand away, which only made Miz Goodpepper laugh harder.

'Oh, stop it, Violene,' Miz Goodpepper said with a snort, offering her hand again. 'It's over. We just cleared up twenty years of bad karma. I feel thoroughly cleansed. This has been a spiritual enema.'

Everyone roared with laughter.

'Come on, Violene,' Miz Goodpepper said, 'let's go home.'

Miz Hobbs crawled to her knees. She reluctantly took hold of Miz Goodpepper's outstretched hand and hissed under her breath, 'Exhibitionist bitch.'

'Tree-murdering tramp,' Miz Goodpepper said with a laugh as she hauled Miz Hobbs to her feet.

Miz Goodpepper turned to my aunt. 'I don't know how I'll ever make this up to you, Tootie, but I guarantee I'll try.'

Aunt Tootie's face was flushed with anger when she walked toward her eccentric neighbors, but her graciousness prevailed when she raised her hands and said, 'It's all right. What are a few broken dishes among friends? Now, y'all go on home and pull yourselves together.'

They limped across the patio in opposite directions, vaulting halfhearted insults at each other. Miz Goodpepper disappeared through the opening in the hedge while Miz Hobbs threw open the garden gate. The congregation of women laughed and clapped while Louie let out a squawk and strutted after Miz Goodpepper.

An elderly woman with a dowager's hump and emerald earrings the size of gumdrops walked toward Aunt Tootie. 'I never thought I'd live to see the day when *any* party could top the one I had back in '37, but this one just did.'

Another woman laughed and said, 'Tootie, you always have

the *best* parties. I can't wait to tell my sister Irene about it – she'll be sick to death she missed it.'

Everyone began talking at once, telling stories of the party disasters they'd witnessed.

One woman told a story of a spectacular wedding catastrophe that involved a missing girdle and a 'marvelously embarrassing' toast given by a drunken best man. The stories had everyone howling, each woman trying to top the story before hers.

While listening to the laughter swirl around me, the strangest thing happened: my whole world turned pink, and an effervescent kind of warmth filled me with a sense of belonging I'd never known.

I turned and looked at Aunt Tootie's house, my gaze traveling to my sleeping porch, up to the huge trees, and into the bright Georgia sky. And as I stood there, soaking in the wonder of my new life, I knew Savannah was my home. I was safe here, I belonged, and I knew I always would.

As angry and hurt as I'd been when my father sealed my fate and sent me to live with Aunt Tootie, I knew he had spoken the truth when he'd said, 'One day you'll thank me for this. Believe me, you will.'

Maybe I'd write him a letter and tell him just how right he was. Not anytime soon, but one day.

From the corner of my eye I saw Miz Obee working her way across the patio, happily gathering beads from Miz Hobbs's broken necklace. She dropped them, one by one, down the front of her dress.

Everyone pretended not to notice.

Later that evening, after we'd all said good night and headed for bed, I stood at my window. The Spanish moss hung from the trees like miles of torn green lace, and far below, the yellow-and-white-striped canopy appeared to float in the air, as if suspended by the buoyant memories of a day that had surely reached the height of garden party infamy. Off in the distance a candle flickered from a table on Miz Goodpepper's porch. A fleeting ghost of white moved across her lawn, and a moment later I heard the squeak of a spigot followed by the splash of water. By the thin light of the moon I watched her lift a glass to her lips and take a slow sip of wine. After pinning up her hair, she pushed her robe off her shoulders. It slid down her body and pooled at her feet like buttermilk. A moment later she stepped into the tub and lowered herself out of sight.

On top of my chest of drawers sat the photographs I'd taken at the party. Carefully I tucked each picture around the mirror frame. From an envelope in the top drawer of my dresser, I removed the picture I'd taken of Lucille and Rosa at their Friday street picnic and slid it alongside the others. I pulled the ribbon from my hair and draped it over the top of the mirror, weaving it around the pictures. When I was done, I stepped back to admire my creation. It looked like a wreath.

From one woman's face to the next I went, studying each smile. And as I did, a strange, nameless feeling brushed over my skin. I walked across the room and pulled my mother's scrapbook from beneath the mattress. Dried-out sheets of protective film crackled as I leafed through the pages – pages that, like my mother's dreams, had become smudged by the passage of time. I turned to the picture of her standing on the pageant platform. Momma's eyes gleamed with hope and promise, and her brunette hair tumbled across her shoulders, lush and shiny. Her perfect white dress was as crisp as a brand-new day, and twinkles of light sparked from her tiara. And, of course, there was that silly green sash she had coveted so much, draped from shoulder to hip: 1951 Vidalia Onion Queen.

Carefully I pulled the picture from the scrapbook. After blowing off a few specks of dust, I took it across the room and leaned it against the mirror. And there they were, all the women in my life. It struck me that, other than Momma and Mrs. Odell, I hadn't known any of them at the beginning of the summer, yet every single woman had pressed her fingers against the pages of my Life Book, making her own unique, indelible impression.

I turned and gazed into the sky. The night was as thick as spilled ink, and high above the trees I could see the faint twinkle of a single star.

'Hi, Momma,' I whispered. 'I hope you made it to heaven all right. Is it pretty there? Do you have a girlfriend to talk with? I figure you already know this, but I live in Savannah with Aunt Tootie. I used to get annoyed when you'd talk about the South all the time, but now I understand why you loved it so much. Mrs. Odell is here too. Did you know that? I start school tomorrow, and I'm a little worried about it. I don't know how things work up there in heaven, but if you can, please send me some good luck. Good night, Momma.'

I wasn't very tired so I curled up in bed with the book Miz Goodpepper had given me. But as wonderful a storyteller as Eugene Field was, his words failed to hold my attention. Every paragraph or two I'd glance over at the photograph of my mother, feeling an odd sense of wonder, as if it were the first time I had ever seen it.

I'd never know why those turbulent storms had raged in her mind, or if, on that brilliant June day, she had slipped her feet into her red shoes and danced into the path of that truck with the intent of freeing herself from a life that had become unbearable. In my heart I wanted to believe it was an accident – that maybe she'd seen something across the road that delighted her, and for a brief, blindingly bright moment, she forgot where she was and what she was doing. I'd like to believe the policeman was right, that it happened so fast she didn't feel a thing.

For the most part I had begun to make peace with the life I had back in Willoughby. But like a deep bruise, the memory of Momma's final day jolts me whenever I bump up against it.

I suspect it always will.

So much about my mother's life and death would forever remain a mystery, but as I lay in bed, sifting through memories of her, there was one thing I knew for certain: even during her wildest moments, when fireworks flashed in her eyes and her hair stood on end, Momma had loved me.

It was with that thought that I sat up, slid open the top drawer of my night chest, and removed the pink satin pouch. Momma's necklace slid into my hand, and I held it beneath the lamplight, admiring its soft luster, and how, when I squinted my eyes, I could see the tiny imperfections in each pearl. Like I'd done so many times before, I smoothed them between my fingers until they grew warm. And I remembered the story Momma had told me – how the oyster had yawned and a grain of sand had lodged in its mouth, eventually becoming a pearl. At the time I had thought it was just something she'd made up, but years later I read a book about the wonders of the ocean, and sure enough, my mother had told me the truth. It was her version of the truth, but the truth just the same.

I turned out the light and lay my head against the pillow, breathing in the fragrant night air, liking the feel of my mother's pearls in my hand. And just as I drifted off to sleep, I heard her words float in with the breeze, *'It's how we survive the hurts in life that brings us strength and gives us our beauty.'*

Thirty

I could hardly believe it. Who was that girl in the mirror? From side to side I turned, a goofy grin on my face, as if I were rehearsing for a toothpaste commercial. But I couldn't help it. This was the first time in my life I felt proud of who I was, and, well – maybe even a little bit pretty. Oletta had washed and pressed my new blouse to perfection, the plaid patterns of my kilt matched exactly from one pleat to the next, and the buttons of my new red blazer gleamed in the early morning light like a row of lucky pennies. As I ran my fingers over the Rosemont School for Girls crest that was sewn to the breast pocket of my blazer, I felt like I was dreaming.

After adjusting my knee socks and folding over the tops, I tied the laces of my new saddle shoes into perfect bows.

'Okay,' I said to myself, taking one last look in the mirror. 'This is it, CeeCee – the biggest day of your whole life. Don't mess it up.'

I took a few deep breaths, squared my shoulders, and headed downstairs.

Aunt Tootie, Oletta, and Mrs. Odell were talking in the kitchen. When I walked in, they turned and looked at me.

'Oh, Cecelia Rose. You look positively adorable,' Aunt Tootie said, getting up from the table. She smoothed her hands over the sleeves of my blazer and plucked a tiny piece of lint from the lapel.

Mrs. Odell reached out and took hold of my hand. 'CeeCee, I can't tell you how happy I am to witness this day.'

Oletta poured a glass of orange juice and handed it to me. 'When I got up this mornin' and looked out the window, I knew the Good Lord himself sent you a nice cool breeze and some sunshine for your first day at school. I believe this will be a mighty fine day for you, child.'

I sat at the table, sipped the orange juice, and wondered what my first day would be like. But more than anything I wondered if Dixie McAllister would be waiting for me at 7:45 like she'd promised.

I was surprised when Oletta served breakfast at the kitchen table and not in the breakfast room. I was also surprised when Aunt Tootie pulled out the extra chair and asked Oletta to sit down and join us, which she did with a wide smile on her face.

And there we were – Aunt Tootie, Mrs. Odell, Oletta, and I – all having a casual breakfast together like a real family, *my* real family.

When the hands of the clock moved to 7:40, I gathered my notebook and headed for the front door. I checked myself in the mirror one last time as Aunt Tootie, Oletta, and Mrs. Odell paraded down the hall, looking anxious and wringing their hands. One by one they wished me luck: Aunt Tootie with a kiss and Mrs. Odell with a hug. Oletta looked at me real serious, smoothed her hand over my shoulder, then winked a slow, gentle kind of wink.

I smiled, said good-bye, and was relieved that they let me walk outside by myself and didn't stand on the front steps to watch.

My veins pulsed with excitement as I pulled the door closed.

Is this really happening? Am I, CeeCee Honeycutt, about to walk to a new school with a brand-new girlfriend?

I took a deep breath, turned, and looked toward the sidewalk. Then my stomach plummeted, and my smile fell away from my face. My worst fear had come true: Dixie McAllister wasn't there.

Stay calm. She'll be here any minute.

I stood on my toes and looked up and down the sidewalk. A few men dressed in suits hurried by, swinging leather briefcases at their sides, and crossing the street by Forsyth Park was a spry old woman walking her dog, but Dixie was nowhere to be seen. Then from around the corner came a quick burst of laughter, and my heart skipped a beat.

Here she comes. Here she comes.

But it was only two girls whizzing by on bicycles.

I searched the sidewalks and chanted, 'Please, Please. Please. Oh, God, please have her be here.'

Knowing I had to leave for school or I'd risk being late, I slowly walked down the steps and opened the wrought-iron gate. When I turned to pull it closed, I saw Mrs. Odell, Oletta, and Aunt Tootie peeking around the fringed edge of the living room curtains. Heat rose to my cheeks. They knew Dixie hadn't kept her promise. I pretended not to see them watching and tried my best to look happy, as if it didn't matter that Dixie wasn't there.

After securing the latch on the gate, I turned and stepped onto the sidewalk. And right there, sitting on the low stone wall, partially hidden by the foliage of Aunt Tootie's front garden, was Dixie. She was hunched over, elbows on her knees, reading a book.

When she looked up and saw me, relief washed over her face. 'Hi, CeeCee. Am I ever glad to see you! I was worried you went to school without me.'

I all but fell to my knees with gratefulness at the sight of her – my new friend who was wearing a brand-new uniform exactly like mine and a smile as wide as the new day.

'Are . . . are you kidding?' I sputtered. 'I couldn't wait to see you again.'

Dixie stood, gathered her book, and surprised me when she stepped forward and laced her arm through mine. 'I was so excited I left my house early. I've been sitting out here since seven-thirty. CeeCee, have you ever read *Murder on the Orient Express*? Oh, my gosh, I can't put it down.'

'Yes,' I said, nodding furiously.

She babbled about how much she adored our new uniforms and how she couldn't wait to see what our reading list would include. As we crossed the street – Dixie all but running as if to keep her feet in pace with her words and me feeling dizzy with an insane kind of gladness – I glanced over my shoulder. And there they were, Aunt Tootie, Mrs. Odell, and Oletta, still hovering at the living room window. The vision of them nearly split my heart open.

As the sunlight raced across the brilliant Savannah sky, the day unfolded like a beautiful yet painfully wrapped gift. Momma had left this world and set herself free, and in doing so, she had set me free too. As much as I missed her and wished I could hear her laughter one more time, I believed she was out there in the big bright *somewhere*, watching me, cheering for me. Loving me.

Acknowledgments

Exceptional people have pressed their fingertips along the edges of this book, and I'm indebted to them all.

Grateful thanks to literary agent extraordinaire Catherine Drayton of Inkwell Management, for opening the window and hanging a star in the October sky. With hearfelt gratitude, I thank a rare jewel in the publishing world – the gracious and enormously talented Pamela Dorman – for her brilliant and inspiring editing. A warm thanks goes to Leigh Butler, Hal Fessenden, Julie Miesionczek, Nancy Sheppard, Shannon Twomey, Carolyn Coleburn, Randee Marullo, Veronica Windholz, Dennis Swaim, and Andrew Duncan for their guidance and kindness. And a big thanks to Clare Ferraro, Susan Petersen Kennedy, and everyone at Pamela Dorman Books/Viking Penguin for believing in CeeCee – and me.

A special thanks to Robin Smith for her sharp eyes, good humor, and friendship. And speaking of friends, had it not been for the support of Marlane Vaicius, Debra Kreutzer, Margaret Vincent, and Marie Behling, I'd surely be making macaroni somewhere in Idaho.

A tender thank-you goes to my husband, Mark, a gentleman of great integrity and kindness.

Sometimes the moon smiles and a surprise lands in our hands. I have known such a surprise and want to thank my friend, Vivienne Dacosta, and my talented editor at Little, Brown Book Group, Jenny Parrott, for bringing CeeCee's story to the UK.